THE ARIZONANS

They forged a state from a beautiful, forbidding territory—a frontier that would challenge the heart, the mind, and the soul.

THE BEST OF THE WEST

Extraordinary stories of the men and women who put themselves on the line of fire and lived up to the promise of a new land.

THE ARIZONANS

Bill Pronzini and Martin H. Greenberg, editors

FAWCETT GOLD MEDAL • NEW YORK

Acknowledgments

"The Hunting of Tom Horn," by Clay Fisher. Copyright © 1962 by Western Writers of America, Inc. First published in the anthology *Legends and Tales of the Old West*. Reprinted by permission of Henry W. Allen.

"One Night in the Red Dog Saloon," by Hal G. Evarts. Copyright © 1953 by Curtis Publishing Co.; copyright renewed © 1981 by Hal G. Evarts. First published in *The Saturday Evening Post*. Reprinted by permission of the author.

"The Tonto Woman," by Elmore Leonard. Copyright © 1982 by Western Writers of America, Inc. First published in the anthology *Roundup*. Reprinted by permission of the author and H.N. Swanson, Inc.

"Two-Gun Farewell," by C.S. Park. Copyright © 1955 by Bard Publishing Corp. First published in *Western Magazine*. Reprinted by permission of Scott Meredith Literary Agency, 845 Third Avenue, New York, N.Y. 10022.

"Way of the Law in Calico," by John Prescott. Copyright © 1956 by Curtis Publishing Co. First published in *The Saturday Evening Post* as "The Landlady's Daughter." Reprinted by permission of Scott Meredith Literary Agency, 845 Third Avenue, New York, N.Y. 10022.

"The Angel of Santa Sofia," by Loren D. Estleman. Copyright © 1989 by Loren D. Estleman. Published by permission of the author.

Introduction

The Arizonans is the third volume in a series of Western fiction anthologies celebrating frontier life in various Western states. It contains stories that are not only set in Arizona, but that fictionally recreate the many aspects of its colorful and exciting history—stories written primarily by authors past and present who have lived within its boundaries.

The thirteen tales in these pages are told through the eyes of cattlemen young and old, drifters, prospectors, ferrymen, bartenders, youngsters, tenderfeet, stock detectives, a deputy U.S. marshal, and a Deputy Collector of Customs. In them you'll visit Tucson and Tombstone and Red Dog, and the Custom House at old Fort Calabasas; you'll travel that part of the Gila Trail known as the Devil's Highway, take a ferry across the Colorado River, wander the vast southwestern deserts; you'll join a hunt for Tom Horn, the most deadly hired gun ever to stalk the West; and you'll find, among other things, both elephants and camels.

Subsequent volumes in the series will take you to New Mexico, Montana, Wyoming, and other western states large and small. In each book you'll discover short Western fiction at its most entertaining and historically accurate, by such writers as Zane Grey, Owen Wister, Elmore Leonard, Loren D. Estleman, Norman A. Fox, John Jakes, and Jack Schaefer.

We hope you enjoy this fictional journey through the Old West, as well as the two which preceded it—*The Texans* and *The Californians*—and all those to follow.

—Bill Pronzini and
Martin H. Greenberg

Stewart Edward White's Arizona Nights *(1907) was one of the first major collections of stories about frontier days in the "Land of Opportunity" and is still highly regarded among scholars and aficionados of Western literature; Walter Van Tilburg Clark called it "a vivid, dramatic Scheherazade of the West." "Buried Treasure" is just one of the many memorable tales to be found in its pages. White, who has been favorably compared to Jack London, James Oliver Curwood, and Rex Beach, authored more than fifty other books of merit about pioneer America. These include such story collections as* Blazed Trail Stories, *and* Stories of the Wild Life *(1906), and such novels as* The Westerners *(1901),* The Riverman *(1908),* Gold *(1913), and* Folded Hills *(1934).*

Buried Treasure

★★★★★★★★★★★★★★★

Stewart Edward White

I. THE OLD TIMER

JUST at dusk one afternoon we finished cutting the herd that our morning's drive had collected. The stray-herd, with its new additions from the day's work, we pushed rapidly into one big stock corral. The cows and unbranded calves we urged into another. Fifty head of beef steers found asylum from dust, heat, and racing to and fro, in the mile-square wire enclosure called the pasture. All the remainder, for which we had no further use, we drove out of the flat into the brush and toward the distant mountains. Then we let them go as best pleased them.

By now the desert had turned slate-colored, and the brush was olive green with evening. The hard, uncompromising ranges, twenty miles to eastward, had softened behind a wonderful veil of purple and pink, vivid as the chiffon of a girl's gown. To the south and southwest the Chiricahuas and Dragoons were lost in thunderclouds that flashed and rumbled.

We jogged homewards, our cutting ponies, tired with the quick, sharp work, shuffling knee-deep in a dusk that seemed to disengage itself and rise upwards from the surface of the desert. Everybody was hungry and tired. At the chuck wagon we threw off our saddles and turned the mounts into the remuda. Some of the wisest of us, remembering the thunderclouds, stacked our gear under the veranda roof of the old ranch house.

Supper was ready. We seized the tin battery, filled the plates with the meat, bread, and canned corn, and squatted on our heels. The food was good, and we ate hugely in silence. When we could hold no more we lit pipes. Then we had leisure to notice that the stormcloud was mounting in a portentous silence to the zenith, quenching the brilliant desert stars.

"Rolls" were scattered everywhere. A roll includes a cowboy's bed and all of his personal belongings. When the outfit includes a bed wagon, the roll assumes bulky proportions.

As soon as we had come to a definite conclusion that it was going to rain, we deserted the camp fire and went rustling for our blankets. At the end of ten minutes every bed was safe within the doors of the abandoned adobe ranch house, each owner recumbent on the floor-claim he had preempted, and every man hoping fervently that he had guessed right as to the location of leaks.

Ordinarily we had depended on the light of camp fires, so now artificial illumination lacked. Each man was indicated by the alternately glowing and waning lozenge of his cigaret fire. Occasionally someone struck a match, revealing for a moment highlights on bronzed countenances, and the silhouette of a shading hand. Voices spoke disembodied. As the conversation developed, we gradually recognized the membership of our own roomful. I had forgotten to state that the ranch house included four chambers. Outside, the rain roared with Arizona ferocity. Inside, men congratulated themselves, or swore as leaks developed and localized.

Naturally we talked first of stampedes. Cows and bears are the two great cattle-country topics. Then we had a mouth organ solo or two, which naturally led on to songs. My turn came. I struck up the first verse of a sailor chantey as possessing at least the interest of novelty:

> Oh, once we were a-sailing, a-sailing were we,
> *Blow high, blow low, what care we;*

And we were a-sailing to see what we could see,
Down on the coast of the High Barbaree.

I had just gone so far when I was brought up short by a tremendous oath behind me. At the same instant a match flared. I turned to face a stranger holding the little light above his head and peering with fiery intentness over the group sprawled about the floor.

He was evidently just in from the storm. His dripping hat lay at his feet. A shock of straight, close-clipped, vigorous hair stood up gray above his seamed forehead. Bushy iron-gray eyebrows drawn close together thatched a pair of burning, unquenchable eyes. A square, deep jaw, lightly stubbled with gray, was clamped so tight that the cheek muscles above it stood out in knots and welts.

Then the match burned his thick, square fingers, and he dropped it into the darkness that ascended to swallow it.

"Who was singing that song?" he cried harshly. Nobody answered.

"Who was that singing?" he demanded again.

By this time I had recovered from my first astonishment.

"I was singing," said I.

Another match was instantly lit and thrust into my very face. I underwent the fierce scrutiny of an instant, then the taper was thrown away half-consumed.

"Where did you learn it?" the stranger asked in an altered voice.

"I don't remember," I replied; "it is a common enough deep-sea chantey."

A heavy pause fell. Finally the stranger sighed.

"Quite like," he said; "I never heard but one man sing it."

"Who in hell are you?" someone demanded out of the darkness.

Before replying the newcomer lit a third match, searching for a place to sit down. As he bent forward, his strong, harsh face once more came clearly into view.

"He's Colorado Rogers," the Cattleman answered for him; "I know him."

"Well," insisted the first voice, "what in hell does Colorado Rogers mean by bustin' in on our song *fiesta* that way?"

"Tell them, Rogers," advised the Cattleman, "tell them—just as you told it down on the Gila ten years ago next month."

"What?" inquired Rogers. "Who are you?"

"You don't know me," replied the cattleman, "but I was with Buck Johnson's outfit then. Give us the yarn."

"Well," agreed Rogers, "pass over the 'makings' and I will."

He rolled and lit a cigaret, while I revelled in the memory of his rich, great voice. It was of the sort made to declaim against the sea or the rush of rivers or, as here, the fall of waters and the thunder—full, from the chest, with the caressing throat vibration that gives color to the most ordinary statements. After ten words we sank back, oblivious of the storm, forgetful of the leaky roof and the dirty floor, lost in the story told us by the Old Timer.

II. THE TEXAS RANGERS

I CAME from Texas, like the bulk of you punchers, but a good while before the most of you were born. That was forty-odd years ago—and I've been on the Colorado River ever since. That's why they call me Colorado Rogers. About a dozen of us came out together. We had all been Texas Rangers, but when the war broke out we were out of a job. We none of us cared much for the Johnny Rebs, and still less for the Yanks, so we struck overland for the West, with the idea of hitting the California diggings.

Well, we got switched off one way and another. When we got down to about where Douglas is now, we found that the Mexican government was offering a bounty for Apache scalps. That looked pretty good to us, for Injin chasing was our job, so we started in to collect. Did pretty well, too, for about three months, and then the Injins began to get too scarce, or too plenty in streaks. Looked like our job was over with, but some of the boys discovered that Mexicans, having straight black hair, you couldn't tell one of their scalps from an Apache's. After that the bounty business picked up for a while. It was too much for me, though, and I quit the outfit and pushed on alone until I struck the Colorado about where Yuma is now.

At that time the California immigrants by the southern route used to cross just there, and these Yuma Injins had a monopoly on the ferry business. They were a peaceful, fine-looking lot, without a thing on but a g-string. The woman had belts with rawhide strings hanging to the knees. They put them on one over the other until they didn't feel too decollotey. It wasn't until the soldiers came that the officers' wives got them to wear handkerchiefs over their breasts. The system was all right, though. They wallowed around in the hot, clean sand, like chickens and kept healthy. Since they took to wearing clothes they've been petering out and dying of dirt and assorted diseases.

They ran this ferry monopoly by means of boats made of tules, charged a scand'lous low price, and everything was happy and lovely. I ran on a little bar and panned out some dust, so I camped a while, washing gold, getting friendly with the Yumas, and talking horse and other things with the immigrants.

About a month of this, and the Texas boys drifted in. Seems they sort of overdid the scalp matter and got found out. When they saw me, they stopped and went into camp. They'd traveled a heap of desert, and were getting sick of it. For a while they tried gold washing, but I had the only pocket—and that was about skinned. One evening a fellow named Walleye announced that he had been doing some figuring and wanted to make a speech. We told him to fire ahead.

"Now look here," said he, "what's the use of going to California? Why not stay here?"

"What in hell would we do here?" someone asked. "Collect Gila monsters for their good looks?"

"Don't get gay," said Walleye. "What's the matter with going into business? Here's a heap of people going through, and more coming every day. This ferry business could be made to pay big. Them Injins charges two bits a head. That's a crime for the only way across. And how much do you suppose whiskey'd be worth to drink after that desert? And a man's so sick of himself by the time he gets this far that he'd play chuck-a-luck, let alone faro or monte."

That kind of talk hit them where they lived, and Yuma was founded right then and there. They hadn't any whiskey yet, but cards were plenty, and the ferry monopoly was too easy. Walleye served notice on the Injins that a dollar a head went; and we all set to building a tule raft like the others. Then the wild bunch got uneasy, so they walked upstream one morning and stole the Injins' boats. The Injins came after them innocent as babies, thinking the raft had gone adrift. When they got into camp our men opened up and killed four of them as a kind of hint. After that the ferry company didn't have any trouble. The Yumas moved up river a ways, where they've lived ever since. They got the corpses and buried them. That is, they dug a trench for each one and laid poles across it, with a funeral pyre on the poles. Then they put the body on top, and the women of the family cut their hair off and threw it on. After that they set fire to the outfit, and, when the poles had burned through, the whole business fell into the trench of its own accord. It was the neatest, automatic, self-cocking, double-action sort of a funeral I ever saw. There wasn't any ceremony—only crying.

The ferry business flourished at prices which were sometimes hard to collect. But it was a case of pay or go back, and it was a tur'ble long ways back. We got us timbers and made a scow; built a *baile* and saloon and houses out of adobe; and called her Yuma, after the Injins that had really started her. We got our supplies through the Gulf of California, where sailing boats worked up the river. People began to come in for one reason or another, and first thing we knew we had a store and all sorts of trimmings. In fact we was a real live town.

III. THE SAILOR WITH ONE HAND

AT this moment the heavy beat of the storm on the roof ceased with miraculous suddenness, leaving the outside world empty of sound save for the *drip, drip, drip* of eaves. Nobody ventured to fill in the pause that followed the stranger's last words, so in a moment he continued his narrative.

We had every sort of people with us off and on, and, as I was lookout at a popular game, I saw them all. One evening I was on my way home about two o'clock of a moonlit night, when on the edge of the shadow I stumbled over a body lying part across the footway. At the same instant I heard the rip of steel through cloth and felt a sharp stab in my left leg. For a minute I thought some drunk had used his knife on me, and I mighty near derringered him as he lay. But somehow I didn't, and looking closer, I saw the man was unconscious. Then I scouted to see what had cut me and found that the fellow had lost a hand. In place of it he wore a sharp steel hook. This I had tangled up with and gotten well pricked.

I dragged him out into the light. He was a slim-built young fellow, with straight black hair, long and lank and oily, a lean face, and big, hooked nose. He had on only a thin shirt, a pair of rough wool pants, and the rawhide homemade *zapatos* the Mexicans wore then instead of boots. Across his forehead ran a long gash, cutting his left eyebrow square in two.

There was no doubt of his being alive, for he was breathing hard, like a man does when he gets hit over the head. It didn't sound good. When a man breathes that way he's mostly all gone.

Well, it was really none of my business, as you might say. Men got batted over the head often enough in those days. But for some reason I picked him up and carried him to my 'dobe shack and laid him out and washed his cut with sour wine. That brought him to. Sour wine is fine to put a wound in shape to heal, but it's no soothing syrup. He sat up as though he'd been touched with a hot poker, stared around wild-eyed, and cut loose with that song you were singing. Only it wasn't that verse. It was another one further along, that went like this:

Their coffin was their ship, and their grave it was the sea,
Blow high, blow low, what care we;
And the quarter that we gave them was to sink them in the sea,
Down on the coast of the High Barbaree.

It fair made my hair rise to hear him, with the big, still, solemn desert outside, and the quiet moonlight and the shadows, and him sitting up straight and gaunt, his eyes blazing each side of his big eagle nose, and his snaky hair hanging over the raw cut across his head. However, I made out to get him bandaged up and in shape; and pretty soon he sort of went to sleep.

Well, he was clean out of his head for nigh two weeks. Most of the time he lay flat on his back staring at the pole roof, his eyes burning and looking like they saw each one something a different distance off, the way crazy eyes do. That was when he was best. Then again he'd sing that Barbaree song until I'd go out and look at the Colorado flowing by just to be sure I hadn't died and gone below. Or else he'd just talk. That was the worst performance of all. It was like listening to one end of a telephone, though we didn't know what telephones were in those days. He began when he was a kid, and he gave his side of conversations, pausing for replies. I could mighty near furnish the replies sometimes. It was a queer lingo—about ships and ships' officers and gales and calms and fights and pearls and whales and islands and birds and skies. But it was all little stuff. I used to listen by the hour, but I never made out anything really important as to who the man was, or where he'd come from, or what he'd done.

At the end of the second week I came in at noon as per usual to fix him up with grub. I didn't pay any attention to him, for he was quiet. As I was bending over the fire he spoke. Usually I didn't bother with his talk, for it didn't mean anything, but something in his voice made me turn. He was lying on his side, those black eyes of his blazing at me, but now both of them saw the same distance.

"Where are my clothes?" he asked, very intense.

"You ain't in any shape to want clothes," said I. "Lie still."

I hadn't any more than got the words out of my mouth before he was atop me. His method was a winner. He had me by the throat with his hand, and I felt the point of the hook pricking the back of my neck. One little squeeze . . . Talk about your deadly weapons!

But he'd been too sick and too long abed. He turned dizzy and keeled over, and I dumped him back on the bunk. Then I put my six-shooter on.

In a minute or so he came to.

"Now, you're a nice, sweet proposition," said I, as soon as I was sure he could understand me. "Here I pick you up on the street and save your worthless carcass, and the first chance you get you try to crawl my hump. Explain."

"Where's my clothes?" he demanded again, very fierce.

"For heaven's sake," I yelled at him, "what's the matter with you and your old clothes? There ain't enough of them to dust a fiddle with anyway. What do you think I'd want with them? They're safe enough."

"Let me have them," he begged.

"Now, look here," said I, "you can't get up today. You ain't fit."

"I know," he pleaded, "but let me see them."

Just to satisfy him I passed over his old duds.

"I've been robbed," he cried.

"Well," said I, "what did you expect would happen to you lying around Yuma after midnight with a hole in your head?"

"Where's my coat?" he asked.

"You had no coat when I picked you up," I replied.

He looked at me mighty suspicious but didn't say anything more—wouldn't even answer when I spoke to him. After he'd eaten a fair meal he fell asleep. When I came back that evening the bunk was empty, and he was gone.

I didn't see him again for two days. Then I caught sight of him quite a ways off. He nodded at me very sour and dodged around the corner of the store.

"Guess he suspicions I stole that old coat of his," thinks I; and afterwards I found that my surmise had been correct.

However, he didn't stay long in that frame of mind. It was along toward evening, and I was walking on the banks looking down over the muddy old Colorado, as I always liked to do. The sun had just set, and the mountains had turned hard and stiff, as they do after the glow, and the sky above them was a thousand million miles deep of pale green-gold light. A pair of Greasers were ahead of me, but I could see only their outlines, and they didn't seem to interfere any with the scenery. Suddenly a black figure seemed to rise up out of the ground; the Mexican man went down as though he'd been jerked with a string, and the woman screeched.

I ran up, pulling my gun. The Mex was flat on his face, his arms stretched out. On the middle of his back knelt my one-armed friend. And that sharp hook was caught neatly under the point of the Mexican's jaw. You bet he lay still.

I really think I was just in time to save the man's life. According to my belief another minute would have buried the hook in the Mexican's neck. Anyway, I thrust the muzzle of my Colt into the sailor's face.

"What's this?" I asked.

The sailor looked up at me without changing his position. He was not the least bit afraid.

"This man has my coat," he explained.

"Where'd you get the coat?" I asked the Mex.

"I ween heem at monte off Antonio Curvez," said he.

"Maybe," growled the sailor.

He still held the hook under the man's jaw, but with the other hand he ran rapidly under and over the Mexican's left shoulder. In the half light I could see his face change. The gleam died from his eye; the snarl left his lips. Without further delay he arose to his feet.

"Get up and give it here," he demanded.

The Mexican was only too glad to get off so easy. I don't know whether he'd really won the coat at monte or not. In any case, he flew *poco pronto*, leaving me and my friend together.

The man with the hook felt the left shoulder of the coat again, looked up, met my eye, muttered something intended to be pleasant, and walked away.

This was in December.

During the next two months he was a good deal about town, mostly doing odd jobs. I saw him off and on. He always spoke to me as pleasantly as he knew how, and once made some sort of a bluff about paying me back for my trouble in bringing him around. However, I didn't pay much attention to that, being at the time almighty busy holding down my card games.

The last day of February I was sitting in my shack smoking a pipe after supper, when my one-armed friend opened the door a foot, slipped in, and shut it immediately. By the time he looked toward me I knew where my six-shooter was.

"That's all right," said I, "but you better stay right there."

I intended to take no more chances with that hook.

He stood there looking straight at me without winking or offering to move.

"What do you want?" I asked.

"I want to make up to you for your trouble," said he. "I've got a good thing, and I want to let you in on it."

"What kind of a good thing?" I asked.

"Treasure," said he.

"H'm," said I.

I examined him closely. He looked all right enough, neither drunk nor loco.

"Sit down," said I, "over there; the other side the table." He did so. "Now, fire away," said I.

He told me his name was Solomon Anderson, but that he was generally known as Handy Solomon, on account of his hook; that he had always followed the sea; that lately he had coasted the west shores of Mexico; that at Guaymas he had fallen in with Spanish friends, in company with whom he had visited the mines in the Sierra Madre; that on this expedition the party had been attacked by Yaquis and wiped out, he alone surviving; that his blanket-mate before expiring had told him of gold buried in a cove of Lower California by the man's grandfather; that the man had given him a chart showing the location of the treasure; that he had sewn this chart in the shoulder of his coat, whence his suspicion of me and his being so loco about getting it back.

"And it's a big thing," said Handy Solomon to me, "for they's not only gold, but altar jewels and diamonds. It will make us rich, and a dozen like us, and you can kiss the Book on that."

"That may all be true," said I, "but why do you tell me? Why don't you get your treasure without the need of dividing it?"

"Why, mate," he answered, "it's just plain gratitude. Didn't you save my life, and nuss me, and take care of me when I was nigh killed?"

"Look here, Anderson, or Handy Solomon, or whatever you please to call yourself," I rejoined to this, "if you're going to do business with me—and I do not understand yet just what it is you want of me—you'll have to talk straight. It's all very well to say gratitude, but that don't go with me. You've been around here three months, and barring a half-dozen civil words and twice as many of the other kind, I've failed to see any indications of your gratitude before. It's a quality with a hell of a hang-fire to it."

He looked at me sideways, spat, and looked at me sideways again. Then he burst into a laugh.

"The devil's a preacher, if you ain't lost your pinfeathers," said he. "Well, it's this then: I got to have a boat to get there; and she must be stocked. And I got to have help with the treasure, if it's like this fellow said it was. And the Yaquis and cannibals from Tiburon is through the country. It's money I got to have, and it's money I haven't got and can't get unless I let somebody in as pardner."

"Why me?" I asked.

"Why not?" he retorted. "I ain't see anybody I like better."

We talked the matter over at length. I had to force him to each point, for suspicion was strong in him. I stood out for a larger party. He strongly opposed this as depreciating the shares, but I had no intention of going alone into what was then considered a wild and dangerous country. Finally we compromised. A third of the treasure was to go to him, a third to me, and the rest was to be divided among the men whom I should select. This scheme did not appeal to him.

"How do I know you plays fair?" he complained. "They'll be four of you to one of me; and I don't like it, and you can kiss the Book on that."

"If you don't like it, leave it," said I, "and get out, and be damned to you."

Finally he agreed; but he refused me a look at the chart saying that he had left it in a safe place. I believe in reality he wanted to be surer of me, and for that I can hardly blame him.

IV. THE MURDER ON THE BEACH

AT this moment the cook stuck his head in at the open door.

"Say, you fellows," he complained, "I got to be up at three o'clock. Ain't you *never* goin' to turn in?"

"Shut up, Doctor!" "Somebody kill him!" "Here, sit down and listen to this yarn!" yelled a savage chorus.

There ensued a slight scuffle, a few objections. Then silence, and the stranger took up his story.

I had a chum named Billy Simpson, and I rung him in for friendship. Then there was a solemn, tall Texas young fellow, strong as a bull, straight and tough, brought up fighting Injins. He never said much, but I knew he'd be right there when the gong struck. For the fourth man I picked out a German named Schwartz. He and Simpson had just come back from the mines together. I took him because he was a friend of Billy's, and besides was young and strong, and was the only man in town excepting the sailor, Anderson, who knew anything about running a boat. I forgot to say that the Texas fellow was named Denton.

Handy Solomon had his boat all picked out. It belonged to some Basques who had sailed her around from California. I must say when I saw her I felt inclined to renege, for she wasn't more'n about twenty-five feet long, was open except for a little sort of cubbyhole up in the front of her, had one mast, and was pointed at both ends. However, Schwartz said she was all right. He claimed he knew the kind; that she was the sort used by French fishermen and could stand all sorts of trouble. She didn't look it.

We worked her up to Yuma, partly with oars and partly by sails. Then we loaded her with grub for a month. Each of us had his own weapons, of course. In addition we put in picks and shovels and a small cask of water. Handy Solomon said that would be enough, as there was water marked down on his chart. We told the gang that we were going trading.

At the end of the week we started and were out four days. There wasn't much room, what with the supplies and the baggage, for the five of us. We had to curl up 'most anywheres to sleep. And it certainly seemed to me that we were in lots of danger. The waves were much bigger than she was and splashed on us considerable, but Schwartz and Anderson didn't seem to mind. They laughed at us. Anderson sang that song of his, and Schwartz told us of the places he had worked. He and Simpson had made a pretty good cleanup, just enough to make them want to get rich. The first day out Simpson showed us a belt with about a hundred ounces of dust. This he got tired of wearing, so he kept it in a compass-box, which was empty.

At the end of the four days we turned in at a deep bay and came to anchor. The country was the usual proposition—very light-brown, brittle-looking mountains, about two thousand feet high; lots of sage and cactus, and pebbly beach, and not a sign of anything fresh and green.

But Denton and I were mighty glad to see any sort of land. Besides, our keg of water was pretty low, and it was getting about time to discover the spring the chart spoke of. So we piled our camp stuff in the small boat and rowed ashore.

Anderson led the way confidently enough up a dry arroyo, whose sides were clay and conglomerate. But, though we followed it to the end, we could find no indications that it was anything more than a wash for rain floods.

"That's main queer," muttered Anderson, and returned to the beach.

There he spread out the chart—the first look at it we'd had—and set to studying it.

It was a careful piece of work done in India ink, pretty old, to judge by the look of it, and with all sorts of pictures of mountains and dolphins and ships and anchors around the edge. There was our bay, all right. Two crosses were marked on the land part—one labelled *"oro"* and the other *"agua."*

"Now there's the high cliff," says Anderson, following it out, "and there's the round hill with the boulder—and if them bearings don't point due for that ravine, the devil's a preacher."

We tried it again, with the same result. A second inspection of the map brought us no light on the question. We talked it over and looked at it from all points, but we couldn't dodge the truth: the chart was wrong.

Then we explored several of the nearest gullies but without finding anything but loose stones baked hot in the sun.

By now it was getting toward sundown, so we built us a fire of mesquite on the beach, made us supper, and boiled a pot of beans.

We talked it over. The water was about gone.

"That's what we've got to find first," said Simpson, "no question of it. It's God knows how far to the next water, and we don't know how long it will take us to get there in that little boat. If we run our water entirely out before we start, we're going to be in trouble. We'll have a good look tomorrow, and if we don't find her, we'll run down to Mollyhay[1] and get a few extra casks."

"Perhaps that map is wrong about the treasure, too," suggested Denton.

"I thought of that," said Handy Solomon, "but then, thinks I to myself, this old rip probably don't make no long stay here—just dodges in and out like, between tides, to bury his loot. He would need no water at the time; but he might when he came back, so he marked the water on his map. But he wasn't noways particular *and* exact, being in a hurry. But you can kiss the Book to it that he didn't make no such mistakes about the swag."

"I believe you're right," said I.

When we came to turn in, Anderson suggested that he should sleep aboard the boat. But Billy Simpson, in mind perhaps of the hundred ounces in the compass-box, insisted that he'd just as soon as not. After a little objection Handy Solomon gave in, but I thought he seemed sour about it. We built a good fire, and in about ten seconds were asleep.

Now, usually I sleep like a log, and did this time until about midnight. Then all at once I came broad awake and sitting up in my blankets. Nothing had happened—I wasn't even dreaming—but there I was alert and clear as though it were broad noon.

By the light of the fire I saw Handy Solomon sitting, and at his side our five rifles gathered.

I must have made some noise, for he turned quietly towards me, saw I was awake, and nodded. The moonlight was sparkling on the hard stony landscape, and a thin dampness came out from the sea.

After a minute Anderson threw on another stick of wood, yawned, and stood up.

[1]Mulege—I retain the Old Timer's pronunciation.

"It's wet," said he; "I've been fixing the guns."

He showed me how he was inserting a little patch of felt between the hammer and the nipple—a scheme of his own for keeping damp from the powder. Then he rolled up in his blanket. At the time it all seemed quite natural—I suppose my mind wasn't fully awake, for all my head felt so clear. Afterwards I realized what a ridiculous bluff he was making: for of course the cap already on the nipple was plenty to keep out the damp. I fully believe he intended to kill us as we lay. Only my sudden awakening spoiled his plan.

I had absolutely no idea of this at the time, however. Not the slightest suspicion entered my head. In view of that fact, I have since believed in guardian angels. For my next move, which at the time seemed to me absolutely aimless, was to change my blankets from one side of the fire to the other. And that brought me alongside the five rifles.

Owing to this fact, I am now convinced, we awoke safe at daylight, cooked breakfast, and laid the plan for the day. Anderson directed us. I was to climb over the ridge before us and search in the ravine on the other side. Schwartz was to explore up the beach to the left, and Denton to the right. Anderson said he would wait for Billy Simpson, who had overslept in the darkness of the cubbyhole, and who was now paddling ashore. The two of them would push inland to the west until a high hill would give them a chance to look around for greenery.

We started at once, before the sun would be hot. The hill I had to climb was steep and covered with *chollas*, so I didn't get along very fast. When I was about halfway to the top I heard a shot from the beach. I looked back. Anderson was in the small boat, rowing rapidly out to the vessel. Denton was running up the beach from one direction and Schwartz from the other. I slid and slipped down the bluff, getting pretty well stuck up with the *cholla* spines.

At the beach we found Billy Simpson lying on his face, shot through the back. We turned him over, but he was apparently dead. Anderson had hoisted the sail, had cut loose from the anchor, and was sailing away.

Denton stood up straight and tall, looking. Then he pulled his belt in a hole, grabbed my arm, and started to run up the long curve of the beach. Behind us came Schwartz. We ran near a mile, and then fell among some tules in an inlet at the farther point.

"What is it?" I gasped.

"Our only chance—to get him—" said Denton. "He's got to go around this point—big wind—perhaps his mast will bust—then he'll come ashore—" He opened and shut his big brown hands.

So there we two fools lay, like panthers in the tules, taking our only one-in-a-million chance to lay hands on Anderson. Any sailor could have told us that the mast wouldn't break, but we had winded Schwartz a quarter of a mile back. And so we waited, our eyes fixed on the boat's sail, grudging her every inch, just burning to fix things to suit us a little better. And naturally she made the point in what I now know was only a fresh breeze, squared away, and dropped down before the wind toward Guaymas.

We walked back slowly to our camp, swallowing the copper taste of too hard a run. Schwartz we picked up from a boulder, just recovering. We were all of us crazy mad. Schwartz half wept and blamed and cussed. Denton glowered away in silence. I ground my feet into the sand in a helpless sort of anger, not only at the man himself, but also at the whole way things had turned out. I don't believe the least notion of our predicament had come to any of us. All we knew yet was that we had been done up, and we were hostile about it.

But at camp we found something to occupy us for the moment. Poor Billy was not dead, as we had supposed, but very weak and sick, and a hole square through him. When we returned he was conscious, but that was about all. His eyes were shut, and he was moaning. I tore open his shirt to stanch the blood. He felt my hand and opened his eyes. They were glazed, and I don't think he saw me.

"Water, water!" he cried.

At that we others saw all at once where we stood. I remember I rose to my feet and found myself staring straight into Tom Denton's eyes. We looked at each other that way for I guess it was a full minute. Then Tom shook his head.

"Water, water!" begged poor Billy.

Tom leaned over him.

"My God, Billy, there ain't any water!" said he.

* * *

V. BURIED TREASURE

THE Old Timer's voice broke a little. We had leisure to notice that even the drip from the eaves had ceased. A faint, diffused light vouchsafed us dim outlines of sprawling figures and tumbled bedding. Far in the distance outside a wolf yelped.

We could do nothing for him except shelter him from the sun and wet his forehead with seawater; nor could we think clearly for ourselves as long as the spark of life lingered in him. His chest rose and fell regularly, but with long pauses between. When the sun was overhead he suddenly opened his eyes.

"Fellows," said he, "it's beautiful over there; the grass is so green, and the water so cool; I am tired of marching, and I reckon I'll cross over and camp."

Then he died. We scooped out a shallow hole above the tide mark, and laid him in it, and piled over him stones from the wash.

Then we went back to the beach, very solemn, to talk it over.

"Now, boys," said I, "there seems to me just one thing to do, and that is to pike out for water as fast as we can."

"Where?" asked Denton.

"Well," I argued, "I don't believe there's any water about this bay. Maybe there was when that chart was made. It was a long time ago. And anyway, the old pirate was a sailor, and no plainsman, and maybe he mistook rainwater for a spring. We've looked around this end of the bay. The chances are we'd use up two or three days exploring around the other and then wouldn't be as well off as we are right now."

"Which way?" asked Denton again, mighty brief.

"Well," said I, "there's one thing I've always noticed in case of folks held up by the desert: they generally go wandering about here and there looking for water until they die not far from where they got lost. And usually they've covered a heap of actual distance."

"That's so," agreed Denton.

"Now, I've always figured that it would be a good deal better to start right out for some particular place, even if it's ten thousand miles away. A man is just as likely to strike water going in a straight line as he is going in a circle; and then, besides, he's getting somewhere."

"Correct," said Denton.

"So," I finished, "I reckon we'd better follow the coast south and try to get to Mollyhay."

"How far is that?" asked Schwartz.

"I don't rightly know. But somewheres between three and five hundred miles, at a guess."

At that he fell to glowering and glooming with himself, brooding over what a hard time it was going to be. That is the way with a German. First off he's plumb scared at the prospect of suffering anything and would rather die right off than take long chances. After he gets into the swing of it, he behaves as well as any man.

We took stock of what we had to depend on. The total assets proved to be just three pairs of legs. A pot of coffee had been on the fire, but that villain had kicked it over when he left. The kettle of beans was there, but somehow we got the notion they might have been poisoned, so we left them. I don't know now why we were so foolish—if poison was his game, he'd have tried it before—but at that time it seemed reasonable enough. Perhaps the horror of the morning's work, and the sight of the brittle-brown mountains, and the ghastly yellow glare of the sun, and the blue waves racing by outside, and the big strong wind that blew through us so hard that it seemed to blow empty our souls, had turned our judgment. Anyway, we left a full meal there in the beanpot.

So without any further delay we set off up the ridge I had started to cross that morning. Schwartz lagged, sulky as a muley cow, but we managed to keep him with us. At the top of the ridge we took our bearings for the next deep bay. Already we had made up our minds to stick to the seacoast, both on account of the lower country over which to travel and the off chance of falling in with a fishing vessel. Schwartz muttered something about its being too far even to the next bay, and wanted to sit down on a rock. Denton didn't say anything, but he jerked Schwartz up by the collar so fiercely that the German gave it over and came along.

We dropped down into the gully, stumbled over the boulder wash, and began to toil in the ankle-deep sand of a little sagebrush flat this side of the next ascent. Schwartz followed steadily enough now, but had fallen forty or fifty feet behind. This was a nuisance, as we had to keep turning to see if he still kept up. Suddenly he seemed to disappear.

Denton and I hurried back to find him on his hands and knees behind a sagebrush, clawing away at the sand like mad.

"Can't be water on this flat," said Denton; "he must have gone crazy."

"What's the matter, Schwartz?" I asked.

For answer he moved a little to one side, showing beneath his knee one corner of a wooden box sticking above the sand.

At this we dropped beside him, and in five minutes had uncovered the whole of the chest. It was not very large and was locked. A rock from the wash fixed that, however. We threw back the lid.

It was full to the brim of gold coins, thrown in loose, nigh two bushels of them.

"The treasure!" I cried.

There it was, sure enough, or some of it. We looked the chest through, but found nothing but the gold coins. The altar ornaments and jewels were lacking.

"Probably buried in another box or so," said Denton.

Schwartz wanted to dig around a little.

"No good," said I. "We've got our work cut out for us as it is."

Denton backed me up. We were both old hands at the business, had each in our time suffered the "cotton-mouth" thirst, and the memory of it outweighed any desire for treasure.

But Schwartz was money-mad. Left to himself he would have stayed on that sand flat to perish, as certainly as had poor Billy. We had fairly to force him away, and then succeeded only because we let him fill all his pockets to bulging with the coins. As we moved up the next rise, he kept looking back and uttering little moans against the crime of leaving it.

Luckily for us it was winter. We shouldn't have lasted six hours at this time of year. As it was, the sun was hot against the shale and the little stones of those cussed hills. We plodded along until late afternoon, toiling up one hill and down another, only to repeat immediately. Toward sundown we made the second bay, where we plunged into the sea, clothes and all, and were greatly refreshed. I suppose a man absorbs a good deal that way. Anyhow, it always seemed to help.

We were now pretty hungry, and as we walked along the shore, we began to look for turtles or shellfish or anything else that might come handy. There was nothing. Schwartz wanted to stop for a night's rest, but Denton and I knew better than that.

"Look here, Schwartz," said Denton, "you don't realize you're entered against time in this race—and that you're a damn fool to carry all that weight in your clothes."

So we dragged along all night.

It was weird enough, I can tell you. The moon shone cold and white over that dead, dry country. Hot whiffs rose from the baked stones and hillsides. Shadows lay under the stones like animals crouching. When we came to the edge of a silvery hill we dropped off into pitchy blackness. There we stumbled over boulders for a minute or so and began to climb the steep shale on the other side. This was fearful work. The top seemed always miles away. By morning we didn't seem to have made much of anywhere. The same old hollow-looking mountains with the sharp edges stuck up in about the same old places.

We had got over being very hungry, and though we were pretty dry, we didn't really suffer yet from thirst. About this time Denton ran across some fishhook cactus, which we cut up and chewed. They have a sticky wet sort of inside which doesn't quench your thirst any but helps to keep you from drying up and blowing away.

All that day we plugged along as per usual. It was main hard work, and we got to that state where things are disagreeable, but mechanical. Strange to say, Schwartz kept in the lead. It seemed to me at the time that he was using more energy than the occasion called for—just as a man runs faster before he comes to the giving-out point. However, the hours went by, and he didn't seem to get any more tired than the rest of us.

We kept a sharp lookout for anything to eat, but there was nothing but lizards and horned toads. Later we'd have been glad of them, but by that time we'd got out of their district. Night came. Just at sundown we took another wallow in the surf and chewed some more fishhook cactus. When the moon came up we went on.

I'm not going to tell you how dead beat we got. We were pretty tough and strong, for all of us had been used to hard living, but after the third day without anything to eat and no water to drink, it came to be pretty hard going. It got to the point where we had to have some *reason* for getting out besides just keeping alive. A man would sometimes rather die than keep alive, anyway, if it came only to that. But I made up my mind I was going to get out so I could smash up that Anderson, and I reckon Denton had the same idea. Schwartz didn't say anything, but he pumped on ahead of us, his back bent over and his clothes sagging and bulging with the gold he carried.

We used to travel all night, because it was cool, and rest an hour or two at noon. That is all the rest we did get. I don't know how fast we went; I'd got beyond that. We must have crawled along mighty slow, though, after our first strength gave out. The way I used to do was to collect myself with an effort, look around for my bearings, pick out a landmark a little distance off, and forget everything but it. Then I'd plod along, knowing nothing but the sand and shale and slope under my feet, until I'd reached that landmark. Then I'd clear my mind and pick out another.

But I couldn't shut out the figure of Schwartz that way. He used to walk along just ahead of my shoulder. His face was all twisted up, but I remember thinking at the time it looked more as if he was worried in his mind than like bodily suffering. The weight of the gold in his clothes bent his shoulders over.

As we went on the country gradually got to be more mountainous, and, as we were steadily growing weaker, it did seem things were piling up on us. The eighth day we ran out of the fishhook cactus, and, being on a high promontory, were out of touch with the sea. For the first time my tongue began to swell a little. The cactus had kept me from that before. Denton must have been in the same fix, for he looked at me and raised one eyebrow kind of humorous.

Schwartz was having a good deal of difficulty to navigate. I will say for him that he had done well, but now I could see that his strength was going on him in spite of himself. He knew it, all right, for when we rested that day he took all the gold coins and spread them in a row, and counted them, and put them back in his pocket, and then all of a sudden snatched out two handfuls and threw them as far as he could.

"Too heavy," he muttered, but that was all he could bring himself to throw away.

All that night we wandered high in the air. I guess we tried to keep a general direction, but I don't know. Anyway, along late, but before moonrise—she was now on the wane—I came to, and found myself looking over the edge of a twenty-foot drop. Right below me I made out a faint glimmer of white earth in the starlight. Somehow it reminded me of a little trail I used to know under a big rock back in Texas.

"Here's a trail," I thought, more than half-loco; "I'll follow it!"

At least that's what half of me thought. The other half was sensible and knew better, but it seemed to be kind of standing to one side, a little scornful, watching the performance. So I slid and slipped down to the strip of white earth, and, sure enough, it was a trail. At that the loco half of me gave the sensible part the laugh. I followed the path twenty feet and came to a dark hollow under the rock and in it a round pool of water about a foot across. They say a man kills himself drinking too much after starving for water. That may be, but it didn't kill me, and I sucked up all I could hold. Perhaps the fishhook cactus had helped. Well, sir, it was surprising how that drink brought me around. A minute before I'd been on the edge of going plumb loco, and here I was as clearheaded as a lawyer.

I hunted up Denton and Schwartz. They drank themselves full, too. Then we rested. It was mighty hard to leave that spring—

Oh, we had to do it. We'd have starved sure, there. The trail was a game trail, but that did us no good, for we had no weapons. How we did wish for the coffee-pot, so we could take some away. We filled our hats, and carried them about three hours, before the water began to soak through. Then we had to drink it in order to save it.

The country fairly stood up on end. We had to climb separate little hills so as to avoid rolling rocks down on each other. It took it out of us. About this time we began to see mountain sheep. They would come right up to the edges of the small cliffs to look at us. We threw stones at them, hoping to hit one in the forehead, but of course without any results.

The good effects of the water lasted us about a day. Then we began to see things again. Off and on I could see water plain as could be in every hollow and game of all kinds standing around and looking at me. I knew these were all fakes. By making an effort I could swing things around to where they belonged. I used to do that every once in a while, just to be sure we weren't doubling back, and to look out for real water. But most of the time it didn't seem to be worthwhile. I just let all these visions riot around and have a good time inside me or outside me, whichever it was. I knew I could get rid of them any minute. Most of the time, if I was in any doubt, it was easier to throw a stone to see if the animals were real or not. The real ones ran away.

We began to see bands of wild horses in the uplands. One day both Denton and I plainly saw one with saddle marks on him. If only one of us had seen him, it wouldn't have counted much, but we both made him out. This encouraged us wonderfully, though I don't see why it should have. We had topped the high country, too, and had started down the other side of the mountains that ran out on the promontory. Denton and I were still navigating without any thought of giving up, but Schwartz was getting in bad shape. I'd hate to pack twenty pounds over that country even with rest, food, and water. He was toting it on nothing. We told him so, and he came to see it, but he never could persuade himself to get rid of the gold all at once. Instead he threw away the pieces one by one. Each sacrifice seemed to nerve him up for another heat. I can shut my eyes and see it now—the wide, glaring, yellow country, the pasteboard mountains, we three dragging along, and the fierce sunshine flashing from the doubloons as one by one they went spinning through the air.

VI. THE CHEWED SUGAR CANE

"I'D like to have trailed you fellows," sighed a voice from the corner.

"Would you!" said Colorado Rogers grimly.

It was five days to the next water. But they were worse than the eight days before. We were lucky, however, for at the spring we discovered in a deep wash near the coast was the dried-up skull of a horse. It had been there a long time, but a few shreds of dried flesh still clung to it. It was the only thing that could be described as food that had passed our lips since breakfast thirteen days before. In that time we had crossed the mountain chain and had come again to the sea. The Lord was good to us. He sent us the water, and the horse's skull, and the smooth, hard beach without breaks or the necessity of climbing hills. And we needed it, oh, I promise you, we needed it!

I doubt if any of us could have kept the direction except by such an obvious and continuous landmark as the sea to our left. It hardly seemed worthwhile to focus my mind, but I did it occasionally just by way of testing myself. Schwartz still threw away his gold coins, and once, in one of my rare intervals of looking about me, I saw Denton picking them up. This surprised me mildly, but I was too tired to be very curious. Only now, when I saw Schwartz's arm sweep out in what had become a mechanical movement, I always took pains to look, and always I saw Denton search for the coin. Sometimes he found it, and sometimes he did not.

The figures of my companions and the yellow-brown tide sand under my feet and a consciousness of the blue-and-white sea to my left are all I remember, except when we had to pull ourselves together for the purpose of cutting fishhook cactus. I kept going, and I knew I had a good reason for doing so, but it seemed too much of an effort to recall what that reason was.

Schwartz threw away a gold piece as another man would take a stimulant. Gradually, without really thinking about it, I came to see this, and then went on to *sabe* why Denton picked up the coins; and a great admiration for Denton's cleverness seeped through me like water through the sand. He was saving the coins to keep Schwartz going. When the last coin went, Schwartz would give out. It all sounds queer now, but it seemed all right then— and it *was* all right, too.

So we walked on the beach, losing entire track of time. And after a long interval I came to myself to see Schwartz lying on the sand, and Denton standing over him. Of course we'd all been falling down a lot, but always before we'd got up again.

"He's give out," croaked Denton.

His voice sounded as if it was miles away, which surprised me, but, when I answered, mine sounded miles away, too, which surprised me still more.

Denton pulled out a handful of gold coins.

"This will buy him some more walk," said he gravely, "but not much."

I nodded. It seemed all right, this new, strange purchasing power of gold—it *was* all right, by God, and as real as buying bricks—

"I'll go on," said Denton, "and send back help. You come after."

"To Mollyhay," said I.

This far I reckon we'd hung onto ourselves because it was serious. Now I began to laugh. So did Denton. We laughed and laughed.

> "A damn long way
> To Mollyhay,"

said I. Then we laughed some more, until the tears ran down our cheeks, and we had to hold our poor, weak sides. Pretty soon we fetched up with a gasp.

> "A damn long way
> To Mollyhay,"

whispered Denton, and then off we went into more shrieks. And when we would sober down a little, one or the other of us would say it again:

> "A damn long way
> To Mollyhay,"

and then we'd laugh some more. It must have been a sweet sight!

At last I realized that we ought to pull ourselves together, so I snubbed up short, and Denton did the same, and we set to laying plans. But every minute or so one of us would catch on some word, and then we'd trail off into rhymes and laughter and repetition.

"Keep him going as long as you can," said Denton.

"Yes."

"And be sure to stick to the beach."

That far it was all right and clearheaded. But the word "beach" let us out.

> "I'm a peach
> Upon the beach,"

sings I, and there we were both off again until one or the other managed to grope his way back to common sense again. And sometimes we crowhopped solemnly around and around the prostrate Schwartz like a pair of Injins.

But somehow we got our plan laid at last, and slipped the coins into Schwartz's pocket, and said good-bye.

> "Old socks, good-bye,
> You bet I'll try,"

yelled Denton, and laughing fit to kill, danced off up the beach, and out into a sort of gray mist that shut off everything beyond a certain distance from me now.

So I kicked Schwartz, he felt in his pocket, threw a gold piece away, and "bought a little more walk."

My entire vision was fifty feet or so across. Beyond that was gray mist. Inside my circle I could see the sand quite plainly and Denton's footprints. If I moved a little to the left, the wash of the waters would lap under the edge of that gray curtain. If I moved to the right, I came to cliffs. The nearer I drew to them, the farther up I could see, but I could never see to the top. It used to amuse me to move this area of consciousness about to see what I could find. Actual physical suffering was beginning to dull, and my head seemed to be getting clearer.

One day, without any apparent reason, I moved at right angles across the beach. Directly before me lay a piece of sugar cane, and one end of it had been chewed.

Do you know what that meant? Animals don't cut sugar cane and bring it to the beach and chew one end. A new strength ran through me, and actually the gray mist thinned and lifted for a moment, until I could make out dimly the line of cliffs and the tumbling sea.

I was not a bit hungry, but I chewed on the sugar cane and made Schwartz do the same. When we went on I kept close to the cliff, even though the walking was somewhat heavier.

I remember after that its getting dark and then light again, so the night must have passed, but whether we rested or walked I do not know. Probably we did not get very far, though certainly we staggered ahead after sunup, for I remember my shadow.

About midday, I suppose, I made out a dim trail leading up a break in the cliffs. Plenty of such trails we had seen before. They were generally made by peccaries in search of cast-up fish—I hope they had better luck than we.

But in the middle of this, as though for a sign, lay another piece of chewed sugar cane.

* * *

VII. THE CALABASH STEW

I HAD agreed with Denton to stick to the beach, but Schwartz could not last much longer, and I had not the slightest idea how far it might prove to be to Mollyhay. So I turned up the trail.

We climbed a mountain ten thousand feet high. I mean that; and I know, for I've climbed them that high, and I know just how it feels, and how many times you have to rest, and how long it takes, and how much it knocks out of you. Those are the things that count in measuring height, and so I tell you we climbed that far. Actually I suppose the hill was a couple of hundred feet, if not less. But on account of the gray mist I mentioned, I could not see the top, and the illusion was complete.

We reached the summit late in the afternoon, for the sun was square in our eyes. But instead of blinding me, it seemed to clear my sight, so that I saw below me a little mud hut with smoke rising behind it and a small patch of cultivated ground.

I'll pass over how I felt about it: they haven't made the words—

Well, we stumbled down the trail and into the hut. At first I thought it was empty, but after a minute I saw a very old man crouched in a corner. As I looked at him he raised his bleared eyes to me, his head swinging slowly from side to side as though with a kind of palsy. He could not see me, that was evident, nor hear me, but some instinct not yet decayed turned him toward a new presence in the room. In my wild desire for water I found room to think that here was a man even worse off than myself.

A vessel of water was in the corner. I drank it. It was more than I could hold, but I drank even after I was filled, and the waste ran from the corners of my mouth. I had forgotten Schwartz. The excess made me a little sick, but I held down what I had swallowed, and I really believe it soaked into my system as it does into the desert earth after a drought.

In a moment or so I took the vessel and filled it and gave it to Schwartz. Then it seemed to me that my responsibility had ended. A sudden great dreamy lassitude came over me. I knew I needed food, but I had no wish for it, and no ambition to search it out. The man in the corner mumbled at me with his toothless gums. I remember wondering if we were all to starve there peacefully together—Schwartz and his remaining gold coins, the man far gone in years, and myself. I did not greatly care.

After a while the light was blotted out. There followed a slight pause. Then I knew that someone had flown to my side and was kneeling beside me and saying liquid, pitying things in Mexican. I swallowed something hot and strong. In a moment I came back from wherever I was drifting to look up at a Mexican girl about twenty years old.

She was no great matter in looks, but she seemed like an angel to me then. And she had sense. No questions, no nothing. Just business. The only thing she asked of me was if I understood Spanish. Then she told me that her brother would be back soon, that they were very poor, that she was sorry she had no meat to offer me, that they were *very* poor, that all they had was *cala-bash*—a sort of squash. All this time she was hustling things together. Next thing I knew I had a big bowl of calabash stew between my knees.

Now, strangely enough, I had no great interest in that calabash stew. I tasted it, sat and thought awhile, and tasted it again. By and by I had emptied the bowl. It was getting dark. I was very sleepy. A man came in, but I was too drowsy to pay any attention to him. I heard the sound of voices. Then I was picked up bodily and carried to an outbuilding and laid on a pile of skins. I felt the weight of a blanket thrown over me—

I awoke in the night. Mind you, I had practically had no rest at all for a matter of more than two weeks, yet I woke in a few hours. And, remember, even in eating the calabash stew I had felt no hunger in spite of my long fast. But now I found myself ravenous. You boys do not know what hunger is. It *hurts*. And all the rest of that night I lay awake chewing on the rawhide of a pack saddle that hung near me.

Next morning the young Mexican and his sister came to us early, bringing more calabash stew. I fell on it like a wild animal and just wallowed in it, so eager was I to eat. They stood and watched me—and, I suppose Schwartz, too, though I had now lost interest in anyone but myself—glancing at each other in pity from time to time.

When I had finished the man told me that they had decided to kill a beef so we could have meat. They were very poor, but God had brought us to them—

I appreciated this afterward. At the time I merely caught at the word "meat." It seemed to me I could have eaten the animal entire, hide, hoofs, and tallow. As a matter of fact, it was mighty lucky they didn't have any meat. If they had, we'd probably have killed ourselves with it. I suppose the calabash was about the best thing for us under the circumstances.

The Mexican went out to hunt up his horse. I called the girl back. "How far is it to Mollyhay?" I asked her.

"A league," said she.

So we had been near our journey's end after all, and Denton was probably all right.

The Mexican went away on horseback. The girl fed us calabash. We waited.

About one o'clock a group of horsemen rode over the hill. When they came near enough I recognized Denton at their head. That man was of tempered steel—

They had followed back along the beach, caught our trail where we had turned off, and so discovered us. Denton had fortunately found kind and intelligent people.

We said good-bye to the Mexican girl. I made Schwartz give her one of his gold pieces.

But Denton could not wait for us to say "hullo" even, he was so anxious to get back to town, so we mounted the horses he had brought us and rode off, very wobbly.

We lived three weeks in Mollyhay. It took us that long to get fed up. The lady I stayed with made a dish of kid meat and stuffed olives—

Why, an hour after filling myself up to the muzzle I'd be hungry again and scouting round to houses looking for more to eat!

We talked things over a great deal, after we had gained a little strength. I wanted to take a little flyer at Guaymas to see if I could run across this Handy Solomon person, but Denton pointed out that Anderson would be expecting just that, and would take mighty good care to be scarce. His idea was that we'd do better to get hold of a boat and some water casks, and lug off the treasure we had stumbled over. Denton told us that the idea of going back and scooping all that dinero up with a shovel had kept him going, just as the idea of getting even with Anderson had kept me going. Schwartz said that after he'd carried that heavy gold over the first day, he made up his mind he'd get the spending of it or bust. That's why he hated so to throw it away.

There were lots of fishing boats in the harbor, and we hired one and a man to run it for next to nothing a week. We laid a course north and in six days anchored in our bay.

I tell you it looked queer. There were the charred sticks of the fire and the coffeepot lying on its side. We took off our hats at poor Billy's grave a minute, and then climbed over the *cholla*-covered hill carrying our picks and shovels and the canvas sacks to take the treasure away in.

There was no trouble in reaching the sandy flat. But when we got there we found it torn up from one end to the other. A few scattered timbers and three empty chests with the covers pried off alone remained. Handy Solomon had been there before us.

We went back to our boat sick at heart. Nobody said a word. We went aboard and made our Greaser boatman head for Yuma. It took us a week to get there. We were all of us glum, but Denton was the worst of the lot. Even after we'd got back to town and fallen into our old ways of life, he couldn't seem to get over it. He seemed plumb possessed of gloom and moped around like a chicken with the pip. This surprised me, for I didn't think the loss of money would hit him so hard. It didn't hit any of us very hard in those days.

One evening I took him aside and fed him a drink and expostulated with him.

"Oh, *hell*, Rogers," he burst out, "I don't care about the loot. But, suffering cats, think how that fellow sized us up for a lot of pattern-made fools; and how right he was about it. Why, all he did was to sail out of sight around the next corner. He knew we'd start across country, and we did. All we had to do was to lay low and save our legs. He was *bound* to come back. And we might have nailed him when he landed."

"That's about all there was to it," concluded Colorado Rogers, after a pause, "—except that I've been looking for him ever since, and when I heard you singing that song I naturally thought I'd landed."

"And you never saw him again?" asked Windy Bill.

"Well," chuckled Rogers, "I did about ten years later. It was in Tucson. I was in the back of a store when the door in front opened and this man came in. He stopped at the little cigar case by the door. In about one jump I was on his neck. I jerked him over backwards before he knew what had struck him, threw him on his face, got my hands in his black hair, and began to jump his features against the floor. Then all at once I noted that this man had two arms; so of course he was the wrong fellow. 'Oh, excuse me,' said I, and ran out the back door."

Those who know Owen Wister's fine, true evocation of the Old West only through his famous novels Lin McLean *(1897) and* The Virginian *(1902) will be surprised to learn that his fiction was not limited in background to the Wyoming range country. He also wrote often and well of other locales—Arizona, for one, as in this good-natured yarn about a man "well seasoned by the frontier, [who] had tried a little of everything: town and country, ranches, saloons, stage-driving, marriage occasionally, and latterly mines." Other of Wister's tales of life on various parts of the Western frontier appear in such collections as* Red Men and White *(1896),* The Jimmyjohn Boss and Other Stories *(1900), and* Members of the Family *(1911).*

Specimen Jones

★★★★★★★★★★★★★★★

Owen Wister

EPHRAIM, the proprietor of Twenty Mile, had wasted his day in burying a man. He did not know the man. He had found him, or what the Apaches had left of him, sprawled among some charred sticks just outside the Cañon del Oro. It was a useful discovery in its way, for otherwise Ephraim might have gone on hunting his strayed horses near the cañon and ended among charred sticks himself. Very likely the Indians were far away by this time, but he returned to Twenty Mile with the man tied to his saddle and his pony nervously snorting. And now the day was done, and the man lay in the earth, and they had even built a fence round him; for the hole was pretty shallow, and coyotes have a way of smelling this sort of thing a long way off when they are hungry, and the man was not in a coffin. They were always short of coffins in Arizona.

Day was done at Twenty Mile, and the customary activity prevailed inside that flat-roofed cube of mud. Sounds of singing, shooting, dancing, and Mexican tunes on the concertina came out of the windows hand in hand, to widen and die among the hills.

A limber, pretty boy, who might be nineteen, was dancing energetically, while a grave old gentleman, with tobacco running down his beard, pointed a pistol at the boy's heels and shot a hole in the earth now and then to show that the weapon was really loaded. Everybody was quite used to all of this—excepting the boy. He was an eastern new-comer, passing his first evening at a place of entertainment.

Night in and night out every guest at Twenty Mile was either happy and full of whiskey, or else his friends were making arrangements for his funeral. There was water at Twenty Mile—the only water for twoscore of miles. Consequently it was an important station on the road between the southern country and Old Camp Grant and the new mines north of the Mescal Range. The stunted, liquor-perfumed adobe cabin lay on the gray floor of the desert like an isolated slab of chocolate. A corral, two desolate stable-sheds, and the slowly turning windmill were all else. Here Ephraim and one or two helpers abode, armed against Indians and selling whiskey. Variety in their vocation of drinking and killing was brought them by the travelers. These passed and passed through the glaring, vacant months—some days only one ragged fortune hunter, riding a pony; again by twos and threes, with high loaded burros; and sometimes they came in companies, walking beside their clanking freight wagons. Some were young, and some were old, and all drank whisky and wore knives and guns to keep each other civil. Most of them were bound for the mines, and some of them sometimes returned. No man trusted the next man and their names, when they had any, would be O'Rafferty, Angus, Schwartzmeyer, José Maria, and Smith. All stopped for one night; some longer, remaining drunk and profitable to Ephraim; now and then one stayed permanently and had a fence built round him. Whoever came, and whatever befell them, Twenty Mile was chronically hilarious after sundown—a dot of riot in the dumb Arizona night.

On this particular evening they had a tenderfoot. The boy, being new in Arizona, still trusted his neighbor. Such people turned up occasionally. This one had paid for everybody's drink several times, because he felt friendly, and never noticed that nobody ever paid for his. They had played cards with him, stolen his spurs, and now they were making him dance. It was an ancient pastime; yet two or three were glad to stand round and watch it, because it was some time since they had been to the opera. Now the tenderfoot had misunderstood these friends at the beginning, supposing himself to be among good fellows, and they therefore naturally set him down as a fool. But even while dancing you may learn much, and suddenly. The boy, besides being limber, had good, tough, black hair, and it was not in fear but with a cold blue eye that he looked at the old gentleman. The trouble had been that his own revolver had somehow hitched, so he could not pull it from the holster at the necessary moment.

"Tried to draw on me, did yer?" said the old gentleman. "Step higher! Step, now, or I'll crack open yer kneepans, ye robin's egg."

"Thinks he's having a bad time," remarked Ephraim. "Wonder how he'd like to have been that man the Injuns had sport with?"

"Weren't his ear funny?" said one who had helped bury the man.

"Ear?" said Ephraim. "You boys ought to been along when I found him and seen the way they'd fixed up his mouth." Ephraim explained the details simply and the listeners shivered. But Ephraim was a humorist. "Wonder how it feels," he continued, "to have—"

Here the boy sickened at his comments and the loud laughter. Yet a few hours earlier these same half-drunken jesters had laid the man to rest with decent humanity. The boy was taking his first dose of Arizona. By no means was everybody looking at his jig. They had seen tenderfeet so often. There was a Mexican game of cards; there was the concertina; and over in the corner sat Specimen Jones, with his back to the company, singing to himself. Nothing had been said or done that entertained him in the least. He had seen everything quite often.

"Higher! skip higher, you elegant calf," remarked the old gentleman to the tenderfoot. "High-yer!" And he placidly fired a fourth shot that scraped the boy's boot at the ankle and threw earth over the clock so that you could not tell the minute from the hour hand.

" 'Drink to me only with thine eyes,' " sang Specimen Jones softly. They did not care much for his songs in Arizona. These lyrics were all, or nearly all, that he retained of the days when he was twenty, although he was but twenty-six now.

The boy was cutting pigeon wings, the concertina played "Matamoras," Jones continued his lyric, when two Mexicans leaped at each other, and the concertina stopped with a quack.

"Quit it!" said Ephraim from behind the bar, covering the two with his weapon. "I don't want any greasers scrapping round here tonight. We've just got cleaned up."

It had been cards, but the Mexicans made peace, to the regret of Specimen Jones. He had looked round with some hopes of a crisis, and now for the first time he noticed the boy.

"Blamed if he ain't neat," he said. But interest faded from his eye, and he turned again to the wall. " 'Lieb Vaterland magst ruhig sein,' " he melodiously observed. His repertory was wide and refined. When he sang he was always grammatical.

"Ye kin stop, kid," said the old gentleman, not unkindly, and he shoved his pistol into his belt.

The boy ceased. He had been thinking matters over. Being lithe and strong, he was not tired nor much out of breath, but he was trembling with the plan and the prospect he had laid out for himself. "Set 'em up," he said to Ephraim. "Set 'em up again all round."

His voice caused Specimen Jones to turn and look once more, while the old gentleman, still benevolent, said, "Yer langwidge means pleasanter than it sounds, kid." He glanced at the boy's holster and knew he need not keep a very sharp watch as to that. Its owner had bungled over it once already. All the old gentleman did was to place himself next to the boy on the off side from the holster; any move the tenderfoot's hand might make for it would be green and unskillful and easily anticipated. The company lined up along the bar, and the bottle slid from glass to glass. The boy and his tormentor stood together in the middle of the line, and the tormentor, always with half a thought for the holster, handled his drink on the wet counter, waiting till all should be filled and ready to swallow simultaneously, as befits good manners.

"Well, my regards," he said, seeing the boy raise his glass; and as the old gentleman's arm lifted in unison, exposing his waist, the boy reached down a lightning hand, caught the old gentleman's own pistol, and jammed it in his face.

"Now you'll dance," said he.

"Whoop!" exclaimed Specimen Jones, delighted. "*Blamed* if he ain't neat!" And Jones's handsome face lighted keenly.

"Hold on!" the boy sang out, for the amazed old gentleman was mechanically drinking his whiskey out of sheer fright. The rest had forgotten their drinks. "Not one swallow," the boy continued. "No, you'll not put it down either. You'll keep hold of it, and you'll dance all round this place. Around and around. And don't you spill any. And I'll be thinking what you'll do after that."

Specimen Jones eyed the boy with growing esteem. "Why, he ain't bigger than a pint of cider," said he.

"Prance away!" commanded the tenderfoot, and fired a shot between the old gentleman's not widely straddled legs.

"You hev the floor, Mr. Adams," Jones observed respectfully at the old gentleman's agile leap. "I'll let no man here interrupt you." So the capering began, and the company stood back to make room. "I've saw juicy things in this Territory," continued Specimen Jones aloud to himself, "but this combination fills my bill."

He shook his head sagely, following the black-haired boy with his eye. That youth was steering Mr. Adams round the room with the pistol, proud as a ringmaster. Yet not altogether. He was only nineteen, and though his heart beat stoutly, it was beating alone in a strange country. He had come straight to this from hunting squirrels along the Susquehanna, with his mother keeping supper warm for him in the stone farmhouse among the trees. He had read books in which hardy heroes saw life and always triumphed with precision on the last page, but he remembered no receipt for this particular situation. Being good, game American blood, he did not think now about the Susquehanna, but he did long with all his might to know what he ought to do next to prove himself a man. His buoyant rage, being glutted with the old gentleman's fervent skipping, had cooled, and a stress of reaction was falling hard on his brave young nerves. He imagined everybody against him. He had no notion that there was another American wanderer there, whose reserved and whimsical nature he had touched to the heart.

The fickle audience was with him, of course, for the moment, since he was upper dog and it was a good show; but one in that room was distinctly against him. The old gentleman was dancing with an ugly eye; he had glanced down to see just where his knife hung at his side, and he had made some calculations. He had fired four shots; the boy had fired one. "Four and one hez always made five," the old gentleman told himself with much secret pleasure, and pretended that he was going to stop his double-shuffle. It was an excellent trap, and the boy fell straight into it.

He squandered his last precious bullet on the spittoon near which Mr. Adams happened to be at the moment, and the next moment Mr. Adams had him by the throat. They swayed and gulped for breath, rutting the earth with sharp heels; they rolled to the floor and floundered with legs tight tangled, the boy blindly striking at Mr. Adams with the pistol butt, and the audience drawing closer to lose nothing, when the bright knife flashed suddenly. It poised, and flew across the room, harmless, for a foot had driven into Mr. Adams' arm, and he felt a cold ring grooving his temple. It was the smooth, chilly muzzle of Specimen Jones's six-shooter.

"That's enough," said Jones. "More than enough."

Mr. Adams, being mature in judgment, rose instantly, like a good old sheep, and put his knife back obedient to orders. But in the brain of the overstrained, bewildered boy universal destruction was whirling. With a face stricken lean with ferocity, he staggered to his feet, plucking at his obstinate holster, and glaring for a foe. His eye fell first on his deliverer, leaning easily against the bar watching him, while the more and more curious audience scattered and held themselves ready to murder the boy if he should point his pistol their way. He was dragging at it clumsily, and at last it came. Specimen Jones sprang like a cat and held the barrel vertical and gripped the boy's wrist.

"Go easy, son," said he. "I know how you're feelin'."

The boy had been wrenching to get a shot at Jones, and now the quietness of the man's voice reached his brain, and he looked at Specimen Jones. He felt a potent brotherhood in the eyes that were considering him, and he began to fear he had been a fool. There was his dwarf Eastern revolver, slack in his inefficient fist, and the singular person still holding its barrel and tapping one derisive finger over the end, careless of the risk to his first joint.

"Why, you little—— ——" said Specimen Jones caressingly to the hypnotized youth, "if you was to pop that squirt off at me, I'd turn you up and spank y'u. Set 'em up, Ephraim."

But the commercial Ephraim hesitated, and Jones remembered. His last cent was gone. It was his third day at Ephraim's. He had stopped, having a little money, on his way to Tucson, where a friend had a job for him and was waiting. He was far too experienced a character ever to sell his horse or his saddle on these occasions and go on drinking. He looked as if he might, but he never did; and this was what disappointed businessmen like Ephraim in Specimen Jones.

But now, here was this tenderfoot he had undertaken to see through, and Ephraim reminding him that he had no more of the wherewithal. "Why, so I haven't," he said, with a short laugh, and his face flushed. "I guess," he continued, hastily, "this is worth a dollar or two." He drew a chain up from below his flannel shirt collar and over his head. He drew it a little slowly. It had not been taken off for a number of years—not, indeed, since it had been placed there originally. "It ain't brass," he added lightly, and strewed it along the counter without looking at it. Ephraim did look at it and, being satisfied began to uncork a new bottle, while the punctual audience came up for its drink.

"Won't you please let me treat?" said the boy, unsteadily. "I ain't likely to meet you again, sir." Reaction was giving him trouble inside.

"Where are you bound, kid?"

"Oh, just a ways up the country," answered the boy, keeping a grip on his voice.

"Well, you *may* get there. Where did you pick up that—that thing? Your pistol, I mean."

"It's a present from a friend," replied the tenderfoot with dignity.

"Farewell gift, wasn't it, kid? Yes; I thought so. Now I'd hate to get an affair like that from a friend. It would start me wondering if he liked me as well as I'd always thought he did. Put up that money, kid. You're drinking with me. Say, what's yer name?"

"Cumnor—J. Cumnor."

"Well, J. Cumnor, I'm glad to know y'u. Ephraim, let me make you acquainted with Mr. Cumnor. Mr. Adams, if you're rested from your quadrille, you can shake hands with my friend. Step around, you Miguels and Serapios and Cristobals, whatever y'u claim your names are. This is Mr. J. Cumnor."

The Mexicans did not understand either the letter or the spirit of these American words, but they drank their drink, and the concertina resumed its acrid melody. The boy had taken himself off without being noticed.

"Say, Spec," said Ephraim to Jones, "I'm no hog. Here's yer chain. You'll be along again."

"Keep it till I'm along again," said the owner.

"Just as you say, Spec," answered Ephraim smoothly, and he hung the pledge over an advertisement chromo of a nude, cream-colored lady with bright straw hair holding out a bottle of somebody's champagne. Specimen Jones sang no more songs, but smoked and leaned in silence on the bar. The company were talking of bed, and Ephraim plunged his glasses into a bucket to clean them for the morrow.

"Know anything about that kid?" inquired Jones abruptly.

Ephraim shook his head as he washed.

"Traveling alone, ain't he?"

Ephraim nodded.

"Where did y'u say y'u found that fellow layin' the Injuns got?"

"Mile this side the cañon. 'Mong them sandhumps."

"How long had he been there, do y'u figure?"

"Three days, anyway."

Jones watched Ephraim finish his cleansing. "Your clock needs wiping," he remarked. "A man might suppose it was nine, to see that thing the way the dirt hides the hands. Look again in half an hour and it'll say three. That's the kind of clock gives a man the jams. Sends him crazy."

"Well, that ain't a bad thing to be in this country," said Ephraim, rubbing the glass case and restoring identity to the hands. "If that man had been crazy he'd been livin' right now. Injuns'll never touch lunatics."

"That band have passed here and gone north," Jones said. "I saw a smoke among the foothills as I come along day before yesterday. I guess they're aiming to cross the Santa Catalina. Most likely they're that band from round the San Carlos that were reported as raiding down in Sonora."

"I seen well enough," said Ephraim, "when I found him that they wasn't going to trouble us any, or they'd have been around by then."

He was quite right, but Specimen Jones was thinking of something else. He went out to the corral, feeling disturbed and doubtful. He saw the tall, white freight wagon of the Mexicans, looming silent, and a little way off the new fence where the man lay. An odd sound startled him, though he knew it was no Indians at this hour, and he looked down into a little dry ditch. It was the boy, hidden away flat on his stomach among the stones, sobbing.

"Oh, snakes!" whispered Specimen Jones, and stepped back. The Latin races embrace and weep, and all goes well; but among Saxons tears are a horrid event. Jones never knew what to do when it was a woman, but this was truly disgusting. He was well seasoned by the frontier, had tried a little of everything: town and country, ranches, saloons, stage-driving, marriage occasionally, and latterly mines. He had sundry claims staked out and always carried pieces of stone in his pockets, discoursing upon their mineral-bearing capacity, which was apt to be very slight. That is why he was called Specimen Jones. He had exhausted all the important sensations and did not care much for anything any more. Perfect health and strength kept him from discovering that he was a saddened, drifting man. He wished to kick the boy for his baby performance, and yet he stepped carefully away from the ditch so the boy should not suspect his presence. He found himself standing still, looking at the dim, broken desert.

"Why, hell," complained Specimen Jones, "he played the little man to start with. He did so. He scared that old horse thief, Adams, just about dead. Then he went to kill me, that kep' him from bein' buried early tomorrow. I've been wild that way myself and wantin' to shoot up the whole outfit." Jones looked at the place where his middle finger used to be, before a certain evening in Tombstone. "But I never—" He glanced toward the ditch, perplexed. "What's that mean? Why in the world does he git to cryin' for *now*, do you suppose?" Jones took to singing without knowing it. " 'Ye shepherds, tell me, have you seen my Flora pass this way?' " he murmured. Then a thought struck him. "Hello, kid!" he called out. There was no answer. "Of course," said Jones. "Now he's ashamed to hev me see him come out of there." He walked with elaborate slowness round the corral and behind a shed. "Hello, you kid!" he called again.

"I was thinking of going to sleep," said the boy, appearing quite suddenly. "I—I'm not used to riding all day. I'll get used to it, you know," he hastened to add.

" 'Have you seen my Flo'—Say kid, where y'u bound, anyway?"

"San Carlos."

"San Carlos? Oh. Ah. 'Flora pass this way?' "

"Is it far, sir?"

"Awful far, sometimes. It's always liable to be far through the Arivaypa Cañon."

"I didn't expect to make it between meals," remarked Cumnor.

"No. Sure. What made you come this route?"

"A man told me."

"A man? Oh. Well, it *is* kind o' difficult, I admit, for an Arizonan not to lie to a stranger. But I think I'd have told you to go by Tres Alamos and Point of Mountain. It's the road the man that told you would choose himself every time. Do you like Injuns, kid?"

Cumnor snapped eagerly.

"Of course y'u do. And you've never saw one in the whole minute-and-a-half you've been alive. I know all about it."

"I'm not afraid," said the boy.

"Not afraid? Of course y'u ain't. What's your idea in going to Carlos? Got town lots there?"

"No," said the literal youth, to the huge internal diversion of Jones. "There's a man there I used to know back home. He's in the cavalry. What sort of a town is it for sport?" asked Cumnor, in a gay Lothario tone.

"Town?" Specimen Jones caught hold of the top rail of the corral. *"Sport?"* Now I'll tell y'u what sort of a town it is. There 'ain't no streets. There ain't no houses. There ain't any land and water in the usual meaning of them words. There's Mount Turnbull. It's pretty near a usual mountain, but y'u don't want to go there. The Creator didn't make San Carlos. It's a heap older than Him. When He got around to it after slickin' up Paradise and them fruit trees, He just left it to be as He found it, as a sample of the way they done business before He come along. He 'ain't done any work around that spot at all, He 'ain't. Mix up a barrel of sand and ashes and thorns, and jam scorpions and rattlesnakes along in, and dump the outfit on stones, and heat yer stones redhot, and set the United States Army loose over the place chasin' Apaches, and you've got San Carlos."

Cumnor was silent for a moment. "I don't care," he said. "I want to chase Apaches."

"Did you see that man Ephraim found by the cañon?" Jones inquired.

"Didn't get here in time."

"Well, there was a hole in his chest made by an arrow. But there's no harm in that if you die at wunst. That chap didn't, y'u see. You heard Ephraim tell about it. They'd done a number of things to the man before he could die. Roastin' was only one of 'em. Now your road takes you through the mountains where these Injuns hev gone. Kid, come along to Tucson with me," urged Jones suddenly.

Again Cumnor was silent. "Is my road different from other people's?" he said finally.

"Not to Grant, it ain't. These Mexicans are hauling freight to Grant. But what's the matter with your coming to Tucson with me?"

"I started to go to San Carlos, and I'm going," said Cumnor.

"You're a poor chuckle-headed fool!" burst out Jones, in a rage. "And y'u can go, for all I care—you and your Christmas-tree pistol. Like as not you won't find your cavalry friend at San Carlos. They've killed a lot of them soldiers huntin' Injuns this season. Good night."

Specimen Jones was gone. Cumnor walked to his blanket roll, where his saddle was slung under the shed. The various doings of the evening had bruised his nerves. He spread his blankets among the dry cattle dung and sat down, taking off a few clothes slowly. He lumped his coat and overalls under his head for a pillow and, putting the despised pistol alongside, lay between the blankets. No object showed in the night but the tall freight wagon. The tenderfoot thought he had made altogether a fool of himself upon the first trial trip of his manhood, alone on the open sea of Arizona. No man, not even Jones now, was his friend. A stranger, who could have had nothing against him but his inexperience, had taken the trouble to direct him on the wrong road. He did not mind definite enemies. He had punched the heads of those in Pennsylvania and would not object to shooting them here; but this impersonal, surrounding hostility of the unknown was new and bitter: the cruel, assassinating, cowardly Southwest, where prospered those jailbirds whom the vigilantes had driven from California. He thought of the nameless human carcass that lay near, buried that day, and of the jokes about its mutilations. Cumnor was not an innocent boy, either in principles or in practice, but this laughter about a dead body had burned into his young, unhardened soul. He lay watching with hot, dogged eyes the brilliant stars. A passing wind turned the windmill, which creaked a forlorn minute, and ceased. He must have gone to sleep and slept soundly, for the next he knew it was the cold air of dawn that made him open his eyes. A numb silence lay over all things, and the tenderfoot had that moment of curiosity as to where he was now which comes to those who have journeyed for many days. The Mexicans had already departed with their freight wagon. It was not entirely light, and the embers where these early starters had cooked their breakfast lay glowing in the sand across the road. The boy remembered seeing a wagon where now he saw only chill, distant peaks, and while he lay quiet and warm, shunning full consciousness, there was a stir in the cabin, and at Ephraim's voice reality broke upon his drowsiness, and he recollected Arizona and the keen stress of shifting for himself. He noted the gray paling round the grave. Indians? He would catch up with the Mexicans and travel in their company to Grant. Freighters made but fifteen miles in the day, and he could start after breakfast and be with them before they stopped at noon. Six men need not worry about Apaches, Cumnor thought. The voice of Specimen Jones came from the cabin, and sounds of lighting the stove, and the growling conversation of men getting up. Cumnor, lying in his blankets, tried to overhear what Jones was saying, for no better reason than that this was the only man he had met lately who had seemed to care whether he were alive or dead. There was the clink of Ephraim's whiskey bottles and the cheerful tones of old Mr. Adams, saying, "It's better 'n brushin' yer teeth"; and then further clinking and an inquiry from Specimen Jones.

"Whose spurs?" said he.

"Mine." This from Mr. Adams.

"How long have they been yourn?"

"Since I got 'em, I guess."

"Well, you've enjoyed them spurs long enough." The voice of Specimen Jones now altered in quality. "And you'll give 'em back to that kid."

Muttering followed that the boy could not catch. "You'll give 'em back," repeated Jones. "I seen y'u lift 'em from under that chair when I was in the corner."

"That's straight, Mr. Adams," said Ephraim. "I noticed it myself, though I had no objections, of course. But Mr. Jones has pointed out—"

"Since when have you growed so honest, Jones?" cackled Mr. Adams, seeing that he must lose his little booty. "And why didn't you raise yer objections when you seen me do it?"

"I didn't know the kid," Jones explained. "And if it don't strike you that game blood deserves respect, why it does strike me."

Hearing this, the tenderfoot, outside in his shed, thought better of mankind and life in general, arose from his nest, and began preening himself. He had all the correct trappings for the frontier, and his toilet in the shed gave him pleasure. The sun came up, and with a stroke struck the world to crystal. The near sandhills went into rose, the crabbed yucca and the mesquite turned transparent, with lances and pale films of green, like drapery graciously veiling the desert's face, and distant violet peaks and edges framed the vast enchantment beneath the liquid exhalations of the sky. The smell of bacon and coffee from open windows filled the heart with bravery and yearning, and Ephraim, putting his head round the corner, called to Cumnor that he had better come in and eat. Jones, already at table, gave him the briefest nod; but the spurs were there, replaced as Cumnor had left them under a chair in the corner. In Arizona they do not say much at any meal, and at breakfast nothing at all; and as Cumnor swallowed and meditated he noticed the cream-colored lady and the chain, and he made up his mind he should assert his identity with regard to that business, though how and when was not clear to him. He was in no great haste to take up his journey. The society of the Mexicans whom he must sooner or later overtake did not tempt him. When breakfast was done he idled in the cabin, like the other guests, while Ephraim and his assistant busied about the premises. But the morning grew on, and the guests, after a season of smoking and tilted silence against the wall, shook themselves and their effects together, saddled, and were lost among the waste, thorny hills. Twenty Mile became hot and torpid. Jones lay on three consecutive chairs, occasionally singing, and old Mr. Adams had not gone away either, but watched him, with more tobacco running down his beard.

"Well," said Cumnor, "I'll be going."

"Nobody's stopping y'u," remarked Jones.

"You're going to Tucson?" the boy said, with the chain problem still unsolved in his mind. "Goodbye, Mr. Jones. I hope I'll—we'll—"

"That'll do," said Jones; and the tenderfoot, thrown back by this severity, went to get his saddlehorse and his burro.

Presently Jones remarked to Mr. Adams that he wondered what Ephraim was doing, and went out. The old gentleman was left alone in the room, and he swiftly noticed that the belt and pistol of Specimen Jones were left alone with him. The accoutrement lay by the chair its owner had been lounging in. It is an easy thing to remove cartridges from the chambers of a revolver and replace the weapon in its holster so that everything looks quite natural.

The old gentleman was entertained with the notion that somewhere in Tucson Specimen Jones might have a surprise, and he
did not take a minute to prepare this, drop the belt as it lay before,
and saunter innocently out of the saloon. Ephraim and Jones were
criticizing the tenderfoot's property as he packed his burro.

"Do y'u make it a rule to travel with ice cream?" Jones was
inquiring.

"They're for water," Cumnor said. "They told me at Tucson
I'd need to carry water for three days on some trails."

It was two good-sized milk cans that he had, and they bounced
about on the little burro's pack, giving him as much amazement
as a jackass can feel. Jones and Ephraim were hilarious.

"Don't go without your spurs, Mr. Cumnor," said the voice
of old Mr. Adams, as he approached the group. His tone was
particularly civil.

The tenderfoot had indeed forgotten his spurs, and he ran back
to get them. The cream-colored lady still had the chain hanging
upon her, and Cumnor's problem was suddenly solved. He put
the chain in his pocket and laid the price of one round of drinks
for last night's company on the shelf below the chromo. He returned with his spurs on and went to his saddle that lay beside
that of Specimen Jones under the shed. After a moment he came
with his saddle to where the men stood talking by his pony, slung
it on, and tightened the cinches; but the chain was now in the
saddlebag of Specimen Jones, mixed up with some tobacco, stale
bread, a box of matches, and a hunk of fat bacon. The men at
Twenty Mile said good day to the tenderfoot, with monosyllables
and indifference, and watched him depart into the heated desert.
Wishing for a last look at Jones, he turned once, and saw the three
standing, and the chocolate brick of the cabin, and the windmill
white and idle in the sun.

"He'll be gutted by night," remarked Mr. Adams.

"I ain't buryin' him, then," said Ephraim.

"Nor I," said Specimen Jones. "Well, it's time I was getting
to Tucson."

He went to the saloon, strapped on his pistol, saddled, and rode
away. Ephraim and Mr. Adams returned to the cabin; and here is
the final conclusion they came to after three hours of discussion
as to who took the chain and who had it just then:

Ephraim. Jones, he hadn't no cash.

Mr. Adams. The kid, he hadn't no sense.

Ephraim. The kid, he lent the cash to Jones.

Mr. Adams. Jones, he goes off with his chain.

Both. What damn fools everybody is, anyway!

And they went to dinner. But Mr. Adams did not mention his relations with Jones's pistol. Let it be said, in extenuation of that performance, that Mr. Adams supposed Jones was going to Tucson, where he said he was going, and where a job and a salary were awaiting him. In Tucson an unloaded pistol in the holster of so handy a man on the drop as was Specimen would keep people civil, because they would not know, any more than the owner, that it was unloaded; and the mere possession of it would be sufficient in nine chances out of ten—though it was undoubtedly for the tenth that Mr. Adams had a sneaking hope. But Specimen Jones was not going to Tucson. A contention in his mind as to whether he would do what was good for himself, or what was good for another, had kept him sullen ever since he got up. Now it was settled and Jones in serene humor again. Of course he had started on the Tucson road, for the benefit of Ephraim and Mr. Adams.

The tenderfoot rode along. The Arizona sun beat down upon the deadly silence, and the world was no longer of crystal but a mesa, dull and gray and hot. The pony's hoofs grated in the gravel, and after a time the road dived down and up among lumpy hills of stone and cactus, always nearer the fierce glaring Sierra Santa Catalina. It dipped so abruptly in and out of the shallow, sudden ravines that, on coming up from one of these into sight of the country again, the tenderfoot's heart jumped at the close apparition of another rider quickly bearing in upon him from gullies where he had been moving unseen. But it was only Specimen Jones.

"Hello!" said he, joining Cumnor. "Hot, ain't it?"

"Where are you going?" inquired Cumnor.

"Up here a ways." And Jones jerked his finger generally toward the Sierra, where they were heading.

"Thought you had a job in Tucson."

"That's what I have."

Specimen Jones had no more to say, and they rode for a while, their ponies' hoofs always grating in the gravel, and the milk cans lightly clanking on the burro's pack. The bunched blades of the yuccas bristled steelstiff, and as far as you could see it was a gray waste of mounds and ridges sharp and blunt, up to the forbidding boundary walls of the Tortilita one way and the Santa Catalina the other. Cumnor wondered if Jones had found the chain. Jones was capable of not finding it for several weeks, or of finding it at once and saying nothing.

"You'll excuse my meddling with your business?" the boy hazarded.

Jones looked inquiring.

"Something's wrong with your saddle pocket."

Specimen saw nothing apparently wrong with it, but perceiving Cumnor was grinning, unbuckled the pouch. He looked at the boy rapidly and looked away again, and as he rode, still in silence, he put the chain back round his neck below the flannel shirt collar.

"Say, kid," he remarked, after some time, "what does J stand for?"

"J? Oh, my name! Jock."

"Well, Jock, will y'u explain to me as a friend how y'u ever come to be such a fool as to leave yer home—wherever and whatever it was—in exchange for this here Godforsaken and iniquitous hole?"

"If you'll explain to me," said the boy, greatly heartened, "how you come to be ridin' in the company of a fool, instead of goin' to your job at Tucson."

The explanation was furnished before Specimen Jones had framed his reply. A burning freight wagon and five dismembered human stumps lay in the road. This was what had happened to the Miguels and Serapios and the concertina. Jones and Cumnor, in their dodging and struggles to exclude all expressions of growing mutual esteem from their speech, had forgotten their journey, and a sudden bend among the rocks where the road had now brought them revealed the blood and fire staring them in the face. The plundered wagon was three parts empty; its splintered, blazing boards slid down as they burned into the fiery heap on the ground; packages of soda and groceries and medicines slid with them, bursting into chemical spots of green and crimson flame; a wheel crushed in and sank, spilling more packages that flickered and hissed; the garbage of combat and murder littered the earth, and in the air hung an odor that Cumnor knew, though he had never smelled it before. Morsels of dropped booty up among the rocks showed where the Indians had gone, and one horse remained, groaning, with an accidental arrow in his belly.

"We'll just kill him," said Jones; and his pistol snapped idly,

and snapped again, as his eye caught a motion—a something—
two hundred yards up among the boulders on the hill. He whirled
round. The enemy was behind them also. There was no retreat.
"Yourn's no good!" yelled Jones, fiercely, for Cumnor was getting out his little, foolish revolver. "Oh, what a trick to play on
a man! Drop off yer horse, kid; drop, and do like me. Shootin's
no good here, even if I was loaded. *They* shot and look at them
now. God bless them ice-cream freezers of yourn, kid! Did y'u
ever see a crazy man? If you 'ain't, *make it up as y'u go along*!"

More objects moved up among the boulders. Specimen Jones
ripped off the burro's pack, and the milk cans rolled on the ground.
The burro began grazing quietly, with now and then a step toward
new patches of grass. The horses stood where their riders had left
them, their reins over their heads, hanging and dragging. From
two hundred yards on the hill the ambushed Apaches showed,
their dark, scattered figures appearing cautiously one by one,
watching with suspicion. Specimen Jones seized up one milk
can, and Cumnor obediently did the same.

"You kin dance, kid, and I kin sing, and we'll go to it," said
Jones. He rambled in a wavering loop, and diving eccentrically
at Cumnor, clashed the milk cans together. " 'Es schallt ein Ruf
wie Donnerhall,' " he bawled, beginning the song of "Die Wacht
am Rhein." "Why don't you dance?" he shouted, sternly. The
boy saw the terrible earnestness of his face, and, clashing his milk
cans in turn, he shuffled a sort of jig. The two went over the sand
in loops, toe and heel; the donkey continued his quiet grazing,
and the flames rose hot and yellow from the freight wagon. And
all the while the stately German hymn pealed among the rocks,
and the Apaches crept down nearer the bowing, scraping men.
The sun shone bright, and their bodies poured with sweat. Jones
flung off his shirt; his damp, matted hair was half in ridges and
half-glued to his forehead, and the delicate gold chain swung and
struck his broad, naked breast. The Apaches drew nearer again,
their bows and arrows held uncertainly. They came down the hill,
fifteen or twenty, taking a long time and stopping every few yards.
The milk cans clashed, and Jones thought he felt the boy's strokes
weakening. "Die Wacht am Rhein" was finished, and now it was
"Have you seen my Flora pass this way?' " "Y'u mustn't play
out, kid," said Jones, very gently. "Indeed y'u mustn't," and he
at once resumed his song. The silent Apaches had now reached
the bottom of the hill. They stood some twenty yards away, and

Cumnor had a good chance to see his first Indians. He saw them move, and the color and slim shape of their bodies, their thin arms, and their long, black hair. It went through his mind that if he had no more clothes on than that, dancing would come easier. His boots were growing heavy to lift, and his overalls seemed to wrap his sinews in wet, strangling thongs. He wondered how long he had been keeping this up. The legs of the Apaches were free, with light moccasins only half way to the thigh, slenderly held up by strings from the waist. Cumnor envied their unencumbered steps as he saw them again walk nearer to where he was dancing. It was long since he had eaten, and he noticed a singing dullness in his brain, and became frightened at his thoughts, which were running and melting into one fixed idea. This idea was to take off his boots, and offer to trade them for a pair of moccasins. It terrified him—this endless, molten rush of thoughts; he could see them coming in different shapes from different places in his head, but they all joined immediately, and always formed the same fixed idea. He ground his teeth to master this encroaching inebriation of his will and judgment. He clashed his can more loudly to wake him to reality, which he still could recognize and appreciate. For a time he found it a good plan to listen to what Specimen Jones was singing and tell himself the name of the song if he knew it. At present it was "Yankee Doodle," to which Jones was fitting words of his own. These ran, "Now I'm going to try a bluff, And mind you do what I do"; and then again, over and over. Cumnor waited for the word "bluff," for it was hard and heavy and fell into his thoughts, and stopped them for a moment. The dance was so long now he had forgotten about that. A numbness had been spreading through his legs, and he was glad to feel a sharp pain in the sole of his foot. It was a piece of gravel that had somehow worked its way in, and was rubbing through the skin into the flesh. "That's good," he said, aloud. The pebble was eating the numbness away, and Cumnor drove it hard against the raw spot, and relished the tonic of its burning friction. The Apaches had drawn into a circle. Standing at some interval apart, they entirely surrounded the arena. Shrewd, half-convinced, and yet with awe, they watched the dancers, who clashed their cans slowly now in rhythm to Jones's hoarse, parched singing. He was quite master of himself and led the jig round the still blazing wreck of the wagon, and circled in figures of eight between the corpses of the Mexicans, clashing the milk cans above each one.

Then, knowing his strength was coming to an end, he approached an Indian whose splendid fillet and trappings denoted him of consequence; and Jones was near shouting with relief when the Indian shrank backward. Suddenly he saw Cumnor let his can drop, and without stopping to see why, he caught it up, and, slowly rattling both, approached each Indian in turn with tortuous steps. The circle that had never uttered a sound till now receded, chanting almost in a whisper some exorcising song which the man with the fillet had begun. They gathered round him, retreating always, and the strain, with its rapid muttered words, rose and fell softly among them. Jones had supposed the boy was overcome by faintness, and looked to see where he lay. But it was not faintness. Cumnor, with his boots off, came by and walked after the Indians in a trance. They saw him and quickened their pace, often turning to be sure he was not overtaking them. He called to them unintelligibly, stumbling up the sharp hill and pointing to the boots. Finally he sat down. They continued ascending the mountain, herding close round the man with the feathers, until the rocks and the filmy tangles screened them from sight; and like a wind that hums uncertainly in grass, their chanting died away.

The sun was half behind the western range when Jones next moved. He called and, getting no answer, he crawled painfully to where the boy lay on the hill. Cumnor was sleeping heavily; his head was hot, and he moaned. So Jones crawled down and fetched blankets and the canteen of water. He spread the blankets over the boy, wet a handkerchief, and laid it on his forehead; then he lay down himself.

The earth was again magically smitten to crystal. Again the sharp cactus and the sand turned beautiful, and violet floated among the mountains, and rose-colored orange in the sky above them.

"Jock," said Specimen at length.

The boy opened his eyes.

"Your foot is awful, Jock. Can y'u eat?"

"Not with my foot."

"Ah, God bless y'u, Jock! Y'u ain't turrble sick. But *can* y'u eat?"

Cumnor shook his head.

"Eatin's what y'u need, though. Well, here." Specimen poured a judicious mixture of whiskey and water down the boy's throat and wrapped the awful foot in his own flannel shirt. "They'll fix y'u over to Grant. It's maybe twelve miles through the cañon. It ain't a town any more than Carlos is, but the soldiers 'll be good to us. As soon as night comes you and me must somehow git out of this."

Somehow they did, Jones walking and leading his horse and the imperturbable little burro and also holding Cumnor in the saddle. And when Cumnor was getting well in the military hospital at Grant, he listened to Jones recounting to all that chose to hear how useful a weapon an ice-cream freezer can be, and how if you'll only chase Apaches in your stocking feet they are sure to run away. And then Jones and Cumnor both enlisted; and I suppose Jones's friend is still expecting him in Tucson.

The Western fiction of Henry Wilson Allen, whether it appears under the pseudonym Clay Fisher or that of Will Henry, has been widely lauded for its provocative exploration of both the myth and reality of the Old West. Testimony to the validity of his praise are the four Western Writers of America Spur awards he has won, two for Best Novel and two for Best Short Story. His books include the novels Who Rides with Wyatt? *(1955),* Where the Sun Now Stands *(1960), and* Alias Butch Cassidy *(1968), as by Will Henry, and* The Big Pasture *(1955),* The Pitchfork Patrol *(1962), and* Black Apache *(1976), as by Clay Fisher; and the short-story collections* The Oldest Maiden Lady in New Mexico and Other Stories *(1962) and* Nine Lives West *(1978), both as by Fisher. In "The Hunting of Tom Horn," he tells a wry tale of an old range detective's encounter with the legendary gunman in Arizona Territory.*

The Hunting of Tom Horn

★★★★★★★★★★★★★★★

Clay Fisher

SOMETIMES a man has to lie to save his own neck, and sometimes to save somebody else's. I had to lie once to save another man's life, and I don't know to this day whether I did right or wrong.

It was on the old Jim Birch stage road about halfway between Lordsburg and Tucson. I was Tucson-bound, coming back from having trailed a bunch of rustled stock for the Association over into New Mexico. In those days we could do that, the cattlemen's associations in both territories being glad to see a cow thief caught, no matter whether by an Arizona detective or a New Mexican one. I will say, though, strictly as an item of professional pride, that we boys from the Arizona side had a little better record for arrests and convictions. Maybe that's why I hadn't gotten too much cooperation from the Lordsburg sheriff just now, and why I was riding back to Tucson empty-handed. Anyway, I was over

52

a week late in getting back, and in no need whatever of further delay. But on a lonely stage line in Arizona Territory, trouble was always as close as the next bend in the road.

In this case, what lay around that next bend was a lynching bee, and when my pony snorted and put on the brakes and that hard-tailed bunch of range riders posed around the kid on the piebald gelding eased off on the rope around his neck and looked my way, mister, you could have heard a drop of sweat hit that roadside dust.

It was trouble, all right, the worst kind. Only question was, was it my trouble or just the other fellow's?

I didn't know yet. But I got down off my horse nice and quiet and went walking toward the lynchers real easy. You see, the way I'm built, I couldn't help myself; I had to find out. I suppose that's the streak of cussedness that made me a stock detective. Anyway, it was the streak that put me to walking up on those flint-faced cowboys, when I ought to have been hightailing it away from them as fast as old Shoofly could carry me. Which was somewhat.

But I was never known for good sense, only for inferior judgment. I picked out the foreman and braced him.

"What seems to be the difficulty?" I asked.

He jerked a thumb over his shoulder, his reply notably unloquacious. "Take a look for yourself," he advised.

I stepped around his horse and complied.

It was a tied-down, two-year-old beef, thrown alongside a small fire. The running, or single-iron, was propped in the flames, still heating. The evidence, though simple, was ample: a brand blotter had been interrupted at his trade. I turned back to the foreman.

"You know a single-iron when you see one, mister?" he inquired, giving me a look as hard as gunhammer steel. "This particular one fits just perfect under this boy's stirrup fender. That satisfy you?"

I tried to trade tough looks with him.

"Not quite," I said. "You can't hang a man just for changing a brand. Not these days. It's eighteen-eighty, mister."

"*I* can hang him," he answered back, not flicking a lid. "I'm E. K. Sanders, managing foreman, Mescalero Land & Cattle Company. Now, how about you?"

"How about me?" I said, eying him back. "I'll tell you about me, Mr. Sanders. I'm against hanging a man without full and fair trial, for *any* reason."

This Mescalero Company foreman was a big man, running a big, notoriously hard-case cattle outfit. He wasn't of the breed to buy any offhand interference.

"Mister," he said, "you open your mouth once more, we'll run you up alongside this hot-iron artist. We been after him six months, and we mean to swing him. *Now*, how about *you*?"

"Do you even know who he is?" I stalled.

"Don't know, don't care. The kid was caught burning a Mescalero cow. We didn't wait for no formal introduction."

It was time for the lie. I had set it up. Now I had to carry it off like the cold-deck bluff it was.

"Well, I do know him," I said. "What's more, I want him, and I mean to take him."

The foreman nodded past me to two of the cowboys behind me. They moved up, flanking me, hands on their holsters.

"And who might you be?" he asked, real quiet.

"Charlie Shonto," I answered, just as quiet.

"From Gila Bend?"

"There's another Charlie Shonto?"

"Don't get smart," he said, "you're flanked. Your fast gun don't mean a thing to my boys. Moreover, we ain't sent for no help from the Arizona Cattlemen's Association. Time comes we can't catch our own cow thieves, we'll let you know."

I shook my head.

"You don't listen good, Mr. Sanders," I said. "This boy has been on our list since last July. That's a year ago, come next month. We're tired of chasing him."

"So?"

"So, he's our boy, and I'm taking him into Tucson. I got to earn my keep, Mr. Sanders, same as you and your boys, here." I eased one step to the side, half turning to get both him and the two hands in pulling view. The other riders were out of it and sitting quiet. "Now, I do hope you don't mean to make me earn it unpleasant," I finished up. "I prefer working friendly."

Sanders gave me a long looking over. Then he waved carefully to his hard-case flankers. He wasn't going to fight the Association—an outfit that had an unmatched reputation in the Southwest—but all the same he felt compelled to go on record, personally.

"All right, Shonto." He nodded. "But you know range law

and you know you had no call to mix in here. We had this kid dead to rights."

It was my turn to nod. I took it on the acid side.

"You pretty near had him dead," I agreed, "but not to rights. Not to *his* rights, anyhow." I gave him three seconds to think about it, then went on. "Yes, I know range law, Mr. Sanders, and I know regular law, too. So I'll tell you, right out, what I mean to do. I'm turning this boy over to Sheriff Gates in Tucson. You want to come in and press cow-stealing charges against him, that will be the place to do it—not out here on the range, with you and your men as judge and jury." I threw him another pause, then nailed him down. "The day of the rope is done, Mr. Sanders. You know it, I know it. And we both know I'm only doing what's right and legal." I bent my crouch a little more toward the two gunhands. "Now, you men get the noose off the boy and cut his hands loose. Hop it!"

They hesitated, looking to Sanders for their yes or no. He gave them another yes, and they cut the rustler free.

"All right, kid," I said, "rein your horse over here."

He did so, and Sanders watched him bitterly.

"You're only putting off the inevitable, Shonto," he told me. "The kid was born to hang. He'll make it without your help, *or* mine." I nodded to that, agreeing with the general idea, then started off with the boy. Sanders raised his voice. "And, Shonto," he warned, "you'd better have him in that Tucson jail when we come after him!" I held up my horse, nettled by his tone.

"He'll be there," I said, flat out, "safe and sound."

"He'll still hang," he persisted tartly. "Range law or regular, he'll end on a rope. Remember I said it."

"I'll remember," I promised. "See you in Tucson, Mr. Sanders."

He held me a minute with that hard look of his, then nodded and said very soft, almost to himself.

"It's a long ways, yet, Mr. Shonto. With that boy you may just never make it."

We were lucky at Cow Creek Station. The weekly stage from Lordsburg was there, hung up with a wheel change. All I had to do was wait around until after supper and ride on into Tucson with my prisoner in style. It was a prospect pleasing in more varieties than getting that kid rustler back of bars. I had been sitting on

Shoofly the better part of two weeks and was good and touchy in the tailbone. Those old Concord seats were going to feel like feather beds. Overcome by the prospect, I offered to take the kid for a walk to sort of let him get the ache out of his own backside before we sat down to eat.

It was deep dusk when we set out down the road below the station. I was preoccupied somewhat. I hadn't been able to get out of my mind the foreman's warning about the boy. There was something about it, and the kid himself, that I kept thinking I ought to remember. I had seen him, or his face, somewhere before, I was certain. But I couldn't remember where for the life of me—and that fact was very nearly the death of me.

He was a big kid, curly-headed, handsome, good-natured as a hound pup. And smiling, always smiling. Polite, too. Polite as a preacher talking to the devil. Like right then, for instance, as we strolled along under a three-quarter moon, just smelling the sweet sage and hot sand cooling off after the daytime swelter.

"Mr. Shonto," he grinned sheepishly, "I wonder if it would trouble you too entirely much, sir, if I was to ask you—well, naw, you wouldn't—excuse me, sir."

"Well, come on, boy," I said. "Don't lead me to the altar like that and then leave me standing there. Speak up, I ain't the sheriff."

"Well, sir, I was just thinking if you would have the trust in me to turn my hands loose for just one good stretch. I'd give you my bounden word, sir."

"You would, eh?" I eyed him good. "All right, I'll just take your word, then. For one stretch."

I undid him—took off the cuffs—and he flexed his hands, worked his shoulder muscles and the like.

"Oh, my," he said, "that certainly is some grand, Mr. Shonto. Thank you ever so kindly, sir."

He put his hands up and took the stretch, long and luxurious. Then lowered his reach and put out his hands toward me, shy-smiling like I'd commuted his sentence, or something. Unthinking, I went to put the cuffs back on him, and he struck at me so fast I didn't know what had happened until I'd landed on my back in the dirt and he'd grabbed my gun off me whilst I was shaking my head to get the cobwebs out of it.

"Indian wrestling trick," he said. "Learnt it from the San

Carlos tribe, over to Fort Apache. Sorry, Mr. Shonto, but I only give you my word for one stretch. Now, ain't that so?''

I made it back to my feet, still groggy.

"You seem to be doing the talking, boy," I replied. "Just keep going."

He smiled, bright-faced enough to shame the moon.

"Yes sir, thank you, sir. Just what I intend doing, soon as we can get back to the station stock corral and pick up my pony. And please move steady and nice, Mr. Shonto. You know how I feel my debt to you."

I had started to edge away from him, to get a set at jumping him. Now I nodded and gave it up.

"Yes, it seems I do, boy," I said, feeling the crick in my back where he had thrown me. "You don't need to fear for me turning on you."

"I reckon that's so, sir," he grinned. "Let's go."

I got his pony out of the corral for him, him directing me from behind the hayshed corner, my own Colt covering me every step of the way. He swung up on the paint back of the shed, stuck my revolver in his belt, told me good-bye and God bless me till I could find more rewarding work.

"Hold on, boy," I said. "I don't believe I caught your name."

"Don't believe you did, either, Mr. Shonto. Didn't toss it."

"Would you mind, son? A man sort of likes to know who his friends are."

"You mean his enemies, don't you, Mr. Shonto?"

"You know what I mean, kid. I'm bound to come after you. I give my word in the Association's name that I'd turn you over to Sheriff Gates in Tucson. I'll do it, too, boy. One way or the other."

He shook his head, the smile still 100 percent uncut good will.

"Some other summer, maybe; not this one, Mr. Shonto—" He started his pony away, then held him up. Obviously another impulse of charity had seized him. He yielded to it with charming grace. "However, sir," he said, "in case you want to send me a picture postal of that Tucson jail, just mail it to General Delivery, Arizona Territory, care of Tom Horn. So long, Mr. Shonto."

This time when he turned the paint and flashed his happy smile, he was gone. All I could do was stand there scratching my thick head and talking to myself in terms of tenderness never meant for mother's ears—his or mine.

Tom Horn! One of the most fantastic badmen the Southwest ever spawned. He didn't look a day over eighteen years old and already had a reputation for cold nerve second to nobody's in the outlaw business. I had seen his smiling likeness on enough wanted flyers to paper a six-room house; and I would rather have gone blindfold into a gopher hole after a rattlesnake than to take out, alone, after that boy. But I had told a deliberate lie to save his life, and I had used the name of the Arizona Cattlemen's Association into the bargain. The fact it was a poor bargain didn't change a thing. It was still up to nobody but Mrs. Shonto's simpleminded boy, Charlie, to make good on its stated terms.

I would have that kid back in Tucson for that Mescalero Land & Cattle Company rustling trial if it was the last ride-down ever I set foot into stirrup for.

The country down below was desolate, brooding, empty; full only of the glare of desert sun and big silence—Apache country. I was bellied down on a high rock scanning it through a pair of field glasses. My nerves were balled up like a clenched fist.

Tom Horn had headed straight into that stillness down there, figuring I wouldn't follow. Odds were, he could have won his bet. That was bad country any time and especially bad just then.

Broken Mouth, called Boca Rota by the local Indians, and, by any name, the poorest friend the white man ever had in Arizona, was making a last move to keep Apacheria for the Apaches. He and his mixed band of New Mexico Mescaleros and local "Cherry Cows," Chiricahuas, had been on the raid since early spring. The old chief had served notice on the U.S. Army at Fort Yavapai that any soldier, or civilian, caught in his hunting preserve would be given the full welcome. In Apache talk that meant they would entertain a man all night, then—well, you could put it this way, that man's first sunrise with Broken Mouth and his red wolf pack would be his last. Still, I had to face the fun.

Tom Horn was down there somewhere. That left me no choice. In my business a man has got to be ready to live by his word, or die by it.

It was late that afternoon when I saw the old dreaded Apache sign, black smoke rolling upward from some burning settler's home or barn. The track line I'd been running on Tom Horn led toward the smoke, and I spurred over the near rise in the wagon road he'd been following, to see if I might be in time to help the poor devils. I wasn't. I no more than topped the rise, then I hauled old Shoofly in.

Coming toward me, up the far side of the rise, was an old farm wagon loaded down with cheap furniture, torn mattresses, chicken crates, all the pitiful remnants of an Indian burn-out, including two red-eyed little kids. On the seat with the kids was a dismounted cavalry trooper doing the driving. Behind the wagon rode seven other troopers, and in front of it came their sergeant. When he saw me, the sergeant threw up his hand and called the halt, and I rode down for the talk.

"You're a little late, mister," he opened. "And so were we."

I nodded, tight-mouthed.

"I can see that. Apaches, eh?"

"Some folks call them that."

"Yeah, I know what you mean." I looked past the sergeant, to the two kids. "Poor little things. I reckon their folks were both—"

"Yeah," said the sergeant, "they were."

"Which Apaches?" I asked. "Do you know for sure?"

"Bronco Mescalero. Some Cherry Cows mixed in. Broken Mouth's bunch. You ever hear of him?"

"Somewhat."

"Well, then, you've heard enough to turn around and follow us back to the fort."

"That depends, sergeant. You haven't by any chance seen a tall, curly-headed boy riding a red sorrel paint, have you?"

"Might be we have. Why so?"

"He's a wanted man."

"You a bounty hunter?"

"Nope. Stock detective for the Cattlemen's Association."

"Oh? Well, yes, we seen your boy. Not thirty minutes down the road." He jerked his thumb over his shoulder toward the smoke, and I turned my horse.

"Thanks, sergeant. Good luck to you."

"Yeah. Sorry I can't say the same to you."

A little puzzled, I held up. "How's that, sergeant?"

"Just that I hope you never catch the kid," he said. "He's the one saved these two little ones here. Rode into the Apache surround, head-on. Broke through it, got into the house, held them off till we hove in sight. Then he lit out like we'd caught him sucking eggs."

"That's like him." I nodded. "Which way did he take?"

"A way I'd advise you not to follow, mister detective; smack-dab in the tracks of them Apaches."

"It's a poor way," I agreed, "but I'm bound to go it."

He shook his head scowlingly, turned his horse to signal the forward-ho to his men.

"Oh, sergeant," I added. "You're a soldier. You ever took on an order you'd rather get horsewhipped than to go through with?"

"Sure. What you getting at?"

"I'm only doing a job of work. It don't pleasure me at times. You buy that?"

"Yeah, I reckon. I dunno. So long, detective." He started to signal his men again, then melted a little. "Happen you get back with your hair in one piece, detective," he grudged, "might be you could still use some help to hold it together. If so, remember Fort Yavapai lies yonder, six miles down the road. They won't chase you past the front gates—I don't think."

"Thanks for the kind thought, sergeant." I grinned. "It'll likely keep me awake all night."

"It better," he answered, with no grin, and yelled at his troopers to move it out. They went over the rise, none of them looking back, and I was left alone with that job which didn't always pleasure me. I clucked to old Shoofly, and we got on with it.

Along about sundown, I got too close to Tom Horn. I jumped him out of a dry wash just shy of some badland hills. Neither of us wanted to shoot, and so it settled into a horse race.

It soon became apparent to Tom that I had the better horse. He had to do something to lose me, and he did. He led me square through the middle of the Apache camp, and left me there to do my own explaining. In a physical way, it was simple. He had spotted the camp from a high point, and I hadn't. He was able to dash his horse right over their supper fire, so sudden did he come on them, and to get on away into the thickening twilight before they realized they'd just missed a certain chance to grab themselves a white man. Thus aroused, they were ready for me and didn't miss their second chance. Old Shoofly ran right into them, but those devils feared no horse and could handle any that was ever foaled, running full tilt or standing. They had him halter-hung and sat on his haunches, and me knocked off his back, in about fifteen seconds. I was lying on the ground alongside their scattered fire, while the beat of Tom Horn's horse's hoofs was still drumming away into the desert dusk. When my head quit swimming and I could sit up and take a look, I found the ugliest one Indian in southeast Arizona bending over me. We didn't need any introductions.

"White man know me," he mumbled through his disfigured lips. It was a statement, not a question, but I felt bound to answer it, no matter.

"Yes," I said, "I know you. You're Boca Rota, the Mescalero chief. The one that's declared war on all the whites."

"Yes," he grunted, acid-bitter. "Me Broken Mouth." He pointed to the terrible scars and purple burn welts that twisted his face. "You know how me get sick mouth? Yes, from white man." He sat down by me, while behind us the other Indians rebuilt the fire. His face, though hideously marked, was not a cruel face. Hard, yes. And bitter as bear gall about something. But not outright vicious and mean, as a man would have expected from his reputation. Now, while I listened, Broken Mouth told me his brief story. And the bitterness and the flint-steel look of him fell into place.

"White man own store, right here, Apache Wells," he began. He pointed to the remains of the old adobe ruin in which his band had camped. I looked around. There were the still-standing walls of two buildings, some nearly complete, some weathered down to three or four feet high. A few cottonwood trees grew near the hand-dug white man's well, which the nomad Apache kept cleaned out for their own use, and which gave the place its evil name. I shivered and nodded. He returned the nod, resumed his tale. "White man store owner he say me steal from store. Me say I no steal. No Apache steal anything from white man when he give word he no do it, I tell him. But he say me lie. He say he teach me no lie any more. His friends hold me by arms. He take branding iron for cow, and heat in stove. Then he burn my mouth like you see. He say, 'There, you no lie no more, you no steal.' But white man wrong. I come back, steal one more time."

He paused to point again. My eyes, following his direction, came to a halt on a weathered wooden headboard surrounded by sagging, sun-warped pickets, just beyond the store.

"I have *my* friends hold *him*. Take out tongue, far back in throat. Then me tell him. 'There, now we even. You no lie no more either.' Next day soldiers come down when see buzzards in sky. Find him dead, all blood run out his body. Soldier Chief he

say, *'Dah-eh-sah,'* death to Broken Mouth. Broken Mouth answer, *'Zas-te!'* kill Soldier Chief. So long time war now. No peace
for Apache people until last soldier gone.''

With this pause, he pointed to me, tapping me on the chest.

''Last soldier no go, until last white man gone. So me say *zas-
te*! all white man, then we have peace again.''

He sat silent after that, and finally I asked him the big one,
using all the control I could.

''Does that mean you're going to kill me, chief?''

''No can help it.'' He shrugged. ''Apache law. Me no hate
you. You look like brave man. Words good, eye steady. But Mescalero law say you die.''

''All right. When?''

''When sun come, first light of day in morning.''

''How about meanwhile, chief?''

''No, you no worry about meanwhile. We no hurt you. We
treat you good. Put you against wall when sun come up, just like
soldier do Apache warrior. You die honorable. Quick. Many bullets through head and belly. All right?''

As he saw it, this was high courtesy. I answered to it the best
way I knew how.

''Yes, certainly. Thank you, chief. I salute you.''

I looked around again, stalling in desperation, hoping for some
miracle to develop, trying the while to tough it out, to ''talk light''
of my coming execution.

''You got any particular wall in mind, chief?'' I asked, backing
it with what I supposed was a tip-off grin.

But the Apache sense of humor wasn't this well developed, it
seemed. Broken Mouth took me literally. He also took his sweet
Mescalero time in the process of so doing, examining the available selection without prejudice, and mighty carefully. Finally he
nodded through the darkness, now fully down, toward a piece of
standing wall with a gaping doorway in it.

''We use that one,'' he said.

Unconsciously my eyes hung on the spot, while his didn't. And
a good thing, too. I only saw the face peering around the edge of
that doorframe for a split-tail second. But the firelight bouncing
past the Apaches squatting around broiling their supper meat had
lit up the happy grin and quick bob of curly brown hair just long
enough.

That was Tom Horn over back of that doorway wall.

* * *

It was an hour later, the moon not yet up but coming any minute. Broken Mouth and I sat along the wall where he was planning to have me shot, he on one side of the empty doorway, I on the other. I was trussed up like a Thanksgiving turkey, he was almost asleep under his black felt hat. On the ground in front of us, scattered in blanketed lumps on the bare dirt, slept the other Apaches. One of them sat hunched upright, dozing on guard at the fire. Of the Horn kid there had been no further sign, and by now I had given up hope of his making a play to break me free.

I had no sooner nodded to myself in mute agreement with this dismal opinion, however, when I saw a white hand slide out past the doorframe, curl itself in my direction, and throw me a sassy finger wave, before pulling back out of sight.

I straightened out both myself and my opinion.

Tom Horn was one of the greatest Indian scouts who ever lived. The Apaches admitted it as well as the whites. To begin with, he apparently had circled back and snuck in to enjoy himself watching me squirm. But he had stayed a little too long for his own peculiar set of morals. Tom was against capital punishment in any form. You might say he was professionally opposed to it. When he heard what he had led me into, that old Boca Rota was meaning to cut me down come daybreak, it just wasn't in his character to set by and wait for sunup; or moonrise, either, for that matter.

As I watched, the hand came out of the doorway again. This time it crept around Broken Mouth's side of the frame. Gentle and deft as a cardsharp palming a spare ace, it lifted the chief's hat off his head and laid it on the ground beside him. Then it disappeared to return with a chunk of adobe brick in it. It raised the brick up and brought it down on Boca Rota's skull. Then it put down the brick, picked up the hat, put it back on the chief's head. With the old devil unconscious, the rest of Tom Horn slid out that doorway and stood sizing up the other Apaches out by the fire. Looking over at me, he nodded and touched the brim of his hat, sober as a circuit judge. Next thing he floated out through the ground-sleepers and came up behind the one at the fire. Easing out his revolver, he took hold both edges of the guard's hat-brim, jammed the hat clean down over his ears, caved in the back of it, nice and quiet, with his pistol barrel. *Then* he grinned over at me and had the gall to tap himself on the forehead with the tip of one forefinger to indicate the overall braininess of the total operation.

When he drifted back to begin slashing me loose, he frowned at the tightness of my bonds, speaking under his breath.

"This here sort of thing is bad for the circulation, Mr. Shonto. A man your age has got to be more careful how he gets tied up."

I handed him a walleyed look and a likewise whisper.

"I'll be a damned sight more careful who I save from the rope hereafter, I'll promise you that, boy," I told him.

"Shucks now, Mr. Shonto," he said reprovingly, "if you hadn't of saved me, who'd be untying you now?"

"Well, that's one way of looking at it," I answered, standing up and working my limbs to get the numbness out of them. "But let's don't quibble it. We can continue auguring your noble unselfishness closer to Fort Yavapai. You any objections to that course?"

He bowed, sweeping off his hat.

"Después de usted, patrón," he said in Spanish. "After you. Age before beauty."

"Thank you," I said, "for nothing."

The rest went pretty good. We got over to the Apache picket line without any fuss being put up by the ponies. We cut them loose and hazed them out into the night with wild yells and arm waves, then ran through the rocks to where Tom had our two saddled horses stashed and waiting. We went aboard them and got long gone from there, as the first angry yelps of the horse-chasing hostiles began to burn the night behind us.

It was the second morning, real early. Tom and I were laid up in some high rocks, looking over the back trail. We were feeling edgy. The kid shook his head.

"Damn," he said, "I wish we had them field glasses of yours, Mr. Shonto."

"I'd rather have your eyes, boy," I told him. "They saved us from getting jumped twice yesterday. How about this morning? You figure we've lost them for good? Maybe they've quit and went home. Who knows?"

"I do, Mr. Shonto," he said. "They never quit and they ain't got no homes. How far we from the fort, you figure?"

"Eight miles maybe. But I don't like the looks of that meadow just ahead. Too many rocks, and too big ones."

He nodded, agreeing.

"It's that way or none, though. Either we go through that meadow, or ride half a day around it. And we ain't got a half day, Mr. Shonto. Look down yonder."

I looked. Far down, looking like sow-bug dots crawling the trail we had just come up, were a dozen Apache.

"You're right, boy," I said. "It's more like half an hour. Let's use it."

Twenty minutes later we were into the first of the meadow rocks. Another few pony steps and we stopped dead. Ahead of us on a ridge closing off the far side of the meadow sat another dozen Apache. We were bottled.

"If you will excuse me, Mr. Shonto," grinned Tom Horn, "I think I will be riding along."

"Just a minute, boy," I said. "You by any chance going on toward Fort Yavapai?"

"Well," he scratched his jaw, "hadn't thought of it, but now you mention it, why not?"

"Why not, indeed?" I gritted, and jumped my horse with his into a hammering gallop toward the Indians ahead. We got up pretty close to them and might have broken through, just on brass alone, when of a sudden I took one through the meat of my right leg and was knocked clean out of the saddle. Horn saw me go and slid his horse to his hocks, turning him to come back for me. He made an Indian-style pickup of me, and we got going again, double-mounted, just as the Apaches came over the ridge behind us, to join those we'd tried to butt through in front.

Now, I'd have thought the cork was in, tight. But not Tom Horn.

"Hang on, Mr. Shonto!" he yelled. "Here we go, double or nothing!"

He was grinning as usual, the threat of death by Apache rifle lead no more impressive to him than that by Mescalero Land & Cattle Company hemp rope. But his high-spirited shout was wasted. Five jumps and his horse took a smoothbore musket ball through the shoulders. He went down hard, us getting free of him on the fall, but forting up behind him the next minute, Tom putting a Colt bullet through his head to quiet his thrashing, while I looked to my hurt leg and our general position.

The leg wasn't bad, only bad enough so that I couldn't run on it. Our setup was not so lucky, but we did have some reasonably good rocks to back us. We also had another little chance. Old

Shoofly was grazing off about fifty paces, with good rocks and brush cover between him and us. I pointed him out to Horn.

"I reckon I can put up enough smoke to hold them off long enough for you to get to him," I said. "Good luck, Tom." It was the first and last time I called him by name, and I saw him react to it. "Fort's not far. I can stick it here till you get back. Now beat it, kid. One hero's enough in the family."

I'd thought he was going to refuse, but he only grinned.

"All right, Mr. Shonto. A boy's bound to respect the wishes of older folks. Hold the thought—I'll be right back!" Which he was. He didn't head for the fort at all but only spurred Shoofly right back to our rocks, slid off of him with his big grin, and announced, "Like I said, Mr. Shonto, double or nothing."

Well, after that I could believe anything and very nearly had to. That crazy kid talked me into another run at those Indians, claiming if I could put him up alongside of one of them, he would guarantee to knock him off his mustang and we'd ride out in style, each with our own horse. He did it, too. And we managed to get a lead on them, I suppose by the out-and-out shock of us having the guts to try anything so empty-headed. It was only a few pony lengths to begin with, but Horn had picked a good scrub, and we soon opened it up to where they quit forcing and firing. Other than lobbing an occasional rifle shot to keep us honest and loping along about a half mile back, they seemed to have lost real heart for closing in. Especially after the kid got two of them and me one in the early hard running. They made a second go at us when we rounded the last butte and saw Fort Yavapai a mile off across the juniper flats, but we lasted them out. I think that next to seeing Tom Horn's hand reach out that doorway and crown Broken Mouth, the next best sight of my life was watching that army sergeant friend of mine yelling down off the catwalk for the gate detail to, "Swing 'em, you bastards—riders coming in!"

Inside I couldn't get out of the saddle and had to be helped down. Horn was there to do it with the troopers siding him. They got me onto the ground just as the sergeant puffed up.

"I just remembered your invitation," I told him. "Sorry we're a little late."

"Better late than never, which you almost was," he answered. Then, frowning it, "I see you brought the kid back."

I looked at Horn, smiling a little wearylike.

"You got that wrong-side-to, sergeant," I said. "The kid

brought me back." Horn ducked his head at this and put on that shy grin of his. I moved over to him and laid my arm on him for support. "I mean what I just said, boy," I told him. "You saved my life." I straightened a little and caught his eye. "But I mean what I said before, too. Nothing can change that. Soon as I'm fit to sit leather, you're going to Tucson. I give my word to put you in that jail, kid, and you're going to be put in it. You hear?"

He'd been looking a mite worried, but now brightened.

"Oh, that!" he said, relieved. "Shucks, now, Mr. Shonto, don't you fret none about that. I understand your situation, sir." Here, he reached a hand to my shoulder, sincere as a Methodist minister. "Moreover, Mr. Shonto, sir, I agree with it wholeheartedly."

"What's that, boy?" I said, surprised.

"A man's got to stand by his word, that's what, sir!"

I studied him a minute, barely able to suppress my astonishment at this about-face. But he didn't crack one inch.

"Well," I finally said, "if that's the case, you won't mind giving me your word that you won't try anything on the way back to Tucson. How about that, boy? You game?"

"As a gouty rooster," he swore at once. "You've got my word, Mr. Shonto, and this time I mean it. You can trust me all the way."

I looked at him good and hard, then nodded.

"All right, remember that, kid. I'll be depending on you." I turned to the troopers. "Come on, boys," I said. "You better get me inside. I'm a shade used up."

We rode up the center of Old Tucson, heading in at the hitchrack in front of the mud-walled jail. We'd come the last five miles on Shoofly, Horn's Apache mustang having suddenly gone lame as a kicked dog. I'd thought maybe it was some trick of the kid's to get me in front of him, mounted double, but he hadn't said boo and was still grinning and saying "yes, sir" to every word when we got down. I threw the reins over the rail, and we marched in, me still watching him sharp as a hawk.

Jim Gates got up from his desk when he came through the door. He knew me, of course, but I could see the kid was a stranger to him. He just had that kind of a sweet face. No matter how many times you saw it on a wanted flyer, you couldn't remember it for a bad one.

"Sheriff," I said, "this here is Tom Horn. I'm turning him in on a cow-stealing complaint by the Mescalero outfit. They'll be in to press charges, if they haven't already."

"They have, Charlie." He nodded, then sized up the kid. "Tom Horn, eh?" he said. "Son of a bitch, he sure don't look it, does he?"

"Oh, I ain't really, sheriff," claimed Horn, with his head-ducking grin. "You see, acherally, I was took at an early age by the Pima Apache, and never heard of Tom Horn till this here Association man come along and—"

I put a hand to his arm and cut him short.

"Save it for the jury, son," I advised him. "The sheriff's got a dozen pictures of you right in his top drawer." I turned to Gates. "Jim," I said, "no matter this kid has got a poor start, he deserves better. He saved my life at a time—two times—when he could have got clean away by himself. But he stuck and then gave his word to come in to Tucson and surrender peaceful, and he's done it. I'm asking you to remember all that when his trial comes up."

Gates took hold of young Horn.

"All right, Charlie," he agreed. "I'll see he gets a total fair trial." He started over to the cell block with the prisoner. At the door into the block the sheriff held up to fuss picking the key out of his ring, and I called to Horn, "So long, boy, and good luck to you." He just looked at me in an odd, sidelong sort of a way, shook his head slightly, and said not a word. "What's the matter with you, kid?" I asked. "Don't you believe in saying good-bye?" Then he grinned, but still wagged his head in that funny way, and said, real soft.

"Not till it's time, Mr. Shonto. Not till it's time—" Then, just as soft but to the sheriff. "Let's go, Mr. Gates, sir. I don't want to keep you from your work."

Jim and me traded looks, then he took the kid on into the cell block, and I said, "See you down the road, Jim," and walked back out in the street to see about some breakfast and a hot-towel shave. The hash house was half a block down, so naturally I went to ride it. I took a minute, maybe two, to tighten Shoofly's cinch, check my bedroll and the like, just as a matter of habit. Then I took hold his reins to mount up. That's when the voice hit me from behind.

"Wait along a bit, Mr. Shonto," it said.

Well, I knew that voice by now, and I made my turn slow and careful. It was Tom Horn, of course, just standing and grinning in the jailhouse door and jangling the Sheriff's keyring in his left hand while his right balanced the office sawed-off in my general direction. As I stayed quiet, eyeing the shotgun, he called back over his shoulder cheerful as a jaybird.

"Now don't you fret in there, Mr. Gates. You told me yourself that it was your best cell."

He moved out onto the boardwalk, scanning the empty street before tossing the keyring into the dirt under the hitch rail. Then he sauntered up to me, ducking his head.

"Sorry, Mr. Shonto but I need *our* horse."

"Boy," I charged him reproachfully, "you gave me your word." He nodded soberly then lit up his 100-carat grin.

"I sure did, Mr. Shonto," he admitted. "but I didn't make no similar promises to that sheriff, did I now?"

He looked at me pure as a choirboy. I couldn't help myself. I'd been taken again, and I hoped I was man enough to appreciate it. I stepped away from old Shoofly.

"Boy," I said, "he's all yours."

He got on the horse, keeping the shotgun my way. I put a hand on his near thigh, easy and light.

"And, boy," I added, "there's something I said in yonder, which I'll repeat out here, scattergun or no scattergun. Good luck to you."

I was sober with it, and it got to him. He looked down an awkward minute, then, impulsive as usual, reached down his hand.

"Mr. Shonto, sir," he said, "if you don't mind—"

He wasn't grinning anymore, and I took his hand. We exchanged a quick, hard grip. Then I stepped back away from Shoofly and Horn was back to his quirky grin just as fast as he'd turned serious the minute before.

"Well, here goes nothing," he said, with the final, sunbright smile. *"Hee-yahhh!"*

With the yell, he spurred the old horse away from the rail and off down the Tucson main stem on the cowboy run, fanning him with his hat on every jump. I stood and watched him go, following him down all the long gallop which took him out of Old Tucson and into his dark future in far-off Laramie County, Wyoming.

They can say what they want about Tom Horn, and it is true

that he did wind up at the end of a rope. But that was twenty years later, and for my part I will always think of Tom Horn as a boy with a grin crackly enough to warm your hands by on a cold day—yes, and more pure nerve to go with it than a train robber with a toy pistol.

I don't know for sure to this day whether I did right or wrong to save Tom Horn's life that time down in Arizona Territory, but I will tell you one thing.

I got a pretty good idea.

Hal G. Evarts's Western fiction is noted for its high drama and well-drawn backgrounds, but another of its successful ingredients is dry, salty humor. "One Night in the Red Dog Saloon" is Evarts at his humorous best—a jovial tale concerning Apaches, the cavalry, a bibulous prospector named Lew Zane, and—yes—"a genuine one-hump camel . . . canted in ribs and flank and ugly as sin." Evarts, whose father, Hal Sr., was also a noted Western writer, has a number of first-rate Arizona-based novels to his credit, among them Apache Agent *(1955),* The Man from Yuma *(1958), and* Colorado Crossing *(1963). Other of his accomplished short stories can be found in his 1955 collection,* Fugitive's Canyon.

One Night in the Red Dog Saloon

★★★★★★★★★★★★★★★

Hal G. Evarts, Jr.

No charge, gents. Drinks are on the house. Every round, yes sir. It's all free, all the likker you can hold. Liquidatin' our stock, so to speak. Sober? Me? No, I don't own this here saloon, I just tend bar. Step up, friend, the whiskey won't last forever. Strangers in Red Dog, ain't you? Thought so. Otherwise you'd know about Lucky Lew Zane.

Lewis Leslie Zane. Lucky 'cause he's still alive, I reckon, after that last Apache ruckus. Not a quieter, milder gent in all Arizona than Lew Zane. Almost shy-like when he's sober. But when he's got a skinful, man, look out! Every six months or so he throws a real stemwinder. Don't blame him none either, considering how he prospects in 'Pache country for his beans and bacon. Man can work up a sizable thirst dodging redskin arrows and a-hanging on to his scalp out in that desert yonder. Folks hereabout allow that Lew owes himself a first-rate blow-out whenever he comes to town. They're glad to see him have a bit of harmless fun, kinda look forward to his visits.

No, thank you kindly. Never touch the stuff myself. But fill your glass, pardner. Here's the bottle. Costs a dime a shot across the street in the Silver Dollar.

As I was saying, it started one afternoon last fall when Lew rode into Red Dog and tied up out front. Soon as word spread, the boys smiled to themselves and got ready. Merchants put up their window shutters, the bartenders took down their mirrors and fancy glasses. Just in case. Lew hadn't hardly more than got settled in the Golden Nugget here when Long Jim Lannigan ambled up to his table.

Maybe Long Jim ain't the best sheriff we ever had but he's a stickler for the law. A tall lanky party, he's as big and tough as Lew and almost as close-mouthed. The difference is, he don't drink, not even a sociable nip. Matter of principle. So now and again he gets a mite impatient with Lew's shenanigans. "Hoddy, Lew," he said.

"Hoddy, Sheriff," Lew said.

"How's the Injuns this trip?"

"Pesky. Had to pacify a few."

Long Jim sighed and looked at the two six-shooters in Lew's holsters. He knew Lew was fixing for a ripsnorter. Lew was too darn unnatural quiet, even for Lew. "You're among friends now," Long Jim said. "How's about letting me keep your guns tonight?"

"I don't reckon, Sheriff," Lew said. "Might want to shoot out some windows later." That seemed reasonable but, like I say, this Lew is a very honest, peace-loving citizen. He pulled a buckskin bag out of his pocket and dumped a trickle of gold dust on the table. "Like to pay in advance," he said. "For the windows, I mean."

Long Jim gave him a sorrowful look and shook his head, then walked out. The sheriff's attitude hurt Lew. It was a point of honor with him to pay his debts. Always did. He just couldn't understand that reproachful look of Long Jim's. Got to brooding so it sort of spoiled his fun. So he wasn't rightly himself when a pair of sharpers drifted over to the table and suggested a game of penny ante. They'd seen that poke of gold dust, too.

Well sir, one thing led to another, and pretty soon Lew had cleaned out every gambler in the house, not caring a hoot. The more he drank the soberer he got, the wilder he bet the more he won, until chips were stacked up chin-high in front of him. Then Acey-Ducey Dugan dealt himself into the game.

Acey-Ducey Dugan was real artistic with a deck of cards. He owned two saloons, a pearl stickpin, the flashiest diamond ring in town, and he couldn't abide lucky amateurs like Lew. When he took a hand we looked for action. First off he lost his cash, next his stickpin, then his ring, and when the next big pot came up he tossed in his deed to the Golden Nugget. Lew called him.

Acey-Ducey laid down four aces and reached for the pot, but Lew smiled and turned up a straight club flush, six high. That's when Dugan made the worst gamble of his life. He reached for his gun. When the smoke cleared away, Mr. Acey-Ducey Dugan was face down on the barroom floor, and I had a new boss.

Lew felt terrible. Here the evening was barely started, and he'd gone and made a peck of trouble for his good friend Long Jim Lannigan. Being such a teetotal dry, Long Jim might be some put out with him. So, to save embarrassment all around, Lew bid the customers good night, tucked a spare quart under his coat, and meandered out to his horse and climbed aboard. Riding down the street, he shot out what few store windows wasn't shuttered, but even that didn't raise his spirits. He done it because it was expected of him, and Lew Zane wasn't a man to disappoint his friends.

Heading back for the hills, he got awful blue thinking about all the pleasurable times he'd had in town before. Now and again he tipped up the bottle to cut the dust, but his heart wasn't in it. Likely Long Jim would be downright peeved.

Near sunrise he stopped at a spring to water, planning to hole up in the rocks come daylight lest some stray Injun cut his trail. He wasn't much popular with the 'Paches, being as how he'd served a hitch as army scout a couple of years back when the cavalry rounded up Chief Black Eagle's tribe and stuck 'em on the reservation. They'd purely love to lift his hair. So he climbed on up the ridge but his horse started acting skittish. Lew gave her a cuff and all of a sudden a big black shape reared off the ground and let out a bellow. The horse jumped straight up in the air and Lew, all loose in the saddle, went sailing off and cracked his head on a rock.

When he woke up, the sun was beating down in his face and

his head was pounding like a tom-tom. He felt the lump behind his ear, then felt in his coat for the bottle, which somehow had been spared. Grateful for that, Lew took a snort and sat up to look for his horse. Instead he saw a big, brown, shaggy critter watching him with mournful eyes not ten yards away. Too big for a bear and too rank-smelling for a cow. Besides it had a green beard and a humped back.

Lew shut his eyes tight, spit out his mouthful of whiskey, and flopped back on the rock. When a man got to seeing camels in the middle of the desert it was time to quit. Past time, 'way past. John Barleycorn was panting down his neck. Lew lay there shivering and sweating but by and by he noticed a strange thing: that animal stink was strong as ever. Cautious-like he opened one eye a crack and sure enough that camel was still a-staring at him.

A weaker man might've cracked right there, but not Lew Zane. He got up shaky on his feet and circled round the beast. It was real, a genuine one-hump camel, hunkered down on its knees. An old male, he guessed, ganted in ribs and flank and ugly as sin. All the teeth was gone and saliva had dribbled down its chin like a moss goatee, but them big, soft eyes had the most piteous look Lew had ever seen, almost human. Someways that look reminded him of Long Jim Lannigan. Finally Lew stepped in close and put a hand on its neck. The camel rolled over on one side and whimpered like a sick dog. Then he saw what the trouble was. A prickly-pear cactus had stuck in the left hind footpad like a pin cushion and the leg was beginning to swell. The poor old brute couldn't walk.

Lew felt relieved to learn he didn't have the fantods after all, but he was mighty puzzled. How come a camel to be way out here? Near as he could recollect camels belonged in Africa, a far piece from Arizona Territory. Runaway from a circus, he thought, but that was silly. He just couldn't figure an answer. One thing sure, old Green Beard had scared off his horse, which meant a long, hot chase on foot, and he'd best be getting at it.

But he couldn't leave the critter all crippled up to die of thirst. Lew was too tenderhearted for that. Had to get it down to the spring. Well sir, he tried everything he knew, but that camel wouldn't budge. He coaxed and wheedled and cussed and kicked, but the camel just kept watching him with those big, sad eyes. After an hour of that his temper frazzled out and he pulled a gun. "You stubborn orn'ry fool!" he shouted. "I'm tryin' to help you."

The camel grunted and rolled over on the other side. Lew felt mean and lowdown but there was only one way to end its misery. He put his muzzle against its head and cocked the hammer and shut his eyes, willing himself to squeeze the trigger. Couldn't do it though, and lucky for him. Sure was his lucky day.

The camel heaved up on its front legs and let out a squall that unnerved Lew so he jumped. Right then a bowstring twanged, and an arrow bounced off the rock where he'd been standing a second before. Ducking behind a boulder, he glimpsed a swarm of redskins up on the sky line. They'd sneaked up to ambush him, but now their ponies were bucking and plunging and neighing crazy. Injuns couldn't control 'em. Before Lew could shoot more than a couple the whole bunch stampeded and raced over the ridge like the U. S. Cavalry was on their tails. He swallowed hard and mopped his face and looked around, but there was just him and old Hump Back.

Soon as he was breathing again Lew crawled up the ridge. The Apaches was hightailing across the desert in a cloud of dust, carrying off their two dead brothers like Injuns do, and they didn't look to be coming back real soon. Some of Black Eagle's braves jumping the reservation, Lew supposed, but he had other problems aplenty to worry him. He was afoot a long way from nowhere, and his head hurt bad. He wished he'd never gone to town.

The camel had settled back on its haunches, looking all forlorn. Lew couldn't bear to shoot it now. "You mangy old buzzard bait," he said. "No wonder them horses lit out when they got a whiff of you."

Then he noticed a kind of scar on one hip. It was furred over, but he squatted down close and saw the brand USA had been burned into the hide. He got to remembering his grandpappy, who'd been a soldier on the frontier 'way back in the fifties, before the war. His grandpappy had seen camels, some of the bunch Jeff Davis had shipped over for the War Department to haul mail out west. Lew scratched his head, trying to recollect the story.

Seemed like the experiment hadn't worked. The camels scared the cavalry mounts, the soldiers hated the camels, and the Army cussed Jeff Davis proper. So they sold 'em off and turned 'em loose, and the camels disappeared. This one, Lew allowed, must've been wandering around on his lonesome for close to thirty years. Didn't seem possible, but there was a U. S. Army brand to prove it.

"You done me a favor, Moss Face," Lew said. "Looks like I got to doctor you up."

So he got out his knife and started on that cactus. It was a messy job prying the stuff loose, and Lew got all stuck up himself, but the camel never let out a bleat, though the spines had worked in deep. Gamest thing he ever did see. But he'd doctored enough horses to know there was still a danger of infection. What he needed was a disinfectant. That's when Lew Zane showed he'd got a heart as big as all creation. Quite a tussle with his conscience but he done it. Picked up his bottle, near half a quart left, pulled out the cork with his teeth, and poured it all on Hump Back's punctured foot. Old Hump blubbered a little but took it like a soldier, like a real old army trooper. Made Lew feel right proud.

The camel lumbered to his feet this time and limped down to the spring. Lew had a drink, too, but the water tasted flat. Gave the beast a friendly slap on the rump and set off to shag his horse. Hadn't gone a hundred yards before the camel hobbled up behind him. "Look," Lew said, "you're in no shape to travel, and I got me a horse to catch."

He went on a little ways and old Moss Face limped right after him. Kinda exasperated, Lew stopped again. "We're even, ain't we? Go on back to water. Git!"

He shied a rock, but the camel didn't move, just watched him with those weepy eyes. Gave Lew the notion it wanted to tell him something. But he figured that any critter who could outlast the 'Paches for thirty years didn't need no more help from him. Regretful, he said, "So long, pardner. I won't catch that horse till a year from Christmas if you tag along."

He ran then, ran hard over the hill and through some boulders where a cripple couldn't follow, and after a spell he shook the camel. Feeling guilty, he walked on hunting for horse tracks. 'Long about dinnertime he was passing a big rock when Long Jim Lannigan stepped out with a rifle. Behind him stood two horses, one of which was Lew's.

"Hoddy, Sheriff," Lew said.

"Hoddy, Lew," Long Jim said.

Lew hoped maybe everything was going to be all right now that Long Jim had caught his horse, and he said, "I'm sorry about Acey-Ducey Dugan."

"What for?"

"Well," Lew said, "he ran a nice, quiet saloon."

"That he did," Long Jim said. "But Acey-Ducey ain't what's botherin' me, Lew. It's the way you sneaked off without payin' for them windows you busted."

Lew could tell the sheriff was riled, the way he kept pointing that Winchester. "Why, plumb slipped my mind, but I'll pay you right now," he said, and shoved a hand in his pocket.

Catch was, he didn't have a nickel. He'd left his money and dust poke on the table in the Golden Nugget the night before. Feeling sheepish, he said, "Reckon you'll have to trust me, Sheriff, till I dig some more dust back in the hills."

Long Jim shook his head. "Hate to say this, Lew, but you own the Golden Nugget now. Never did trust a saloon keeper."

Lew's face went pale. He knew Long Jim didn't hold with drinking but he'd clean forgot that handsome straight club flush. Just couldn't believe he'd won the Golden Nugget. Great roarin' Jupiter! His own saloon! "Can't you trust me till we get to town?" he said.

"Have to." Long Jim wrinkled his nose. "What's that smell on you? Skunk?"

Lew sniffed at his shirt. "Camel," he said. "Darndest thing happened to me—"

When he got done explaining, a funny look came over Long Jim's face. He tugged at his ear and scuffed his boot in the dirt and coughed loud. "Hmm," he said. "You run off a dozen Injuns?"

"Thereabouts," Lew said.

"You and this critter with the whiskers?"

"Yup."

"Then you poured a quart of good whisky on its foot."

"Half a quart," Lew said.

Long Jim's face got longer than a hound dog's. "Lew," he said, "I'll be fifty-three next June, and I ain't never seen a camel. Let's go take a look."

They rode back, not talking on the way, but when they reached the spring there wasn't a sign of old Moss Face. Lew tramped up and down the ridge, but he couldn't find a single track amongst all the rocks. Couldn't even find that 'Pache arrow. "Must be close by," he told Long Jim. "With that sore foot."

Long Jim gave him another sorrowing look and picked up the empty whisky bottle and smashed it on a boulder. "What color you say that beard was?"

"Green," Lew said. "Man wouldn't hardly believe it."

Long Jim sighed and said in a soothing voice, "Sure I would, Lew boy." Then he clipped Lew behind the ear with his six-gun and roped him on the horse.

When Lew came to he was lying on a bunk in the Red Dog jail. Sunlight was streaming through a barred window, and Doc Spires was bending over him with a stethoscope. "Acute alcoholic poisoning," Doc said. "Heat prostration and nervous shock. Needs complete rest."

"That's what I calc'lated, Doc," Long Jim said. He was leaning against the door with a toothpick in his mouth. "Sad case."

Doc tapped a finger to his head. "If he goes into deliriums again, send for me. Might turn violent."

Lew sat up with a jerk. "You're not talkin' about me, Doc?"

Doc backed off quick and hurried out of the cell. "Lay back easy, Lew," Long Jim said. "Anything you want?"

Lew's head was feeling fuzzy, and he said, "Sure could use a drink, Sheriff."

Long Jim took out his toothpick and stared at the end of it. "Nope."

"Ain't my credit good?" Lew demanded. "When a man owns a whole saloon—"

"You heard the doc," Long Jim said. "You're sick, Lew."

"Just one little drink?"

Long Jim shook his head.

That got Lew's dander up then, and he said, "I'll be dogged if I pay for any windows till I get out!"

Long Jim talked to him real gentle, like a father to his son, "Lew," he said, "you got the wrong attitude. I'm trying to help you."

"I don't want no help!" Lew yelled. "Lemme out of here and I'll show you who's crazy. That camel—"

"There you go again." Long Jim closed the cell door and stomped into his office, leaving Lew to holler and bang on the bars.

The news spread fast. Next day everybody in Red Dog knew that Lew Zane had slipped his hitch. A pity, folks said. They'd miss his antics, but you couldn't turn a man loose in that condition. Might go clear off his rocker. Long Jim padlocked the Golden

Nugget and went around all gloomy-faced. As Lew's good friend it pained him, but he done his duty as he saw it.

That night he went back to the jail for another try. "Lew," he said, "why don't you admit you had one too many and we'll forget this."

Lew was mighty sick of that cell and might've backed down, stubborn as he was, but just then some kid sung out under the alley window:

> "Lew, Lew, crazy ole Lew!
> Drunk a mess of camel stew!"

Lew's jaw jutted out. Couldn't understand why his friend was treating him so. Got an idea Long Jim might be trying to reform him complete. "I'm still waiting on that drink," he said.

Long Jim drew a deep breath, being stubborn, too. "You'll set here a spell then."

"You'll wait a spell for your window money, too." Lew glared at him. "I seen what I seen, and nobody can tell me different."

So it ended in a draw. Neither would budge an inch. Lew sulked around the jail, and Long Jim gave up arguing with him. Lew didn't really want that drink, but he figured his reputation was at stake. Maybe he couldn't prove he wasn't loco, but he wasn't going to admit it, not to Long Jim or nobody else. Never live it down. Old Hump Back had landed him in some fix.

No telling how long it might have dragged on like that but next week the Injuns busted off the reservation again. Came swarming through the hills, burned a couple of ranches, ran off some horses, and headed south for Mexico. Chief Black Eagle himself, cute and sly as a coyote. Cut the telegraph wires so we couldn't send for the Army. Long Jim rounded up a posse to catch 'em.

Trouble was, he needed a scout, and the only man in town who knew the 'Pache country was Lew Zane. Knew every hill and gully, every bush and rock, and talked the lingo, too. Even looked Apache. Without Lew along to guide, Long Jim might as well go chase after the wind as Black Eagle.

"Tell you what, Lew," he said. "Let's make a deal."

Lew gave him a sour look, being in no mood to dicker. Had the sheriff over a barrel. What he wanted was a chance to find that camel and prove he was sane and sober as the next citizen. Make Long Jim eat a fair-sized hunk of crow.

"I'm appealin' to you as a red-blooded American," Long Jim said. "Help me corral them hostiles back on the reservation."

Lew tapped a finger to his head. "I'm crazy, Sheriff. You heard what Doc said. You don't want a crazy man."

" 'Pears like I was a trifle hasty," Long Jim told him. "Anyways, you ain't that crazy."

"I don't walk through that door," Lew said, "till you fetch me a drink."

Long Jim hustled over to the Silver Dollar, where his posse was waiting, and bought a bottle. First drink he'd ever bought in Red Dog. Hustled back to the jail with it. "Now," Lew said, "you write out a notice like I tell you."

That stuck in Long Jim's craw, but he done it. Had to. He wrote out, "I'm as crazy as Lew Zane." Signed it, "James Lannigan, Esq., Sheriff," and tacked it on his bulletin board alongside the reward dodgers, where all the town loafers gathered.

But Lew wasn't satisfied yet. "No sir, Sheriff," he said. "I don't leave town without them windows is paid for. Folks'd claim I was weaselin' out of my debts."

Long Jim slapped down a handful of double eagles on the bunk. "You got me this time, Lew boy," he said real grim. "But you ever throw another shindig in Red Dog, I'll lock you up for keeps."

He meant it, too. Lew knew his drinking days in Red Dog was done. Well, there was a lot of other towns with sheriffs not so fussy. He'd made his bargain, and he'd keep it. But he hated to have his friend Long Jim rankled with hard feelings.

So that's how come he walked out of jail, strapped on his guns, and led the posse out of town. Nobody cracked a smile. Drunk or crazy or cold sober, Lew Zane wasn't a man to tangle with. He picked up the tracks of Black Eagle's bunch, about twenty strong, and followed 'em south into the badlands all that day. After sundown he turned into a short cut he knew, thinking the redskins would stick to the long route by way of water. When they came to a notch through the hills, Lew split the posse in half and spread 'em on either side of the trail and settled back to wait.

It was a good scheme and might've worked, but by and by Lew got fidgety. Couldn't understand what was taking the redskins so long. He was bound and determined to do this right, show Long Jim he hadn't lost his grip. Matter of pride. 'Long about daybreak he sneaked off by himself on a back track toward the next spring to see if Black Eagle had outsmarted him.

He was riding along careful, peering out for Injun sign, when his nose began to twitch. His horse got one sniff, r'ared up and bucked him off, and lit out. Laying on his back, Lew saw old Hump trot out from behind a bush, spry as a pup. "Oh, no!" he groaned, and rubbed his eyes.

No mistake though. Couldn't be two camels that ugly. Moss Face seemed glad to see him, but Lew didn't feel the same. Any minute the 'Paches might come along, which was no fix for a man without a horse. "Dang your worthless hide!" he said. "Ain't you caused me enough trouble?"

But the camel paid his ungratefulness no never-mind. Snuggled up close and gave his face a great big drooly lick. It came over Lew then that this reunion wasn't a coincidence. These desert water holes was old Hump's home range, and he was showing Lew his appreciation. Might not be pretty but sure was one smart camel. Smart and shy, Lew figured. Prob'ly didn't trust white men or redskins neither.

"Listen, pardner," Lew said, "here's your chance to prove I'm not a liar."

He started back toward the posse, but old Hump didn't follow. Didn't move a muscle. Stood there watching Lew. Must be awful shy with strangers, Lew thought, and the stubbornest critter on four legs. That's when he got his big idea.

The sky was beginning to pale. No time for a man to be caught by Black Eagle's braves, specially not Lew Zane, who'd killed a gracious plenty over the years. So he climbed up on old Hump bareback, got a tight hold around the neck, turned the head toward where he'd left Long Jim's posse, and give that beast a solid boot in the ribs. But Moss Face had a notion all his own. He swung around and headed north instead of south, straight for the water hole. Traveling fast, too, now his foot had healed. Lew tried to turn him back, yanking at his ears, but Hump let out a long wobble-jointed stride and after that Lew was too busy hanging on to steer.

Used to fancy himself as a bronc stomper, Lew did. Gentled quite a few in his day. But he'd never ridden camel flesh before, and never will again. Like to fractured both his legs and shook his insides fierce. Too paralyzed to let go and fall off. So he went a-bouncing and a-jouncing right into the 'Pache camp a mile or so down the pass, just as Black Eagle was crawling out from under his blanket. Pounded through the horse herd, scattered Injun ponies right and left, and sent 'em squealing flat-eared for the hills.

Then old Hump stopped dead. Right smack in the middle of twenty bug-eyed Injuns. Collapsed on his knees, and Lew slid off all dazed and shaky. He'd been in many a tight spot before but not one like this. For a long minute they stared back at him, being too sleepy and surprised to rush and maybe scared, too. They'd never seen a camel close up, and Moss Face smelled like bad medicine. Bad enough to stampede all their horses.

A shriveled-up old codger in a breechclout and raggedy shirt, Black Eagle didn't look to be the most fearsome Apache in Arizona. But he hadn't got to be chief by his sweet, forgiving nature. Soon as he recognized Lew his eyes went mean and wicked. He'd lost his horses but he aimed to pay off a few old scores. He grabbed up his bow and motioned his braves to close in.

Automatic Lew's hand dropped to his gun butt. He might squeeze off a shot or two before they stuck him full of arrows. He looked at old Hump, and his mouth went dry. Lew wasn't what you'd call a pious man but he decided to turn over a new leaf. He couldn't rightly blame a camel. Whiskey and his own mule-headed nature had led him into this scrape. He breathed a little prayer and made his vow. Right then he swore off red-eye permanent—if he lived that long.

Black Eagle raised a hand for silence. Lew looked around at the ring of hot-eyed bucks, clutching their bows and rifles and war clubs, and he wet his lips. They'd string this out to torment him, 'Pache style, unless he got the jump, so he played his hole card first, knowing only one thing had ever licked 'em: Uncle Sam.

"The Great White Chief in Washington is angry with his red brothers," he said. "He sends me to order you to return to the reservation."

Black Eagle's eyes bored into his, and Lew said louder, "Fifty blue coats on fresh fast horses are waiting for my signal behind that hill. One shot from my gun will bring them. Do you want your squaws wailing in your lodges tonight?"

Black Eagle squinted up at the empty hills and grunted. Maybe he believed it but chances were he didn't. Nothing for Lew to do but stretch his bluff. A shot would bring Long Jim's posse on the run but what they'd find was one dead paleface. "The Great White

Chief will not punish you for stealing horses," Lew said, "but if you disobey his orders his vengeance will be swift."

The young bucks were getting impatient with all this palaver, itching for the fun to start, but Black Eagle scowled them down. He didn't hanker to be trapped afoot in any blue-coat ambush. "You lie," he growled. "I cut the wire that talks to Washington."

Old Hump heaved up onto his feet with a holler and the 'Paches scattered back. All along that camel had been trying to tell Lew something, and at last he got the message. Black Eagle was teetering on the edge, yes or no, but white-men talk wouldn't push him over. What he needed was an Injun sign.

"You cut the wire that talks, yes, but the voice of the Great White Chief is like the voice of thunder over the land when his brothers make him angry." Lew drew a long breath and shoved in his last chip. "My chief has spoken. Here is the great seal of Washington." He pointed to the brand on Hump Back's rump and folded his arms.

Black Eagle stepped up close and clawed at the fur. His eyes got round, and he popped a hand over his mouth. The others crowded in to stare grunting and jabbering with excitement. They knew what that USA meant. They'd seen it on army mounts and stockades and on beef rations their agent handed out. That was the Voice all right, though a camel's hind end might seem a peculiar place to find it.

Black Eagle quieted his boys with a snarl. They muttered and grumbled some, but he was boss. "You are the enemy of my people," he said to Lew, and gave him a murdering look. "If you ever come to our reservation, we will kill you."

Lew had sense enough not to crowd his luck. Fact was he'd sweated clear through his coat. Kept mum and watched Black Eagle and his bunch shuffle off through the rocks on their long walk home. A few looked back like maybe they were going to potshoot him, chief or no chief, but pretty soon they was out of sight in the hills. If ever a man needed a drink then it was Lew, but he'd made his promise. Also he'd lost that bottle during all the fuss.

He wiped his face and said, "Old friend, you done the U. S. Army proud today. Too bad Jeff Davis wasn't here to see it."

He turned around, but Moss Face wasn't there. Loping off through the hills in the other direction. "Hey, come back!" Lew hollered, but that camel never stopped. In a minute he was gone over the sky line. No use chasing him, Lew knew. He could outrun a mustang. He'd done his duty, and all he wanted now was to be let alone. Like the song says, "Old soldiers never die, they just fade away," and that's what old Hump done.

Real thoughtful, Lew walked back up the trail. When he came to the pass Long Jim Lannigan and his posse climbed out from behind their rocks. They wasn't in a humor to be trifled with, being some provoked that Lew had sneaked off and left 'em short a guide.

"Hoddy, Sheriff," Lew said.

"Hoddy, Lew." Long Jim gave him the cold eye. "See you lost your horse again."

"Yup," Lew said.

"Didn't happen to see any redskins on the loose, Lew boy?"

"Now you mention it," Lew said. "I did. Black Eagle and his bucks. Walkin' back toward the reservation."

"Well now," Long Jim said, and his voice sounded like a fresh-honed razor, "I reckon you scared 'em off with a quart of whiskey."

Lew opened his mouth to explain, then took another look at Long Jim. Sometimes, he figured, friendship is more important than the truth. "Why no," he said. "Me and Black Eagle kinda agreed to call a truce. Had a friendly talk, and we both seen the light."

Natural enough, Long Jim was skeptical. But a man can't argue with facts. Black Eagle went back to the reservation and stayed there. Ain't been off since. So Lew and Long Jim are friends again. No bad feelings over them windows. And if Lew ever bumps into old Hump on his prospecting trips into the badlands, he don't say so. Learned his lesson in more ways than one. Hasn't touched anything stronger than lemon soda from that day to this.

What's all that racket you hear? I reckon that'll be Lew now, shooting up the Silver Dollar across the street. Red Dog folks expect it of him when he comes to town. Man's privilege to give away his whiskey if he gets the notion but he can't hardly shoot up his own saloon. Matter of ethics. Like I say, Lew Zane kept his word.

So pour yourself another drink, gents, before the supply gives out.

The cinematic quality of Elmore Leonard's writing is evident in the fact that many of his novels and short stories have made outstanding films. In the Western genre, these include 3:10 to Yuma, *from the story of the same title;* The Tall T, *from the novelette "The Captives"; and* Hombre *and* Valdez is Coming, *from a pair of highly praised novels of the same titles. "The Tonto Woman," about Ruben Vega, a rustler, horse thief, and self-confessed fornicator of "many women, maybe eight hundred," is vintage Leonard—and that makes it very good indeed.*

The Tonto Woman

★★★★★★★★★★★★★★

Elmore Leonard

A TIME would come, within a few years, when Ruben Vega would go to the church in Benson, kneel in the confessional, and say to the priest, "Bless me, Father, for I have sinned. It has been thirty-seven years since my last confession. . . . Since then I have fornicated with many women, maybe eight hundred. No, not that many, considering my work. Maybe six hundred only." And the priest would say, "Do you mean bad women or good women?" And Ruben Vega would say, "They are all good, Father." He would tell the priest he had stolen, in that time, about twenty thousand head of cattle but only maybe fifteen horses. The priest would ask him if he had committed murder. Ruben Vega would say no. "All that stealing you've done," the priest would say, "you've never killed anyone?" And Ruben Vega would say, "Yes, of course, but it was not to commit murder. You understand the distinction? Not to *kill* someone to take a life, but only to save my own."

Even in this time to come, concerned with dying in a state of sin, he would be confident. Ruben Vega knew himself, when he was right, when he was wrong.

* * *

85

Now, in a time before, with no thought of dying, but with the same confidence and caution that kept him alive, he watched a woman bathe. Watched from a mesquite thicket on the high bank of a wash.

She bathed at the pump that stood in the yard of the adobe, the woman pumping and then stooping to scoop the water from the basin of the irrigation ditch that led off to a vegetable patch of corn and beans. Her dark hair was pinned up in a swirl, piled on top of her head. She was bare to her gray skirt, her upper body pale white, glistening wet in the late afternoon sunlight. Her arms were very thin, her breasts small, but there they were with the rosy blossoms on the tips, and Ruben Vega watched them as she bathed, as she raised one arm and her hand rubbed soap under the arm and down over her ribs. Ruben Vega could almost feel those ribs, she was so thin. He felt sorry for her, for all the women like her, stick women drying up in the desert, waiting for a husband to ride in smelling of horse and sweat and leather, lice living in his hair.

There was a stock tank and rickety windmill off in the pasture, but it was empty graze, all dust and scrub. So the man of the house had moved his cows to grass somewhere and would be coming home soon, maybe with his sons. The woman appeared old enough to have young sons. Maybe there was a little girl in the house. The chimney appeared cold. Animals stood in a mesquite-pole corral off to one side of the house, a cow and a calf and a dun-colored horse, that was all. There were a few chickens. No buckboard or wagon. No clothes drying on the line. A lone woman here at day's end.

From fifty yards he watched her. She stood looking this way now, into the red sun, her face raised. There was something strange about her face. Like shadow marks on it, though there was nothing near enough to her to cast shadows.

He waited until she finished bathing and returned to the house before he mounted his bay and came down the wash to the pasture. Now as he crossed the yard, walking his horse, she would watch him from the darkness of the house and make a judgment about him. When she appeared again it might be with a rifle, depending on how she saw him.

Ruben Vega said to himself, Look, I'm a kind person. I'm not going to hurt nobody.

She would see a bearded man in a cracked straw hat with the

brim bent to his eyes. Black beard, with a revolver on his hip and
another beneath the leather vest. But look at my eyes, Ruben Vega
thought. Let me get close enough so you can see my eyes.

Stepping down from the bay he ignored the house, let the horse
drink from the basin of the irrigation ditch as he pumped water
and knelt to the wooden platform and put his mouth to the rusted
pump spout. Yes, she was watching him. Looking up now at the
doorway he could see part of her: a coarse shirt with sleeves too
long and the gray skirt. He could see strands of dark hair against
the whiteness of the shirt, but could not see her face.

As he rose, straightening, wiping his mouth, he said, "May
we use some of your water, please?"

The woman didn't answer him.

He moved away from the pump to the hardpack, hearing the
ching of his spurs, removed his hat and gave her a little bow.
"Ruben Vega, at your service. Do you know Diego Luz, the
horsebreaker?" He pointed off toward a haze of foothills. "He
lives up there with his family and delivers horses to the big ranch,
the Circle-Eye. Ask Diego Luz, he'll tell you I'm a person of
trust." He waited a moment. "May I ask how you're called?"
Again he waited.

"You watched me," the woman said.

Ruben Vega stood with his hat in his hand facing the woman
who was half in shadow in the doorway. He said, "I waited. I
didn't want to frighten you."

"You watched me," she said again.

"No, I respect your privacy."

She said, "The others look. They come and watch."

He wasn't sure who she meant. Maybe anyone passing by. He
said, "You see them watching?"

She said, "What difference does it make?" She said then, "You
come from Mexico, don't you?"

"Yes, I was there. I'm here and there, working as a drover."
Ruben Vega shrugged. "What else is there to do, uh?" Showing
her he was resigned to his station in life.

"You'd better leave," she said.

When he didn't move, the woman came out of the doorway into
light, and he saw her face clearly for the first time. He felt a shock
within him and tried to think of something to say, but could only
stare at the blue lines tattooed on her face: three straight lines on
each cheek that extended from her cheekbones to her jaw, mark-

ings that seemed familiar, though he could not at this moment identify them.

He was conscious of himself standing in the open with nothing to say, the woman staring at him with curiosity, as though wondering if he would hold her gaze and look at her. Like there was nothing unusual about her countenance. Like it was common to see a woman with her face tattooed and you might be expected to comment, if you said anything at all, "Oh, that's a nice design you have there. Where did you have it done?" That would be one way—if you couldn't say something interesting about the weather or about the price of cows in Benson.

Ruben Vega, his mind empty of pleasantries, certain he would never see the woman again, said, "Who did that to you?"

She cocked her head in an easy manner, studying him as he studied her, and said, "Do you know, you're the first person who's come right out and asked."

"Mojave," Ruben Vega said, "but there's something different. Mojaves tattoo their chins only, I believe."

"And look like they were eating berries," the woman said. "I told them if you're going to do it, do it all the way. Not like a blue dribble."

It was in her eyes and in the tone of her voice, a glimpse of the rage she must have felt. No trace of fear in the memory, only cold anger. He could hear her telling the Indians—this skinny woman, probably a girl then—until they did it her way and marked her good for all time. Imprisoned her behind the blue marks on her face.

"How old were you?"

"You've seen me and had your water," the woman said, "now leave."

It was the same type of adobe house as the woman's but with a great difference. There was life here, the warmth of family: children sleeping now, Diego Luz's wife and her mother cleaning up after the meal as the two men sat outside in horsehide chairs and smoked and looked at the night. At one time they had both worked for a man named Sundeen and packed running irons to vent the brands on the cattle they stole. Ruben Vega was still an outlaw, in his fashion, while Diego Luz broke green horses and sold them to cattle companies.

They sat at the edge of the ramada, an awning made of mesquite, and stared at pinpoints of light in the universe. Ruben Vega asked about the extent of graze this season, where the large herds were that belonged to the Maricopa and the Circle-Eye. He had been thinking of cutting out maybe a hundred—he wasn't greedy—and driving them south to sell to the mine companies. He had been scouting the Circle-Eye range, he said, when he came to the strange woman. . . .

The Tonto Woman, Diego Luz said. Everyone called her that now.

Yes, she had been living there, married a few years, when she went to visit her family who lived on the Gila above Painted Rock. Well, some Yavapai came looking for food. They clubbed her parents and two small brothers to death and took the girl north with them. The Yavapai traded her to the Mojave as a slave. . . .

"And they marked her," Ruben Vega said.

"Yes, so when she died the spirits would know she was Mojave and not drag her soul down into a rathole," Diego Luz said.

"Better to go to heaven with your face tattooed," Ruben Vega said, "than not at all. Maybe so."

During a drought the Mojave traded her to a band of Tonto Apaches for two mules and a bag of salt, and one day she appeared at Bowie with the Tontos that were brought in to be sent to Oklahoma. Among the desert Indians twelve years and returned home last spring.

"It put age on her," Ruben Vega said. "But what about her husband?"

"Her husband? He banished her," Diego Luz said, "like a leper. Unclean from living among the red niggers. No one speaks of her to him, it isn't allowed."

Ruben Vega frowned. There was something he didn't understand. He said, "Wait a minute—"

And Diego Luz said, "Don't you know who her husband is? Mr. Isham himself, man, of the Circle-Eye. She comes home to find her husband a rich man. He don't live in that hut no more. No, he owns a hundred miles of graze and a house it took them two years to build, the glass and bricks brought in by the Southern Pacific. Sure, the railroad comes and he's a rich cattleman in only a few years."

"He makes her live there alone?"

"She's his wife, he provides for her. But that's all. Once a month his segundo named Bonnet rides out there with supplies and has someone shoe her horse and look at the animals."

"But to live in the desert," Ruben Vega said, still frowning, thoughtful, "with a rusty pump . . ."

"Look at her," Diego Luz said. "What choice does she have?"

It was hot down in this scrub pasture, a place to wither and die. Ruben Vega loosened the new willowroot straw that did not yet conform to his head, though he had shaped the brim to curve down on one side and rise slightly on the other so that the brim slanted across the vision of his left eye. He held on his lap a nearly flat cardboard box that bore the name *L. S. Weiss Mercantile Store.*

The woman gazed up at him, shading her eyes with one hand. Finally she said, "You look different."

"The beard began to itch," Ruben Vega said, making no mention of the patches of gray he had studied in the hotel room mirror. "So I shaved it off." He rubbed a hand over his jaw and smoothed down the tips of his mustache that was still full and seemed to cover his mouth. When he stepped down from the bay and approached the woman standing by the stick-fence corral, she looked off into the distance and back again.

She said, "You shouldn't be here."

Ruben Vega said, "Your husband doesn't want nobody to look at you. Is that it?" He held the store box, waiting for her to answer. "He has a big house with trees and the San Pedro River in his yard. Why doesn't he hide you there?"

She looked off again and said, "If they find you here, they'll shoot you."

"They," Ruben Vega said. "The ones who watch you bathe? Work for your husband and keep more than a close eye on you and you'd like to hit them with something, wipe the grins from their faces."

"You better leave," the woman said.

The blue lines on her face were like claw marks, though not as wide as fingers: indelible lines of dye etched into her flesh with a cactus needle, the color worn and faded but still vivid against her skin, the blue matching her eyes.

He stepped close to her, raised his hand to her face and touched the markings gently with the tips of his fingers, feeling nothing. He raised his eyes to hers. She was staring at him. He said, "You're in there, aren't you? Behind these little bars. They don't seem like much. Not enough to hold you.''

She said nothing, but seemed to be waiting.

He said to her, ''You should brush your hair. Brush it every day . . .''

''Why?'' the woman said.

''To feel good. You need to wear a dress. A little parasol to match.''

''I'm asking you to leave,'' the woman said. But didn't move from his hand, with its yellowed, stained nails, that was like a fist made of old leather.

''I'll tell you something if I can,'' Ruben Vega said. ''I know women all my life, all kinds of women in the way they look and dress, the way they adorn themselves according to custom. Women are always a wonder to me. When I'm not with a woman I think of them as all the same because I'm thinking of one thing. You understand?''

''Put a sack over their head,'' the woman said.

''Well, I'm not thinking of what she looks like then, when I'm out in the mountains or somewhere,'' Ruben Vega said. ''That part of her doesn't matter. But when I'm *with* a woman, ah, then I realize how they are all different. You say, of course. This isn't a revelation to you. But maybe it is when you think about it some more.''

The woman's eyes changed, turned cold. ''You want to go to bed with me? Is that what you're saying, why you bring a gift?''

He looked at her with disappointment, an expression of weariness. But then he dropped the store box and took her to him gently, placing his hands on her shoulders, feeling her small bones in his grasp as he brought her in against him and his arms went around her.''

He said, ''You're gonna die here. Dry up and blow away.''

She said, ''Please . . .'' Her voice hushed against him.

''They wanted only to mark your chin,'' Ruben Vega said, ''in the custom of those people. But you wanted your own marks, didn't you? *Your* marks, not like anyone else . . . Well, you got them.'' After a moment he said to her, very quietly, ''Tell me what you want.''

The hushed voice close to him said, ''I don't know.''

He said, ''Think about it and remember something. There is no one else in the world like you.''

* * *

He reined the bay to move out and saw the dust trail rising out of the old pasture, three riders coming, and heard the woman say, "I told you. Now it's too late."

A man on a claybank and two young riders eating his dust, finally separating to come in abreast, reined to a walk as they reached the pump and the irrigation ditch. The woman, walking from the corral to the house, said to them, "What do you want? I don't need anything, Mr. Bonnet."

So this would be the Circle-Eye foreman on the claybank. The man ignored her, his gaze holding on Ruben Vega with a solemn expression, showing he was going to be dead serious. A chew formed a lump in his jaw. He wore army suspenders and sleeve garters, his shirt buttoned up at the neck. As old as you are, Ruben Vega thought, a man who likes a tight feel of security and is serious about his business.

Bonnet said to him finally, "You made a mistake."

"I don't know the rules," Ruben Vega said.

"She told you to leave her be. That's the only rule there is. But you bought yourself a dandy new hat and come back here."

"That's some hat," one of the young riders said. This one held a single-shot Springfield across his pommel. The foreman, Bonnet, turned in his saddle and said something to the other rider who unhitched his rope and began shaking out a loop, hanging it nearly to the ground.

It's a show, Ruben Vega thought. He said to Bonnet, "I was leaving."

Bonnet said, "Yes, indeed, you are. On the off end of a rope. We're gonna drag you so you'll know the ground and never cross this land again."

The rider with the Springfield said, "Gimme your hat, mister, so's you don't get it dirty."

At this point Ruben Vega nudged his bay and began moving in on the foreman who straightened, looking over at the roper, and said, "Well, tie onto him."

But Ruben Vega was close to the foreman now, the bay taller than the claybank and would move the claybank if the man on his back told him to. Ruben Vega watched the foreman's eyes moving and knew the roper was coming around behind him. Now the foreman turned his head to spit and let go a stream that spattered the hardpack close to the bay's forelegs.

"Stand still," Bonnet said, "and we'll get her done easy. Or you can run and get snubbed out of your chair. Either way."

Ruben Vega was thinking that he could drink with this ramrod and they'd tell each other stories until they were drunk. The man had thought it would be easy: chase off a Mexican gunnysacker who'd come sniffing the boss's wife. A kid who was good with a rope and another one who could shoot cans off the fence with an old Springfield should be enough.

Ruben Vega said to Bonnet, "Do you know who I am?"

"Tell us," Bonnet said, "so we'll know what the cat drug in and we drug out."

And Ruben Vega said, because he had no choice, "I hear the rope in the air, the one with the rifle is dead. Then you. Then the roper."

His words drew silence because there was nothing more to be said. In the moments that Ruben Vega and the one named Bonnet stared at each other, the woman came out to them holding a revolver, an old Navy Colt, which she raised, and laid the barrel against the muzzle of the foreman's claybank.

She said, "Leave now, Mr. Bonnet, or you'll walk nine miles to shade."

There was no argument, little discussion, a few grumbling words. The Tonto woman was still Mrs. Isham. Bonnet rode away with his young hands, and a new silence came over the yard.

Ruben Vega said, "He believes you'd shoot his horse."

The woman said, "He believes I'd cut steaks, and eat it, too. It's how I'm seen after twelve years of that other life."

Ruben Vega began to smile. The woman looked at him and in a few moments she began to smile with him. She shook her head then, but continued to smile. He said to her, "You could have a good time if you want to."

She said, "How, scaring people?"

He said, "If you feel like it." He said, "Get the present I brought you and open it."

He came back for her the next day in a Concord buggy, wearing his new willow-root straw and a cutaway coat over his revolvers, the coat he'd rented at a funeral parlor. Mrs. Isham wore the pale blue and white lace-trimmed dress he'd bought at Weiss's store, sat primly on the bustle and held the parasol against the afternoon sun all the way to Benson, ten miles, and up the main street to the Charles Crooker Hotel where the drummers and cattlemen and railroad men sitting in their front-porch rockers stared and stared.

They walked past the manager and into the dining room before Ruben Vega removed his hat and pointed to the table he liked, one against the wall between two windows. The waitress in her starched uniform was wide-eyed taking them over and getting them seated. It was early, and the dining room was not half-filled.

"The place for a quiet dinner," Ruben Vega said. "You see how quiet it is?"

"Everybody's looking at me," Sarah Isham said to the menu in front of her.

Ruben Vega said, "I thought they were looking at me. All right, soon they'll be used to it."

She glanced up, and said, "People are leaving."

He said, "That's what you do when you finish eating, you leave."

She looked at him, staring, and said, "Who are you?"

"I told you."

"Only your name."

"You want me to tell you the truth, why I came here?"

"Please."

"To steal some of your husband's cattle."

She began to smile, and he smiled. She began to laugh, and he laughed, looking openly at the people looking at them, but not bothered by them. Of course they'd look. How could they help it? A Mexican rider and a woman with blue stripes on her face sitting at the table in the hotel dining room, laughing. He said, "Do you like fish? I know your Indian brothers didn't serve you none. It's against their religion. Some things are for religion, as you know, and some things are against it. We spend all our lives learning customs. Then they change them. I'll tell you something else if you promise not to be angry or point your pistol at me. Something else I could do the rest of my life. I could look at you and touch you and love you."

Her hand moved across the linen tablecloth to his with the cracked, yellowed nails and took hold of it, clutched it.

She said, "You're going to leave."

He said, "When it's time."

She said, "I know you. I don't know anyone else."

He said, "You're the loveliest woman I've ever met. And the

strongest. Are you ready? I think the man coming now is your husband.''

It seemed strange to Ruben Vega that the man stood looking at him and not at his wife. The man seemed not too old for her, as he had expected, but too self-important. A man with a very serious demeanor, as though his business had failed or someone in his family had passed away. The man's wife was still clutching the hand with the gnarled fingers. Maybe that was it. Ruben Vega was going to lift her hand from his, but then thought, Why? He said as pleasantly as he was able, "Yes, can I help you?"

Mr. Isham said, "You have one minute to mount up and ride out of town.''

"Why don't you sit down," Ruben Vega said, "have a glass of wine with us?'' He paused and said, "I'll introduce you to your wife.''

Sarah Isham laughed; not loud but with a warmth to it, and Ruben Vega had to look at her and smile. It seemed all right to release her hand now. As he did he said, "Do you know this gentleman?''

"I'm not sure I've had the pleasure," Sarah Isham said. "Why does he stand there?''

"I don't know," Ruben Vega said. "He seems worried about something.''

"I've warned you," Mr. Isham said. "You can walk out or be dragged out.''

Ruben Vega said, "He has something about wanting to drag people. Why is that?'' And again heard Sarah's laugh, a giggle now that she covered with her hand. Then she looked up at her husband, her face with its blue tribal lines raised to the soft light of the dining room.

She said, "John, look at me. . . . Won't you please sit with us?''

Now it was as if the man had to make a moral decision, first consult his conscience, then consider the manner in which he would pull the chair out—the center of attention. When finally he was seated, upright on the chair and somewhat away from the table, Ruben Vega thought, All that to sit down. He felt sorry for the man now, because the man was not the kind who could say what he felt.

Sarah said, "John, can you look at me?''

He said, "Of course I can.''

"Then do it. I'm right here."

"We'll talk later," her husband said.

She said, "When? Is there a visitor's day?"

"You'll be coming to the house, soon."

"You mean to see it?"

"To live there."

She looked at Ruben Vega with just the trace of a smile, a sad one. Then said to her husband, "I don't know if I want to. I don't know you. So I don't know if I want to be married to you. Can you understand that?"

Ruben Vega was nodding as she spoke. He could understand it. He heard the man say, "But we *are* married. I have an obligation to you and I respect it. Don't I provide for you?"

Sarah said, "Oh, my God—" and looked at Ruben Vega. "Did you hear that? He provides for me." She smiled again, not able to hide it, while her husband began to frown, confused.

"He's a generous man," Ruben Vega said, pushing up from the table. He saw her smile fade, though something warm remained in her eyes. "I'm sorry I have to leave. I'm going on a trip tonight, south, and first I have to pick up a few things." He moved around the table to take one of her hands in his, not caring what the husband thought. He said, "You'll do all right, whatever you decide. Just keep in mind there's no one else in the world like you."

She said, "I can always charge admission. Do you think ten cents a look is too high?"

"At least that," Ruben Vega said, "But you'll think of something better."

He left her there in the dining room of the Charles Crooker Hotel in Benson, Arizona—maybe to see her again sometime, maybe not—and went out with a good conscience to take some of her husband's cattle.

Arizonan C.S. Park knows the Mexican border country well, as he demonstrates in this suspenseful tale of old Fort Calabasas and of Claybourne Lankford, "cavalryman, Indian Agent, Deputy United States Marshal, and now Deputy Collector of Customs . . . one weathered veteran guarding a stretch of border from El Paso to Yuma where whole armies once did 'round-the-clock duty." Park is the author of numerous stories set in his native state, as well as such novels of both the old and the contemporary west as Border Valley *(1959) and* Gun in the Dust *(1967).*

Two-Gun Farewell

★★★★★★★★★★★★★★★

C.S. Park

BLUE lightning flashed and thunder rattled the loose adobes in the walls of the Custom House at old Fort Calabasas. The telegraph sounder, part of a communication system installed by a departed army, clacked to a power surge somewhere north along the line.

Claybourne Lankford laid his leather-bound copy of the *Tariff of 1883* on the table. Clay got up, a straight, slender shape in the room's afternoon dimness, and limped over to stand in the doorway to feel the coolness rushing ahead of the summer storm.

The scent of wet dust and rainwashed mesquite was on the wind that swept the old parade ground. The wire stretching away from the Custom House swung in long loops, and from it Clay had earlier picked a laborious message in slow code: Dee Pruitt had assaulted Frisco Bozark in the Oriental Saloon at Fort Lowell, cleaned out the safe, kidnapped Bozark's woman, and lit for Mexico.

Clay looked at his watch. From La Osa to Coyote Pass there was only one direct way through the table-topped Atascosas into Sonora, and that was down the narrow twisted gut of Calabasas

97

Canyon. A fast horse with a pushing rider could make it from Fort Lowell in ten hours. Clay had done it himself.

In the gray wall of approaching rain the vague outlines of two riders showed briefly. Clay picked up his hat and stepped out rapidly across the parade ground so as to reach Shy Kelso's International Hotel well ahead of the two riders. Rain in ropy sheets draped his shoulders and splashed his boots before he gained shelter.

Shy Kelso looked up from a month-old newspaper with no pleasure. "They comin', Clay?"

"Somebody is coming."

Kelso lifted his large arms to light a lamp in deference to company and an early dusk. "All the men Bozark has cheated will be hoping Pruitt gets away."

"Pruitt won't." Clay leaned against the short bar and thought back over his thirty-four years with the government.

Cavalryman, Indian Agent, Deputy United States Marshal, and now Deputy Collector of Customs. Now he was just one weathered veteran guarding a stretch of border from El Paso to Yuma where whole armies once did 'round-the-clock duty.

Time is a collapsible thing. When the years fold back upon each other a decade can seem no longer than the week just passed.

There had been a wagon plundered outside Fort Lowell, and the smell of wood smoke had turned Clay Lankford off the path near his own small, neglected ranch. There had been a burning wagon, a man down, and a blond woman of unbelievable beauty with a frightened boy that she called Dee facing three badmen embarked upon their final baseness before slipping off into trackless Mexico. It seemed no further past than yesterday's noon, that quick kick of a new Army Colt against Clay's hand.

A splashing in the muddy road outside the saloon sounded like a man getting down off a horse. Clay concentrated all of his attention upon the doorway. Kelso lowered his arms.

Dee Pruitt stepped carefully sidewise into the room, carrying a small woman. His soft young face froze into a hard young face when he felt Clay Lankford's light-eyed stare. Dripping rainwater formed a spreading puddle on the floor between Dee's soggy boots.

"She's give out, Clay. She's got to rest!" Paleness around Dee's mouth told of personal exhaustion.

Clay held silence.

Kelso's voice was the rasp of a file in the quiet room. "Then carry her upstairs, Dee."

Dee Pruitt circled Clay, defiance displacing the faded look of a forlorn hope in his tired eyes.

Kelso yelled for his Mexican wife and puffed up the stairs with an armload of towels, leaving Clay to the cold pleasure of his calling and the sourness of memory. . . .

Ten years ago, Dee was a towheaded kid hugging his mother's thigh and staring in wide-eyed fear while Clay Lankford shot it out with three badmen within the short space of thirty seconds. Then, gratitude blinded the woman to Clay's graying temples, while a mist in Clay's tawny eyes must have blinded him to the twenty years between their ages.

They both learned that gratitude mistaken for love is a poor substitute for honor and obedience. Where his flint and steel had never raised a spark in a year and more of marriage, someone else found wildfire overnight. That left Clay alone with the exacting demands of an earlier love: Law and Order. . . .

He stepped over to a table and pulled out a chair and sat down astride it, and the thoughtful cigaret he rolled was a mechanical gesture. There was much in today's Dee Pruitt to remind him of the younger one. He stared at the wall and did not know how long he had been sitting there when he heard Kelso clump down the stairs. He rediscovered the cigarette and lit it with steady fingers.

He said to Kelso, "I'll hold them for the sheriff, Kelso."

"Dee gambled you'd be somewhere along the border like you gener'ly are, Clay. His luck run out on him. But you could go now, and nobody would be the wiser. Give 'em a few minutes rest. I'll guarantee they won't be here when you come back."

Law and order above all things. Never easy, often harder. "Does it make sense that a man sworn to enforce laws would aid a fugitive who violated them? I'll hold them for the sheriff."

"Then every miner and cowpoke this side of the Gila will think it's because of what his maw did to you ten years ago. Yellow-eyed dog or yellow-eyed man, neither one worth a damn, that's what they'll be sayin'."

Clay Lankford shrugged in irritation. "Dee broke the law!"

"Gettin' back money stolen in Bozark's cheatin' games? Whippin' the man that stole it? Takin' that little lady upstairs away from him?" Kelso's fat lips framed a rude word.

Even solid friendship is a fragile thing when it is caught in the turbulence of an exploding temper. Clay's broad hand slammed the bar. "Kelso!" His anger soared, choking off talk. Yet in a moment he hit the bar again, but softly, and turned away and walked across to the door.

The short storm was past. The heavy clouds were following the sun. Two horses stood drenched and dejected with lines trailing in the mud. Clay read the dismal signs of patched and mended saddles; this boy hadn't been doing so well. Anger seeped away, leaving him feeling worn and empty.

There was the muted murmur of water trickling in the washes and into Shy Kelso's dirt tank, which was there above his garden patch and his corral. Over the talk of rivulets Clay heard the sloppy sound of hoofs squashing mud. He moved out to loosen the cinches of Dee's sorry saddles and from there got a better view of the advancing rider.

Frisco Bozark, roaring vengeance driving him, was an angry man with swollen eyes in a bruised face. A checkered vest and derby attested his hurried departure from Fort Lowell. Looming high on a tall sorrel, sitting the saddle stiffly, Bozark surveyed the Custom House, Kelso's, the tank, garden, and trail-sore animals. Then he was studying Clay's badge, gun, and eventually his light-eyed gaze.

With everything located and placed inside his mind, Bozark swung down in the way of a man who has ridden many punishing miles. Clay eased quickly back to the door. Bozark's boots sucked mud as he turned hurriedly to watch him.

Clay faded into the interior gloom. Bozark bulked darkly against the orange sky and then came into the hotel with his hand well away from his gun.

Kelso said, "Bozark," and casually placed a bottle and a glass on the bar. Bozark lifted bottle and glass and strode on to a table and turned to face them with solid wall at his back. He grinned.

"Hello, Kelso."

Frogs around Kelso's tank raised their croaking chorus in anticipation of night.

Clay Lankford thought he heard more arriving hoofs in the

mud, but his narrowing concentration closed off all outer distraction.

Glass clinked on glass as Bozark filled and drank and filled again. Then there was the filtered murmur of voices from the floor above. The scraping sound of boot leather.

Bozark lowered bottle and glass to the table and wiped his hands in an upward motion along his vest. Dark moisture on the dirt floor told a story where soaked boots had laid a plain trail. Bozark's eyes followed it to the stairway. Muscle jumped at the angle of his jaw. He tilted his head to the cottonwood beams of the low ceiling, then slanted his gaze down to Clay Lankford's badge.

"Dee Pruitt?"

"My prisoner," said Clay.

"What about my woman?"

To shock a man off balance and keep him there is elementary offense. Clay did it with, "You legally wed?" and watched the color pull out of Bozark's face to leave it all staring eyes and bruised lips drawn back from yellow teeth.

"What the hell has that got to do with it?"

"You couldn't rightly say she's yours, if you aren't."

There wasn't any mirth in Bozark's short laugh. He hung his watchful gaze on Clay and began a slow pivot toward the stairway. "I've got all the right I need, Collector."

The forces of opposition boiled up strongly in Clay. It wasn't that he felt any responsibility toward the woman. But Bozark and Dee Pruitt in the same room meant trouble, and it was to the law that wanted Dee Pruitt that Clay was responsible. "I'm holding the boy for the sheriff, Mister. Keep away from those stairs."

There is a connection between a man's eyes and his actions, but Bozark's lids were drooped too low for Clay's look to dig under them. All of his attention converged upon a spot two buttons down the front of Bozark's vest.

Two taut men standing bent-kneed. Each searching out the other's intent. Waiting through a shrieking space in time. All of the unfinished tag ends of a life sweeping up into one intense moment hanging on a trigger pull.

Then Bozark quit cold. He shrugged and picked up his bottle. "You feel that way about it, Collector, I'll just wait for the sheriff."

The whole room came back into focus for Clay, instead of just Bozark's vivid vest.

Kelso stood in stiff protest, tension flattening the rounded lines of his gross body.

But there had been too many peaceful days in old Fort Calabasas, dulling the edge of caution where it should have been razor sharp.

Bozark flipped the bottle end over end and went for his gun.

Drawing and firing were Clay's conditioned reflex. Dodging the bottle was not. It ruined his aim. The bottle struck his forehead and carried him down.

He lay stunned, bleeding. But in a fighting man the energy of a fighting spirit keeps him going. Clay's hand came up, his thumb cocking the Army Colt.

Now time had slowed to a crawl again. Kelso, shouting with wide mouth, his shout unheard above the roar in Clay's ears, bent for the sawed-off under the bar. Bozark swung the muzzle of his gun around on Kelso, making of himself a wide-open target for Clay.

Caught between the ebb of action and the flow of returning consciousness, Clay struggled to give the gentle tug on the trigger that would reverse this rushing tide.

Then from the corner of his eyes to the center of his vision, from the wings of the stage to the footlights, blurred fury with blazing eyes launched from the catapult of the stairway, slight Dee Pruitt hurled violently into heavy Frisco Bozark. Dee Pruitt turned the tide.

Dee Pruitt backed away, with Bozark's gun shaking in his hand. Bozark hung on the bar, supported by wide-spread arms and sagging legs.

Now Clay could stir. Now he could brace himself and push up from the floor, could shake the stinging fluid from his eyes and spatter the dust with the red shower.

Bozark slid along the bar behind Clay, using him as a shield from that trembling gun in Dee's hand.

Once more Kelso shouted, swinging his ugly shotgun. "Stop, Bozark!"

But Bozark shoved away and plunged out the door with Dee jumping after him.

The flat echo of a shot came back across the dim canyon to meet Clay limping stiffly through the doorway with Kelso treading on his bootheels. Bozark's crumbling figure by the low dirt dike of Kelso's tank was a silent, falling shadow. Dee was a slender shape moving dully out of the evening.

The night wind passed damp and cool across Clay's throbbing forehead, lifted his thin, gray cowlick.

Dee stopped five paces away. Probably he had just saved two lives, and one of them was Clay Lankford's own. But Clay's unclear thinking clung obstinately to the groove of a lifetime: law and order. *An unarmed man had been shot.*

The flat taste of his words was brassy on his tongue. "I'm holding you for the sheriff, Dee."

"But he had a hideout gun, Clay!" Through his dullness, Clay sensed the stiffening resistance in the boy, the nearness of new violence.

Kelso said, "You'll not hold him long, Clay. Sheriff's already here." The bitterness of his tone left his words hanging heavily in the dusk.

Dim figures came away from the corners of the saloon. Some went to the quiet mound by the tank, others converged upon Dee. Sheriff Jay Einmann's bass grumble reached out of the moist darkness.

"We saw you, Dee. And Bozark didn't have no hideout."

"I tell you he had one, Jay! He turned right there and threw down on me!"

"We'll go over the ground. If he had one, we'll find it."

At eight there was no more light in the western sky and no moon to help the feeble rays of a lantern. No hideout gun, either.

Possemen, straying across the border where in the little settlement of Calabasas they could find entertainment and quarters away from home, found them and sent back snatches of laughter mixed in with the shrill voices of women and the howling of mangy dogs disturbed by the strange night noises. These were sounds that couldn't reach Dee's ears behind the thick walls of the detention cell.

Clay faintly heard the revelry as he sat in Kelso's and half listened to Einmann's rattling tongue. The bandaged knob on Clay's forehead throbbed to every slurred word.

Sometimes a tired man's liquor hits him harder than he likes. Turgid veins imparted cherry color to Einmann's long nose, and his cheeks were as red as blood. His dissatisfaction was finding expression in speech.

"Been on the run since morning. Got the man I'm after. Far as I'm concerned, what he did this morning's in his favor. 'N's far's the girl's concerned there was no kidnapping. She tells me Bozark kept her locked up so she couldn't leave whenever she wasn't singing in the Oriental Saloon. Showed me marks where he hit her. She come away with Dee Pruitt voluntary." The sheriff's hand went unsteadily across his face, swabbing the tired look, and the scrape of the bristles on his chin was a loudness in the silent room. He went on:

"It's against everything human in me, but I'll take Dee Pruitt in. He'll get a decent trial, even with reformers packing the jury."

Kelso's fat lips fluttered in faint, derisive sound. Einmann turned too quickly and grabbed Clay's shoulder for support. Kelso's eyes were closed; his lips fluttered again.

Einmann said, "Look at that! Bartender asleep on his feet. Hey! *You Kelso!* Wake up and give a man a drink to pound his ear on."

Kelso moved sleepily. "You goin' to drain my tank in the morning, Sheriff?"

"We won't find any hideout gun there, but if I don't look I couldn't live with my conscience." His head rolled around, his gaze was not quite clear, and his voice carried its note of aggressive accusation. "If I take Dee Pruitt in, it's for murder. I saw it. Maybe you could have eased him on across the border and saved us all a lot of trouble, huh? People going to remember about you and his mother, Clay."

The tightness in Clay's throat squeezed into his voice. "What would you have done?"

Einmann pushed away from the bar. "I'm a politician. This thing may bring criticism from some sources. I'd have told him to keep movin'. I'd do it now if I had half a chance." He spat on the floor. "But not you, I guess. Not the best lawman in the West." He whirled away and lined out for the door where he turned, braced himself against the wall. "I sure's hell wouldn't want to live with your conscience." He backed through the doorway and vanished into the darkness of the parade.

Clay rolled a slow cigarette and absently placed it between his dry lips, sunken deep in reflection. The girl's mellow voice came at him like an extension of his own thoughts:

"Men remember Dee's mother. You aren't her only mistake, she made a lot more after you. Like mother like son, they say.

And was there ever a community so hell-bent on reform as one where too many men have a skeleton in their closets?''

Clay turned around. He cuffed his hat back onto his aching head, feeling the tightness of the white cloth that bound it.

The girl Dee had brought to Calabasas had hair that was as black and glossy as a raven's back and eyes that were glowing lumps of coal. Neither angry nor sorrowful, she talked straight at Clay.

"You knew they wouldn't let Dee keep a decent job. They tried every way to run him off. Out of sight, out of mind, d'you see? But he stayed on." She moved in closer, looking up to him. "He told me it was *you* that made him that way. Never give up, you used to tell him. Live honest and square so you can look any man in the eye. Talked to him like the father he never had, I guess." Her voice went soft. "Why don't you let him out of that cell?"

This girl's words were a dull lance probing into an unhealed wound left from that earlier period—the shadowy memory of a friendly little fellow as eager and loyal as a setter pup.

Law and Order. Sometimes easy, often harder. Sometimes a man can take nothing more without coming apart at the seams. Clay wished he knew how to put into words what he felt: that no honest lawman could serve two masters and remain honest. But he never could talk about such things. So he walked out on her and away from Kelso's silent disapproval.

Out in the quiet night, Clay said over his shoulder, not knowing if they heard or understood, "There is nothing I can do now. He isn't my prisoner."

Half of a white moon stood big and round above the rim of the canyon, its bottom edge trimmed with the ragged black embroidery of silhouetted junipers. A mournful coyote solo filtered down the miles on the soft wind out of Mexico, a lonely crying in the night. It brought melancholy retrospection to Clay Lankford. . . .

There had been that one more time, riding hard down the Santa Cruz with a warrant in his pocket. Catching up to a fleeing horse thief and a stolen woman and her boy as they rode on horses wearing the Lankford brand. Seeing in his mind that rash young man turning at the sound of running hoofs, seeing him draw his gun—then riding through a rain of lead to get in one true shot.

So that man in the dust hadn't ever troubled his conscience. He had died resisting arrest. Neither had the woman's look of fear and loathing. But the haunting quality in Dee's young eyes staring again on the violence that made hating strangers out of trusted friends was ever a troublesome thing in a sleepless night. . . .

The dog population across the border hashed up the coyote aria in a senseless clamoring chorus that returned Clay to the old fort by the edge of the pool where Bozark had fallen.

Clay stood in deep meditation, staring into the muddy water. Dee's future depended upon whatever lay—or did not lie—beyond its opaqueness to back up the story of a hideout weapon. A bullfrog bellowed once. In the night the sound was followed by a gurgling splash.

Then somewhere behind Clay there was a sound. He turned to see Kelso's bulky form large against the lamplighted doorway. The night's air after the rain had put a stiffness into Clay's joints. Along the way to his quarters he passed Kelso, said his, "Good night," and got the fat man's sardonic:

"Pleasant dreams, Clay."

Lying clothed and tense-muscled in the darkness of his room, Clay traced back down the route of his years and found no instance in his loyalty to the law he served where he had compromised with the other side. He was too old to start now. And there was still the home place back in the hills with the mavericks running wild in the arroyos. Thought milled on.

Sure that he would not sleep this night, Clay was surprised by sunlight. He swung his legs over the edge of the bed. He pulled on his boots and found his hat, and on his feet felt a little less like a man dragged through a knothole. From the washstand by his door he saw the sheriff's posse shoveling a spillway for the water in the tank. He watched a moment before he angled across the broad sunny parade to join Kelso at breakfast.

Chorizo and eggs and strong black Mexican coffee make the kind of a meal a man can rely on to tide him over until lunch. He ate methodically, finishing with a cigaret rolled thin in the Mexican manner, and was smoking thoughtfully when Sheriff Einmann walked in.

There was a red tracery of veins in the sheriff's eyes, a survivor of last night's excess. "I may have said something I didn't mean, Clay." He laid a wet Army Colt on the table.

"But I would have bet a hundred to one there'd be no gun in that pond. Funny we didn't see so big a gun in Bozark's hand before Dee shot him."

"Too dark to see well." Clay let his look slide over to Kelso. "Now you've got your chance to let the kid go. If you don't take it—I wouldn't want to live with *your* conscience." It might have been a small smile that twitched the corners of his mouth.

Einmann nodded. "We're pulling out, Clay. Dee saw a gun, and he shot in self-defense. There won't be charges of robbery or assault—the complaining witness is dead. So I have no prisoner. Thanks, anyway." He turned and went out, boot heels thumping.

Kelso's fat face wrinkled up. He touched the gun with a big forefinger. "One of the first guns of this kind to be made. If I hadn't given it to you myself some years ago, I might not know that you've got a big, soft heart in your chest instead of the *Revised Statutes*."

Clay stood up and tucked the damp gun into his waistband, wanting to tell Kelso that as of last night he no longer considered the *Revised Statutes* his Bible. But Sheriff Einmann reappeared in the doorway, holding a wet derringer up between thumb and forefinger. The sheriff said:

"You might like to know we found this in the tank, too."

It was exactly the kind of small, deadly weapon a shifty gambler might carry up his sleeve like an extra ace. Einmann grinned, lifted his hand, said, "I'm going to leave before we find maybe a sawed-off shotgun in the drink," and vanished from the doorway.

Kelso said softly, not moving, "Dee didn't lie, Clay."

"Go get that girl, Kelso!"

You can still see the crumbled walls of Kelso's International Hotel beneath the west rim of Calabasas Canyon and those of the Custom House under the east. A hundred paces separate them, and if some brush has grown up between them now, there was none when the black-haired girl ran across the parade and into Dee's waiting arms. Over by the corral, the sheriff's men turned around and cursed their horses in muffled tones and tended strictly to saddling up.

Clay came away from the Custom House, limping slowly, knowing he should say something apologetic. But he hadn't ever been good at saying his mind when it had to do with this kind of thing. So he called softly when he was near enough, "The old place needs someone to look after it, son," and stopped, fearing to the bottom of his soul that Dee wasn't listening to him.

Then Dee turned the girl. Together they moved toward Clay standing with the early morning sunlight glinting on his hatless gray head. And Clay stood steady, for this was a moment a yellow-eyed man could savor the rest of his days.

This unusual tale of the last days of an elderly Arizona cowboy makes effective use of a number of different elements, among them nostalgia and fantasy. Its realistic background stems from the fact that Jay Lucas was himself an Arizona cowboy in the early years of this century. Prior to World War II Lucas was a frequent contributor to such pulp magazines as Western Story *and* Blue Book. *He also authored a number of novels with authentic Arizona settings, among them 7 Bar 7 Ranch (1934),* The Arizonan *(1934),* Blaze McGee *(1935), and* Boss of the Rafter C *(1937).*

Black Horses

★★★★★★★★★★★★★★

Jay Lucas

HEAT —dry, glaring and windless. The scorched waste of Mendoza Flat stretched to a level horizon above which came another horizon of low, jagged, dark-blue mountains.

The herd streamed slowly on in a great cloud of dust, approaching the weathered corrals of the X Bar Y. There was the din of bawling cows, calves, steers, each to its own note; and sometimes came the high trumpeting of a bull. Now and then rose the shrill, wearied yelp of a cowboy.

A dust-gray horse swung out from the cloud, on its back a withered, dust-powdered old man who loped ahead of the point, tiredly slapping his quirt against his tattered chaps. He shouted hoarsely from a dry throat:

"Ho-o-old up! Ho-o-old up!"

The point stopped. Like the current of a slow river, the swing came on and pressed against it. Last came the drag—mostly shaggy, big-paunched calves that stumped doggedly on short legs, heads hanging and mouths open. Cows turned, bawling brokenly for calves lost in the press; the herd was stopped and began milling slowly.

Men, eyes red-rimmed from the biting dust, shouted to each other above the din. The old man called to a passing rider:

"Sam, would you mind holdin' the cut awhile?"

This, then, was an old-fashioned outfit; there were no orders to cowboys, merely requests—perhaps a relic of the day when the hoarse voice of Judge Colt made all men equal here in Arizona.

There began the usual business of working a herd. A long-legged calf went flying; behind him a racing pony, a whirling loop. The calf was dragged back to the herd—he went in stiff hops, stiff legs thrust far out, strangling; this was his first lesson in bunch-breaking.

Now the old man was wearily mopping his lined face with a red, white-dotted handkerchief. Hard day—never seen a bunch more ornery to drive. But you could hardly blame 'em—shore hot, hotter'n the hinges of hell!

Another man, thickset, perhaps forty, came loping up on a sweat-streaked sorrel. He spoke gently:

"Dad, we can handle 'em all right now; you better go up to the house an' rest."

"Believe I will, son—believe I will. I'm tired—tired. Reckon I'm gettin' a mite old to stand this work."

Old Ernie Tompkins turned his horse quickly; that pain in his chest had caught him again, and he did not want Clay to see his face. Of course, all that ailed him was that dust and heat. . . .

He did not unsaddle at the corrals; he did not want to walk to the house—he was tired, very tired. Some of the young squirts could unsaddle for him when they got through working the herd. They wouldn't mind, being as how he was getting sort of old. They were good kids—not like the cowboys of the old days, of course, but good kids, anyway.

Stiffly he swung from his shabby saddle, dropped the reins, and slowly climbed the three steps to the wide, old-fashioned porch. He kicked off his tattered chaps—bat-wings—and hung them on a nail against the wall.

He left his spurs on—ancient spurs, silver-mounted, with straight shanks. His dusty boots were tiny and trim; he hadn't walked a mile since he was a boy back in Texas. Big Bend Country of Texas; shore used to be wild. Bad men a-plenty! They said it wasn't so doggone' tame back there yet! Likely not, likely not—them kind of men didn't *get* tame; they could only get shot.

He eased himself slowly into a rawhide-bottom rocker. He reached to his shirt pocket and drew out a long piece of thin corn-shuck, trimmed with scissors. He tapped a little stream of tobacco along it and rolled a cigaret. Funny how he'd got back to corn-shuck cigarets this last year or so; nobody else smoked them any more. Used to smoke them back there in the Big Bend Country when he was a kid—him and Steve.

He inhaled deeply. Dang it! There went that pain in his chest again. That dust was enough to give anybody pains in the chest.

He stiffly crossed his thin knees and sat staring down at his boots. He wore them, of course, with the tops outside his trousers; it was them movies made in California that had most of the young fellers wearing their boots inside their pants now—and them crazy wide cuffs on their pants. And the big feet most of 'em had now— you could see plain how much *they'd* walked. Only a few, like Clay, reared on cow outfits, had small feet and wore their boots outside.

Old Ernie surveyed a foot. He wore fives. Steve had used to wear fives, too. They'd sometimes swap boots, and sometimes they'd try which could sneak out of bed first in the morning to grab the best pair. . . . Steve—Steve.

He slowly raised his head and looked out across the corrals to where the boys were working his herd. At that distance his eyes were still almost as keen as they had been fifty, sixty years ago. Course, he didn't see things close as well as he used to, but outside of that—

Seventy-two—seventy-two last Friday—and still able to make a hand. Not many men could say that! Course he couldn't top a bronc' any more, and it was none of his business to flank calves— that was for the young squirts; but he could still make a hand. He was proud of it; he knew people talked about it—"Seventy-two, and look at him head that calf!" Yes sir, and still ran his little outfit without a foreman.

Little outfit? Well, one had to admit that it wasn't so little at that—not big exactly, but comfortable, comfortable. And danged good white-faces. Funny, sorter, to look back on the long-legged, long-horned devils he'd started out with—wild as jackrabbits, and you might as well try to get beef on a racehorse. No money in critters of that kind, but he'd had the range when white-faces began to come into the country—English cattle they used to call them at first.

See Clay, heading that cow back into the herd! Good rider and a good boy; he had a good head for cattle. Clay was well-educated, too; clear up to the eighth grade and could read pretty near anything and write fine letters to buyers. Jim, the young one, was even smarter, even if he hadn't gone to school quite as much as Clay; he was range-boss for the big Tyson Cattle Company and drew down a fine check every month. Uh-huh—both his boys was smart; he was lucky.

Uh-huh—good boys; didn't care about anything, only working with cattle; they'd got it from him. So many young fellers nowadays was so rattle-headed; looked like all they wanted was to listen to that danged thing they called a saxyphone. Squealed like a stuck hog, it did—call *that* music? Now a good fiddler, and another feller with good lungs to call the figgers—

Old Ernie's head had jerked up once; it was drooping again slowly. His eyes were closing.

"Swi-i-ing yore partners!"

Two fiddles were wailing lustily. It was "Money Musk"—right pretty piece; you couldn't beat it. Whirling, stamping figures weaved in and out. Silvery jingle of spur rowels, swish of long skirts. Nell was shore pretty tonight—right pretty!

"Hi-yuh, Nell!"

Swish and swing of voluminous skirts, tight bodices heaving, cheeks pink from the fast dance. Gosh, but Nelly Greaves was *pretty*—and good sense, too, which all girls that pretty didn't have. And how she could dance!

"Nell, yo're shore dancin' tonight!"

"Now, Ernie!"

Was she really mad at him or only acting? Her face had turned pinker, and she had looked away. She looked back once, quickly, and then away again. Dance! Nothing could dance like Nell's eyes, or shine like 'em. Huh? He was thinking things like a poetry feller!

"Nell, let's show that Badger Creek bunch real *dancin'*!"

Real dancing was faster dancing. Wild whirl. Small feet twinkling beneath her long skirt. Her laugh of pure joy.

Excitement, high spirits. Now and then the shrill, high-pitched yelp of a cowboy ringing against the rafters of the little schoolhouse. Pure joy of life, of course; the most rowdy of them would not think of going to a dance when he'd had a drink or two—not among decent girls. Why, if he did, a girl wouldn't touch him even to slap his face; the other boys would attend to him, plenty!

A soft voice:

"Ernie, yo're no slouch at dancin' yoreself."

Shyly, with a single flash of those clear blue eyes. And what pretty yellow hair she had!

The music was over, and he had taken Nell back to her place. A hand tapped him quietly on the shoulder from behind.

"Ernie, come outside. I want to talk to you."

That was Steve—never was a partner like Steve Mullins. Raised together in the Big Bend; ran away together to join a herd going "up the trail." Panhandle—Dodge City—Montana. Out to the wild Arizona Territory, side by side, singing and laughing as they rode, and sometimes getting into tomfoolery as young fellers will—did many things they shouldn't. Working on one outfit after another; summers passing, and winters. Steve six feet tall—handsome cuss—and wore the same size boots as his shorter partner. And could Steve fork a bronc'!

"Want to talk to you."

Walking across the floor, side by side, him and Steve. Nell staring after them with wide, scared eyes, her face white and one hand up to her heaving bodice. Out through the door, out into the clear, cold moonlight where buckboards stood, and horses with saddles high on their humped backs. Steve! *Steve!*

Huh? Dang near fell out of his chair! Must have been sort of asleep. And—dreaming about Steve. Funny, he had dreamt about Steve so much this last year or so; seemed like Steve was near him. But the dream always stopped before—

That wouldn't do; had to think about something else.

Wonder if that young college feller was coming back to stay with him again this summer? He had an invite and shore was welcome. Nice sort of young feller; too bad if he had TB like the doctors thought he might be getting. Liked to sit there on the porch and read to an old cattleman that was just a mite shy on book learning. Could even read things in Latin and Greek—read it slow, because he had to say it in English.

There was Castor and Pollux—he remembered them well because the book had a colored picture of them. On two fine white horses with sort of silvery manes and tails. Right pretty horses, looked like Arabs. No other horse could ever be as pretty as an

Arab, even if they were kind of small—teeny little muzzles and slim legs; pretty as spotted pups. Two fellers riding side by side on white horses—side by side, like him and Steve. . . . Huh! Mustn't think of Steve.

That young feller said the old Romans used to believe in 'em. Well, it was poor business to make fun of any man's religion— who knew the truth about that sort of thing? Some people stuck up their noses at the Mormons or used to a few years ago, but what if they *had* found them tablets of gold like they said? Anyway, they'd turned out to be mighty fine people; you couldn't beat 'em.

Elysium Fields? Wasn't that what the young college feller had called it? Fields—any cattle in 'em? Or cowboys? Or old stove-up cowboys? Golden harps—that didn't seem like much fun somehow; a place with horses would be better. Back in the old days, when Steve—

"Well, Ernie?"

A big man with a big cigar in one corner of his mouth was speaking to him across a battered desk.

"Well, I—I reckon I *might* take that sheriff job—but I got to get a hundred a month. I—uh—I'm savin' a little stake to get an outfit o' my own."

"Batchin' outfit, Ernie?"—gravely.

"Aw, shet up, Jedge—you gimme a pain!"

"Haw—haw! Well, ol' man Greaves's gal is right pretty."

"Aw, you gimme a pain! Do I get the hundred?"

"You danged—! Oh, well—pin this on yore chest."

Now, that sheriff job—

"Well, what you going' to do about it, Ernie?" Coolly, sarcastically.

The gaunt towheaded young man with the dissipated face was standing opposite him on the board sidewalk, grinning down at him tolerantly because he was so short. Whitey Remsen was *bad*; he'd killed Sheriff Cox, whom nobody had wanted to replace until Judge Laviter had talked to Ernie; and they said Whitey'd shot Walter Nunn just to see him kick.

"I'm a-goin' to see that you git out o' town in five minutes, Whitey. That rough stuff don't go here no more."

"Oh! Think yo're tough since you got that tin badge?"

"I don't think nothing—only that yo're a-gittin' out an' quick."

"What if I don't go, Ernie?"

"We-ell, *one* of us is goin', Whitey—feet first, if we have to."

A flash of hands . . . Whitey's gun was clattering on the boards of the sidewalk, and Whitey was holding his right elbow with his left hand; he'd never make another fast draw. Blood was streaming through Whitey's fingers and dripping down the front of his trousers. . . .

And there went Whitey, riding down through the thick dust of the street, a dirty bandanna tied around his arm. Yeah—that was right; go after the toughest one first, and then the others wouldn't give him no bother. . . .

"Spike, don't you think the climate o' Californy might be what you need awhile?"

"Reckon it might be, at that, Ernie—yo're the doctor."

Slim, good-looking Spike was grinning at him recklessly, carelessly, with a brown cigaret dangling from his mouth. Spike Driscoll was a good kid, only that he'd got in with the wrong bunch.

"Have a drink with me, Spike, before you go—jest to show there's no hard feelin's?"

"Hell, yes. Yo're all right, Ernie. If I was half as slick with a gun as you are—"

And there went Spike Driscoll, riding off, whistling. Heck, he'd straighten out yet—he'd meant what he promised back there in the saloon.

Ouch!

That pain in his chest had woke him up—sort of shooting around there inside him, not in one spot. Course it was only the dust—that dust all day, and the heat, and working so hard would give anybody pains in the chest. Well, he hadn't been dreaming about Steve that time; that was a good thing. Some day he'd finish that dream about Steve; and when he did— No, he must never finish that dream about Steve—never! Because if he did— Well, he *must* not finish it. Have to stop thinking about him, even—about Steve and that night.

What was it he'd been figgering about? Oh, yes—religion and that sort of thing.

Take them Hopi Indians with their snake dance: he'd never seen anybody look more plumb religious than the snake priests. They'd go dancing along nearly naked with big live rattlesnakes in their mouths—*hop-hop* one foot, *hop-hop* the other. Dang near naked, with gray fox skins hanging down behind; the gray fox was sacred with them, like the grizzly bear. All painted up with colored mud. Sounded crazy, but shore powerful solemn and religious, even to a white man that didn't understand a word of the chants. And two solemn-faced gray-haired old priests helping the old, old medicine man, who was so old that he was all dried-up and blind and stooped away over.

That snake dance was to bring rain to their little patches of fields miles apart on the desert—a Hopi would run twenty miles and back in a day to look after a little field no bigger than the floor of a small bedroom. Little fields with a flat rock stuck up to shelter each young melon vine from the desert sun; why anything grew there, or how the Hopis knew where to plant, no white men ever could figure out—no more than they could figure out why a snake priest never died of snakebite; that had the doctors puzzled, but they never could find out.

Uh-huh—them snake priests were so religious and believed it so much that one of them wouldn't open his eyes or miss a step even when a big rattler bit him clear through the cheek into the tongue. Could anything be wrong, when anybody believed it so strong as them priests? And if they *were* wrong, believing it that way, then everybody must be wrong and there was nothing—But that didn't sound right: must be *something*. . . .

Seventy-two. Maybe live ten, fifteen years more—mighty healthy for his age; hardly ever ailing. His grandfather had lived to eighty-six, and his father might have, if a horse hadn't fell on him and killed him. Fifteen years, and after that? Shore, there had to be something!

Was that two teeny little dark clouds coming up over the mountain way off there, side by side? Side by side—that's how him and Steve used to ride. Funny—*danged* funny—that he couldn't get Steve off his mind today. Him and Steve back there—him and Steve and Nell. Nell Greaves, she was then. . . .

Two little dark clouds, way off across Mendoza Flat . . . Had to rain soon and break this heat . . . Two little dark clouds coming toward him.

"Ernie—Ernie! I'm goin'! Ernie!"

"Nell, hon! You'll feel better in the mornin'. The doctor said—"

"The boy, Ernie? The boy?"

"Kickin' like a yearlin', Nell—husky young-un."

"You—you'll call him Jim, after my dad?"

"Shore, Nell—*we* will."

"No! *No!* Ernie—I can't—can't see you. *Ernie!*"

"Hon, I'm right here. You go right to sleep, an' you'll wake up all right."

Tears streaming down his face, an awful lump in his throat. But he had to keep his voice steady; wouldn't do to scare poor Nell—used to be Nell Greaves. He was squeezing a white, thin hand that felt clammy and cold.

"I won't—wa-wake. . . . *Ernie! He's comin'!*"

She was sitting up, white as the white sheets. And she was falling back, lifeless as the sheets themselves.

"Oh, my God! My God!"

Mrs. Saunders was leading him from the room; he crashed into the doorjamb and stood facing it blindly an instant before he knew how to go around it. *Nell!*

And whom had she seen coming? He'd never figured it out.

Huh! Why, he'd dang near fell out of his chair. But it wasn't pain in his chest that woke him up; it hadn't come that time. Funny that he should be dreaming so much about things that had happened so long ago—now Jim was range-boss for the big Tyson Cattle Company and drew down a fine check every month. Jim was a smart boy, and so was Clay.

His cowboys were unsaddling down by the corrals now; some throwing their saddles over the top log, some laying them neatly on their sides on the ground with the sweat-drenched blankets spread on top to dry. Shore wet blankets today; this heat was hard on horses, like it was on men. Old Brownie had fell dead under Slim Sullivan—queer that a horse should fall dead that way! But it was shore hot, and kind of choky. . . .

That college feller—there was a picture in one of his books of a feller called Pluto; he drove great black horses and took dead people down into a great, endless cave somewheres back in the old countries. That's what the Romans used to believe, but it sounded like foolishness. But what if the Romans and the Mormons and the Hopi snake priests were all of them right? Might be different things—sounded reasonable; we don't all like the same things. Now, if he had his choice, and could go with good horses—

No, them wasn't clouds—couple fellers coming riding across the Flat. Likely a couple boys from the Diamond T outfit coming to pick up their strays. He'd better make 'em stay all night; the cattle had had driving enough for one day, it so hot—one cow had "melted" on them and dropped dead; fine, fat cow, too. But it was beginning to cool off a mite now, seeing as it was about sunset.

"Want to see you outside, Ernie."

Crisp, cool night of an Arizona October, with clear, brilliant moonlight as nowhere else.

Empty buckboards; saddled horses with humped backs and trailing reins. Two men stopped facing each other—two slim, trim young cowboys, one a good deal taller than the other.

"Ernie, Nell Greaves is my gal—*sabe*?" Quietly.

"See here, Steve—Nell's free, white, an' eighteen. She can go with anybody she wants to."

"I was goin' with her first!"—in a voice that was dry, harsh.

"How often?" A scoffing tone, still held in restraint. "Not what you could rightly call *goin'* with a gal, Steve."

"I don't give a damn! You lay off!" Crisp, bitter.

"Steve, us two—"

"Aw, lay off, you fellers; let's go back into the dance."

"Ed, we're a-goin' to settle it right now. Listen here, Ernie—"

"Steve, I ain't a-listenin' to nothin'. I'm a-goin' with Nell Greaves all she'll go with me, an' if you don't like it—"

The sentence meaningly unfinished. A pause . . .

"Stop 'em, for God's sake!"

A tang of biting black powder in the still air—a little whitish cloud drifting off in the brilliant moonlight. Steve on the ground on his back; he moved only once—sort of rolled over and drew up one knee a little bit. Something dark spreading down the side of the white shirt he'd worn for the dance. A man with a badge on his chest coming running from the schoolhouse where now the music had stopped suddenly.

"What? For God's sake—"

"Steve started it; we all saw it. He called Ernie out—"

"No use—plumb through the heart."

The man with the badge pointing a stern finger:

"You git home—the judge'll want to see you in the mornin' anyway."

"Wait, Ernie! You don't have to quit the country; go on home for the night. We'll all sw'ar he started it, an' it was an even break."

"Break be damned! I've killed—Steve. . . . !"

"Self-defense. Prisoner discharged. You, Ernie Tompkins: I'm a-warnin' you. . . . Too danged quick on the trigger. Jest as much to blame as him."

"Thanks, Jedge. I—mebbe I was a mite hasty. Steve—"

"You young cowpunchers! I should send you up for it; but then, when two of you— Well, git out! Next case; that gal from the red-light—"

And they'd buried Steve under the big juniper up on the hill, where he could have seen for miles and miles, if he could have seen at all. He'd have liked that. Steve—Steve—his pardner.

This time he woke up slowly, stupidly, with cold beads of sweat on his forehead, with that pain clutching and gnawing at his chest as it never had before.

So he'd finished the dream at last—the thing he'd dreaded all down those long years. Many a night he'd woke up in a cold sweat just as they were walking out of the little schoolhouse, Nell staring after them, her eyes big and scared—he'd always woke up then, shivering, with sweat on his forehead.

Them was wild days—many a young cowboy got shot for less. If Steve hadn't been his pardner—

From out toward Mendoza Flat came a quick spatter of sound. *"Yip-ee! Yip-yip-yip!"*

Why, it was just like Steve's coyote yell! A rider was dashing by the corrals and toward him, leading a spare saddled horse. How he rode! Some young fool that hadn't better sense than to ride a good horse to death a hot evening like this. That coyote yapping—

Dusk was settling; the sleepy, eerie hoot of a great owl came from a ledge.

Arab horses! No others could have such slender legs and such dainty muzzles—muzzles hardly large enough for the flaring, quivering nostrils. Black manes whipping—black Arabs—he didn't know there were any black Arabs! Coal black, jet black—the blackest, shiniest things you ever saw.

And how they came! They'd easy take any race in Prescott or—

Huh! Them was too big for Arabs; nearly twice too big, but they shore had the lines. Great black tails streaming in the wind of their own speed.

Here they were, sliding to a stop in a cloud of dust, the lead horse rearing and pawing once—pretty! The rider was leaning back with the grace of an old-time cowboy who had lived his life in the saddle; he was smoking a brown cigaret.

"Ready to drift, Ernie?"

"Huh? I ain't a-goin' nowhere, son."

The young man in the saddle threw back his head—a well-shaped head—and laughed. It was a merry, reckless laugh. Ernie though he recognized it vaguely; was it that new bronc'-twister from the Bar Heart come over after strays? His face looked sort of blurry, like things did at close range these late years; a man of seventy-two couldn't see close things so very well.

"Hurry up, Ernie!"

It came to him suddenly. The young fellow wanted to sell him one of the horses; wanted to try it out. Everybody knew he was a fool about good horses and the fool price he'd pay if one suited him. Well, he'd buy one of 'em, if it took the price of the herd he'd gathered that day; it would last him the rest of his life, if he took care of it. But he was foxy; he wouldn't let on to be too anxious—he'd have to pay a-plenty at the best.

"Ain't tryin' to sell one o' them horses to me, are you, son? Showin' 'em off that way."

Again that merry, wholly reckless laugh—seemed to be a nice sort of kid; wonder if he could hire him?

"Climb on an' try one, Ernie."

As well as he could see so close, the kid seemed to be grinning at him—seemed to know some great joke. Uh-huh; seemed to be a right nice kid.

"Well, I got too many horses now, kid; I can't afford— Oh, might as well see what gaits he has!"

It seemed difficult to lift himself out of his chair with both hands; he barely did make it. He had to lean one shoulder against the wall as he slowly pulled on his old chaps. Across the porch now and down the three steps—it seemed miles. His old chaps flapped dismally, and his rusty spurs clinked. . . . Now he had the rein—he could hardly see it—and the saddle-horn. Now, if he could get his foot up into the stirrup . . .

Huh! The horse reared suddenly, pawed the air; the great black mane whipped across old Ernie's face, blinding him. And something happened: a terrible pain in his chest that didn't last no time; a blinding flash of white-hot light that swept around him; a mighty crack in his ears.

And here he was, seated firmly in the saddle; he could just remember swinging up instantly like a young feller—or better. He flushed with pride. Who'd say he couldn't make a hand—and he seventy-two!

"Let's *go*!"

His breath caught; he gasped. Why, that sounded just like Steve's voice, just as it used to, 'way back in them days—And he could have sworn he saw somebody falling down flat beside the horse just as he went up—some little withered feller in torn bat-wing chaps. He'd have looked down, but he didn't have time. . . . They were going, going! Over the fence like two swallows.

"*Yip-ip! Yip-ip-ip!* Let's drift, Ernie!"

Fear was clutching at him—if that wasn't Steve— And under them the swift rattle of hoofs like the very fast roll of soft little drums. Streaks of yellow passed under them, and dark lines, and then a wide streak of silver, so fast that things were all blurry; he could not tell where they were going. And—and they had started west, but the sun was rising ahead of them! Why, it was nearly clear over them now!

A terrible fear seized Ernie, a fear such as he had never known. If that *was* Steve—

Swift rattle of hoofs—what mighty horses these blacks were! The silver streak had fallen behind; dark land fled under them, as they went on, side by side.

He began to tremble. What had happened? Why, he was all limber and active, like a young-un fresh out of bed of a cool morning. He—but he felt sort of queer; he didn't feel right!

His eyes came suddenly to his hand holding the reins. What! Why, his hand looked white and soft, like the hand of a young cowboy who had always worn gloves, like the old-timers did! Why, it wasn't *natural*! And he could see his hand so plain; it should look blurry. Something was wrong. . . . Fear clutched at him, horror. His head swung slowly, stiffly, and his eyes fell full on the face of the other rider.

"*Steve!* But—I shot you!"

Steve's calming, quiet voice—yes, it was Steve, just as he used to be:

"Heck, what of it, pardner? It had to be one of us; I ain't got no hard feelin's."

"But, Steve, yo're *dead*!"

A little friendly, twisted grin. How well he remembered that little twist down to the left corner of Steve's mouth.

"So are you, pardner. They picked me to go for you, so's you wouldn't get too scared—us bein' pardners always. An' she said to tell you—"

Darkness ahead; a gaping hole: they shot into it. Cold, damp, clutching darkness, but the black horses never paused. And then a soft glow of light before them, growing larger with astonishing swiftness. The blacks were slowing down now of their own accord.

Ahead Ernie could see a horse that seemed to be molded of burnished silver—what a wonderful long mane and tail he had! And—that was a young girl riding him, waving her hat and coming at a lope as though she'd been waiting.

A whisper from Steve:

"That's her. I'll swing off."

He was gone, somewhere. Ernie leaped from his saddle before the silver had stopped. His arms were extended.

"Nell! Hon!" In his strong young arms, her body was warm, soft; her face was flushed with happiness.

"Ernie!"

The black horse and the silver nuzzled each other in greeting. Across the rich, short grass there came a puff of scent-laden air; petals fluttered gently to the ground.

Ernie's eyes closed; a little groan of happiness came from his lips. So *this* was death!

Although born in Michigan, John Prescott moved to Arizona in 1951 to be closer to the scenes of his fiction and to uphold a family tradition: his father and grandfather also lived in the state, installing machinery in the mines of Ajo, Bisbee, and Tombstone. Prescott's short fiction appeared in numerous pulps and in such slick-paper magazines as The Saturday Evening Post, *where "Way of the Law in Calico" was first published. Prominent among his novels is* Journey by the River, *which won a WWA Spur for Best Western Historical of 1954.*

Way of the Law in Calico

★★★★★★★★★★★★★★

John Prescott

EVERY spring when school let out in Calico and I could help my mother and sister run our boardinghouse, my father went into the mountains to dig in our mine. It was required that he do so much assessment work each year to keep the claim. Sometimes he would be away a week and other times a month or more; and the year that Mr. Dean arrived in Calico, Father was gone for seven weeks. The reason for this variation was not related to the quantity of gold he was removing, but to the quality of fishing when the assessment work was finished.

As a matter of fact, through all the years we held our claim, my father found no gold whatever, though he often worried that he might. Since we had come to Arizona for his health, he felt that he could handle only certain kinds of labor, and he developed a fear of finding a paying vein. He came to believe that a real bonanza might so interfere with fishing that his recovery would be threatened.

So while he was away my mother would collect the money and do the cooking, Elaine would do the cleaning and the beds, and I would be the outside man.

It was on a day that I was being this outside man that Mr. Dean appeared. I was sweeping the gallery clean of dirt from muddy boots when I heard someone speak.

"Such ardent labors are worthy of that other Hercules in the famed Augean stables."

I looked, and there he was. First I saw the bright yellow shoes, then his flowered waistcoat, then way above all that his high, gray beaver. He was young and willow tall, and his smile and dress were those of a drummer.

I told him my name was Sammy, that this was Bayley's Boardinghouse.

His name was Dean. "A fair place," he then said of our boardinghouse. "Aye, it brings to mind the palace of Fontainbleau."

He seemed surprised that I should ask him what that was. Setting down his carpetbag, he crossed his arms and examined me.

"You know not," he asked, "the seat of the Frankish kings?"

It was not the usual thing to hear a question of that kind in Calico. I shook my head. I'd never seen the seat of any king.

"What, then, do you know of that noble Roman, Caesar?"

But I could only shake my head at Caesar, too.

"Can we converse upon Ulysses, friend?"

I felt really bad.

"Have you knowledge of Galileo?" When I said I hadn't he clicked his tongue. "What of James Watt, then? What of Dante? What of Burke?"

There were more, and they were all, I guess, the ringing names of emperors and dragon slayers, or the chemical names of scientists, the papery names of poets and philosophers. His voice rose and fell, his arms moved in the air, but I didn't know any of them.

Mr. Dean laughed gently and made another gesture.

"Their greatness lay in their aspirations, Samuel. They were of high heart, children of wonder."

He fixed his hand in a fist and beat upon his own high heart. He smiled again and raised a finger.

"Mayhap I should be your mentor, Samuel. Together we might give pursuit to the wonders they wrought. Aye, and many another marvel, too. In time you could be educated."

I began to say that school in Calico was educating me for nearly six months every year, but at that moment my mother and sister came out of the door.

"Ah," said Mr. Dean, sweeping off his beaver and bending

like a reed, "the fair Penelope; and lo, a vestal virgin in attendance."

This made my sister turn the color of sunset, but my mother had been in the boarding business quite a while. All she did was primp a little at her hair.

"What are you selling?" she said to Mr. Dean. "I'll hear you out, but I give no promise to buy."

"Good madam, I come not peddling trifles to your annoyance," Mr. Dean said, his thumbs now in the armholes of his waistcoat. "My traffic is all of replevins, torts, briefs and letters testamentary. Permit me, if you will"—and he bowed again—"the name is Dean, Edwin Corinthian, barrister, solicitor, counselor-at-law. I seek in this salubrious clime a haven from my wanderings. I seek lodgings at your hands."

When he finished, my mother looked at him for some time. In Calico, where people did their litigating with their fists or with an ax handle sometimes, lawyers were unknown. Elaine looked at him, too, and I remembered a doe I had startled in the hills one time when I was hunting with father.

"It's a lawyer you are, I gather," Mother said in a moment. "And you want a room."

"Precisely," said Mr. Dean with still another bow.

My mother regarded him again.

"Very well; I have a room if you wish to see it," she said. "It's small, though, and at the back."

"Lead on," Mr. Dean replied. "Let us see to the appointments of the suite."

Although that song about the first man up being the best man dressed is stretching the rope, a boardinghouse is still an interesting kind of place. While individuals like my father often had their little gopher pockets, Calico depended on the Copper Princess for its bread and butter, and the men who lodged with us were hunkies at the Princess. They were men with complicated names who dug and drilled all week, and then, on Saturday nights, engaged in terrible recreation in the honky-tonks. On these nights of payday revels they would drink, swear, prance, and fight. Often mother locked them out, and other times the marshal, Mr. Bolt, would lock them up. Sometimes it was necessary for Mr. Bolt to damage them, and there was none among them he hadn't beaten up at least once; he liked his authority understood. Other evenings they sat wearily on the gallery, each beside his cuspidor, where they could see the roasters fill the night with flame and hear the stamp mills pounding out the gold and silver and copper.

Besides the lodgers there were some who only boarded with us, men like Mr. Bolt, who came to take his supper at evening. My father used to say that we would all be better off, Elaine especially, if Mr. Bolt spent more of his time at the jail. It was a curious thing how other men became discouraged when Mr. Bolt came calling.

Now it might be thought a man like Mr. Dean would feel himself a stranger in such an atmosphere, but the odd thing of it was that he got on well with everyone—leastways for quite a while.

I expect this was because he had a way of making people laugh. On those evenings when the men were sitting by their cuspidors, he told them stories. Sometimes they were animal tales which had been written long ago by Mr. Aesop. They always laughed to hear about the fox and grapes, and the dog that dropped the meat on seeing his own reflection in the river. There were quite a few like that, and yet, when thought of later, some of them had parts that didn't seem so funny as they had at first.

Maybe it was just the way he told them that was funny, waving his arms about and making his hands go high and low. Once, when he was doing a part in an old-time play he called Hamlet, the men went black in the face with laughing.

Then there were the things he'd say. One time when Elaine went riding in a rig with Mr. Bolt, the horse was so slow in starting that Mr. Bolt was forced to smack it with a club. It was after they'd gone on that Mr. Dean remarked there would come a time when a rig would run without a horse. Another occasion, when they were speculating on the blind side of the moon, he said a man would one day go and look at it!

You can see how anyone who talked in that way would be appreciated in our boardinghouse. Some of the lodgers even bragged him up to those of other houses not so lucky as to have a Mr. Dean to entertain them. In a couple of weeks, when he began to play the Game with them, they came even to look upon him as a kind of regular.

As the test of skill, the Game was played to see which man could stream a cheekful of Old Puma Pelt the farthest into the yard, with the loser going down to the Apex for a bucket of beer. In a while he got so good at this that on occasion he bested even

Mr. Bolt, a master. The only time he wouldn't play was when Elaine was on the gallery. When that was understood by Mr. Bolt he made his greatest efforts in those moments.

But it wasn't all sitting on the gallery with Mr. Dean. In those early days when mandamuses and habeases were slow in coming, I sometimes tramped the countryside in his company; and there would often come a moment high on some hill when he would waft me off to other lands.

"Samuel, let us sail the ocean blue," he'd say. "What do you see below us there?"

"Grass," I said, for I did not see any ocean blue. "It looks white and shining in the sun."

"Aye, the burnished look; the glint the westering mariner sees upon the face of the sea."

I looked very hard but couldn't tell if he was right or not, until he launched a ship.

"Let us consider that we sail upon that vessel there," he said. "It is very small, a caravel, not like the ironclads we know today. And the men who sail with us are frightened, for they go upon an unknown water in whose deeps may lurk great serpents and which ends in a timeless void at the lip of the world."

I closed my eyes, and when I opened them again, it was as he said. The ship was frail and made of wood. The scuppers ran with smelly water, and little bugs crept out upon the planks. The eyes of the men showed white and wide, and they scratched themselves. It was strange how I could feel the pitching decks and hear the storm winds howling in the yards and the flapping of the sails when we lay panting in a calm. Sometimes the men bent over the rails in agony, other times they cursed the captain. But the captain simply stood above us, resolute and tall, and it was hard to tell if he, too, feared the serpents. Mr. Dean said the captain's name was Columbus.

Another time he pointed off at faraway mountains.

"How tall would you say they were?" he asked.

"Close to a mile, my father told me."

"Then, imagine them at twice that elevation. Nay, make it two and a half times, close to thrice."

I did, and they lifted until they filled the sky. The rocky flanks soared sheer beyond the timber line, the peaks remote and icy with eternal winter.

"Now, let us look for elephants," he said.

It took some doing to see elephants in Arizona, but when I
found them we weren't in Arizona any more. We'd gone to the
middle of Europe and were in the Alps. It was very cold, and the
wind shrieked through the mountain passes. In certain places there
were chasms, and when an elephant would slip and fall over, I'd
hear him trumpeting away on down to the bottom. The people,
dark and small, gathered up their cloaks for warmth. Some of
them wore leopard or lion skins, and their shields were made of
bullock hide and even the hide of crocodiles. A few of them
slipped over, too, with their burnooses streaming out behind.
They carried spears and swords, and at the head of them was
Hannibal.

Mr. Dean made other pictures, too. It sometimes seemed to
me as though he opened up great doors and windows, and when
looking through them I was near to thoughts and meanings which
would be too big to know once they were closed again.

They weren't all in distant places. Once I took him up a canyon
to an Indian ruin I knew about. There was nothing left but broken
pottery, some old metates, a few adobe walls now nearly melted
into the earth; but he was able to build these things into what they
were in the beginning. He put people in them, too; and for a
while I saw them work and play, heard shouts and laughter in that
place where there had been no sound for nearly a thousand years.

That was the time he found the pot. He pulled it out of one of
the walls, and though there wasn't much to it, he gave it to Elaine
when we returned that evening. He gave a little poem with it—
"Ode to a Grecian Urn," he called it. All the while he talked
Elaine held onto that dirty pot as if it was made of purest gold.
When he finished, none of the hunkies knew if they should laugh
or not. In some way it was different from other things he'd said.

Later, though, when Mr. Bolt was helping wipe the dishes with
Elaine and broke it on the floor, they did. It was always good for
a laugh when Mr. Bolt was being useful.

A peculiar time had its beginning with that pot. Take the conversations Mr. Bolt began to have with Mr. Dean.

"Mr. Dean," he said to him one evening on the gallery, "there's
things you don't seem to know about this country."

"How lamentably true that is," said Mr. Dean. "But then, are
we not all of us slaves to ignorance in some fashion? I can but
hope time brings familiarity."

"Calico ain't so big," said Mr. Bolt. "P'raps there ain't enough to it to make your stayin' on worth while."

"Oh, even the smallest of things have virtues and significance," said Mr. Dean.

Prying the nail of his thumb between his teeth, Mr. Bolt removed a shred of beef and flicked it over the railing.

"I been thinking, Mr. Dean," he said, "that a pettifogger's a surprising thing to find in Calico."

"The world is full of surprises, Mr. Bolt. They stand among the pleasures of life."

"That's as may be," said Mr. Bolt. "But it never seemed to me that Calico law was suitable for argufying."

"Mr. Bolt, I wonder if your thinking on that point is not disorganized?" said Mr. Dean. "I think it is clear the law in these United States is vested in the Constitution. Men have worn themselves down to an early grave through arguing about that document."

"Arguing the law in Calico has done the same for others, Mr. Dean," said Mr. Bolt.

That was the kind of talk Mr. Bolt began to make. On the face of it, it didn't look too much, and yet there was an undercurrent too; a kind of uncomfortable feeling. Whenever they talked that way, the men kept still by their cuspidors. Elaine would listen at the door, and even my mother, who never set foot on the gallery in the evening for fear they might be playing the Game, would bring her broom and sweep, no matter that I'd swept it all before.

Take the things my mother said to Mr. Dean one day when he came into the parlor to pay his weekly rent. After she'd put it in the book, she held him there for a moment of talk.

"Mr. Dean, as a man of culture, I expect you've seen far places in your travels."

"Indeed," said Mr. Dean, "I have been privileged to journey widely. It has been a passion with me."

"I wonder, Mr. Dean, if you've ever been to California? I've heard so many interesting things about it."

"No, unhappily not," said Mr. Dean. "I've never been into this western part of our country before."

My mother smoothed her dress across her knees. "I should think a man of your interests would never rest until he'd seen it all. How I'd love to stand on the shores of the Pacific Ocean."

I'd never heard her speak before of California, and yet she made it sound as if a visit there might be a prime wish with her.

"Oh, I daresay California is a splendid place," said Mr. Dean, "but I have come to the point of thinking that travel is a search for something, and I feel my own particular search has ended. I would be pleased to spend the rest of my life right here."

"Oh," my mother said. "Oh, dear!"

Even Elaine was acting differently. She gave up joking and talking with Mr. Dean. He was just as nice to her as ever, but she was stiff and pale, hardly speaking at all unless there was need. Once I asked her why she'd turned so rude, and she went to her room and cried an hour.

So maybe it was that pot that stood in back of it all. Maybe the pot was *chindi*, in the way that relics of the Old Ones are said to be among the Navahos. Maybe the pot was just a sign, the way an ore outcrop may show what lies below the surface. It was hard to put your finger on.

It took a burro to bring it into the open. It was one of those which Mr. Kee kept taking home with him. Mr. Kee was an old Chinaman who came each week to talk with Mr. Dean in what was called the Canton dialect. Mr. Kee knew only a little English because a mine cave-in had hurt his head and, until the coming of Mr. Dean in Calico, there'd been nobody he could talk to.

So on Sundays Mr. Kee would stand there pulling at his queue and smile as if a warm light lay all over him while they talked of nobody could say what. Sometimes it seemed that there were tears in the eyes of Mr. Kee, but Mr. Bolt said that could not be, since Celestials had no feelings.

Sometimes Mr. Kee came with a black burro, sometimes with a gray one, other times with something else. Mr. Kee's own burro hadn't come out of the cave-in, yet he seemed to think that he would find it if he only looked enough. These that he took home did not belong to him, but after he'd had them for awhile, he'd come to see that for himself and take them back to their rightful owners. Nobody ever cared about it. Calico was full of burros.

Mr. Kee had brought a reddish one this time, and Mr. Dean was showing his admiration in the Canton dialect when Mr. Bolt came up. At first he made as if to walk up on the gallery where the hunkies all sat blinking in the sunlight of the morning after, but a couple of yards beyond the burro he turned around and looked at it. He studied it for some moments, and the hunkies all edged forward in their chairs.

"Say," said Mr. Bolt, "I seen that jack on a rope somewhere. Where'd you get him, chink?"

Mr. Dean spoke to Mr. Kee; Mr. Kee pulled at his queue and spoke to Mr. Dean, and Mr. Dean then said, "It is a wanderer, Mr. Bolt. In his compassion, Mr. Kee has fed and watered it."

"Yair?" said Mr. Bolt He backed off a ways from the burro while he squinted at it. "That thing come from Sig Czerney's place; I'd know it anywhere."

Mr. Dean didn't speak to Mr. Kee; instead, he spoke to Mr. Bolt. "If it has, it shall return," he said. "Mr. Kee has always found their proper homes. Everybody knows that."

"Yair?" said Mr. Bolt. "All I know is that he's got an animal as don't belong to him. That chink's got a long record of stock theft in this town, and stock theft is a hanging crime."

It was strange to hear a burro elevated to the dignity of cows and horses, but nobody laughed. This began to look as if it might be going beyond the burro business now. In a way it seemed that Mr. Bolt was using the burro for something else. On the gallery men were leaving their chairs, coming down the steps as if they saw a treat in store. My mother and sister came to the door.

Mr. Dean considered Mr. Bolt a moment before he spoke to Mr. Kee. Then when Mr. Kee, looking unhappy and confused, had wrung his hands and nodded, Mr. Dean said to Mr. Bolt, "I have been retained as counsel. In order to charge a theft the plaintiff must identify the evidence."

"I one time mentioned there was things you didn't seem to know about in Calico, Mr. Dean. Stand aside."

Mr. Bolt began to walk toward Mr. Kee, but Mr. Dean did not stand aside.

"You'll not take him into custody without due process, Mr. Bolt. You cannot jail or hang a man on allegations."

"Get out of the way," said Mr. Bolt.

"Under constitutional guarantee, Mr. Kee enjoys a freedom from unreasonable search and seizure." Mr. Dean raised up his finger. "You'll not infringe upon his rights of person."

No one had ever talked that way to Mr. Bolt before. Mr. Dean had a marvelous way with words, but as this hardly seemed to be the right time for them, I felt uneasy. This was a good deal different from yarning on the gallery or walking about in the hills.

"I'm takin' him, Mr. Dean," said Bolt.

But Mr. Dean stood firm in front of Mr. Kee. Mr. Bolt came up, and when his arm came over his fist caught Mr. Dean beside the jaw. Mr. Dean sat down in the road. His mouth began to bleed. Mr, Kee jumped all around him in agony and the hunkies yelled and shouted.

On the gallery Elaine began to cry. My mother pushed her through the door, then she brought her broom to the road and began to hit out right and left. Never had she done a thing like that in another fight, but they paid her no attention.

"Stop them!" she kept shouting the whiles she swung the broom, but no one listened. They just shouldered her off her swats and swore. At last she cried, "Scum! Monsters!" and fumed back into the house.

By this time Mr. Dean was on his feet again. He held his arms before him and danced about in so elegant a manner that, for a moment, I forgot to be fearful for him. Mr. Bolt was fighting Calico style—arms low, face pushed ahead of him like a stump. It was the hunky style, but Mr. Dean's approach was new. The bunch of them laughed uproariously.

When Mr. Dean went down the third time he didn't get up so quickly. His nose was bleeding, he didn't dance around so much. Mr. Bolt had fists as large as melons. Whenever he caught Mr. Dean with one, Mr. Dean would sway as if a high wind was blowing. Except that he was tall and springy, Mr. Dean would long ago have been out. Mr. Bolt was widely known for his strength.

But Mr. Dean was wearing down. Each time he fell, he was slower rising. By now the whole of his face was bloody; he had given up his dancing but managed to stay in front of his client. If he had just stayed on the ground when he went down it would have ended. He seemed more intent on watching out for Mr. Kee than in watching out for himself.

That was when I remembered to be afraid for him. I knew certain things about him then that hadn't so clearly shown before. I was frightened for him, for Mr. Bolt was raging like a bull. As if one of the doors that Mr. Dean had shown me had swung open, I knew Mr. Dean would never quit. There was his high heart and his aspiration. Those had been fine words describing men of other times and places; but now I understood them to have expensive and dreadful meanings.

And I knew certain things about miners, too. I knew them to
be callous, hard men of fleshly appetites and lusts. They enjoyed
a fight above all things and could take a beating in stride. Mr. Bolt
had beaten all of them, and so they didn't mind that Mr. Dean
should be beaten, too.

When Mr. Dean went down again he stayed down; but it
didn't end with that. Mr. Bolt, now backing off a few yards,
made a run at him. But the badness in him threw him off stride,
so that the kick he aimed at Mr. Dean went wide, and the force
so made him slew around, he lost his balance and fell to the
ground beside him. When, with such strength as he had left,
Mr. Dean pi...ed down the legs of Mr. Bolt, Mr. Bolt went
for his gun.

It seemed to me that time stopped then, and there was in the
air a silence like none I'd ever heard. That gun kept coming up
and out, and all the while no one moved or spoke. Then I heard
a shout, and it was me. I started running—that, too, surprised
me. I don't guess I thought to be afraid of what might happen; I
was bent on stopping murder. Mr. Dean had been kind and good
to me. He had opened up new thoughts and places, and now they
would never be opened again.

So I ran toward Mr. Bolt, had almost reached his arm when
one of the hunkies caught me by the middle and swung me back.
At the same time, and with his other hand, he grabbed the barrel
of Mr. Bolt's revolver, wrenching it out of his grasp to fling it far
over the road. Then he bent to peer at Mr. Bolt.

"Nah, there, Mr. Bolt," he said, "you'll fight him fair. He's
shown his mettle, and the beating he's had at your hands has made
him one of ourselves. So we'll no more stand for his killing than
for that of another among us."

This was something strange to hear, and Mr. Bolt did not believe it until he'd pulled himself up and looked at each miner in
turn. Then he did believe it, and there came over his face a terrible
look. He stood for the whole of a minute while the knowledge of
danger grew in him, and then he whirled and went quickly down
the road. He didn't even stop for his gun.

Mr. Dean lay up in his room for seven days and, as Elaine was
doing for him every minute of it, dust balls floated around like
tumbleweeds, and everybody slept in rumpled sheets and blankets.

My mother set a penance on the miners, too. Every night that Mr. Dean was in bed she fed them cold potatoes. It made no difference how they pleaded; she held them to be full of beastly sin for being so slow in helping Mr. Dean, and all of the evenings of that week they sat glumly on the gallery with the cold potatoes inside them. Nobody played the Game. None of them went a-wallowing in the honky-tonks when Saturday came. Not till Mr. Dean was well enough to play the death of Romeo did any of them laugh again.

I guess I blubbered some when I was allowed to see him, and he said I was a foolish but gallant boy. That was when I told him of the doors and windows, and how I'd been scared I'd never get to see through them again.

"Ah, the doors," he said in a smile that looked all out of shape on his battered face. "You were able to see. And they made you want to know? They made you curious?"

"Oh, yes!"

"Ah, blessed curiosity. It is the mark of the educated man."

It was on the day that Mr. Dean got out of bed and came down that my father returned from the assessment work and the fishing that inevitably followed. He was not a bookish man, but he had gained a deal of learning and, as he looked suspiciously at Mr. Dean, I sensed an encounter of powerful minds.

"Mr. Dean," my father said, when he was told of all that had happened and had drawn conclusions from the way Elaine was taking care of the invalid, "I'm going to ask you one question."

As best he could with his injuries, Mr. Dean drew himself up and waited.

My father closed his eyes for a moment.

Then he said, "Given a sprightly day in May beside a tumbling mountain creek, what would the finding of a stone nymph suggest to you?"

Oh, it was a devilish question, and I feared again for Mr. Dean, but Mr. Dean was not afraid. For a moment, though, a vein stood out at his temple with the weight of his thinking.

"I would take the stone nymph," he began, "and I would put it on a small hook and cast it out."

"Ah," my father said, but then he sharpened again. "Downstream?"

"Nay," said Mr. Dean. "Up. Against the current and just below a rapids, where the trout feed best."

"Ah," my father said again, and this time he smiled benignly at Mr. Dean and at Elaine, too. "What a pleasure it will be to have a man of wisdom in this family."

Loren D. Estleman has won numerous awards (including three Spurs from the Western Writers of America) and high acclaim for his Western fiction. His most recent historical Western, Bloody Season *(1987), has been lauded as "hard bone and real blood, as real as the barrel on a Frontier model Colt pistol." The same can be said of his other novels, four of which—*The High Rocks *(1979),* Stamping Ground *(1980),* Murdock's Law *(1982), and* The Stranglers *(1984)—are narrated by United States deputy marshal, Page Murdock. "The Angel of Santa Sofia," to date Estleman's only Page Murdock short story, is cast in the same mold of hard, raw realism as Murdock's longer adventures.*

The Angel of Santa Sofia

★★★★★★★★★★★★★★★

Loren D. Estleman

THE Pinkerton was a lean kid with a rusty fringe along his upper lip and a passion for plaid vests and tequila taken without salt and buxom, dark-eyed *señoritas* twice his age. He was working on one at his table now who he claimed was involved with a case, but her bedroom eyes and the fierce glances the couple was drawing from a mustachioed Mexican at the bar said different. Well, he was old enough to take care of himself.

"I hate to keep interrupting," I told him patiently, "but I've come six hundred miles, and I'd sort of like to be reassured that it wasn't for nothing."

"Who'd you say you were again?" He sipped his tequila without taking his eyes from the handsome *mujer.*

I laid the badge, which I never wear, atop the warrant I'd been carrying since Montana. "Page Murdock, U.S. deputy marshal. Ten days ago you wired Judge Blackthorne in Helena that you had Dale Sykes under surveillance here in Santa Sofia. Where is he?"

"In a mission down by the river." He had scarcely glanced at either of the items. "You can't miss him. He fits the description on that dodger you had out on him."

Some persuasion seemed in order. I was muddy with dust and perspiration and exhausted from eighteen straight hours in the saddle, not counting the other one hundred and sixty I had spent there over the past ten days. I drew my English revolver from its holster and clanked it down in front of him. "Show me."

He gave the weapon rather more attention than he had my other credentials. Then he sighed, kissed his disappointed companion's hand, and snatched his plug hat from the table.

A short ride from town found us on a rise overlooking an adobe chapel awash in the old gold rays of the setting sun. The only things stirring in the yard were a tobacco-colored dog yawning and stretching from a day spent dozing in whatever shade was available and a couple of Yaqui Indians busy rehanging the building's arched oaken door. You could see the same thing in pueblos all over that part of Arizona. We had been watching for about ten minutes when a figure in a brown hooded robe came out past them carrying a bucket in the direction of the river. The Pinkerton, whose name was Walsh, pointed at him.

"You're joking," I said.

He shook his head. "He's Sykes, down to the stiff elbow and strawberry mark on his left cheek. Around here he's known as Brother Dale. The locals know who he is and what he's done and don't care."

"It's wonderful what a little money can do. The conductor he shot in that mail-train robbery two years ago is still chained to a bed. He'll be there the rest of his life."

"As I understand it," said Walsh, "there's no money involved. According to the townspeople I questioned, a local farmer found him lying beside the road a mile north of here about two weeks after the robbery. He had four bullets in him. There isn't a doctor for a hundred miles, so he was taken to the old padre. He was delirious by that time, and it wasn't long before everyone knew his life history. The padre calls his recovery a miracle. The Yaquis think tequila had more to do with it. At any rate, instead of heading down across the border as expected when he was strong enough, Sykes paid for his keep by doing odd jobs around the mission, fixing things up, things like that. Claimed he had seen the light. Last year he was at the river washing that brown robe the padre gave him when a little girl playing along the bank fell in. He jumped in and saved her from drowning. Since then he's been something of a folk hero hereabouts."

I squinted through the failing light at the man kneeling on the riverbank. His stiffened right elbow was made obvious by the way he manipulated the bucket while filling it. The bone had been shattered by a bullet during a shootout at a botched-up bank robbery five years before. "This is going to be easier than I thought," I said.

"That's what you think," snorted the Pinkerton. "As far as the people of Santa Sofia are concerned, he's an angel."

"Angels fall."

The sheriff, a dark, thickset Mexican who shooed his wife and daughters away from the dinner table while he spoke with us, had a habit of waving both arms over his head when agitated, which appeared to be his normal state. He became even more so when I requested his assistance in arresting Dale Sykes.

"Lo siento, señores!" he cried, narrowly missing the coal-oil lamp suspended from the ceiling with a flying right hand. "This is something I cannot do. The election, she is but *tres semanas*— three weeks—away. To help apprehend the most popular man since Miguel Hidalgo would be to commit what you *norteamericanos* would call political suicide. I will let you house him in my jail, as no peace officer can refuse another the use of his facilities, but I dare not go further."

I could have persuaded him to cooperate, but it was obvious that he would have been worse than no support at all. I did get him to lend me a pair of horses from the string of three he kept in a corral behind his home, left my own exhausted mount to the care of his son-in-law, and with Walsh riding beside me and the third horse in tow I returned to the mission.

No guards were posted out front, and the door was unlocked. Inside the chapel was a cavern saved from absolute blackness by a hundred tiny flames that danced wildly in the disturbed air. One of the flames at the far end was moving, propelled by the hands of an old man standing behind the altar, who was busy lighting candles with a long taper. He wore a robe like the one we had seen on Sykes with the hood thrown back to reveal a head of colorless hair curling over a black skullcap and a face like ancient oilcloth. Bright eyes observed our approach.

"I am Father Mendoza. May I help you?" As he spoke his

wasted features leapt into sudden prominence as if illumined by his holy spirit, but it was only the reflected glow of the flaming taper as he brought it to his lips. He blew it out.

I showed the badge. He nodded sadly.

"He told me you would come."

"God?" asked Walsh.

"Brother Dale. He said that someday men would come to take him back to atone for his sins."

"Where is he?" I demanded. Piety brings out my bad side.

"In the back. Firearms will not be necessary."

I ignored him, drawing my gun as I strode toward the arch dimly outlined in the back wall. A tremendous bulk blocked my path. I looked up into the stern features of one of the Yaquis I had seen at work in the yard earlier. "Call him off," I told Mendoza. "Before his blood defiles the sanctity of the church."

"For God's sake, Murdock!" breathed the Pinkerton.

"Let him pass, Diego," Mendoza said.

The Indian stepped aside with a grunt, and I pushed past, Walsh at my heels. We were in a dank corridor, heavy with mildew and lit only by a pale glow beyond a half-open door to the right. There were two others, both closed. I chose the open one.

Dale Sykes, looking much as he had in the old rotogravure Judge Blackthorne had distributed among the marshals only heavier and more sinister with the strawberry mark on his cheek an angry red blaze, was seated on the edge of a stone pallet strewn not too generously with straw, reading a worn Bible in the light of a candle guttering on a rickety table at his elbow. He, too, had peeled back his hood, exposing a skullcap and a wealth of ill-kept black hair. He looked up as we entered and made a move toward the book with his clumsy right arm.

"Stop!" My bellow rang off the walls of the cramped cell. "Get that Bible."

Walsh glanced at me strangely but stepped forward and wrenched the black-bound volume from Sykes's hand.

"I was only marking my place," said the man on the pallet.

I accepted the Bible and riffled through it while Walsh covered Sykes with a baby Remington he had taken from a special pocket beneath his left arm. The book had no hollow where a gun could be hidden. I tossed it onto the pallet. "Keep him covered while I search him," I told the Pinkerton.

There was nothing on him but a small belt purse containing a few coins. "Who shot you?" I asked him.

"My partners." His tone was low, apologetic. "We argued about how to divide the money from the mail-train job. I lost, and they left me for dead."

"The same way you left that conductor," I said.

"He didn't die? Each night I pray that he did not."

"I'm sure he prays every night that he did. Get going." I moved away from the door and waved him toward it with my gun.

The sheriff, who lived across the alley from the jail, muttered a string of gentle blasphemies in Spanish as he unlocked the door to the only cell. The key grated. Jails don't get a lot of use in border towns. When it was open I shoved the prisoner stumbling over the iron cot in the corner.

"There's no call to be so rough," the Pinkerton protested.

"We'll keep an eye on him tonight if it's all right with you," I told the sheriff. "If that son-in-law of yours is any good with horses we'll be able to pull out in the morning."

"What do you mean, 'we'?" Walsh's embryonic mustache bristled.

"The Great Northern Pacific has placed a thousand dollars on Sykes's head. I thought you might want to split it."

He made no reply.

We were interrupted only once during our vigil when someone rapped on the front door. I came up out of a sound sleep on the sheriff's cot, drawing my gun. Walsh, who was standing first watch, was at the door with his Remington in hand. "Who is it?"

There was a muffled response. The Pinkerton opened the door and stepped back, displaying the gun. A short Mexican with a drawn, tragic face, attired in the sandals and shapeless white cotton shirt and trousers that comprise the male uniform down there, moved inside timidly, sombrero clutched in both hands. Just before Walsh closed the door behind him I caught a glimpse of a crowd of men in similar costumes and drably clad women gathered in front of the building.

In a voice scarcely above a whisper, our visitor said, "I have come, good *señores*, to petition for Brother Dale's release."

Walsh snorted. I said, "Who are you?"

"Francisco Vargas, *Señor* Marshal. I am the man whose little daughter Brother Dale rescued from the river last year. Because of this it was decided that I speak for the citizens of Santa Sofia."

"The whole town's with you on this?" I was standing over him now. He was trembling. He was old enough to remember Maximilian and the days when all authority was considered evil.

"Go home, Francisco." Sykes had both hands on the bars of his cell. "I have sinned and must accept my punishment. Go home, and tell everyone else to do the same."

"*Hermano* Dale!" Vargas stepped toward the prisoner. Their hands were almost touching, when I lunged and sent the Mexican reeling with a backhand slash across his face.

"Murdock!" cried Walsh, outraged. He thrust his revolver at me. I leveled mine. He stopped.

"Search him!" I snapped, indicating the Mexican cowering across the room. "That sombrero alone could hide an arsenal."

Somewhat subdued, the Pinkerton put away his gun and turned to the task. When he was finished he fixed me with an accusing glare. "He's not carrying so much as a nail file."

A stone crashed through the barred window in the door. Angry shouts drifted in through the jagged aperture.

"Now you've done it!" Walsh barked.

I flung an arm around Vargas's neck and dragged him into the center of the room. "Tell them if they aren't gone in five minutes, I'll scatter your brains!" I placed the muzzle of my revolver against his right temple.

He did as directed. I remembered enough Spanish from my cowpunching days to know that nothing slipped past me. Walsh, watching at the window, told me when the last of the spectators had left. I let the Mexican go with the assurance that further incidents would mean Sykes's life and took the next watch without comment. That seemed to suit the Pinkerton.

Dawn found the sheriff conspicuously absent, which was more than I could say for the rest of the town. It was out in force as we marched our prisoner out to where the son-in-law waited with our horses and the one I had bought from the sheriff the night before. I tossed the young man a five-dollar gold piece for their care and was ordering Sykes to mount up when a Mexican girl of about ten stepped out of the crowd bearing flowers "*por el Hermano Dale.*" I saw Francisco Vargas standing nearby and knew who she was.

"No gifts," I said, stepping between her and Sykes.

An angry murmuring arose from the crowd.

"Please," said Sykes, "may I speak to her?"

"Don't you have a heart?" Walsh demanded. "Let him."

I looked the girl over. "Just a second," I said, and tore the flowers from her grasp. I pulled apart the paper wrapping. Flowers fluttered to the ground, nothing more. The crowd laughed nastily. "Make it quick," I snapped.

The girl was crying. Bending over her, Sykes said a few soothing words in Spanish and raised a hand to tuck a stray tendril of hair inside her scarf. He fanned his fingers, made a fist beside her ear, and asked her to hold out her hand. When she did so, four coins dropped into it from his fist. She laughed delightedly. He kissed her and turned toward his horse.

"Where'd you pick that up?" I demanded.

"My father taught it to me. The children love it."

We left Santa Sofia at a trot, Sykes in the middle. Walsh reined in after half a mile.

"What's the matter?" I drew rein. "Are we being followed?"

"No, and we're not likely to be. I'm going back."

"Meaning?"

"Meaning I don't like your kind of law, Murdock." His face was flushed. "This isn't the same man who robbed that mail train two years ago. His name may be Sykes, and it may have been his finger that pulled the trigger on that conductor, but he isn't the same. But that doesn't make any difference to you, does it?"

"Is it supposed to?"

He looked at me sadly. "If you don't know the answer to that, you're beyond help."

"Suit yourself. Casa Grande is full of good men with guns who'll be willing to help collect that reward."

He wheeled and cantered off without another word.

A handful of lights were still burning in Santa Sofia as I rode ploddingly down its only street, leading the second horse with its burden slung across the saddle. As I neared the sheriff's home, a fresh yellow glow spread from one of the windows. The lawman emerged carrying a shotgun and struggling to tug his suspenders up over his red-flanneled shoulders. "*Señor* Deputy!" he called. I kept going.

Another figure came trotting out the door of the cantina. This proved to be Walsh. "Murdock, what is it?" He took hold of my bridle. "What are you doing back? You just left this morning."

A crowd was gathering. A lantern was produced, and the dead

man on the other horse was examined. "It is Brother Dale!" someone exclaimed. There was an ominous rumbling.

"You killed him!" Walsh looked horrified.

"He pulled a gun," I said. "Ten miles north of here. He got off a shot. So did I. I didn't miss."

"He has been shot in the back!" said the sheriff.

"His horse panicked. He was turning to rein it back around when I plugged him." I had to shout to be heard above the furious babble of voices.

The Pinkerton was livid. "You're not only a murderer, but a liar as well! Where would he get a gun?"

"I wondered about that, too. I think Vargas passed it to him last night just before I jumped him. You saw Sykes's sleight-of-hand trick with the coins. He could have plucked it out of the sombrero just as easily without us seeing him and hidden it out until it would do him the most good."

"Hogwash! You hated him and took advantage of the first opportunity to kill him. You'll hang for this, Murdock, badge or no badge!"

"Then why did I come back?" While he was puzzling that one out I drew my revolver. "Let go of that bridle."

He obeyed. "Where are you going?"

"To the mission."

The whole town had turned out by the time I reached the chapel, shouting *"Asesino!"* and brandishing machetes and pitchforks. The padre and the two Yaquis were standing in front. I had to back inside, rotating the gun right and left. I don't remember if I had cleared the threshold before I collapsed.

Later Father Mendoza told me he'd taken twenty-seven stitches in the gash Brother Dale's bullet had carved along the right side of my rib cage.

Best known as today's premier writer of detective short stories, Edward D. Hoch occasionally turns his talents to the frontier yarn. He is especially good at melding the two genres in his series about drifter Ben Snow, who may or may not be Billy the Kid. "The Tombstone Hearse," set in Tombstone in 1890 and concerning, among other things, the fanciest hearse in the West, is Hoch and Ben Snow at their most entertaining.

The Tombstone Hearse

★★★★★★★★★★★★★★★

Edward D. Hoch

THE town of Tombstone, Arizona Territory, had been a thriving center for the mining of gold and silver during the 1880s, boasting a population of 10,000 at one point. All that was before the flooding of the mines in 1890 by various underground tributaries of the San Pedro River. By the time Ben Snow visited Tombstone a few years later, the inevitable decline had already set in. The courthouse, the O.K. Corral, and even Boot Hill Cemetery had begun to take on a look of benign neglect.

When Ben Snow paused on his horse Oats to study the town from the top of a sandy rise, he saw that a funeral was in progress. A pair of coal-black horses with black plumes on their heads were pulling a fancy, glass-sided hearse up the road to the cemetery on Boot Hill. A handful of mourners followed behind in carriages and on horseback, winding around a cluster of waxy white yucca plants.

Ben rode down to join them, keeping toward the rear, where a middle-aged cowhand with a weathered face sat astride his chestnut horse smoking a thin Mexican cigar. The cigar suggested to Ben that the man was merely a disinterested observer like himself. "Who died?" he asked.

"Fella named Deng Ping, a Chinaman."

"Not many of those around here," Ben commented.

144

"More than you'd think. They come over to work on the railroad up north. He was the only one in Tombstone, though."

Ben became aware of a sobbing woman dressed in black who might have been Oriental. "That the widow?"

"Yeah." The man took a drag on the cigar. "She's pretty broken up about it. She's part Chinese, too, I guess, but American."

"How'd he die?" Ben asked, watching the undertaker and the pallbearers as they slid the coffin from the hearse.

"Shot dead durin' a robbery. Can't trust these Chinamen, you know."

Ben grunted and rode closer for a better look. He was more interested in the fancy hearse than in the funeral itself, and he dismounted to walk nearer to it. The lettering on the side read *Watt & Tarbell Undertaking Parlor, Tombstone*, and as he ran a hand over the sterling-silver trim with its gold decorations a voice behind him asked, "Admiring our hearse, stranger?"

Ben turned to confront a man in a black suit with a bushy brown moustache. "It's a nice one, all right. You Mr. Watt or Mr. Tarbell?"

"Neither one. I just work for them. Name's Gus Blaine."

"This real gold trim on the hearse?"

Blaine glanced over to where the minister was saying a few words at graveside. "Twenty-four karat gold leaf. And the rest of the trim is sterling silver. Hearse was made for us by the Cunningham Brothers back east in Rochester, New York. They only made eight like it and sold them for eight thousand dollars each back in 1881. See this curved glass on the sides? It's the first ever manufactured for a vehicle."

"It must be almost a pleasure getting your last ride in one of these. Too bad Mr. Ping couldn't appreciate it."

The undertakers' assistant frowned. "Did you know him?"

"No. I was just passing through when your hearse caught my eye."

"I seen you talkin' with Harv Maxwell up on the hill over there."

"Anything wrong with that?"

"No, except that he's the one who shot the Chinaman."

"He didn't tell me that." Ben glanced up in the direction from which he'd come, but Maxwell and his horse had gone. "He said Ping was shot during a robbery."

Gus Blaine smoothed down his mustache. The brief funeral

service had ended, and a pair of gravediggers were starting to shovel dirt onto the coffin. Deng Ping's widow began to sob and cry out. "Well, I suppose that's true enough," Blaine said. "Maxwell was trying to rob his laundry. Deng Ping tried to stop him and got killed."

"Isn't there any law in Tombstone?"

"Oh, sure. The sheriff'll get around to arrestin' Harv one of these times, I suppose. But he always claims his shootings are self-defense, and no one's ever argued with him."

When the funeral procession headed back down Boot Hill, Ben rode on ahead. It wasn't the killing of Deng Ping that had brought him to Tombstone.

"Did you see the hearse?" the old man asked Ben as he finished pouring two cups of tea. They were in a little adobe house at the edge of a nearby reservation.

"I saw it. There was a funeral on Boot Hill this morning."

The old man's name was Joseph Running Bear. His father had been a Sioux warrior up in the Dakotas, but that was a long time ago. Joseph Running Bear had fought with the Union forces during the Civil War and settled into a peaceful existence since then. Ben had met him once on a Texas trail, around 1880, and now the old Indian had managed to contact him, quite by chance, since Ben had never been one to leave a forwarding address.

"You told me once that you owed me a favor, Ben Snow," the Indian said, taking a sip of his tea. "Did you mean it?"

"I meant it. You saved my life back in Texas."

Joseph Running Bear said, "You would have gone on living without me. But I need your help now."

"The hearse?"

"Exactly."

"You want me to steal it?"

"I want what's inside. A man who worked with Gus Blaine at the funeral home was named Simon Glohart. Either he or an accomplice stole fifty gold bars, worth a thousand dollars each, from the Chiricahua Apaches on the reservation here. The gold is hidden in the hearse."

"How do you know that?"

"A man named Maxwell tipped off the Apaches that Glohart had the gold and was fleeing south. Three renegade bucks escaped from the reservation and caught Glohart near the Mexican border. Before he died, he told them the gold was in the hearse.''

"Maxwell," Ben murmured. "Why don't the Apaches go after the hearse themselves?"

"They would if they still had Cochise to lead them. But they are only reservation Indians now. Even those who fought with Geronimo have been transported to confinement in Florida. The three who hunted down Glohart and forced him to talk are now in prison, awaiting sentencing for murder.''

"And you know their secret."

"I visited them in prison, and one of them told me. I am too old and too slow to go after the gold myself."

"What will you do if I get it back for you?"

"Return it to the tribe. They came by it honestly."

Ben finished his tea. "I'll see what I can do for you."

Ben spent the rest of the afternoon roaming the town, stopping at the O.K. Corral to see the spot where the Earp brothers shot it out with the Clanton gang back in '81. It was near the courthouse that he was approached by a slim blond woman in her early twenties dressed in a fashionably long skirt and carrying a parasol to shield her face from the hot afternoon sun. Ben had seen young women wearing such costumes in San Francisco and New Orleans, but never in a frontier town like Tombstone.

"Pardon me," she said in a voice that carried a hint of a British accent. "Would you be Mr. Ben Snow?"

"That's me," he admitted, tipping his hat to her.

"My name is Victoria Miller. I saw you at the cemetery this morning. You were speaking to the funeral director, Mr.—"

"Blaine. Gus Blaine. Apparently he manages the place for the owners."

"I know. It was a position my uncle held before his untimely death."

"Your uncle?"

"Simon Glohart. He was tortured to death by your Red Indian savages."

"Maybe we should go somewhere and talk," Ben suggested. "How about the Tombstone Cafe?" It was right across the street from the courthouse and seemed a likely suggestion.

"I don't often drink hard liquor."

"I'm sure they'll have something else for you, ma'am. Let's go see."

When they had settled down at a wobbly wooden table near the door, Ben ordered a glass of tonic water for her and a straight whiskey for himself. "Thank you," she said, standing her folded parasol against the wall. "It feels good to be out of the sun. How do people live here the year round?"

"They seem to manage."

"You're a cowboy, aren't you? A gunfighter."

"I carry a gun. You can see that."

"Some say you might be a U.S. marshal, sent to Tombstone under cover to arrest Harvey Maxwell."

"I heard that he shot the man who was buried today."

"That is the least of it, Mr. Snow. I believe Maxwell was also responsible for the death of my uncle and another man named Jud Firness."

"You'd better explain that."

"Jud Firness was working at the funeral parlor with my uncle. He drove the hearse and sometimes acted as a pallbearer when they needed one. He was a close friend of my uncle, and the two of them did some drinking together. Uncle Simon often mentioned him in his letters."

"He wrote you often?"

"Every few months. Recently he began hinting that he and Firness had stumbled onto a great deal of money. He said something about gold."

"From the mines?"

"I don't think so. The mines were flooded and closed by that time."

"What were his relations with the Indians around here?"

"All right, as far as I know. Personally I haven't noticed many Indians in Tombstone. They all live on reservations, don't they? They're certainly buried there, because Uncle Simon's funeral home never handled them. That's why it was such a shock to me when they killed him."

"You said he was tortured."

"With flaming embers. When the cavalry patrol found his body near the Mexican border, it was badly burned. They tracked down the killers quickly enough—three Apaches who'd escaped from the reservation. They're in prison now, awaiting sentencing for their crime. It's expected they'll be hanged."

"Did they say why they killed your uncle?"

"No, but they must have forced some information from him before he died."

"What about this friend you mentioned, Jud Firness?"

"Jud was stabbed to death at the funeral home just a day or two before my uncle's death. The sheriff thinks it was an attempted robbery, though nothing was stolen."

"The letters you mentioned—do you have them with you or are they back in England?"

She smiled sweetly. "I haven't lived in England for over ten years, Mr. Snow. My home is in Chicago now. I'm a hostess at a popular restaurant there. I came to Tombstone because Uncle Simon had no one else to care about him once he was dead."

"Life can be cheap on the frontier," Ben admitted.

"I do have the letters in my hotel room, if you wish to see them."

"I do. You said Maxwell might be responsible for both deaths. What did you mean?"

"Gus Blaine told me Maxwell set the Apaches on Uncle Simon's trail. I hope you've come here to arrest him, Mr. Snow. I'll give you all the help I can."

"I'm not what you think I am, Miss Miller—"

"You may call me Victoria."

"I'm Ben."

"Ben."

"Will you be at the hotel this evening?"

"I'll be in my room after dinner."

"I may come calling to see those letters."

Darkness came suddenly in desert regions, without the lingering twilight Ben knew from farther east. There were oil lamps burning on the second floor of the funeral home, indicating that Gus Blaine or someone else must live there. But the shed that held the hearse was separated from the main house by a hundred feet, and Ben could be pretty certain no one would hear him prowling about. He entered through a rear window that yielded to a sharp tap from his pistol butt on the frame.

Though the hearse was kept here, the horses were boarded at a stable down the road, and there was nothing to disturb Ben as he went about the task of searching the vehicle, inside and out, for the Indian gold. It became clear almost at once that there was no possible hiding place for fifty bars of gold, even if they were fairly small. Ben had assumed they'd be in the wooden floor of the vehicle, the platform upon which the coffin rested for its journey to Boot Hill, but the wood was solid and the space between it and the metal frame of the hearse was barely thick enough for a sheet of paper. The metal roof was thin and solid, the four corner posts supporting it were equally solid, and the sides were of the curved glass that so impressed Gus Blaine. There was no hiding place for gold in any of it.

Ben turned his attention to the hearse's undercarriage and wheels, but the results were the same. He had only the moonlight coming through the shed's windows for illumination, but it was enough to convince him that nothing was hidden on the underside of the vehicle. Even the tongue where the horses were attached yielded nothing. Simon Glohart had kept his secret to the end, even under torture, and Joseph Running Bear was going to be disappointed.

He left the shed the way he had come and hurried across the barren earth to the dirt street that led back to the center of town. Heading for the hotel where Victoria Miller was staying, his attention was attracted to a nearby laundry shop where lamplight revealed unusual evening activity. As he drew nearer, he realized it was the shop of Deng Ping, and friends were paying their respects to his widow.

Ben entered the laundry and waited unobtrusively until the woman in black was alone. Then he introduced himself, and said "I'm sorry about your husband. I was at the burial this morning."

The woman's vaguely Oriental features dissolved as she managed a slight smile. "I am Lotus, wife of Deng Ping. Thank you for coming."

"I never knew your husband, but I was shocked by the story of his death. Had he been long in Tombstone?"

"Too long by a day, for him. He came from China last year. We met in San Francisco and were married. I am only half Chinese." Her voice was pleasant even in grief, with an unusual, lilting quality. "I had some money, and we came here to open the laundry. He worked hard at it, even driving his wagon out to the reservations once a week, but it was a bad life. Deng Ping was the only Oriental here besides myself, and he was not suited to frontier life. Men like Maxwell were constantly bullying him. He could not yet read English, and though I helped him with the record-keeping as much as I could, it was a source of torment for him." She placed a delicate hand on her waist. "We have a child on the way, and he wanted the best for it. Sometimes he talked of returning to China, but I told him America is my home."

"How did Maxwell happen to shoot him?"

"No one saw it, but I think he was trying to rob us. Everyone thinks so. My husband would not have stood for that. He kept a six-shooter behind the counter there. Maxwell claims he fired in self-defense, and the sheriff believes him. No one else does."

"Will you remain in Tombstone?"

"There is nothing to keep me here, and I cannot run the business alone. I will return to San Francisco as soon as I can."

"I wish you luck," Ben told her.

He left as some others entered the shop and continued down the street to the Yucca Flats Hotel. It was only three stories high, with no more than twenty rooms, but it served the needs of a town that had fewer visitors with each passing year. The desk clerk said Miss Miller was in and directed him to Room 14.

It was obvious she'd been expecting him. She had a small flask of whiskey and two glasses on a bedside table, and she poured him a drink at once. "I don't know what this will do for my reputation, entertaining a man in my room."

"In Tombstone it'll only make you popular. You'll probably have a line of men outside by tomorrow."

"That's what I mean." She went over to her suitcase and removed a packet of letters. "Here's the correspondence from Uncle Simon. You may read through it if you wish."

Ben skimmed quickly, finding nothing of real interest until he reached the final letter Victoria had received. It was dated nearly two months earlier. "This would have been shortly before he left Tombstone pursued by the renegade Apaches," he said.

"That's right. In fact, the news of his death reached me in Chicago one day before the letter itself arrived."

Ben reread one passage. "My dear little niece, I should tell you that I have recently come into a great deal of money, which is here at the funeral home with me. Some of it may be yours one day. Since I don't consider it a crime to steal from a sneaking yellow thief, I feel I have all rights to this gold myself. My friend Firness has been giving me some trouble, though, and I may take my treasure to the bank in Bisbee." The letter went on briefly to other matters and then ended with a promise to write again soon.

Victoria Miller took a sip of whiskey. "I suppose now you think it was the mention of gold that brought me out here."

"It's no business of mine what brought you, but I'm certainly glad you came, Tell me one thing—could your uncle have stabbed Jud Firness before he fled south?"

"Uncle Simon wasn't above a shady deal once in a while, but he wouldn't harm a fly. That's why what happened to him is so shocking."

"What about the Indians? Could they have killed Firness?"

"The sheriff says they deny it. They admitted killing Simon, but that was all."

Ben poured himself a little more whiskey. The night was still young, and he wasn't the least bit sleepy.

In the morning Ben stopped by the funeral parlor after breakfast and sought out Gus Blaine. He found the man back in the shed, polishing the silver and gold trim on the hearse, and was pleased that there seemed to be no sign of his entry the night before. "Can I speak with you a moment?" he asked.

"What?" Gus Blaine looked up from his labors. "Oh, you're the fella from Boot Hill yesterday."

"Ben Snow's my name. I guess we weren't properly introduced."

"What can I do for you, Snow?"

"I wanted to ask about two of your employees who got themselves killed—Jud Firness and Simon Glohart."

"Simon was killed by Apaches. Don't know much about that. Jud was stabbed to death right here in this shed."

"Here? I thought he was killed in the house."

"No, it was here. Funny thing, it was the next morning that Simon took off, heading for the border. Some folks thought he must have killed Jud, but anyone who really knew him could tell you Simon wouldn't hurt a fly."

"So I've heard."

"What are you so interested for?"

"I'm a friend of his niece."

"Sure—I should have figured that. A looker like her wouldn't be traveling alone. She was in to see me, too. Asked about her uncle. I told her the same thing—he talked rough at times, called Indians a bunch of red savages, but he didn't mean anything by it."

"Might he have stolen from them?"

"Don't know about that. I never knew him to take what wasn't his."

"Did Simon ride down to Bisbee very often?"

"Not that I know— Wait a minute, I think he did go down there one day a week or two before he left town for good. Said he had some business, and he was quite pleased when he got back."

"You must be short-handed here, losing two men at almost the same time."

"We were for a while. Mr. Tarbell, one of the owners, had to ride over from Tucson to help out. Now I got a couple of young fellas helpin' me. I still do all the work on the bodies, though, and drive the hearse and hire the pallbearers."

"Did you have to hire some yesterday for Mr. Ping?"

"Sure did. It ran up the bill. Don't know how the widow will pay it."

"Maybe Harv Maxwell should give her the money."

"I didn't suggest that," Blaine answered nervously. "I feel like livin' a while longer."

It was less than twenty-five miles into Bisbee, and Ben and Oats made the journey in an hour and a half. There was only one bank in the town, a mining community that seemed to be faring better than Tombstone. The vice-president was friendly and accepted Ben's story about seeking his lost uncle, but he insisted there were no accounts under the name of Simon Glohart.

Ben had another idea. "How about Victoria Miller?"

"No, sorry."

"Do you rent safe-deposit boxes?"

The banker shook his head. "You'd have to go into Tucson for that. We don't have a big enough vault."

"Thanks for your help," Ben told him. He ate a light lunch at the local bar and then headed back north, detouring to stop at the house on the edge of the reservation where Joseph Running Bear lived, trapped between the worlds of the red man and the white.

"Have you brought me good news?" he asked from the porch as Ben rode up.

"I'm afraid not." Ben dismounted and looped Oats's reins around the hitching post. "Despite what Glohart told his killers before he died, the gold isn't hidden in that hearse."

Joseph frowned slightly. "The man who told me certainly believed it to be true."

"Why? Because he tortured the information out of Glohart before killing him?"

The old Indian raised his head. "I do not condone such methods any more than I condone such theft."

"All right," Ben said, settling his anger. The man was a friend and had taken no part in Glohart's killing. "Still, there's no gold in the hearse. I thought I'd traced it to a bank in Bisbee but that turned out to be a dry well. The gold is simply gone, I don't know where."

"Is it possible the man lied with his dying words?"

"Maybe your blood brother in prison is the liar. Maybe he hopes to escape and claim the gold for himself."

"No, my information was accurate."

"I don't think Glohart stole the gold in the first place. I think someone else took it." Ben told Joseph about Glohart's letter to his niece.

"Who could he mean?"

"Almost anyone. Maybe he was pointing the finger at Harv Maxwell. Do you know him?"

"I know him," Joseph replies through tight lips. "He is an enemy of the red man."

"An enemy of all men, from what I've heard. Could he have stolen the gold?"

"It was taken from a house on the Apache reservation. A man like Maxwell would never be allowed onto the land. It is still patrolled by the cavalry, you know."

"If Glohart stole the gold, he has been punished for it. What more do you want, Joseph?"

"The gold must be restored to its rightful owners."

"You're a hard old man."

Joseph Running Bear smiled slightly. "But then you already knew that."

Ben had only one place left to look, and the fact that he'd looked there before didn't deter him. The hearse was the key to it. Simon Glohart had died saying so, and Ben finally believed his words. He rode back into Tombstone and headed for the funeral parlor.

By daylight the shed at the back stood open, and Ben walked casually inside. There was no sign of Gus Blaine. Ben set about examining the wooden floor of the vehicle, where in the darkness he'd noticed a space barely deep enough for a sheet of paper. He took a hunting knife from his saddlebag and slipped it between the wood and the metal bottom of the hearse. Something was there, all right.

Not gold, but, in very fact, paper.

With some difficulty he extracted two engraved certificates. They were negotiable government bonds, issued by the Arizona Territorial Bank at Bisbee. Each was in a denomination of twenty-five thousand dollars. "I'll be damned," Ben said almost to himself. "He traded the gold in for government bonds."

And there was something else visible along the right edge of the engraved certificates—dark-reddish stains that could only have been blood. The bonds had been examined by someone with a blood-stained right hand.

"I'll take those, cowboy."

The voice cut through the quiet of the shed, and Ben turned to stare into the barrel of a pistol. Harv Maxwell stood in the doorway of the shed, blotting out the sun with his broad body.

"I don't believe they belong to you."

Maxwell smiled and cocked the hammer of his six-gun. Deftly Ben rolled sideways under the hearse as the first shot hit the ground where he'd been. He had his own gun out now, but Maxwell had retreated around the corner of the doorway, and there was no opportunity to return the fire.

Then Ben saw something he hadn't noticed before. There were wooden wedges beneath the front wheels of the hearse. That might mean the ground sloped slightly here. He kicked one wedge away and then the other, diving back quickly as Maxwell fired a second shot. "Is this another case of self-defense?" he yelled out to the gunman.

The hearse began to roll ever so slightly, then gradually gained momentum. Maxwell fired again, his bullet smashing one of the glass sides as he spotted Ben running out behind the vehicle. Then Ben stopped running, and as the hearse rolled clear he fired two quick shots. Maxwell spun around and toppled to the ground.

The shooting had attracted Gus Blaine's attention, and he came running from the funeral parlor carrying a shotgun. "What's happening here?" he demanded, watching while his hearse curved slightly and rolled gently into an eight-foot-tall yucca plant.

"Just a little shooting," Ben told him. "You'd better go get the sheriff."

Harv Maxwell died of his wounds before the sheriff could question him, but listening to Ben's account of the shooting, Gus Blaine and Victoria Miller were both convinced the mystery was solved. "Maxwell stole the gold from the Apaches," she reasoned, "and then my uncle took it from him. When he became worried about hiding it, he took it to the territorial bank and had it changed into negotiable bonds. He hid them in the hearse, and Maxwell killed Jud Firness trying to find them. That's when my uncle decided to flee to Mexico and those Apaches caught him. Maxwell followed you here today and saw you discover the hiding place of the bonds."

It was a simple explanation, and with Maxwell dead no one cared about questioning it. Maxwell had killed Deng Ping, if no one else, and even the sheriff wasn't anxious to defend him. He patted Ben on the shoulder and pronounced it self-defense. "You really did the town a favor. There's no room for people like Maxwell in Tombstone anymore." He only paused a moment before he added, "I expect you'll be leavin' town right quick yourself, Mr. Snow."

"Tomorrow," Ben confirmed.

Later Victoria walked back to her hotel with him. "I suppose the money will have to go back to the Apaches now. It never really belonged to Uncle Simon."

"No, it didn't. You told me he wouldn't hurt a fly, and maybe that's true, but in some ways he was a bad man."

She looked up sharply. "You don't think he killed Jud Firness?"

"No, but then neither did Maxwell."

"What are you saying? I thought you agreed with what I told the sheriff back there!"

"It's a good enough explanation for the record, but the Indians tell me Harv Maxwell would never have been allowed on the reservation—he couldn't have stolen the gold. Also, there were bloody fingermarks along the edges of those bonds. Firness died instantly, so he didn't handle them after he was stabbed. Unless there was another bloody event in that shed, the fingermarks must have been made by Firness's killer, whose right hand would have been bloodied when he repeatedly stabbed him."

"It still could have been Maxwell."

"No, because he would have taken the bonds when he saw them—he wouldn't have come back to the shed weeks later and tried to steal them from me."

"It doesn't make sense. If Jud Firness was killed for the money, why didn't the murderer take it when the bonds were in his hands?"

"There can be only one explanation. He didn't know what he had. He was looking for gold and those pieces of paper meant nothing to him—because he couldn't read them."

"What?"

"I think the killer of Jud Firness, and the original gold thief, was illiterate in the English language. I think he was a man I never met, a man beyond the reach of the law for all time. It was the man they buried on Boot Hill yesterday, Deng Ping."

At first she would have none of it. "Even if I accept the fact of the killer being unable to read English, there are probably hundreds of people in Tombstone who qualify. Why does it have to be Deng Ping?"

"Because Maxwell told me he was the only Chinese, and his wife confirmed there were no other Orientals. When your uncle said in his letter he'd stolen the gold from a sneaking yellow thief, he was referring to the color of the man's skin, not his cowardice. A man who'd steal gold from the Apaches might be called a fool, but never a coward. And I know your uncle referred to Indians as red savages. Deng Ping's wife Lotus told me he couldn't read English, and she also told me he needed money because she was expecting a child."

"She might have done it. She's part Chinese."

Ben shook his head. "She was born and raised in San Francisco, and she did the record-keeping. Obviously she can read English. But there's more. Who could have gotten onto the reservation, past the cavalry guards, to steal the gold? Not Maxwell—they wouldn't have let him past the gates. Not your uncle, nor Firness, nor Gus Blaine, because we know the Indians bury their own and never used the services of the funeral parlor. But Lotus told me her husband took his laundry wagon to the reservations once a week, giving him a perfect opportunity to steal the gold and transport it past the soldiers."

"I still can't believe it, and yet I know it must be true."

"Deng Ping heard of the hoard of gold and stole it on one of his regular trips to the reservation. But he needed money for his wife and the baby, so I think he must have asked your uncle about disposing of the gold. Simon simply stole it from him, as he wrote you. Then the trouble really began. Deng Ping wanted the gold back, Maxwell was nosing around, and, judging by his letter to you, Jud Firness was suspicious, too. Plus the Apaches themselves, of course. Simon converted the gold to bonds and hid them in the hearse. Firness must have seen him do it and found them later—only Deng Ping came into the shed then and stabbed him. Simon panicked and headed south, where the Apaches caught up with him."

"Why did Maxwell shoot Deng Ping in his laundry?"

"To make it look like a robbery. In a way Maxwell was telling the truth when he said the Chinaman was shot during a robbery. He was speaking of the gold robbery, of course, and he killed Deng Ping to clear the way to the gold. He'd set the Apaches after Simon, and now he shot Deng Ping. All he had to do was find the gold for himself—and he almost did, by following me to the shed."

"Is the killing over at last?"

They'd reached Victoria's hotel, but when he turned to stare down the street Ben could still see the road to Boot Hill. "I don't think it'll ever be over in Tombstone," he said.

Born and raised in Arizona, Brian Garfield has written often and impressively about his native state, both in the Western and suspense genres. His first Western novel, Range Justice, *was published in 1960 when he was just twenty-one years old; exceptional among those that have followed are the historicals* The Lawbringers *(1962),* Sliphammer *(1970),* Tripwire *(1973), and* Wild Times *(1978); and the Western-flavor suspense novels set in modern Arizona,* Relentless *(1972) and* The Threepersons Hunt *(1974). Although numbering only a few, Garfield's frontier short stories have the same authentic ring as his novels; witness the following tense account of one of the more eventful crossings at Yaeger's Ferry on the lower Colorado River.*

The Toll at Yaeger's Ferry

★★★★★★★★★★★★★★

Brian Garfield

HEAT glittered on the muddy flow of the river. Yaeger came tramping along in his heavy knee boots and gave Lupe the brisk nod he reserved for his employees. "Woolgathering, Lupe?"

"Breathing," she answered. "It is hot, *Señor* Patron."

"Aye," said Yaeger judiciously. "But I never knew you to mind the heat." The skin of the girl's pretty eyes was creased; she squinted across the wide, flat river. Out there Bill Calhoun was poling the empty ferry half against the current; his arms made hard ripples. Yaeger said, "Calhoun, there—you think he'll work out, Lupe?"

"Yes."

"My feeling," said Yaeger. "I was half a mind not to hire him, but he's got a good pair of arms, and he don't slack. I wonder where he came from?" Yaeger took a fresh grip on his water bucket and carried it back toward the mule sheds.

Lupe stood between the trampled bank and Yaeger's adobe inn, her brown arms folded meditatively. Calhoun advanced slowly; the shallow boat pulled the guy rope taut, and she could hear, over her head, the pinging of the stretched hemp fibers. Beyond Calhoun, the brush-bobbed bottomlands stretched away in a monotony of sun-bleached yellows and tans.

Calhoun poled the ferry into its landing and made fast with quick, expert loops of the rope. Lupe considered him boldly. He climbed ashore, a big-boned man in butternuts and half boots, shirtless; his chest was sun-whacked like old leather. He had a lot of brown hair and a face like a mountain crag—rocky, strong, here and there broken.

Calhoun dried his face with a swipe of his arm and stood arrested, wrist over his eyes, looking at Lupe. He had a studious expression, the face of a man to whom silence could be important. Lupe's head dipped in a modest gesture, but she flashed a quick little smile. She went back into the inn, skirts flowing.

The dusty, hoarse shouting of a drill sergeant floated vaguely down from the army compound above. Inside the inn, Calhoun heard the gentle rattle of dishes: Lupe laying the table. Overriding those sounds was the steady advancing chug of a two-stroke steam engine—a harsh, alien noise in the desert. Yaeger clumped down from the mule sheds, heavy boots stirring the dust, and stopped by Calhoun. "I didn't expect him until tomorrow."

"Strong currents this time of year," Calhoun said.

Bereft of cabin or any superstructure, the odd little steamer rounded the northern bend and made stately progress toward them: the *Colorado*, drawing only two-and-a-half feet of water. On deck at the stern were three men, slowly taking shape as the steamer neared the landing.

"Riding high," Yaeger observed. "Couldn't have been much freight at Ehrenburg."

"He's got a passenger."

Yaeger looked at him. "You get a faraway look when something comes from around the horizon, Bill. Figuring to push on soon?"

"Haven't made up my mind."

"Hard to find a good boatman hereabouts," Yaeger said. "I'm past the age for poling the damned thing all day."

"I've made no plans," said Calhoun, and abruptly his eyes narrowed.

Yaeger said, "You recognize somebody?"

"Maybe." Calhoun kept his eyes on the steamer while it turned across the current, its wheels churning brown stains in the river. Smoke chuffed from it precarious stack. Captain 'Lonzo Johnson stood at the tiller with his sea-captain's cap at a rakish angle. Light of foot, an Indian youth ran across the gunwales and gathered a coil of rope at the bow. Calhoun moved out onto the dock, ready to catch the line.

Captain 'Lonzo Johnson's hearty call sailed across the closing gap; he waved his arms, and Yaeger waved back. Lupe was at the inn doorway—Calhoun had time to notice that before he caught the flung line and braced his shoulders to haul the bow in tight. Captain 'Lonzo Johnson shut off the wheels and leaned on the whistle cord to lower the boiler pressure: the whoop of the steam whistle shot startlingly along the banks.

In the stern stood a rawboned young man with yellow hair and a reckless grin, eyes brightly on Calhoun, who paid no notice until he had the line secured. Thereupon Calhoun walked along the dock to the stern. "Hello, Chris."

The blond man tipped back the bill of his soft cap. The butt of a Navy revolver showed at his waist. His grin spread across the width of his easy, sensuous face. "Wonderin' where you'd buried yourself, Bill. Help me out of this contraption—damned things make me seasick."

Calhoun gave him a hand. The man called Chris planted both feet solidly on the planks and stood bolt-still, as if to get his land legs after a long voyage. His grin flickered on and off.

Down at the landward end of the dock Captain 'Lonzo Johnson was talking to Yaeger:

"Didn't even pay expenses this trip. I got provisions for the fort, then I'll have to take her across to put off some pelts for San Diego. Damned hot workin' around a boiler under this sun. I'm thinking of rigging a couple parasols over the boat. Two ladies refused to take passage out of Ehrenburg, fearing the heat stroke. Time we made a respectable outfit out of this."

Yaeger nodded absently and then spoke in a low tone, intended to reach no farther than 'Lonzo Johnson's ears: "Know anything about your passenger?"

"Picked him up some miles above Castle Dome. Said his horse had bust a leg, and he'd had to shoot it."

The towheaded newcomer was hauling up saddle and rifle as the Indian ship's mate handed them to him. Yaeger said, "Carries a gun."

"So do most everybody. Gent said he come out of Tonto Apache country—packing a redskin scalp to prove it, too. Reckon I'd rather not tangle with him. Says his name's Chris Roark."

Yaeger's head rocked back. "That so?"

"You mind the name?"

"All kinds of talk around here—everybody passes by here."

"Wild man maybe?"

"Well, now, I guess a man'd be pretty wild to choose riding through Tonto Apache country." Yaeger's speculative attention lay on the blond Chris Roark, coming forward with saddle across his shoulder. Calhoun tagged along with Roark's rifle and possibles, and when they had gone beyond earshot up toward the inn, Yaeger said, "My boatman seems to know the gent."

"That good or bad?"

"We'll see," Yaeger muttered.

'Lonzo Johnson turned to the Indian youth. "Paco, get on up to the fort and tell them lazy soldiers to come down here and get their provisions unloaded."

Inside Chris Roark stood blinking, accustoming his eyes to the dim, cool interior. Lupe came out of the kitchen with a jug of water. As she stretched to set it in the middle of the long plank table, her dress pulled tight against her. She was long-waisted, long-necked; she thought herself too thin. When she turned, she found the eyes of the two young men on her. The stranger was grinning; Calhoun was looking at her soberly. Lupe retreated from the room.

"How about that?" Chris Roark said, and did not notice Calhoun's troubled frown. "Now. Where can a man buy a horse?"

"What happened to yours?"

"Broke his wind. Had to shoot him."

Yaeger's shadow filled the door. "You told the captain your horse had broke a leg."

For an instant Roark's eyes flashed. Then he shrugged. "Same difference. I had to shoot him."

Yaeger said mildly, "Bed and board one dollar, if you're fixin' to spend the night."

Roark dug into his pocket and got a silver dollar. It was shiny with newness. Yaeger looked at it curiously. "Lupe!"

The girl appeared; Yaeger said, "Show him the way to Room Six."

Wordlessly Lupe went across the length of the room to the back door and turned down the corridor. Roark hoisted his saddle and, grinning, went after her. When they were gone, Yaeger said to Calhoun, "You know him?"

"Used to."

"That's a brand-new 'fifty-eight dollar. Could have come from the express office at Mesilla. Butterfield man said they was a holdup two, three weeks ago."

"Maybe," Calhoun said.

"I mind my own business strictly. Ain't none of my never-mind where he got it. But don't encourage him to stay on, Bill."

"No."

Yaeger nodded, tossed the dollar once, and went out.

Calhoun, his head tipped a little in thought, went out back to his shanty and rummaged through his duffel. He found what he was seeking—a cumbersome Dragoon revolver—and checked its load; he capped the six nipples, laid the hammer between two chambers, and thrust it into the waistband of his butternuts.

In a little while the Butterfield coach rattled in from Tucson, and at the same time Calhoun saw dust across the river where the stage from Warner's Ranch was coming on at a good clip. On schedule, both of them. It was Calhoun's job to ferry the Tucson stage across, wait for the Warner's Ranch coach, and bring it back.

He was helping the Butterfield driver lash down the stagecoach wheels on the ferry's narrow deck when Chris Roark ambled on board. "Thought I'd ride across with you. Can I lend a hand?"

"Tie down that off front wheel."

The driver glanced at Roark, said, "Obliged," and ignored the blond man thereafter. The Butterfield mules thumped the decking with nervous hoofs. Yaeger came out on the dock and spoke to Calhoun:

"Ready?"

"Cast off."

Yaeger tossed down the rope and went forward to unfasten the bowline. Calhoun settled the end of his pole against the dock and threw his weight against it. Sluggishly the ferry moved out into the current. The wind braced against the top-heavy coach and might have capsized the ferry but for the restraint of the shore-to-shore guy rope along which the ferry rode on pulleys. Walking backward from bow to stern, Calhoun poled with even strength. Chris Roark sat cross-legged in the shade of the coach, tipped his cap back, and said, "Must be easier ways."

"Sure," Calhoun said, and didn't spend his breath on more talk. They reached the far side, untied the wheels, and watched the driver whoop his stage up the bank. Clattering and bucking, it rammed away into the brush bottoms. The farther coach, coming forward from the dunes, would be another fifteen or twenty minutes.

Chris Roark said, "You got a relief man?"

"Sometimes Yaeger spells me on a long day."

"Maybe," Chris Roark said idly, "tomorrow will be a long day." He stretched out in the shade, laid his cap across his eyes, and smoked a cigaret. "What ever happened to Johnny Santee?"

"Vigilantes hanged him."

"That a fact? Shame, shame. Whereabouts?"

"Tuolumne County someplace," Calhoun said.

"Crying shame," Chris Roark said again, and grinned. "Recall when the three of us tore Shanssey's saloon apart. High old times. That's where you got that break in your nose." He rolled over and propped himself up on one elbow, cupping the cigaret. "Damn it, Bill, I got to say you don't seem particularly glad to see a man."

"You tend to remind me of things I want to forget."

"Gone straight and narrow, hey?"

"I served my time," Calhoun said. "And that's the end to it."

"So now you break your back every hour pushing this hunk of planks back and forth. Where's the joy in that, Bill?"

"Joy enough," Calhoun replied, "in covering the day at a steady pace and not causing regrets. I learned that much."

Almost angry, Chris Roark said, "You got big muscles—what else you got to show for it?"

Calhoun shrugged. "I don't have to show anybody anything."

"You exasperate a man," Chris Roark said, and lay back. By the time his cigaret was finished, the coach from Warner's Ranch was pitching down on them with a swell and a rush.

Calhoun used up most of the day ferrying a wagon train across the river. At three the *Colorado* cast off and crossed the river to unload Captain 'Lonzo Johnson's cargo of pelts. A freight outfit arrived to pick it up and transferred to the boat a shipment of Indian trade items and gunpowder kegs. Johnson's ridiculous little steamer then chugged upstream, struggling against the current, intending to make four miles before dark. When the *Colorado* was gone, a dust-muffled silence settled over the encampment,

broken only by occasional bully shouts from the barracks uphill.
At intervals during the afternoon Lupe stood at the kitchen window watching Calhoun pole the ferry back and forth. On the
porch Chris Roark sat whittling.

At sundown Calhoun lashed the ferryboat tight and went up to
his shanty to put on a shirt. He kept the revolver in his belt despite
the discomfort, only changing the loads against the possibility
that river moisture might have spoiled the powder during the afternoon.

Half-a-dozen guests had drifted into the inn during the course
of the afternoon, awaiting the next day's stage to San Diego. A
drummer of ladies' underthings, a family of farmers, a prospector. Yaeger sat at the head of the table, Calhoun at the foot. Chris
Roark had chosen a seat where his right hand was free and his
back protected by a wall; his eyes never stood still; now and then
he grinned at Calhoun down the length of the table. Lupe moved
in and out of the room, serving; when she laid Calhoun's plate
before him, her arm brushed his shoulder. He looked at her, not
smiling, seeing the pulse beat at her throat. She moved away with
a cool, supple sway. Calhoun noticed Chris Roark's brash grin
when the girl served him; Roark's shoulder moved—his hand was
out of sight under the table. The girl stepped back quickly, her
eyes angry; she tossed her head and walked back into the kitchen,
and Chris Roark chuckled.

A drone of dulled conversation ran around the table. Chris
Roark bought a bottle of forty-rod whiskey from Yaeger's bar and
splashed it into his cup in place of coffee. Calhoun watched
expressionlessly.

A sound arrested him lifting his cup: the weary pat-pat of hoofs
in the dust outside. He looked at Roark and saw that once again
Roark's hand had dropped off the edge of the table, out of sight.
Lupe came in with a tray of pie and stopped in the door; everyone
was that way—frozen, waiting. The horse whickered out front,
and they could hear it nuzzling water in the trough. Boots hit the
steps, then the porch. A man's heavy shape blocked out the doorway—a gray-haired man in range clothes, carrying a brace of
single-shot percussion pistols in hip holsters, butts forward.
"Evening, Lou."

Yaeger inclined his head. "How are you, George?"

"Tired and dusty. And I expect too late for supper."

"I'll warm something up," Lupe said.

"That's kind," the stranger said, and came inside; the corset drummer made a space for him on the bench. Calhoun was still watching Chris Roark, who sat stiffly, both hands under the table, watching the newcomer with unnatural brightness. The stranger's equitable, perceptive attention moved from face to face. "Saw 'Lonzo's boat headed upstream three miles back."

"You came down from Ehrenburg?" Yaeger asked conversationally.

"No. Castle Dome. I came overland from Alamillo—wore out three horses."

"Long ride," Yaeger said. "Smack through Tonto country."

Yaeger was looking just then at Chris Roark, who stared back with bland innocence. Yaeger said: "This here's George Zane. Bill Calhoun down at the end there, my boatman. Gent on my left name of Roark. I'm afraid I don't know the rest of you."

They spoke their names, and George Zane nodded courteously to each. Lupe set a bowl of soup before him. When she stood back, her glance shuttled from Zane to Calhoun to Chris Roark. Her shoulders straightened, and she stood behind Zane, looking at Calhoun, whose eyes lifted to meet hers. Calhoun gave no perceptible signal. The girl went to the kitchen. Calhoun set down his coffee cup and pushed his chair back slightly. The revolver dug at his ribs.

George Zane said, "Express holdup at Mesilla a while back. Four gents. We got three. I tracked the other one as far as Castle Dome." From his pocket he took a badge and pinned it to his shirt. "Don't ordinarily wear this travelin'—sun tends to tarnish it some."

Chris Roark's eyes were bright, restless. "Looks like you had a long ride for nothing then."

"Maybe," George said. "You never can tell."

"This gent you want—know his name or what he looks like?"

"No."

"Didn't his partners talk?"

"They chose to fight. We had a nine-man posse. The odds were poor."

"All three of them dead?"

"That's right," Zane said, meeting Chris Roark's stare. "All dead. It happens that way to the easy-money kind. Sooner or later they all end up out in the brush with a bullet in them or a rope around their Adam's apples."

Lupe brought in a plate of steak and peppers for the marshal. Zane ate with hearty gusto; he seemed oblivious to the currents he had set up in the room. The farmer and family went away to bed. When Zane finished his meal, the others were smoking. Zane said to Yaeger, "Anybody come down from Castle Dome way last day or two?"

"You know my policy, George."

Zane was looking at Chris Roark when he answered. "I can't blame you for minding your own business, Lou. But this fellow I'm after is a killer. Shot down the agent during that holdup."

"I'm sorry about that," Yaeger said, and stood up. "Stage arrives early, folks. I'd recommend you turn in."

The gathering broke up. Lupe turned down the lamps and cleared the table. Calhoun drifted outside and sat down on the porch, propping his legs up on the rail, enjoying the easy relaxation that followed a meal, the cool breeze that came off the river after dark, the slow scud of thin clouds across the night sky. Two men came out—Yaeger followed by Chris Roark. They didn't notice Calhoun in the shadows. Roark said, "I might even be the man the marshal wants, for all you know."

"You might," Yaeger said.

"Captain Johnson told you where he'd picked me up."

"Yes."

"Then I'm obliged you didn't say anything."

"All right," Yaeger said.

"Why don't you go ahead and ask me whether I'm the man he's after?"

"Like I said," Yaeger murmured, "it's not my affair." He went off into the night, his final words drifting back: "I'd appreciate it if you'd consider moving on tomorrow."

Chris Roark moved across the porch; he had, after all, seen Calhoun there—his shrewd eyes didn't miss much. He said, "How about you? He ain't curious, but maybe you are."

"No," Calhoun said.

"Well, just for your information, amigo, it wasn't me robbed any express office or killed any agents."

"All right."

When Roark lighted a cigaret, the match exploded brightly, throwing his facial bones into cruel relief. "I want a favor from you."

"What favor?"

"Let somebody take over for you tomorrow afternoon."

"Why?"

The blond man said gently, "Around here it ain't considered good manners to get curious, remember?"

"What have you got in mind, Chris?"

But Roark moved away without reply. Calhoun listened to Lupe work in the kitchen, cleaning up. Down by the wharf he could see the red tip of Roark's cigaret, dimming and glowing. Presently it arced out and went dead in the river. The current lapped gently. Roark came up to the porch again and said, "I'm just trying to do you a good turn for old times' sake, Bill," and went inside the inn.

Calhoun was still puzzling it over when Yaeger came up from the corrals, and said, "We're just about out of axle grease. Remind me to put in an order. Listen, Bill, don't let that hairpin toll you into anything rash."

"I'm like you," Calhoun said. "Just minding my own business."

"George Zane acts kind of slow, but he don't miss anything worth the mention. Your friend would be smart to move out of here tonight."

"I guess he's the best judge of that."

Yaeger shook his head. "You get to be my age, you get weary of fools. Good night, Bill."

In time Calhoun uncoiled and wandered inside. Crossing the dining room, he stopped, noticing that a light still burned under the closed kitchen door; not a sound came from there. Calhoun walked softly to the door and flung it open, catching Chris Roark in the act of forcing Lupe back against the hot stove. Roark had red-streaked scratches down one cheek, and the girl's hands were raised in claws. Roark wheeled, touching his gun.

"That's enough," Calhoun said quietly.

Roark said with wicked intensity. "Don't come at me like that."

"Been a long day," Calhoun said. "You look tired, Chris."

"For a country where people mind their own business—" Chris Roark began, and trailed off.

Calhoun looked at the girl. "Do you want him here?"

She shook her head. Calhoun said, "On the run, then, Chris."

Roark's eyes widened. "This your property? Whyn't you say so?"

"Go on, Chris."

Roark grinned. "I never meant to step on your toes, Bill." He walked out. Calhoun listened to his steps and heard the bedroom door.

Lupe's breasts rose and fell with her breath. Calhoun said, "I let him think that so he'd let you alone."

She nodded quickly, nervously. Behind the studied composure she was badly shaken; he could see that. He touched her shoulders gently, and she looked up at him like a cornered bird. Calhoun said, "You and me, how many words we said to each other? Not so many, I reckon."

She said, "That man is trouble for you, not just for me."

"He'll be pushing on." Calhoun took his hands away from her shoulders. "You got a man, Lupe?"

"No."

"All right, then," he said, and took her to him. She bunched up against him, small fists clenched on his chest; she didn't cry, but he could feel the tautness in her. He said, "That was a rotten thing for a man to try. You want me to give him a boost out of here?"

When she answered, her voice was muffled by his chest: "Leave him alone, let him go. If you make him angry, it will mean trouble for you."

"Trouble's the only language Chris understands. I know—I used to be the same way."

"Not you," she said. "Not the same as him." They stood holding each other, silent, motionless.

In the morning Marshall George Zane came down to the landing where Calhoun was lashing a wagon on the ferry. Zane said, "Yaeger tells me you been working here three, four weeks."

"That's right."

"Mind telling me where you came from before that?"

Calhoun considered him. Finally he said, "Kansas penitentiary."

Zane nodded. If he was surprised, he didn't show it. "That where you knew this Roark fella?"

"No. That was in Texas, some years back."

"Haven't seen him since, then?"

"Not until yesterday," Calhoun said.

"He come down on 'Lonzo Johnson's boat?"

Calhoun smiled slightly and went forward to lash down another wheel. The marshal followed and said, "You're like Lou, eh? Not talking. Well, it's all right. I found out up at the fort that Roark came in on the boat. He could be the man I want. Seen him around today?''

"No."

"No horses missing. He couldn't have gone far unless he's a good swimmer. Reckon I'll poke around.''

Calhoun straightened. "You have any evidence on him?''

"No. I just want to talk to him. Sometimes you ask a few questions, and they get rattled.''

"Take it slow," Calhoun advised. "He knows how to handle that Navy Colt.''

"Why," George Zane said, "I appreciate that.'' He scratched his jaw. "Mind telling me what you were in prison for?''

"Armed robbery.''

Zane nodded and went away. Calhoun could see Lupe in the kitchen window. She raised a hand and waggled it; Calhoun grinned at her and cast off and plunged his pole into the ooze-bottom of the river, throwing his weight against it.

All morning there was a steady stream of traffic coming out of the desert or down the Gila. One Mexican cattleman from Sonora had five hundred longhorns that had to be ferried across in bunches. Calhoun sweated right through his trousers. At lunch-time Yaeger spelled him for half an hour, and when Calhoun came back aboard, Yaeger said:

"Want me to keep on an hour or two? You're pretty bushed.''

"That's all right," Calhoun drawled. "It's what you pay me for.'' He had occasion to recall Chris Roark's strange warning. In a moment he said, "I've been thinking about something you said yesterday.''

"And?''

"I might like to stay on here, only there's one thing you ought to know about me.''

Yaeger said, "My policy—out here a man's past don't count. I'd be pleased to have you stay on.'' He turned away. Calhoun took the pole.

At two-thirty a pair of bearded toughs rode up to the inn, teth-ered their horses, and went inside to the bar. They didn't reappear until four, when the light brougham stagecoach from the Gila Bend country came. The shotgun guard stepped down to help Calhoun jockey the coach onto the boat; the driver walked away— his replacement waited on the other side. The guard set his scattergun down, and said, "Let's tie her down good. Got gold bullion on board. We capsize, it'll sink ten feet in the mud, and the State of California will be missin' its payroll."

It tightened Calhoun's jaw. He made his knots fast and shifted the weight of the Dragoon revolver in his belt. It could hardly be coincidence that the two toughs chose this moment to lead their saddled horses onto the ferry. They paid passage with shiny new 1858 silver dollars. Calhoun had a fair idea where those had come from. But there was no sign anywhere of Chris Roark. The two toughs made their way into the bow and hunkered against the gunwales, apparently unconcerned. Calhoun glanced at the shotgun guard, who stood by the coach, six feet from his shotgun. Calhoun said softly, "Mind your hardware, Chet."

Chet's glance passed across the two toughs. He nodded and moved without hurry, picking up the shotgun, cradling it in the bend of his elbow. Up at the inn, Yaeger was talking to Marshal George Zane, and Lupe was filling the hanging water *olla* under the porch roof. Calhoun braced the pole against the dock and pushed off.

He knew now what Roark's warning had meant, and he poled steadily with all his nerves gone bowstring-tight, sweeping both banks with his alert attention, for that was where the trouble would come, from the banks—the toughs wouldn't start anything, not in midriver where they could be pinned down. But it was fairly certain what Roark must have in mind.

'Lonzo Johnson's *Colorado* came chugging around the bend at top speed, and that was odd: it should have been miles upriver by now. Calhoun had time to shout a single phrase at the shotgun guard, but the phrase was cut off by the crack of a high-speed rifle shot. The bullet, fired from concealment on the western bank, fanned air like dragonfly wings above the ferry. There was another shot, and yet another; either the concealed marksman had an armful of rifles or he had a repeating weapon of some kind.

The guard's shotgun lay toward the two toughs in the bow, who half smiled and did not move. Calhoun found the puffs of muzzle smoke on the far bank and fired a couple of pistol shots at it, but the bobbing of the boat made precise aim impossible. Then one of the rifleman's bullets parted the guy rope, cutting it cleanly.

Expecting that, Calhoun wheeled toward the stern pulley. The broken end of the guy rope whipped like a bullwhip, lashing up and down in violent loops. In a moment it would run out through the pulley, the ferry would pick up momentum and ride away downstream on the fast current. Calhoun leaped for the rope. His hand caught the shredded end and half-hitched it quickly around the stern cleat. He could see the *Colorado* bearing down a quarter-mile distant, billowing smoke. Its whistle screamed steadily.

The rope ran through the pulley, caught up with a snap, and jerked the ferry around savagely, all but upsetting it. Calhoun felt the rope slipping through his hasty half-hitch; he braced both feet against the cleat and bent his back to the struggle, gripping the frayed end with both fists. Below the inn Yaeger and George Zane were running downstream on shore; Lupe was coming down from the inn, skirts lifted. The steamer loomed upstream. The ferry careened, held by the broken guy rope; it swung in toward the west bank, drawn hard against the rope by the force of the current. Calhoun said, "Brace, Chet. We're going to hit."

Chet spoke sharply to the two toughs, but when the ferryboat rammed into the bank with a crunch of wood, and despite his stance against the coach, Chet sprawled. At the moment of impact, Calhoun let go the rope and scooped up his revolver. He heard the double roar of Chet's shotgun, one after the other, followed by the lighter crack of a handgun. Coming around the coach, Calhoun saw one of the toughs pitch off the stern, all but cut in half by the shotgun blast; the second tough, a gun smoking at his feet, had raised his free hand in astonishment to the bloody mass where his right eye had been.

Chet had dropped his empty shotgun in favor of a horse pistol from his belt. He began to walk toward the wounded tough.

Calhoun said, "Heads up—there's one on the bank."

That was when Chris Roark came out of the brush with a revolving-cylinder rifle. "Drop your gun, Chris." His words were all but drowned in the roar of the steamboat whistle; it was just above the landing now. Chris Roark's finger was white on the trigger.

Calhoun threw himself behind the coach; Roark's bullet splintered the corner of it, blasting slivers of wood into Calhoun's cheek. Calhoun fired blindly around the coach, dropped belly-flat, and crawled underneath, protected by the height of the gunwale.

Across the river, George Zane's rifle was talking harshly, but Chris Roark kept the ferry interposed between himself and that threat. The steamboat was docking upstream, across the river, and that seemed to puzzle and infuriate Roark. He said, "Toss out your gun, Bill, and cast this thing off!" His voice was a feverish shout. On the heels of it came the thunder of Chet's big horse pistol from somewhere up in the bow. Roark laughed. "That went wide, shotgun—now you're all empty. Stand up and push this thing into the river."

"She's solid aground," Chet answered. "You're all done here. Don't you see that?"

"You think so?" Roark cried. Calhoun put his head up in time to see Roark swinging his rifle toward the shotgun guard. Calhoun said in a brittle voice, "Chris."

Roark's rifle came back, moving toward him; Calhoun tipped his Dragoon up and pulled the trigger.

It was obvious, by the way he fell, that Chris Roark was dead.

Across the river Yaeger was yelling. In the bow the bearded tough sat moaning, face in hands; the other one was floating face down, drifting away downstream. Chet went after him.

Calhoun moved forward carefully; the ferry was beginning to list, one side caught fast against the bank where it had rammed. When Chet came up to look at Roark, Calhoun said, "That's one way to end it. Like Zane said—out in the brush with a bullet in him."

"This fellow a friend of yours?"

"That was somewhere else," Calhoun murmured, "a long time ago." His tone was sour.

Yaeger and Zane came over in a skiff to pick them up. Yaeger shook his head. "Holy Judas, what a puking mess." He looked away and added, "Couple of buckos jumped 'Lonzo's boat last night and tried to force him to turn around and come down here. 'Lonzo and the Indian got the drop on them, brought them down here to find out what the ruckus was about."

"Roark's idea," Calhoun told him. "Chris figured to cut the ferry loose and let it drift downstream. He was going to use the steamboat to pick up the bullion and get away downriver, probably to Mexico."

Looking across the river, he saw Lupe on the bank, shading her eyes, looking across. Yaeger was talking to him: "Maybe this changes things for you, Bill. Ain't a pretty memory, all this."

Calhoun was still looking at the girl. He said, "Nothing's changed. Let's go."

In addition to editing or co-editing more than twenty-five anthologies of Western fiction, Bill Pronzini is himself an accomplished writer in the field. His Western novels include The Gallows Land *(1983), which is set in Arizona;* Starvation Camp *(1984),* Quincannon *(1985),* The Last Days of Horse-Shy Halloran *(1987), and* The Hangings *(1989). Among the best of his frontier short stories is this deceptively simple tale of a bereaved drifter who encounters a desert settler's wife near El Camino Real del Diablo—the Devil's Highway—in southern Arizona.*

Decision

****

Bill Pronzini

THE day was coming on dusk, the sky flame-streaked and the thick desert heat easing some, when I found the small, hardscrabble ranch.

It lay nestled within a broad ring of bluffs and cactus-strewn hillocks. Crouched beside a draw leading between two of the bluffs was a pole-and-'dobe cabin and two weathered outbuildings. Even from where I sat my steeldust high above, I could see that whoever lived there was not having an easy time of it. Heat had parched and withered the corn and other vegetables in the cultivated patch along one side, and the spare buildings looked to be crumbling, like the powdering bones of animals long dead.

There were no horses or other livestock in the open corral near the cabin, no sign of life anywhere. Except for the wisps of chimney smoke rising pale and steady, the place had the look of abandonment. It was the smoke that had drawn me off El Camino Real del Diablo some minutes earlier; that and the fact that both my waterbags were near empty.

Most days there seemed to be a fair amount of traffic on the Devil's Highway—the only good road between Tucson and Yuma, part of the Gila Trail that connected California with points east

174

to Texas. Over the past week I'd come on pioneers, freighters, drifters, a Butterfield stagecoach, a company of soldiers on its way to Fort Yuma, groups of men looking for work on the rail line the Southern Pacific had begun building eastward from the Colorado River the previous year, 1878. But today, when I needed water and would have paid dear for it, the road had been deserted.

It was my own fault that I was low on water. I could have filled the bags when I passed through the town of Maricopa Wells last night, but I'd decided to keep on without stopping; it had been late enough so that even the saloons were closed, and I saw no need to go knocking on someone's door at that hour. It was my intention to buy water at the next way station for the Butterfield line, but when I got there, close to noon, the stationmaster had refused me. His main spring had gone bad, he said, and they had precious little for their own needs. He'd let me stay there for most of the afternoon, waiting in the shade by the corral; not a soul had passed by the time I rode on again at five o'clock. And I had seen no one since, either.

I hoped the people who lived down below had enough water to spare. If they didn't I would have to go back to the Devil's Highway and do some more waiting; neither the steeldust nor I was fit enough for moving on without water. I could see the ranch's well set under a plank lean-to in the dusty yard, and I licked at my parched lips. Well, I had nothing to lose by riding down and asking.

I heeled the horse forward, sitting slack in the saddle. Even traveling mostly by night, and even though it was not yet the middle of May, a man dries out in the desert, wearies bone-deep.

But the desert also had a way of dulling the mind, which was just the reason why I had decided to ride alone instead of traveling by coach through these Arizona badlands. I didn't want company or conversation because they would only lead to questions and then sharpened memories I did not care to dwell on. Memories that needed to be buried, the way I had buried Emma four months and six days ago in the sun-webbed ground outside Lordsburg.

People I knew there, friends, said the pain would go away after a while. All you had to do was to keep on living the best you could, and time would help you forget—forget how she'd collapsed one evening after a dozen hours' hard toil on our own hardscrabble land, and how I'd thought it was just the ague because she'd been complaining of chest pains, and that terrible time when I came back from town with the doctor and found her lying in our bed so still and small, not breathing, gone. Heart failure, the doctor said. Twenty-eight years old, prime of life, and her good heart had betrayed her. . . .

Maybe they were right, the friends who'd given their advice. But four months and six days of living the best I could hadn't eased the grief inside me, not with everything and everyone in Lordsburg reminding me of Emma. So a week ago I had sold the farm, packed a few changes of clothing and some personal belongings and a spare pistol into my saddlebags, and set out west into Arizona Territory. I had no idea where I was going or what I would do when the three-hundred-and-eighty dollars I carried in my boot dwindled away. I had nothing, and I wanted nothing except to drift through the long days and longer nights until life took on some meaning again, if it ever would.

The trail leading down to the ranch was steep and switchbacked in places, and it took me the better part of twenty minutes to get to where the buildings were. The harsh daylight had softened by then, and the tops of the bluffs seemed to have turned a reddish-purple color; the sky looked flushed now, instead of brassy the way it did at midday.

I rode slowly toward the cabin, keeping my hands up and in plain sight. Desert settlers, being as isolated as they were, would likely be mistrustful of leaned-down, dust-caked strangers. When I reached the front yard I drew rein. It was quiet there, and I still wasn't able to make out sound or movement at any of the buildings. Beyond the vegetable patch, a sagging utility shed stood with a padlock on its door; the only other structure was a long, pole-sided shelter at the rear of the empty corral. In back of the shed, rows of pulque cactus stood like sentinels in the hot, dry earth.

I looked at the well, running my tongue through the dryness inside my mouth. Then I eased the steeldust half a rod closer to the cabin and called out, "Hello the house!"

Silence.

"Hello! Anybody home?"

There was more silence for a couple of seconds, and I was thinking of stepping down. But then a woman's voice said from inside, "What do you want here?" It was a young voice, husky, but dulled by something I couldn't identify. The door was closed, and the front window was curtained in monk's cloth, but I sensed that the woman was standing by the window, watching me through the curtain folds.

"Don't be alarmed, ma'am," I said. "I was wondering if you could spare a little water. I'm near out."

She didn't answer. Silence settled again, and I began to get a vague feeling of something being wrong. It made me shift uncomfortably in the saddle.

"Ma'am?"

"I can't let you have much," she said finally.

"I'll pay for whatever you can spare."

"You won't need to pay."

"That's kind of you."

"You can step down if you like."

I put on a smile and swung off and slapped some of the fine powdery dust off my shirt and Levi's. The door opened a crack, but she didn't come out.

"My name is Jennifer Todd," she said from inside. "My husband and I own this ranch." She spoke the word "husband" as if it were blasphemy.

"I'm Roy Boone," I said.

"Mr. Boone." And she opened the door and moved out into the fading light.

My smile vanished; I stared at her with my mouth coming open. She was no more than twenty, hair the color of near-ripe corn and piled in loose braids on top of her head, eyes brown and soft and wide—pretty eyes. But it wasn't any of this that caused me to stare as I did. It was the blue-black bruises on both sides of her face, the deep cut above her right brow, the swollen, mottled surface of her upper lip and her right temple.

"Jesus God!" I said. "Who did that to you, Mrs. Todd?"

"My husband. This morning, just before he left for Maricopa Wells."

"But *why*?"

"He was hung over," she said. "Pulque hung over. Mase is mean when he's sober and meaner when he's drunk, but when he's bad hung over he's the devil's own child."

"He's done this to you before?"

"More times than I can count."

"Maybe I've got no right to say this, but why don't you leave him? Mrs. Todd, a man who'd do a thing like this to a woman wouldn't hesitate to kill her if he was riled enough."

"I tried to leave him," she said. "I tried it three times. He came after me each time and brought me back here and beat me half-crazy. A work animal's got sense enough to obey if it's whipped enough times."

I could feel anger inside me. I was thinking of Emma again, the love we'd had, the tenderness. Some men never knew or understood feelings like that; some men gave only one kind of pain, never felt the other kind deep inside them. They never realized what they had with a good woman. Or cared. Men like that—

Impulsively I put the rest of the thought into words. "A man like that ought to be shot dead for what he's done to you."

Something flickered in her eyes, and she said, "If I had a gun, Mr. Boone, I expect I'd do just that thing—I'd shoot him, with no regrets. But there's only one rifle and one pistol, and Mase carries them with him during the day. At night he locks them up in the shed yonder."

It made me feel uneasy to hear a woman talking so casually about killing. I looked away from her, wondering if it was love or some other reason that made her marry this Mase Todd, somebody who kept her like a prisoner in a badlands valley, who beat her and tried to break her.

When I looked back at Mrs. Todd she smiled in a fleeting, humorless way. "I don't know what's the matter with me, telling you all my troubles. You've problems of your own, riding alone across the desert. Come inside. I've some stew on the fire, and you can take an early supper with me if you like."

"Ma'am, I—"

"Mase won't be home until late tonight or tomorrow morning, if you're thinking of him."

"I wasn't, no. He doesn't worry me."

"You look tired and hungry," she said, "and we don't get many visitors out here. I've no one to talk to most days. I'd take it as a kindness if you'd accept."

I couldn't find a way to refuse her. I just nodded and let her show me inside the cabin.

It was filled with shadows and smelled of spiced jackrabbit stew and boiling coffee. The few pieces of furniture were hand-hewn, but whoever had made them—likely her husband—had done a poor, thoughtless job; none of the pieces looked as though it would last much longer. But the two rooms I saw were clean and straightened, and you could see that she'd done the best she could with what she had, that she'd tried to make a home out of it.

She lighted a mill lantern on the table to chase away some of the shadows. Then she said, "There's water in that basin by the hearth if you want to wash up. I'll fetch some drinking water from the well, and I'll see to your horse."

"You needn't bother yourself. . . ."

"It's no bother."

She turned and went to the door, walking in a stiff, slow way but holding herself erect; her spirit wasn't broken yet. I watched her go out and shut the door behind her, and I thought: She's some woman. Most would be half-dead shells by now if they'd gone through what she has.

I crossed to the basin, washed with a cake of strong yellow soap. Mrs. Todd came back as I was drying off. She handed me a gourd of water, and while I drank from it she unhooked a heavy iron kettle from a spit rod suspended above a banked fire. She spooned stew onto tin plates, poured coffee, set out a pan of fresh corn bread.

We ate mostly in silence. Despite what she'd said about not having anyone to talk to, she seemed not to want conversation. But there was something I needed to say, and when I was done eating I got it said.

"Mrs. Todd, you've been more than hospitable to share your food and water with me. I can't help feeling there must be something I can do for you."

"No, Mr. Boone. There's nothing you can do."

"Well, suppose I just stayed until your husband gets home, had a little talk with him—"

"That wouldn't be wise," she said. "If Mase comes home and finds a strange man, he wouldn't wait to ask who you are or why you're here. He'd make trouble for you, and afterward he'd make more trouble for me."

What could I do? It was her property, her life; this was business between her and her husband. If she'd asked for help, that would have been another matter. But she'd made her position clear. I had no right to force myself on her.

Outside, in the silky, moon-washed purple of early evening, I thanked her again and tried to offer her money for the food and water. But she wouldn't have any of it. She was too proud to take payment for hospitality. She insisted that I fill my waterbags from the well before riding out, so I lowered the wooden bucket on the windlass and did that.

As I rode slowly out of the yard, I turned in the saddle to look back. She was still standing there by the well, looking after me, her hands down at her sides. In the silvery moonlight she had a forlorn, fixed appearance—as if she had somehow taken root in the desert soil.

An hour later I was once again on the Devil's Highway, headed west. And a mounting sense of uneasiness had come to ride with me. For the first time in four months and six days, it was someone other than Emma who was disturbing my thoughts; it was Jennifer Todd.

Like an echo in my mind, I heard some of the words she had spoken to me: *If I had a gun, Mr. Boone, I expect I'd do just that thing—I'd shoot him, with no regrets. But there's only one rifle and one pistol, and Mase carries them with him during the day.*

I listened to the echo of those words, and I thought about the way she'd been watching me inside the cabin when I first rode in, the way she'd suddenly opened the door and come outside. Why had she come out at all? Beaten the way she was, most women would have stayed in the privacy of the cabin rather than allow a stranger to see them that way. And why had she talked so freely about her husband, about the kind of man he was?

Then I heard other words she'd spoken—*I'll fetch some drinking water from the well, and I'll see to your horse*—and I drew sharp rein, swung quickly out of the saddle. My fingers fumbled at the straps on the saddlebags, pulled them open, groped inside.

My spare six-gun was missing.

And along with it, three or four cartridges.

I stood there in the moonlight, leaning against the steeldust's flank, and I knew exactly what she had begun planning when she saw me ride in, and what she was planning for when her husband came home from Maricopa Wells and tried to lay hand to her again. And yet, I couldn't raise anger for what she'd done. She had been driven to it. She had every right to protect herself.

But was it really self-defense? Or was it cold-blooded murder?

In the saddle again, I thought: I've got to stop her. Only then Emma came crowding into my thoughts again. Gone, now—gone too young. So many years never to be lived, so many things never to be done; the child we had tried so hard to have never to be born. There had been nothing I could do to save her. But there was something I could do for another suffering young woman on another hardscrabble ranch.

I made my decision.

I kept on riding west.

*W.C. Tuttle's career as one of the most prolific and popular writers
of traditional Westerns spanned more than half a century, beginning
with stories for the pulps during World War I. His first novel,* Reddy
Brant, His Adventures, *appeared in 1920; his last,* Medicine Maker,
*in 1967, two years before his death. During the twenties and thirties,
his series about roving cowboys-cum-detectives, Hashknife Hartley
and Sleepy Stevens, was especially well received. The hallmarks of
his fiction, fast action, humor, and detective-story plot lines, are am-
ply in evidence in the rollicking tale of one Rheinlander Strong Pollinger's descent on Dry Lake, Arizona, which follows. Tuttle's life,
chronicled in his 1966 autobiography* Montana Man, *was every bit
as unusual and interesting as his Western stories; among other things
he was president of the Pacific Coast Baseball League from 1935 to
1943.*

The Code of Arizona

★★★★★★★★★★★★★★★

W.C. Tuttle

NATURE had not been very kind to Rheinlander Strong Pollinger. He was exactly twenty-two years of age, six feet,
five inches tall, and weighed a bare hundred-and-forty-five
pounds. His face was long and lean and heavily freckled, his hair
roan, rather than red. His nose was long, his mouth entirely too
wide for his narrow face, and he wore horn-rimmed glasses over
his blue eyes, which always seemed a bit amazed at the world.

Both ears flared a bit, the left a trifle more than the right, as
though cocked forward, listening. Rheinlander had been an or-
phan for five years, during which time he had managed to grad-
uate from school; and the last five months he had spent in running
down newspaper want ads, trying to find a job.

He owed his landlord a month's rent, owed for meals, owed
the last installment on a suit and overcoat, which were now in
pawn, along with his watch and ring.

As for relatives, Rheinlander Strong Pollinger was entirely un-incumbered. Out in Arizona lived an uncle—an ogre sort, so he understood; and a cousin, somewhere west of the Mississippi River.

Rheinlander had written this uncle, asking him if there was any chance for an ambitious young man to get work in Arizona, but the letter had never been answered.

Rheinlander had at last obtained a position as a filing clerk in a suburban bank, and this was his first day. Even the twelve dollars a week looked like a million. In a few weeks, if everything went well, he reflected comfortably, he could pay up his delinquent room rent, reclaim the suit and overcoat, and look the world in the face.

Never in his life had he been outside a city, and yet his most prized possessions were a pair of fancy high-heel cowboy boots, a five-quart felt hat, and a bulldog-type revolver. The hat and boots had been given him by his father, who had never worn them. The bulldog gun that completed the ensemble had cost him one dollar and fifty cents.

Rheinlander had no delusions of cowboy grandeur. Never did he dream of riding the open ranges; nor was he a throwback of pioneer stock. Perhaps he was prompted by seeing a handsome, dashing hero in a stage play. He did not smoke, drink or swear; and he had seldom had physical combat with any person. His spree consisted of wearing the big hat, the uncomfortable boots, and carrying that heavy revolver in a hip pocket, causing a terrible strain on his suspenders.

Weary from his first day at the bank, he made his way to his rooming house, where he entered fearfully, because of his long overdue room rent, and went carefully up to his room. And there he found a letter under his door.

He saw at a glance that it was not the usual communication from the landlord, but a regular letter, postmarked Dry Lake, Arizona. Eagerly he slit open the envelope. Inside was a queer communication, written in a feminine hand.

Dear Sir:
   Your uncle died yesterday, and I believe he willed you the Seventy-six. Look out for a small, dark man, who looks like a cowboy. I believe he will try to kill you. I am not sure of this, but be on your guard and shoot first.
                                        Ann Unknown.

Rheinlander's Adam's-apple jerked violently. He removed his glasses, polished them vigorously, and reread the letter.

"My goodness!" he exclaimed helplessly. "A man coming to kill me! And I haven't done a thing!"

Trance-like, he sat there a long time, staring into space.

"And just when I have got a job!" he mused inanely. "I like the work, too."

He looked at the date mark on the letter.

"My goodness!" he breathed. "Uncle has been dead a week! For all I know, the murderer might be right here in Chicago by this time!"

Hardly conscious of what he was doing, he removed his shoes and put on his boots. He put the bulldog revolver in his right hip pocket, after which he teetered over to the washbasin, where he began to remove the inkstains from his long fingers.

Suddenly his telephone rang shrilly, and Rheinlander nearly fell over. Taking a deep breath, he viewed the inoffensive telephone as a man might consider a rattlesnake which had suddenly buzzed a warning.

"Hello," he said weakly; and a voice drawled in his ear:

"Is this Mr. R. S. Pollinger?"

"Ye-yes," stammered Rheinlander.

"That's fine. I'm a Mr. Smith from Arizona, an old friend of yore uncle Jim Strong. I promised him I'd look you up and have a talk with you."

"Uh—well—I—I see," choked Rheinlander. "Wh-when did you see my uncle?"

"Oh, a couple days ago. I'll be up pretty soon, and tell you all about it. So long."

The man hung up, leaving Rheinlander weak in the knees.

"A—a couple of days ago," muttered the young man. "He lied. That must be the murderer. Good Lord, what will I do?"

Rheinlander never conceived the idea of leaving his room and keeping away from this man; nor did the loaded gun in his pocket mean anything to him. He read the letter again and became somewhat panicky, after which he put on his big sombrero and sat very straight in a chair listening.

Suddenly it did occur to him that there was a police department and that as a citizen he was entitled to protection. Teetering on his high heels, he crossed the room to the telephone—and was reaching for the directory as a loud knock rattled his door.

The man from Arizona! With the desperation of a cornered rat, Rheinlander staggered across the room toward the door, picking up a chair en route. He was not conscious of picking up the chair; but the next moment he was against the wall beside the door, and he heard his own voice saying: "Come in!"

The door was flung open; a man strode in—and the chair descended, crashing down upon the head of a man who sprawled into the room, knocked cold. Trembling so badly that the sombrero wiggled around on his head, Rheinlander stared wide-eyed at his victim.

"My God!" he exclaimed hollowly. "The landlord!"

The man had been knocked cold. Desperately Rheinlander looked around, trying to think what to do next. It was a nightmare to him. Then he stepped over the prostrate body, yanked the door shut, and bolted down the hallway, heading for the stairs.

There was another man halfway up the stairs, a rather smallish man, wearing a sombrero. Rheinlander checked his headlong rush to prevent a crash.

"I beg yore pardon," drawled the man. "I'm lookin' for a man named Pollinger."

"Oh!" exclaimed Rheinlander, and he deliberately fell against the man, shoving him violently with both hands.

The attack was so sudden that the man went over backward, clutching wildly at Rheinlander; and together they bumped and rolled all the way down to the parlor of the rooming house, where they fell apart.

Rheinlander got to his feet, dazed, bruised, his breath whistling in his throat. But the small man did not get up. On the floor were a number of objects which had fallen from their pockets, and Rheinlander mechanically picked them all up. One was a man-sized revolver and another was a brown leather wallet.

Rheinlander, in his dazed condition, pocketed everything in sight.

A woman had been seated at the old piano in the parlor all during this fall down the stairs, and now she looked at Rheinlander, opened her mouth, and after several attempts, screeched weakly. He looked at her, adjusted his glasses, straightened his hat, and said:

"Really, there is no use, madam. I bid you good evening."

And then he walked out, down the stone steps to the dark street, where the enormity of it all dawned upon him, and he began running—not very fast, because of those high heels, and with no definite destination in mind. Those two heavy guns sagged his pants, and the big hat proved quite a problem, but he managed to put several blocks between himself and that rooming house.

Finally he halted in the illumination from a drugstore window, tried to remove a handkerchief from a pocket, and discovered the wallet, which he looked at curiously. In it were several pieces of currency, some silver, and a return ticket to Dry Lake, Arizona.

"My goodness!" he muttered. "This is remarkable, to say the least."

For a long time he stood there, trying to adjust his thoughts. He was sure he had killed the landlord, and there was a possibility that he had killed the man from Arizona. At any rate, he realized he must get out of town as quickly as possible.

Hailing a cab, he rode to the station, where he approached the ticket clerk.

"Hu-how soon will there be a train to Dud-Dry Lake, Arizona?" he gulped with an effort.

Stifling a smile at his customer's appearance, the clerk looked through a schedule, consulted a paper-bound book, and then informed Rheinlander that Dry Lake was on a stage line.

"You go by train to Oro Grande and by stage from there to Dry Lake," he explained. "A ticket is good on both train and stage; and a train leaves in about ten minutes."

"Thank you very kindly," said Rheinlander.

"Do you want a ticket?"

"N-no, not exactly. I—I had a round-trip ticket, you see; and I'm just returning."

"You're just—oh, I see."

The clerk stared at the retreating Rheinlander, clattering uncertainly on his high heels, his sombrero cocked over one eye, and turned to a brother clerk, who was grinning widely.

"You might tell the information girl that since the price of beef has gone down, they're turning to nuts in Arizona."

* * *

"I hear," said the bartender, "that Jeff Kirk is goin' to heir Jim Strong's Seventy-six spread."

"Rosie" O'Grady, a little button-nosed cowboy, looked at "Cinch" Cutter, a lean, gaunt-faced cowboy who leaned on the bar, one heel locked over the rail, while he peered through a glass of whiskey. Cinch lifted his brows slightly, turned his head, and looked inquiringly at Rosie.

"Goin' to air?" queried Rosie. "You mean ventilate?"

"Quite a powerful undertakin', seems to me," said Cinch.

"I mean, he's goin' to git the Seventy-six," said the bartender. "Don't be so damn' iggerent."

"In reply to yore question of recent date," said Rosie, "we can say that we ain't been advised about Jeff Kirk gettin' the Seventy-six. Trustin' that this will find yore nose full of mud, we beg to remain. Signed by O'Grady and Cutter, C.P.E."

"What's them letters C.P.E. ?" asked the bartender.

"Cowpunchers Extraordinary. Give us a drink, Heel-you-tripe."

"I'll give you credit for a drink."

"Amounts to the same thing," said Cinch. He cuffed his hat over one eye, twisted his lean neck, and looked toward the open doorway.

"My Gawd!" he breathed. "Oh, I hope not! Rosie, don't lie to me. Look toward the doorway and tell me what you see."

Rosie turned slowly, jerked up suddenly, and as slowly turned back.

"I don't think it's my eyes," he muttered. "Must be my stummick. Lightnin' Lewis has been mournin' so hard for Jim Strong that he's burned every meal."

"It's still there," whispered Cinch. "Should we ought to speak to it, Rosie?"

Framed in the doorway was Rheinlander Strong Pollinger, looking exactly as he had when he left that rooming house except that his shirt was dirty and he needed a shave.

"May I come in?" he asked meekly, making a weak gesture with one hand.

"You better duck yore head a little," replied Rosie.

"Thank you, sir," said Rheinlander, making a slow approach.

"Weepin' Willer, where'd you come from?" asked Cinch.

"Off the train," replied the young man, looking rather bewildered. "I—I just came, you see. My name is Rheinlander Pollinger."

"Do you mind if we call you Shorty?" asked Rosie. "My name's Rosie O'Grady, and this horse-faced bunkie of mine answers to the name of Cinch Cutter. Ain't a missionary, are you?"

"Oh, no, indeed. I—I'm not much of anything, really."

"Never can tell," mused Rosie, looking critically at Shorty. "That's a good-lookin' hat yo're wearin', feller; and them boots ain't no drawback. You don't happen to be somebody in disguise?"

"Sorry, but I don't understand what you mean."

"I think we ought to have a drink, before goin' into this thing any further," said Cinch. "Step up, Shorty, and name yore poison."

"Poison?"

"Liquor. The handsome lad with the damp curls is an expert on anythin', such as drawin' beer or givin' you straight liquor. Ask for what you want—and take what you git, Shorty."

"Why, I never took a drink in my life," protested Shorty. "If it is customary—of—course—"

"Whiskey," said Rosie. He poured the extra drink and gave it to Shorty Pollinger, who watched them empty the glass at a gulp. With a flip of his wrist he flung the raw liquor down his throat.

Luckily none of it went down his windpipe. He stood there stiff as a statue for several moments with mouth closed, eyes wide. Then his eyes closed and his mouth flew open. Several times this was repeated. Then he took out a handkerchief, removed his glasses, and polished them, after which he put the glasses in his pocket and essayed to put the handkerchief on the bridge of his nose.

"Sorry," he said huskily, and replaced his glasses. He took a deep breath, tilted his hat a trifle, and said:

"I believe I like this place. It really is—well, different."

"Yeah, that's right," admitted Rosie. "But you should have seen it before they fixed that broken place in the sidewalk. You wouldn't know that Oro Grande was the same place. And then they took away that cinder-pile beside the depot, too, which made a lot of difference. I really didn't know the old town, did you, Cinch?"

"Did I?" retorted Cinch. 'Didn't me and you ride right through here, never knowin' we was in Oro Grande, until we saw the railroad tracks?''

"Stranger," said the bartender, "I'd just like to warn you that these two are the biggest liars that ever came out of Dry Lake Valley. Nobody ever believes 'em.''

"Professional jealousy, Shorty," asserted Rosie, and Shorty giggled.

"I—er—really, I should purchase a drink," said Shorty.

"Yo're a reg'lar feller," said Rosie. "Whiskey, Heel-you-tripe.''

"Some day I'm goin' to poison you for callin' me that," declared the bartender.

While the glasses were filled, Shorty Pollinger fumbled in that leather wallet. Rosie got a look at the outside leather, on which had been burned the initials *T. C.* The little cowboy's expression changed. He gnawed at the corner of his lip and looked speculatively at Pollinger, who paid for the drinks and replaced his wallet.

But this time he had no difficulty with the drink of whiskey, except that it caused him to grimace and take a deep breath.

"I am going to Dry Lake," he told them. "I have an uncle there, whose name is Strong.''

"Jim Strong?" asked Rosie quickly.

"Yes," Shorty agreed. "He is my mother's brother.''

"Uh-huh," said Rosie, a shade of sarcasm in his voice. "There's a family resemblance, all right. Two legs, two arms . . . So yo're goin' to Dry Lake, eh? Goin' to see your uncle, eh? Would it amaze you a whole lot, Shorty, if we told you that yore uncle was dead?''

"Not at all," replied Shorty expansively. The strong liquor had started percolating. "In fact, I should be surprised if you said he was alive.''

Rosie cuffed his hat over one eye and squinted at Shorty, who was leaning on the bar, looking at his own reflection in the backbar mirror.

"That mirror needs cleaning," declared Shorty. "Either that or it's 'nawful poor piece of glass.''

"Do you know Jefferson Kirk?" asked Rosie.

"Not pers'nally," admitted Shorty, a trifle thick of speech.

"You've heard of him?" asked Rosie.

"Once," nodded Shorty.

"When was that, Shorty?"

"Jus' now.''

The bartender's jowls jiggled with unholy glee, and he wiped his eyes. Rosie looked helplessly at Cinch, who choked slightly.

"It's kinda got me pullin' leather," admitted Rosie. "Let's have another drink."

"If you do," declared the bartender, "you two will have to take care of Shorty. I can't have him clutterin' up my place."

"I nev'r cluttered in my life," declared Shorty, "and I don't inten' to ev'r do any cluttering. I feel fine—except my feet."

"What's wrong with your feet?" asked Cinch.

"I can't get my boots off. For four nights and days, I've tried to take off my boots." Shorty smiled wryly. "But they have eluded me."

They had the drink, which left Shorty in an expansive daze.

"How you goin' to git to Dry Lake?" asked Cinch.

"On a stage, of course," said Shorty.

"Well, what you goin' to do in Dry Lake?" asked Rosie.

"I really haven't gone deep in the shubject," replied Shorty. "You see, I'm—I'm fug'tive from jushtish."

"He-e-ey!" yelled a voice at the doorway. "Som'er's around this town, I've got a passenger for Dry Lake."

It was "Exactly" Wright, the stage driver, a short, bowlegged old rawhider.

"I'm the party," admitted Shorty. And to his companions:

"I'm ver' glad to've met you. A pleasure, I 'sure you."

He collided with the side of the doorway as he went out, made one complete turn, caught his balance in some remarkable gyrations, and followed Exactly across the street to the stage depot.

Rosie and Cinch got their horses at the hitchrack and rode away ahead of the stage.

"I never did see anybody funnier nor dumber in my life," said Cinch.

"Boy, you can't always tell by the label," replied Rosie. "If you only knew it, that funny jigger has a gun in each hip pocket, and he's carryin' Tex Cole's pocketbook."

"Tex Cole's? What do you mean?" queried Cinch.

"Tex Cole was the only puncher I ever seen carryin' a pocketbook. It's one of them kind that folds up, and it's got T. C. burned on the outside. I *know* that pocketbook."

"How the hell would he git a pocketbook off Tex Cole?"

"I hope to tell you, there's somethin' crooked about it, Cinch."

Tex Cole went away a few days ago. We all know that Tex is a bad boy, and he came here to do some private gunnin' for Jeff Kirk. All right. Tex disappears, and in comes this queer, iggerent-lookin' jasper who claims to be a nephew of Jim Strong—said jasper packin' two pocket-guns and Tex Cole's pocketbook.''

"Admittin'," added Cinch, "the fact that he's a fugitive from justice."

"And lookin' like he might be a fugitive from a circus. What did he say his name was, Cinch?"

"I dunno. Somethin' like Finlander Stillinger. We better make him write it out in case Jeff Kirk objects to his claims, 'cause I've got a hunch that Jeff might not like the idea of somebody else tryin' to cut in on the Seventy-six."

"Well," sighed Rosie, "if Jeff Kirk ever gits the Seventy-six, I hope to tell you that me and you are out of jobs. It all depends on what Judge Reid has got in his safe."

"What you mean?"

"Well, they're sayin' that Jim Strong had Judge Reid write out a will. Nobody knows for sure, and they won't know until the Judge gits back from Maine and opens his safe."

"I wonder why Harvey Good can't open it, Rosie? He's runnin' the office while the Judge is away."

"I dunno."

"Don't they record wills?"

"I heard 'em talkin' about that, too. Mebbe they do. Anyway, the Judge mebbe didn't have time to do it. I don't know anythin' about law."

Where the road forked to the Seventy-six, they met Jeff Kirk. He would have tried to avoid them if possible, for he was in no mood to talk with people he did not like. Kirk was just past thirty years of age, a big, burly cowboy, owner of the JK outfit, east of Dry Lake.

Just now Jeff Kirk was slightly disfigured. One eye was swollen shut; his nose and chin had received cuts; and his left ear was red and swollen. Rosie and Cinch looked him over curiously.

"Hyah, Jeff," said Rosie. "Been out to the Seventy-six?"

"I reckon I've got a right to go out there!" snapped Kirk.

"Nobody sayin' you haven't," replied Rosie. "Horse kick you?"

"No, a horse didn't kick me," replied Kirk, and without another word he reined his horse and rode away.

"No," said Cinch seriously, "a horse didn't kick him, Rosie."

"Well, he's sure awful peevish about somethin'." They rode on, wondering.

At the Seventy-six they found "Lightning" Lewis, the old cowboy cook, sitting on the veranda of the ranch house, feet cocked up on the railing, and a meat cleaver beside his chair. The two cowboys unsaddled and came up to the house.

Lightning was sixty, skinny as a rail, but "whalebone warp and bull hide fillin'," as he described himself. He eyed the boys severely.

"Prodigal sons come home to eat!" he grunted.

Rosie glanced at the cleaver.

"Waitin' for somebody to bring on the meat?" he asked.

"Mebbe."

"We met Jeff Kirk at the forks," said Cinch. "He looked unhappy."

"Yea-a-ah?" drawled Lightning. "Unhappy, eh? He stood down there at the gate and fired me. First time I ever got fired at that distance."

"Fired?" queried Rosie curiously.

"It didn't take," said the cook. "Jeff Kirk comes here, tryin' to tell me how he wants things done. Me! I was feedin' men when he was wearin' three cornered pants and eatin' from a bottle. Ask me what I done, will you?"

"What'd you do?" asked Rosie.

"What'd I do? Well, I smote him, hip and thigh, I did. I hit him on the ear, and I hit him on the nose, and I hit him on the eye. Then I got me a meat cleaver, and I chased him out of the house. He jist hit the ground six times between here and the gate, and as he was a-hittin' the ground he says, 'If—you—wasn't—so—damn'—old—' and there he was at the gate. Then he turned around and fired me."

"Ungrateful son-of-a-gun," murmured Rosie. "After all you'd done *to* him! Sometimes I lose faith in human nature, Lightnin'."

"Go ahead and be funny," sighed Lightning. "He said he was firin' both of you fellers, and Brad Ellis, jist as soon as he got around to it. I—" Lightning craned his neck, looking down the road. "By the holy horned toad!" he exploded. "What's comin'?"

It was Rheinlander Pollinger, lately known as Shorty, walking up the dusty road. He had left the stage at the forks and was coming to the ranch on foot.

"That," replied Rosie, "is the Mystery of Dry Lake Valley."

The three men sat in silence while Shorty came up to them with an apologetic smile on his lean face.

"I am sorry to intrude," he said. "But the driver of the stage said this was the road to my uncle's ranch; so I walked over. There was really no need for me to go on to the city."

"Uncle?" queried Lightning. "Whose uncle?"

"Mine," replied Shorty. "Jim Strong."

Lightning stared at Rosie, one eye closed tightly.

"His uncle—that's all I know," said Rosie, shrugging.

"Goodness!" exclaimed Shorty. "That whiskey made me queer."

"Blame it on whiskey," sighed Cinch.

"Well, hell!" exploded Lightning. "Will somebody explain things? All this talkin'! I'm beginnin' to think it was me instead of Jeff Kirk that got hit. Rosie, you bug-headed, bat-eared rannahan, will you explain all this to me? Quit laughin', will you?"

Lightning reached for the cleaver, and Rosie sobered quickly.

"You tell him, Shorty," urged Rosie. "Tell him who you are, where you came from, and, why you came."

"Well"—Shorty sat down on the steps and wiped his brow. "My name is Rheinlander Strong Pollinger."

"Gawd!" breathed the cook.

"I beg your pardon?" said Shorty.

"Don't mind him," said Rosie. "He's full of sody."

"Oh, I see. I came here from Chicago, where I was working in a bank. That is, I worked one day. I received a peculiar letter, and—well, I would rather not tell the rest of it."

"Down in Oro Grande you spoke of bein' a fugitive from justice," reminded Cinch.

"That is true—I believe," agreed Shorty.

"Disturbin' the peace?" asked Rosie.

"Oh, no—it may be possible that I killed two men."

Lightning opened his mouth, closed it tightly, and after a few moments' silence he asked:

"Have you ever had any expert instructions?"

"In what?" asked Shorty.

"Plain and fancy lyin'."

"Why, I—I really didn't know one could get instructions in lying."

"I reckon I better cook supper," said Lightning. "I need somethin' to take my mind off things."

He went shuffling back to the kitchen.

"Well," said Rosie, "yo're here, Shorty—win, lose, or draw. Come on back to the bunkhouse, and I'll show you where we do our sleepin'."

"Show him a front bunk," said Cinch. "I sure don't want to be between him and the front door, in case anythin' breaks."

The combination of whiskey and stage travel had tired Shorty, who stretched out on a bunk. Rosie and Cinch left him alone and went down to the stable.

"I dunno," declared Rosie. "He's got me fightin' my hat, Cinch. He's funny to look at, and he sure acts dumb, but—I dunno. Two guns—and Tex's pocketbook. Killed two men—mebbe."

"Nobody but a damn' fool would admit that," said Cinch.

"Not if it was true. I dunno. He don't seem like a bad sort of a feller. Mebbe he *is* Jim Strong's nephew. Jist between me and you, I hope he is, 'cause I'd hate to see Jeff Kirk get this ranch.

In the Cascade Saloon in Dry Lake, the stage driver, Exactly Wright, was telling about his latest fare from Oro Grande when Jeff Kirk came in. The men looked curiously at Kirk, who offered no explanation for his condition.

"This here half-breed orstrich was stewed to the gills," declared Exactly. "Him con-sortin' with Rosie O'Grady and Cinch Cutter, over in the Payday Saloon; and I has to go git him. He confides that he never took a drink before, and I says: 'Well, you've made up for yore long dry spell.'

"He's got a hawg-leg in each hip pocket, and when he starts to climb up over a wheel, his suspenders busted and he almost lost his pants, them guns saggin' awful heavy on his rear end. He wanted me to sing with him, but I didn't know any of his songs; so he sang alone.

"Then he tells me his name. But he's pretty drunk, and mebbe he made a mistake or two in the tellin'. Then he says he's a nephew of Jim Strong, comin' out here to claim the Seventy-six."

"What name did he give you?" asked Jeff Kirk sharply.

"I don't remember, except that the middle name was Strong."

"Where is he now?"

"Out at the Seventy-six, I reckon. I let him off at the forks."

"He's an impostor and a damn' liar," said Kirk. "I'd like to know what his game is and who sent him in here. I'm the only nephew Jim Strong had, the only relative."

"I just been thinking," said the bartender, and the interest turned quickly to him. "Several weeks ago—mebbe a couple months—Jim Strong was in here, havin' a drink with Lige Blackstone, the Sheriff. They got to talkin' about relations. Lige said he had so many he couldn't remember half of 'em. Jim Strong said: 'I thought I only had one, but I reckon I've got two.' He took out a letter and was goin' to show it to Lige, but somebody came in at that time and the talk changed."

"That's news to me," said Jeff Kirk. "But it don't change things, as far as I'm concerned. Let's have a drink."

"What's to be done about the Seventy-six?" asked Exactly after they drank. "There ain't nobody runnin' it, is there?"

"No—damn it!" snapped Kirk. "Them cowpunchers are layin' around doin' nothin'. There ain't nobody bossin' the outfit. Judge Reid is lawyer for the outfit—but he ain't here."

"What about Harvey Good?" asked the bartender. "Ain't he Reid's pardner?"

"Mebbe he is," growled Kirk, "but he ain't got no authority to do anythin' about the Seventy-six. I've got a good mind to move my outfit over there and take charge."

"Before the law gives it to you?" queried Exactly. "You musn't forget that the ownership ain't been settled. If Jim Strong left a will—"

"He never left no will," replied Kirk. "The Seventy-six is mine."

"What became of Tex Cole?" asked Exactly. "I ain't seen him around for quite a while."

"He pulled out," replied Kirk. "Got tired punchin' cows, I guess. Tex is sort of a rambler. I'll buy another drink."

Lightning Lewis wiped his face with his flour-sack apron and went to the doorway where he stood looking toward the corrals. He had noted the expression on Rosie O'Grady's face when Shorty Pollinger mentioned learning to ride horseback; and he had seen the tenderfoot going down to the stable with Rosie, Cinch, and Brad.

He saw several horses circling the corral, and he saw Rosie toss a loop around the neck of a dun-colored gelding known as Smoky. The old cook nodded with evident satisfaction. Smoky was well broken and reliable. At least the boys were not intending to play any jokes on Shorty. Not that Shorty meant anything to Lightning, but he hated to see a tenderfoot take a bad spill.

Lightning rolled a cigarette and leaned against the doorway. The boys were saddling Smoky now, and Cinch was holding tightly to the hackamore. Lightning thought that was queer, because Smoky was gentle.

"Mebbe they're jokin' with the kid," he thought. "Tryin' to make him think Smoky is a bronc."

Shorty was wearing a pair of Rosie's big bat-wing chaps which were too short for him. Brad went over and opened the corral gate, while Rosie seemed to be giving Shorty some last-moment instructions. Lightning grinned. From a corner of his eye he saw a horse and buggy coming through the big gate.

He glanced back toward the corral. Shorty was in the saddle, while Cinch still clung to the hackamore. The horse and buggy were nearing the house, when Lightning heard one of the cowboys yelling. The dun-colored horse and his tall rider were coming out of the corral; and in range parlance, the horse was gnawing at his own tail.

It was the gentle Smoky, gone wild; and strange as it may seem, the tenderfoot was still in the saddle but grabbing with both hands. Some one yelled shrilly in warning; the buggy horse almost sat down in the shafts trying to avoid a collision but too late. Smoky and his clawing rider tried to pass between the horse and the front of the buggy.

A shaft splintered; one front wheel dished, upsetting the buggy; and Shorty Pollinger landed sitting down, almost against the house. The other shaft broke off square, and the frightened buggy horse headed straight for the corral gate, where it entered, skidded to a stop, and stood there kicking blindly.

The cowboys and the cook ran to the wrecked buggy, where a man and a girl were trying to get out. Neither of them was injured. The girl's hat was knocked down over her face, but she cuffed it back and wanted to know if the cyclone had gone past. The man was indignant, spluttering, feeling himself all over. Shorty Pollinger still sat there in a semidaze, a queer expression on his long face. Smoky stopped against the front porch and was looking around as though wondering what it was all about. Dangling from the rear of the saddle was a narrow strap, which had broken.

"My Gawd!" breathed Rosie O'Grady. "You ain't hurt, Ann?"

"I'm all right," laughed the girl. Cinch was talking fast, trying to alibi them.

"Can you imagine Smoky actin' thataway? Never bucked before—not since he was broke. I can't figure what happened. You see—"

"Must have been somethin' he et," said the girl soberly.

"I jist can't understand it," declared Brad. "Are you hurt, Harvey?"

"No thanks to anyone around here," replied Harvey Good. "You might have killed all of us—both of us. Are you all right, Ann?"

"I'm not hurt," replied Ann Reid, looking at Shorty Pollinger, who was getting carefully to his feet.

"Miss Reid," said Rosie, "I'd like to make you used to Shorty Pollinger. Shorty, this is Miss Reid."

Shorty adjusted his glasses and smiled foolishly at the girl.

"It is a pleasure, I assure you, Miss Reid," he said. "You are really the first young lady I ever ran across. I'm sorry, Miss Reid—but that was my first horseback ride."

Then Shorty became red of face and embarrassed. He began backing away from the group, backed into the kitchen steps and sat down hard. But he got up, climbed the steps backward, fell into the kitchen and disappeared, leaving the crowd to stare after him.

"Knocked loco!" exclaimed Rosie.

"Mebbe his rudder is busted, and he thinks he's goin' ahead," suggested Brad.

"The right answer," said Lightnin' soberly, "is that he discovered that you can't slide very far on the seat of yore pants and still retain said seat."

"Well, what the devil is it all about, and who is the freak?" asked Harvey Good, looking with disapproval at Ann Reid, who was convulsed with mirth.

Ann Reid was not pretty, but she was attractive. Eighteen years of age, a decided brunette, capable of riding a horse or cooking a meal, she was easily the most popular girl in the county. Rumor said that she was to marry Harvey Good, who had studied law, and was now working with her father, Judge Reid. However, no engagement had been announced. Good was twenty-four, a tall, blond young man, who took law studies seriously, played poker occasionally, and was not adverse to an occasional drink.

"The freak," replied Rosie, "is Rheinlander Strong Pollinger, late of Chicago, who claims Jim Strong was his uncle."

"Oh!" exclaimed Ann softly.

Good looked curiously at her. "Did you ever hear of him, Ann?" he asked.

"How could she hear of him?" asked Rosie. "Nobody around here ever heard of him. I doubt if Jim Strong ever heard about him."

"An imposter, eh?" said Harvey Good.

"I never said he was," replied Rosie. "I never call a card until it's turned, Harvey."

"But that claim must be ridiculous, O'Grady."

"I reckon I better dig up a pair of pants for the lad," said the cook, and went into the house.

He found Shorty sitting in a chair, and found a pair of overalls for him.

"Is her name Ann?" asked Shorty as he changed.

"Yeah," nodded Lightning. "But she'll prob'ly want you to call her Miss."

"Certainly," agreed Shorty. "I'm sorry for what happened—really. But I had no control over that horse. I—I hope it wasn't injured."

"Them Levis are a little short in the waist for you, but they've got a good seat in 'em," said the cook, as he inspected Shorty.

"Thank you very much, Lightning. I—I hope they won't expect me to go out and talk with them again. That's the most I ever talked with a girl. Perhaps I was a little dazed. Would you mind giving them my regrets?"

"Give 'em nothin'," replied the cook. "They never came out here to see you. The man is Harvey Good, a lawyer, and the girl is the daughter of Judge Reid, who was lawyer for Jim Strong. Hell, they didn't even know you was here."

"I suppose you are right. No apologies necessary; so I'll sit here."

Lightning went outside, where Harvey Good and Ann Reid

were talking with Rosie. Brad and Cinch had caught the buggy horse and were examining the smashed buggy.

"I just got a letter from my father, Lightning," said Ann. "He was leaving the next day; so he should be here tomorrow or next day."

"I wanted to speak to you about a certain matter, Lightning," said Harvey Good. "Jeff Kirk was in my office last evening, and he said—"

"I know what he said," interrupted Lightning. "And you can tell him for me, in case he don't hear very good, that he can keep away from the Seventy-six until he's got a legal right to come here."

"But," protested the young lawyer, "you must understand that it is merely a legal formality. As far as the Seventy-six is concerned, it belongs to Jeff Kirk. I advised him to come out here and see that things were running right."

"What authority have you got to advise him?"

Good's face flushed hotly. "In the absence of Judge Reid, I believe it is my duty to handle such things."

"He didn't wire you to take charge, did he?"

"Oh, what's the use arguing with a bullheaded cook?" sighed Good.

"No use," admitted Lightning. "But just the same, Jeff Kirk ain't runnin' this ranch—yet."

"We can't fix that buggy," asserted Rosie. "You'll have to take the ranch buggy to go home in, Ann."

"Well, that's all right, Rosie," said the girl.

"That clumsy ox!" said Good disgustedly.

"I thought he was quite graceful," said Ann. "He made a perfect flip-flop. I'm glad he wasn't hurt. Anyway, I'm not blaming him."

"You're not? Then who is to blame?"

"The party who put that flank-strap on the horse. It apparently busted in the smash-up."

"Guilty," said Rosie. "It was a joke that kinda backfired."

"So you put a flank-strap on the horse, eh?" said Good. "You deserve a good kick for that, O'Grady."

Rosie's eyes narrowed quickly. "Do I?" he asked softly. "Well, I wish *you* would try it, Harvey."

"Stop it," said Ann quickly. "I'm not hurt, and I'm sure Harvey isn't. Anyway, as long as no one was hurt, it was fun."

"I fail to see any humor in the situation," said Good. "If you boys will let us have the other buggy, we will go back to Dry Lake."

He walked down to the shed to help Brad and Cinch run the buggy out into the open. Ann looked seriously at Rosie for a moment, and they both laughed.

"Rosie, what do you know about that young man—Pollinger?" she asked.

"Just about as much as you do, Ann. He's iggerent of everythin' down here—but he ain't dumb. I can't figure him out. I tell you, he had me stumped. One reason I put that flank-strap on Smoky was to find out if he was lyin'. If he was a puncher, he'd have seen the strap; and if he was playin' 'possum, he'd have rode Smoky. Now I feel sure he's a plain tenderfoot, pure and simple."

"Didn't he tell you anything about himself?"

"Not much—except that Jim Strong was his uncle. But I'm tellin' yuh somethin', Ann: he's got Tex Cole's pocketbook, and he's got two guns. One is one of them bulldog guns, worth about two-bits; but the other is a real man-sized one, which has been used a lot."

"Tex Cole's pocketbook?" queried Ann. "What would that mean?"

"You answer it," said Rosie seriously.

"Where is Tex Cole?"

"*Quien sabe?*"

"Does Jeff Kirk know about him?"

Rosie shrugged his shoulders. "I'll be glad when yore father gets back, Ann; mebbe he can straighten all this out for us. We'll all be lookin' for jobs, when Jeff Kirk gets the Seventy-six."

Ann nodded and looked toward the stable. "I guess Harvey is about ready," she said.

"I wish I'd studied law," sighed Rosie.

Ann smiled at him. "Why, Rosie?"

"Well, you—you kinda took up with a lawyer, you know, Ann."

"Took up?"

"Well, you know what I mean, Ann. They're sayin' that you are goin' to marry Harvey Good—and that's why—" Rosie grinned sourly. "Oh, well, I'd make a hell of a lookin' lawyer, anyway."

"At least," replied Ann softly, "you'd have a sense of humor,

Rosie. Tell Mr. Pollinger I hope he is not hurt, and that I hope to see him again."

"Yeah, I'll tell him, Ann. He'll prob'ly polish his glasses and say, 'My goodness!' That's all the profanity he knows."

"Give him time," smiled Ann. "He'll acquire plenty."

Shorty Pollinger stood in the front doorway and watched them drive away. Rosie came up on the porch.

"I'm sorry about that flank-strap," said Rosie. "You see, Shorty, I was tryin' an experiment."

"An experiment? Oh, I see. Well, did it work?"

"Yeah, I reckon it did. Yo're a queer sort of a jigger, Shorty. Here we play a dirty joke on you, and you don't even git sore."

"No one made me get on that horse."

"I know that. But we told you he was gentle."

"Yes, I believe you did, Rosie."

Shorty went back into the house, picked up Rosie's chaps, and brought them out on the porch.

"I must get me a pair of those things," he said, examining them at arm's length. "But I'd prefer a pair with a seat in them."

Rosie choked, and a tear glistened in his eyes.

"Shorty, I'm for you," he managed to say.

"In what way?" queried Shorty.

"All four ways from the jack, feller. I don't care who you are, nor who sent you here—I'm backin' yore play. And you'll get along all right in this country, even if you are a tenderfoot, so long as you mind your own business. That's the one thing to remember: no matter what you see, nor how queer it looks, you just keep on 'tendin' to your own affairs, and you'll get along O.K."

"That is nice of you, Rosie," said Shorty simply.

"Nice, hell! Listen, Shorty; I'll learn you to ride—and no foolin'. Smoky *is* gentle. We put a flank-strap on him to make him buck. Pull on them chaps, and I'll give you a lesson. I'll learn you how to dab a loop on a horse, how to cinch on a hull, and how to set on a saddle."

"Will you, really?"

"Yeah, I will," drawled Rosie thoughtfully. "But before we start the lessons, you've got to tell papa somethin', Shorty."

"Tell you something?" queried Shorty.

"Yeah. I want to know where in hell you got Tex Cole's pocketbook."

"Tex Cole's pocketbook? Oh, you mean this one?"

Shorty took it from his pocket and handed it to Rosie.

"That's her, pardner. See them initials, *T. C.*?"

"I noticed them," nodded Shorty. "Who is Tex Cole?"

"Don'tcha know him?"

"I'm sure we've never been introduced."

"Uh-huh," drawled Rosie. "But you've got his pocketbook."

"Well, you see," said Shorty, "the man who owned that pocketbook came to murder me, I believe; so I—I whipped him, took his gun and pocketbook, and—well, here I am."

"Lovely dove!" breathed Rosie. "You whipped Tex Cole?"

"He may have died," said Shorty. "I—I knocked one man down with a chair; and this—this Tex Cole—I didn't have any chair—then."

"Let's go learn somethin' about horses," said Rosie. "That is, unless you already know more than I do about 'em."

"Well," Shorty smiled weakly, "I don't know much. You see, I've only had one short ride—and most of that was in the air."

It was the second day after Shorty's disastrous ride; and Shorty, wearing a new pair of overalls and new chaps, was sitting on the kitchen steps, trying to master the art of rolling a cigaret.

Lightning Lewis leaned lazily against the door jamb, a smile on his leathery old face.

"When I was yore age, Shorty, I could roll 'em with my toes," he said.

"I haven't tried it with my toes yet," replied Shorty. "Oh goodness! Spilled it all again!"

"No stick in yore spit," said the old cook. "Shorty, why don't you learn to cuss like a man?"

"It sounds like hell," replied Shorty dryly.—"There! That's not so bad."

Shorty held up his latest cigaret creation for the cook's admiration.

"I can roll a better one out of sagebrush and tar paper."

"With your toes, Lightning?"

"Yeah—one foot."

"I guess it isn't so very good, then. Perhaps I'd better go for a ride."

"If you only knowed how many dudes I've seen ride away and

never come back. Dozens of 'em. If their bones was laid end to end, they'd—they'd surprise you, Shorty.''

"I'm not hard to surprise. Here comes somebody.''

Two men were riding into the yard. Lightning squinted hard at the two riders and said sharply to Shorty:

"If yo're guilty, either start runnin' or shootin'! Here comes the law.''

"Hello there, you old bat-eared dough-puncher!'' yelled one of the riders.

"Bloodhounds of the law!'' snorted the cook. "Hyah, Lige. Well, well, well! If it ain't Irish McClung, the handsome deputy!''

Lige Blackstone, wiry little sheriff, swung down from his saddle, dropped his reins, and came up to the doorway. Irish McClung, the deputy, six feet, two inches tall, redheaded, with a moonlike face besprinkled with freckles, came along, slapping his dusty hat against his chaps.

"Hyah, Lightnin','' he grinned. "How's the bur-r-rnin' question?''

"I never burned food in my life, you redheaded rannahan.''

Irish grinned widely and looked at Shorty with open curiosity.

"Gents,'' said Lightning seriously, "I'd like to make you used to Shorty—Shorty—well, what the hell is yore name, Shorty?''

"My name is Rheinlander Strong Pollinger,'' replied Shorty.

"Git used to him,'' said the cook. "Shorty, this is Lige Blackstone, the sheriff, and Irish McClung, his deputy.''

"Oh, yea-a-ah!'' exclaimed the sheriff. "You're the tall tenderfoot they was tellin' me about in Oro Grande. Exactly Wright was tellin' about you. Are you workin' here now?''

"I'm thinking of owning the ranch,'' replied Shorty.

"You ain't aimin' to buy the Seventy-six, are you?'' asked Irish.

"You see,'' explained Lightning quickly, "he *thinks* he's a nephew of Jim Strong.''

"Well, that's all right,'' said Irish hastily. "I knowed a feller once who thought he was Napoleon. He was a awful big thinker. I was awful strong for him, until he mistook me for a feller named Wellin'ton. The way he acted about it, you'd think that Wellin'ton had pistol-whipped him sometime, when his hands was tied.''

"Wellington bested Napoleon at Waterloo,'' said Shorty.

"When was that?'' asked Irish.

"On June the eighteenth, eighteen hundred and fifteen."

"Now," said Irish triumphantly, "I know he wasn't Napoleon. This feller wasn't over thirty. Well, how are things goin' since Jim Strong died, Lightnin'?"

"Oh, jist fair, Irish. We're kinda sparrin' around, waitin' to see who owns us."

"You won't have to wait long now," said the sheriff. "Judge Reid's back. Got in last night at Oro Grande and drove in from there. We thought we'd ride in and see how things are goin'."

"Huh!" snorted the cook. "In my day, a Arizona deputy had to be a *man*. All you fellers have to do these days is ride back and forth! Why, doggone you, Irish, I remember the time—"

"I know," interrupted Irish. "Yo're the feller that loaned George Washin'ton the silver dollar he throwed across the Rio Grande."

"The dollars I've throwed away down on the Rio Grande!" sighed Lightning.

"Let's go, Lige," said Irish. "This danged old doughgod burner is wound up like a clock. Pleased to have met you, Mr. Rollinger."

"The name is Pollinger," corrected Shorty. "And it wasn't the Rio Grande. Historians disagree, classing the episode with the one about the cherry tree."

"Yeah, I guess we *better* be goin'," agreed the sheriff. "*Adios.*"

"They are rather ignorant of history," declared Shorty as the two officers rode away.

"Still," replied Lightning reflectively, "you can't say that it makes 'em unhappy. The way I look at it is this: if Washin'ton wanted to throw silver dollars across the Rio Grande—let him do it. If the biggest battle of the Boer War was fought on the outskirts of Brownsville, Texas—let it be there. Shorty, yo're goin' to find that geography ain't worth a damn down here."

"I don't believe I understand," said Shorty.

"You don't, eh? Well, you ought to hear Shotgun Slim tell about the Battle of San Juan Hill. Shotgun don't even know where San Juan Hill is; so he makes it jist outside Flagstaff. Shotgun tells it good, and we can all understand it, 'cause we *know* them hills. Do you see what I mean now?"

"In other words, you localize it."

"Localize? Oh, yeah, I reckon that's it. Well, I've got cookin' to do."

"I think I shall ride out to Sidewinder Springs," said Shorty, "where Rosie and Brad went—I know the way there."

After some experimenting Shorty managed to cinch the saddle on Smoky, and rode slowly away from the ranch.

Brad had loaned him a belt and holster, and he was wearing a pair of glaringly new chaps. Rosie had pointed out the trail which led to Sidewinder Springs, but he neglected to tell Shorty that it would be easy for the uninitiated to get off on a wrong trail. Two miles from the ranch, Shorty ran into a maze of cattle trails, but blithely took his pick, continuing as nearly as possible a straight line which led him to the southeast when he should have turned northeast.

It was Shorty's first horseback ride alone. He stopped to look at the queer-shaped rocks in the cañons, admired the ocotillo blossoms—and almost lost his horse when a rattler buzzed from beside the trail, and Smoky leaped nimbly aside. The afternoon shadows were very long when Shorty discovered that he was not on any trail and that he did not know the way back to the ranch.

Shorty sat there and considered his problem calmly. Somewhere he had heard that if you give a horse its head, the horse will go home. But Smoky merely lowered his head and began cropping the sparse grass, showing no desire to go anywhere.

"Another theory exploded," said Shorty. "Horse sense merely means a desire for a full stomach. Go home, Smoky!"

Smoky shook his head and reached for more grass. Shorty stood up in his stirrups and considered the sun.

"That must be the west," he told the horse. "Standing thus, with arms extended, the right hand points north. That is perfectly simple. If I only knew which way I had traveled to reach this point—which I do not. Undoubtedly I am north of the road, which runs from Oro Grande to Dry Lake. Therefore, if I travel south, I must strike that road. Simple reckoning. Proceed, Smoky."

After traveling a few hundred yards due south, he came to the rim of a cañon. Rather than lose his direction, Shorty spurred the horse down a worn cattle trail into the depths of the cañon, where they were far below the last rays of the sun. They crossed the floor of the cañon and struck another old trail, which led up a side cañon through a jumble of boulders and tangled brush.

They broke into a wide opening, and to the left, in against the wall of the cañon, was an old dugout, half cabin, half cave, built years ago by a varmint hunter. Shorty's unpracticed eye did not perceive that it was an abandoned place. It looked like a human habitation, and there might be some one there to guide him back to the Seventy-six ranch.

He halted Smoky at the front, dismounted heavily, and walked over to the half-closed door hanging on one hinge. He shoved the door open, and said:

"I beg your pardon—"

A muffled sound from inside the dugout caused him to step inside the doorway. In the dim light he saw the figure of a man on the floor; a man bound with ropes and with a cloth gag covering his mouth. As Shorty stared at him, the man made queer, gurgling noises behind the gag.

"My goodness!" exclaimed Shorty, and backed outside hurriedly.

Rosie O'Grady had repeatedly told Shorty:

"No matter what you see down here, keep yore mouth shut and mind yore own business—unless it affects you personally."

"This surely doesn't affect me personally," Shorty told himself, and climbed quickly into his saddle. Giving Smoky his head, they were soon out of the cañon but with plenty of hills and brush ahead. That man in the dugout worried him plenty, but it certainly was not his business. Probably he was some criminal arrested by the sheriff and left there for safekeeping.

It seemed only a few minutes since sundown, but the stars were already twinkling overhead, and as far as directions were concerned, Shorty was thoroughly lost. An hour later they found the road. Smoky turned left, and Shorty was willing to leave directions to the horse—which, several hours later, took him to Oro Grande, at least twenty-five miles from the Seventy-six ranch.

Shorty had foresight enough to put his horse in the livery stable and make his tired way to the hotel, where he paid a dollar for a room and went to bed, wondering what the boys at the ranch would think when he did not come home.

As a matter of fact, the Seventy-six outfit was worried. The three cowboys had come straight home from Sidewinder Springs, but they had not seen Shorty Pollinger.

"Well, don't blame me!" snapped Lightning, as he dished up supper. "I ain't' dry-nursin' this So-and-So Pollinger. If that slab-sided, owl-eyed high-pockets wants to git himself lost, it's his business. I told him not to go alone. What the hell do you reckon I should have done—cut off one of his legs? Set down and eat it, before I throw it out."

"We don't want to lose him," said Rosie. "He's m' inspiration."

"Inspiration? What do you mean?" asked Brad.

"Well, every time I git to feelin' that I don't amount to much, I look at Shorty Pollinger."

"You could work the same idea with a jackass," said Lightning.

"Well, I like him," declared Rosie.

"Tastes differ," remarked Cinch.

"Well, you iggerent, hard-hearted scorpions!" blurted Rosie. "Not a damn' one of you seem to care about this lost child. You can all go to the devil. As soon as I finish my supper, I'm goin' huntin' for him."

"Aw, he'll show up," grinned Brad. "He can't git lost."

"The hell he can't! How many miles square does a feller need to get lost in?"

"Yeah, that's true. If he went north—it's a long ways. Yeah, and he could go a mighty long ways west or east. If he went south, he'd cut the road. Mebbe we better go to Dry Lake after supper. If Lige Blackstone and Irish McClung are there, they'll have to help us hunt."

"I'll start out too, as soon as the dishes are washed," offered Lightning. "I kinda like the damn' fool myself."

But there was no use of their going to Dry Lake, because the sheriff and deputy came to the ranch before the boys had finished their meal.

"We just dropped in to tell you that we'll be needin' you boys in the mornin'," announced the sheriff. "Judge Reid came to Oro Grande last night, hired a rig to come home in—but he ain't never got home. We've been huntin' all afternoon for him. Jeff Kirk, Dave Hall, Blizzard Storms, and Harvey Good have gone on to Oro Grande to start searchin' this way early in the mornin', while we start from this end."

"Well, my Gawd!" exclaimed Lightning. "We're gittin' to be the most careless people on earth, Lige. We lost a feller today too."

"You lost a feller? What you mean?"

"Shorty Pollinger strayed away today," said Rosie. "We was comin' to Dry Lake to ask you to help us find him."

"I'm goin' to open a bureau of missin' men," said Irish. "Say! That grub smells awful good, Lightnin'."

"Grab a chair!" grunted the cook.

Both officers obeyed quickly, while the cowboys plied them with questions about Judge Reid, who was a general favorite.

"There ain't a single reason for anybody to harm the old judge," said the sheriff. "My the'ry is that he drove off the grade."

"Didja talk with Ann?" asked Rosie.

The sheriff nodded. "She wanted to ride with us. Early in the mornin' we'll make a good search. With a bunch of us workin' both ways on the road, we'll sure find him. Mebbe we'll find yore missin' man too."

"I wouldn't be surprised," said Lightning. "He's jist damn' fool enough to git lost, ride all over hell's half-acre to find the road, and then fall off the grade."

Shorty Pollinger awoke fairly early that morning. He wanted to start back to the ranch as soon as possible; so he got his horse at the livery stable, tied the animal in front of the hotel, and went in to get his breakfast.

Fifteen minutes later he stepped outside—and ran face to face with the man he had knocked down the stairs in the rooming house. The man looked rather seedy and dirty, but Shorty recognized him in a flash. Apparently the recognition was mutual. For an instant they stared at each other. But the smaller man was the first to make a move.

His right hand jerked to the waistband of his pants, flinging his old coat aside and grasping the butt of a revolver; and at the same moment Shorty's right fist, swinging in a wild arc, struck the man abaft the jaw.

The shock of the blow shook the man to his heels, and his hand fell away from his gun. The force of the blow turned Shorty halfway around, but he came back, swinging with all his power, with his left fist this time, and it crashed true on the man's chin.

Down went the man, knocked cold, the gun falling from his waistband. Like a man in a daze, Shorty picked up the gun, put it into his pocket, and stepped over to his horse, which he quickly mounted. Men were coming across the street and up the street. Hammering Smoky's ribs with his heels, and clinging tightly to the saddle-horn, Shorty rode out of town at a mad gallop, heading back for the ranch.

The man was just coming to when the crowd gathered around him. Jeff Kirk and his two men, Dave Hall and Blizzard Storms, were among the crowd. The man was recognized as Tex Cole.

They helped Tex to his feet, and he looked around blankly, feeling of his aching jaw. He swallowed heavily and tentatively wiggled his lower jaw.

"Where's my gun?" he asked weakly.

"I seen that tall feller put it in his pocket," said a man who had seen the incident from the hotel window.

"Again?" wailed Tex. "That's two!"

"Two what?" asked Jeff Kirk. "You mean—teeth, Tex?"

"Na-a-aw—two guns!"

"C'mon with me; I want to talk to you, Tex," said Kirk. "Yo're all right, now?"

Tex nodded, and they walked slowly away from the crowd.

"I spent the last cent I had for that gun," said Tex painfully, "and I had to hobo my way back. That sand-hill crane took my money and my other gun after knockin' me colder than a bartender's heart."

"Forget it, Tex. I'll buy you a good gun."

"If you do, I'm goin' to hide it where that funny-lookin' jiggernaut can't git his hands on it. I tell you he's bad medicine, Jeff."

"He'll be soothin' syrup when I git through with him."

"And I'll be a corpse," groaned Tex. "Buy me a breakfast. That damn' human orstrich took all my—"

"That's all right, Tex. Brace up."

"I aint et for three days—how the hell can I brace up? I tell you, that feller is a hoodoo, Jeff. My back is—"

"All right. Let's go down to a chink restaurant, where we can have a talk. I've got a lot to tell you."

"Well, I've only got one thing to tell you, and that is—look out for that long-legged accident, 'cause if he happens to you like he's happened to me twice—Gawd help you."

It was about nine o'clock that morning when Judge Reid, pale and weary-looking, slid down through the brush and got to his feet on the grade about three miles from the Seventy-six ranch. Rosie O'Grady, Lige Blackstone, and Irish McClung, searching along the road, saw him at a distance and hurried to reach him.

The Judge was a short, heavyset man, his round face stubbled with gray whiskers, his clothes dirty and torn. He told them a queer tale of starting out alone from Oro Grande, and only proceeding a few miles when two masked men stopped him and made him prisoner. They unharnessed the horse and turned it loose after hiding the buggy behind a mesquite thicket. They had searched the judge for weapons, gave him back his wallet, which contained considerable money, and then took him to a dugout in the hills, where they tied him up and talked with him regarding a ransom.

He had assured them that there was no possibility of anyone's paying any amount of money to them for his safe return; but they did not seem to believe him. They had left him alone, without food or water.

"Last night," he said, "one of them came back, looked in on me, but went away. Later two men came. They gave me a drink of water and went away. Several hours later one man came back, heavily masked. He said they had quarreled, and that he was turning me loose. After cutting the ropes, he disappeared. Since that time I have been trying to get out of the hills."

The old judge was quite exhausted; so they put him on the deputy's horse while the deputy rode double with the Sheriff, and they all went back to Dry Lake.

Brad and Cinch had ridden toward Sidewinder Springs, trying to get some trace of Shorty Pollinger; and old Lightning was the only one at the Seventy-six when Shorty came home.

"Jist about where in hell have you been, feller?" yelled the cook. Shorty unsaddled and came up to the house.

"Oh, I went for a little ride up to Oro Grande," said Shorty. He took Tex Cole's gun from his pocket and placed it on the table.

Lightning looked at the gun in Shorty's holster and at the gun on the table.

"Where didja get that gun?" he asked.

"Oh, I got that in Oro Grande."

"Did you buy it, Shorty?"

"No, I didn't; I knocked a man down and took it away from him."

"You—uh—did, eh? I'll be a dirty name! Who was he?"

"I believe his name is Tex Cole."

"Tex Cole? You knocked—wait a minute, Shorty! I happen to know Tex Cole; *and you never took no gun away from him.*"

"Sorry," replied Shorty stiffly, "but this is the second one I have taken away from Tex Cole. I have also whipped him twice."

Lightning looked sadly upon Shorty.

"You ort to lay down and try to git some sleep," he said kindly. "This here Arizony sun is shore hard on you, when you ain't used to it. Are you hungry?"

"Not very," replied Shorty. "I am a little fatigued. Perhaps I should lie down and take a little nap before luncheon."

Lightning shook his head sadly as he watched the lanky young man going to the bunkhouse. A few minutes later Rosie and Irish McClung came back from Dry Lake. Lightning ran down to meet them at the stable.

"We found the judge," said Rosie. "He was kidnapped, but one of the kidnappers turned him loose."

"That's fine," replied Lightning. "But here's more news: Shorty Pollinger's back—and he's as crazy as a bedbug."

"What?" snorted Rosie. "Crazy, you say, Lightning?"

"The Imperial Sword Swallerer of the Loco Lodge," nodded the old cook. "Rode in like Napoleon at the battle of Bunker Hill. He throwed a strange forty-five on my table, and he says:

" 'I've whipped Tex Cole twice, and that's the second six-gun I've took away from him.' "

"Gawd's sake!" murmured Irish.

"I knowed I had to humor him," continued Lightning, "so I says: 'You better lay down and take a little rest.' He says: 'Perhaps I should, 'cause I'm a little fatty-gued.' "

"What did he mean by that?" asked Irish.

"I dunno," replied Lightning. "I tell you, he's crazy."

"Where is he now?" asked Rosie.

"Over in the bunkhouse, restin' his fatty-gue, I reckon."

"You better let me talk to him alone, boys."

"Can you handle him alone?" queried Irish.

"I think I can, Irish."

"He's as cracked as a hotel washbasin, I tell you," insisted Lightning. "Him lickin' Tex Cole and takin' away his gun!"

"It don't sound accordin' to Hoyle," agreed Irish. But Rosie was apparently unafraid and went boldly up to the bunkhouse where he found Shorty stretched out on his bunk.

"Hello, Rosie," he grinned. "Were you worried about my absence?"

"No," lied Rosie. "We never gave you a thought. What's this I'm hearin' about you whippin' Tex Cole and takin' away his gun?"

"Entirely correct."

"Did you really whip him, Shorty?"

"I suppose I did. He tried to draw a gun, and I struck him with my right hand and then with my left hand—and he—I suppose he fainted. At any rate, I took his gun and—and came home."

Rosie's expression was one of mystified amazement.

"Did anyone else see this, Shorty?"

"There were several men around there. I really did not wait to ask them if they observed the incident. I suppose I was a trifle perturbed. You see, I am not used to that sort of thing."

"Lovely dove!" breathed Rosie. "Took his gun!"

"I left in on the kitchen table," said Shorty wearily. He yawned and blinked.

"Well, you better wrap up a yard or two of shut-eye," said Rosie as he left.

Irish McClung was telling Lightning all about the kidnapping of Judge Reid, but they stopped their conversation to hear about Shorty Pollinger.

"He'll be all right," said Rosie, as he sat down with them.

"Never!" exclaimed Lightning. "Even a damn' fool can tax his brain too far and it'll snap jist like a fiddle string. I've seen a lot of 'em go thataway!"

After supper that night Shorty wanted to go to Dry Lake.

"I have been thinking things over," he told Rosie, "and I would like to have a talk with Judge Reid about my inheritance."

"Shorty, can you prove that Jim Strong was yore uncle?" asked Rosie.

"I don't really know, Rosie. I have always taken it for granted. I wrote him sometimes ago, but I never received any answer. It is a queer situation—really. Perhaps Judge Reid might be able to tell me how I could prove my relationship."

"Well, it's worth tryin'," admitted Rosie. "We'll ride in to-night."

They left their horses at the Cascade Saloon hitch rack and went down to Judge Reid's home, where Ann welcomed them. Shorty grew red in the face, stammered, and hesitated.

"Shorty wants to see yore father, Ann," explained Rosie.

"Yes," said Shorty, "that is it, Miss Reid. You see—"

"Well?" said judge Reid brusquely, stepping into the room.

"Howdy, judge," said Rosie. "How you feelin' tonight?"

But the Judge did not answer, for he was staring at Shorty—staring and scowling, his hands clenched. Shorty shuffled his feet and backed hastily away, alarmed at the Judge's menacing attitude.

"You!" exclaimed the old jurist. "You damned rascal, I'll have you hanged, sir!"

"Father!" exclaimed Ann. "Why, what is wrong?"

"Wrong? Wrong? Why, damn it, that man is one of the kidnappers! Seize him, O'Grady!"

Rosie did not seize him because of the fact that Shorty had whirled, flung open the door, and was galloping toward the little picket fence, which he cleared by several feet, and went pounding toward the main part of Dry Lake.

"Get the sheriff!" yelled the judge. "Don't stand there like a damn' ninny!"

"Wait a minute, judge," begged Rosie. "That boy 'ain't no kidnapper."

"No?" roared the judge. "Damn it, O'Grady, he was the only one of the bunch that forgot to put on a mask. Would anyone mistake that face and figure for anyone else? I tell you, I saw him. I can positively identify him. He came into the dugout last night, looked at me, and then rode away."

"Well, I'll be an uncle to a horn toad!" blurted Rosie.

"But you know where he was last night, don't you, Rosie?" asked Ann.

Rosie shook his head slowly.

"He wasn't at the ranch, Ann. We think he got lost."

"Don't think!" roared the Judge. "Act! We must make an example of that rascal."

"I—I'll do what I can," stammered Rosie, hurrying for the main street.

Shorty Pollinger did not stop to analyze anything. A Superior Court judge had sworn to hang him, and this badly frightened young man was taking that threat literally. Running at top speed, he reached the main street, hat in hand and gasping for breath.

Moonlight aided the illumination of the street, and it seemed to Shorty that everybody in Arizona was on that street. As a matter of fact, there were possibly a dozen people in sight. The lights from the Cascade Saloon illuminated the hitch rack, where a dozen saddle horses were tied.

Shorty had but one idea—flight.

Running blindly to the hitch rack, he yanked the tie-rope on a dun-colored horse, paying no attention to the horse other than the color and no attention to the riding rig. The animal snorted at him, which, in his normal senses, would have frightened Shorty; but he whirled the animal around and got into the saddle.

Somewhere a man was yelling:

"Git off that bronc! Git off that bronc, I tell you!"

Two cowboys were running across the street toward him. Shorty spurred his horse, which promptly bucked straight toward the two cowboys. Shorty was about to be pitched off over the animal's right shoulder when one of the cowboys threw his big hat into the animal's face, causing the bucker to switch directions and literally jerk Shorty back into the saddle.

Two more lunging bucks flung Shorty forward on the horse's neck, and they lurched across the flimsy sidewalk straight into the wide doorway of the Cascade Saloon. There were several men at the bar, two five-handed poker games in operation, and four cowboys playing pool at the far end of the room.

Everyone tried to move at the same time, and chairs went flying, when that squealing dun bronco landed among them. Shorty was flung aside, landed sitting down on top of the polished bar, where he skidded its full length at high speed, with legs and arms flying, and catapulted halfway to the back door.

The room was a kaleidoscope of movement for several moments. The bucking horse broke through the flooring, crashed through a card table, turned over, and stopped upside down, with its rump against the pool table, where it proceeded to do a thorough job of upside-down kicking.

A cowboy dived in and fell across the animal's head, pinning it down and yelling for ropes. Men picked themselves up from corners. One man was walking in a circle with the back of a chair hung around his neck. Gradually order was restored. No one seemed to know who had bucked the horse into the saloon.

One of Kirk's cowboys was trying to tell that it was his horse and that somebody had tried to steal it. Jeff Kirk was walking around, his left eye swollen and purple. Tex Cole was sitting on the floor, his head and shoulders against the wall, rubbing his throat with both hands.

He looked up at Jeff Kirk and made funny noises.

"Horse kick you?" asked Kirk painfully.

"That—damn'—thing," whispered Tex. "He—kicked—me—in—the—neck."

"Pollinger?"

"Yuk," choked Tex. "Didn't—I—tell—yuh?"

The boys were getting the frightened horse to its feet, and the crowd was giving it a wide berth. Rosie O'Grady was trying to check up on what had happened, when in came Judge Reid. Some one pulled him aside while the horse was led through the doorway.

"It was Pollinger on that horse," declared Jeff Kirk.

"Where is the sheriff?" asked the judge. "I want him to arrest that man."

"You mean Pollinger?" asked Kirk.

"That's the man I mean. He was one of the men who kidnaped me, and I want him arrested."

The crowd forgot the damage wrought by the bucking horse and gathered around the judge. By that time the sheriff and his deputy had arrived and listened to what the judge had to say.

"But where does Pollinger fit into the deal?" asked the sheriff. "He's a stranger here. Who could the other men be, I wonder?"

"I don't care for theories nor explanations," spluttered the judge. "I saw this man last night at that dugout. I'm not mistaken. I'll swear on a stack of Bibles that he is the man. He came alone, to see if I was still a prisoner, I suppose. Go and get him."

Sheriff Blackstone scratched his head and looked around.

"Did anybody see where he went?"

"I did," replied one of the pool-playing cowboys. "He dived out that back winder, and he took the sash right along with him."

True enough, the window had been smashed out and part of the frame was missing. Lige Blackstone turned and looked curiously at Rosie O'Grady.

"What do you know, Rosie?" he asked.

"Not a thing. Pollinger wanted to see Judge Reid; so I came with him. Judge Reid accused him of bein' one of the kidnapers, and the tenderfoot cleared Reid's four-foot fence by five feet. That's the last I seen of him."

"Well, damn him, he tried to steal my bronc," declared Dave Hall, of Kirk's outfit.

"They hang men for that," said Kirk.

"Kidnapin' and horse-stealin'," murmured the Sheriff. "Not to mention the fact that he smashed up the Cascade Saloon."

"Yeah," said Jeff Kirk; "and if you don't git him, we will."

"I don't guess he'll be hard to get," said the Sheriff. He turned to Rosie O'Grady.

"He'll go back to the ranch, won't he, Rosie?"

"Don't ask me what he'll do, Lige."

"You might ask me," suggested Tex Cole painfully, as he leaned against the bar. "He kicked me in the neck when he slid down the bar. Damn near killed me."

"He must have it in for you, Tex," said Rosie. "Didn't he knock you out in Oro Grande this mornin'?"

"So he's braggin' about it, eh?"

"C'mon, Tex," said Jeff Kirk; "we're goin' home."

"Put some raw beef on that eye, Jeff," grinned Rosie.

"What did that slat-shaped pelican have to say about me?" demanded Tex.

"Never mind what he said," interrupted Jeff. "C'mon."

"Well, I'll tell you," grinned Rosie. "He asked me what the hell you was doin' in Chicago."

"I never was in Chicago—the damn crazy galoot!" snapped Tex.

He turned on his heel and followed Jeff Kirk out of the saloon. Lige Blackstone looked curiously at Rosie.

"Well, are you going to do something about capturing Pollinger?" asked the judge testily. "Or are you going to stand around in this saloon and—"

The judge's question was interrupted by the sound of a shot. It came from out by the hitch rack. Following the first shot were two more, closely spaced. Everyone ran toward the doorway. They could hear some one yelling, running. One—two—three shots, spaced at regular intervals. They ran out to the hitch rack. Several horses had jerked loose their tie-ropes and were milling around the street.

Flat on his back on the ground near the rack was Tex Cole, shot through the chest. Some distance away, two shots rang out. A lighted lamp was brought from the saloon, and the sheriff examined Tex. There was no need of sending for a doctor. After calling the attention of everyone to the position of the body, the sheriff had it carried into the saloon.

They had just placed the body on the floor when Jeff Kirk came stumbling in, panting heavily.

"I—I couldn't—catch—him!" he panted. "Tex—did he get Tex?"

"Who was it, Jeff?" asked the sheriff.

Jeff Kirk shook his head, as he gasped for breath.

"I didn't see him, Lige. He was there—at the corner, in the dark. He fired the first shot, and Tex was fallin' into me. It scared me for a moment, but I drawed my gun. He shot and missed me, and I—I reckon I missed him. It was too dark.

"Then I—" Jeff stopped to catch his breath. "Then he started runnin', with me after him. But you can't hit a man in the dark when both of you are runnin' thataway."

"He got Tex all right," said the sheriff grimly. "Hit him dead center. Was it that tall tenderfoot?"

"I tell you, I couldn't see him. But I do know he can run like hell."

"Now," said the judge coldly, "will you make an effort to get that man, Sheriff?"

"Why would he kill Tex Cole?" asked Rosie.

"Don't ask me," replied Jeff Kirk. "I don't know that he did."

"You couldn't tell anythin' about his height, nor anythin', eh?" said the sheriff.

"Not a thing," admitted Jeff. "It was too dark."

"C'mon, Irish; we've got a job," said the sheriff.

"If yo're goin' out to the Seventy-six, I'll ride along," said Rosie.

"How about more of us goin' along?" asked Kirk.

"No," replied the sheriff. "I'll handle this, Jeff."

The three men mounted and rode away, after assuring themselves that Smoky was not at the hitch rack.

"Another tenderfoot gone wrong," said the sheriff. "Or is he a tenderfoot, Rosie?"

"I wouldn't swear to anythin'," replied Rosie as they galloped toward the ranch. "I wouldn't even make a guess, Lige."

"It looks like his goose was cooked—if we catch him."

"Yeah, it does look thataway. But damn it, Lige, I like the feller. He talks like a dictionary, and he acts so danged iggerent! He's either the best actor or the biggest darn' fool I ever met."

"What did he want to see Judge Reid about?"

"Oh, about provin' he was a nephew of Jim Strong."

"What proof has he got?"

"None—I guess. Oh, I don't know anythin' about it. But why would the feller dry-gulch Tex Cole? That shore makes me paw my hat."

At the entrance to the Seventy-six ranch they found Smoky. The tie-rope had been looped around the saddle-horn, and Smoky was coming home alone. They caught the animal and unsaddled him at the stable.

"You won't find Shorty Pollinger here," declared Rosie.

"Anyway," said the sheriff, "it's a good place to spend the night. And if he comes later, we'll get him . . ."

"Didn't I tell you he was crazy?" said Lightning, pointing a frying pan at Rosie next morning. "You can't tell me nothin' about crazy people; I know 'em from A to Z. How do you like yore eggs, Lige?"

"Fried on the flat side," replied the sheriff.

"Another candidate for the Loco Lodge," grunted the cook.

"Gee, I wish I'd been there!" exclaimed Brad. "I'll bet there was a scramble when that bronc came into the saloon."

"But can you imagine that four-eyed dude upsettin' the whole town! Man, he's a dinger, that feller!"

"Crazy as a loon," declared Lightning. "He'll never hang; they'll send him to the asylum. The first time I ever set eyes onto him, I says to me: 'Lightnin', if that dood ain't loco, yore eyes need fixin'.'"

"He 'ain't crazy—he's playful," said Rosie soberly. "Pass me the fried latigo."

"That bacon 'ain't so awful good," admitted Brad as he passed the dish to Rosie.

"She's reg'lar hawg bacon!" snorted the cook.

"Cut off a Texas javelina, you mean."

"Well, I've got to be movin'," said Irish, shoving back from the table. "Got to ride to Oro Grande and git the coroner."

"Are you aimin' to inquest Tex Cole?" asked Lightning.

"The law says you have to do it," nodded the sheriff.

"Lige, what's the penalty for kidnapin'?"

"I dunno—about twenty years, I suppose."

"Uh-huh. And a hundred years for murder. How much for ridin' a bronc into a saloon?"

"Thirty days in jail," replied the sheriff.

"Gawd! A hundred and twenty years and thirty days."

"They'll prob'ly knock off the thirty days for good conduct," said Irish.

"Well, I suppose every little helps. Here comes somebody."

It was Judge Reid and Harvey Good, driving up to the ranch in a buggy. The boys went out to meet them.

"You mean to say that you haven't captured him yet?" asked the judge.

"He never came out here, judge," replied the sheriff.

"I suppose he will," remarked the young lawyer sarcastically.

"Yeah," nodded Rosie. "He wouldn't think of goin' away without tellin' us good-bye. How are you, Harvey?"

"I'm disgusted over the way things are handled," he replied.

"We need efficiency in the sheriff's office," said the judge.

"There's no use of us quarreling, judge," said sheriff Blackstone. "I'll get the boy."

"At least, make an effort," said Good. "When you did not find him out here, why didn't you look elsewhere?"

"Since when did you buy a stack of chips in this game, Good?" asked the sheriff. "Wait'll yo're dry behind the ears before you start asking questions of men."

"Turn the horse around, Harvey," ordered the judge. "We are going back to town."

Good nearly upset the buggy in making a short turn. The sheriff looked sourly after them and shook his head.

"I have never seen the judge that mad before. Irish, you go to Oro Grande and get the coroner; I'm goin' to Dry Lake."

Rosie, Cinch, and Brad all decided to go with him, and in a few minutes the four rode away. Lightning went into the kitchen and was washing the breakfast dishes when a shadow darkened the doorway, and he looked up to see—Shorty Pollinger.

"Aw, for gosh sakes!" exploded the cook. "Are you back here?"

Shorty nodded slowly. "I waited until they were all gone."

"Waited? Where was you waitin'?"

"In the hayloft. I slept there last night. Oh, it wasn't bad. But my feet are very sore from walking out here last night."

Lightning leaned against the wall and considered Shorty.

"Why didn't you ride Smoky instead of turnin' him loose?"

"I didn't turn him loose. Didn't you hear what Smoky did in the saloon?"

"That wasn't Smoky; it was a dun-colored bronc from the JK."

"You—you mean, I got the wrong horse?"

"You shore did. But didn't you turn Smoky loose, after that?"

"Certainly not. I was too busy getting out of town."

Lightning hitched up his overalls, spat through the doorway, and turned to him.

"Why did you kill Tex Cole, Shorty?" he asked bluntly.

"My goodness!" Shorty straightened up quickly. "Did Tex Cole get shot?"

"Shorty, are you crazy?"

Shorty's eyes wandered about the room, but came back to the old cook.

"Now that you mention it," he replied, "I wonder."

"Wait a minute, now. Think hard. Do you remember helpin' one or two other men kidnap Judge Reid?"

Shorty rubbed his nose, adjusted his glasses, and cleared his throat.

"Lightning, have you gone crazy, too?" he asked huskily.

" 'Too?' " countered Lightning.

"Judge Reid is crazy," confided Shorty. "He accused me of the same thing."

"Yeah, and you ran like hell."

"You would run, too, if a judge swore to hang you, Lightning."

"Yeah, mebbe I would, at that. Are you hungry?"

"I really am, Lightning."

"Set down and rest yore feet, feller; and don't forget that this might be the last meal you'll ever eat on this side of the bars."

"Tell me about Tex Cole."

"All I know is what I heard, Shorty. Somebody dry-gulched him at the hitch rack. They also took a crack at Jeff Kirk, but missed."

"That is really too bad."

"You mean—missin' Jeff Kirk?"

"I mean the killing of Tex Cole. Murder is deplorable."

"I dunno," sighed the cook, turning back to the stove. "You've got me whipped, Shorty. I'd hate to see you hung for killin' Tex Cole."

"So would I," replied Shorty thoughtfully. "Do you know, sometimes I wish I had never come to this country. I seem to do everything wrong. I'm really sorry about that horse, you know. I never intended riding the animal into the saloon. It must have been disconcerting to the inhabitants, to say the least."

"It scared the hell out of 'em, too," said Lightning. "You go and take a wash and by that time breakfast will be on the table."

Lightning sat down across the table from Shorty and explained the situation which confronted him.

Shorty ate calmly as he listened.

"Was my uncle very fond of Jeff Kirk?" he asked after a while.

"Fond? Hell, he hated Jeff Kirk. They never got along."

"This ranch is really valuable property, isn't it, Lightning?"

"I'd tell a man! The cattle alone are worth thirty, forty thousand dollars. The deed covers ten sections. I'd say it was plenty valuable."

"I am very dumb—don't you know it, Lightning?"

"Well, yeah, I wouldn't say you was overly bright, Shorty."

"You're very charitable, Lightning. If I'd only been born a nephew of somebody else! Fate is a queer thing. After all, I was contented with being a filing clerk in a small bank. I didn't ask to own a ranch. In fact, if a good fairy had granted me three wishes, I would never have thought to wish for a ranch. My whole life has been changed."

"You'll git another change, soon as they catch you, Shorty."

"I suppose they will—" Shorty got quickly to his feet. Some one was dismounting at the kitchen doorway. Lightning stepped over quickly and looked outside.

"Well, well!" he exclaimed softly. "Ann Reid!"

"Hello, Lightning," she said, and came into the kitchen. Shorty was standing beside the table, staring at her.

* * *

Ann was dressed in riding clothes and carrying a quirt looped to her wrist.

"Gug-good morning, Miss Reid," said Shorty.

"So you *are* here!" she said, after taking a deep breath.

"Anybody comin' after him?" asked Lightning quickly.

"There is plenty of talk," she replied. She turned to Shorty.

"Why does my father accuse you of being one of the kidnapers?"

Shorty drew a deep breath and smiled widely.

"Miss Reid, I have figured that all out. That night, I—I got lost. I found that dugout and went there to see if anyone could direct me back to the ranch. There was a man in there, gagged and bound. I—I—well, you see, Rosie told me that any time I saw or heard anything that did not directly concern me, to not do or say anything—so I went on about my business."

Ann stared at him, a curious expression in her eyes. Suddenly she choked, and tears filled her eyes. Lightning looked as if he were suffering from an attack of cramps.

"I'm sorry if I have hurt you," said Shorty soberly.

Ann held both hands over her heart and blinked at Lightning.

"I should have explained it to your father," said Shorty.

"Mine's hay fever, Ann," wheezed Lighting. "I git it every year."

None of them heard another rider come up to the door. Harvey Good, the young lawyer, stepped into the kitchen, and Ann turned to see him. His eyes shifted to each one of the three, but he spoke directly to Ann.

"I suspected that this was your destination," he said coldly.

"So you followed me out here," said Ann accusingly.

"I did."

"Why?"

"I heard you talking to your father last night, trying to excuse this imposter. Even after your own father positively identified him as a kidnaper, you defended him. You know he is a fugitive from justice, hunted by the officers; and still you sneak out—"

"I don't like that word, Harvey," interrupted the girl warmly. "I did not sneak."

"Well, you came secretly."

"Is it any of your business what I do, Harvey?"

"Well, I felt that—"

"You felt!" said Ann angrily.

"Ann, I don't want to quarrel with you," he said. "But you don't understand. What will folks think of you coming out here to see a man, who is already as good as convicted as a kidnaper, murderer, and an impostor. They will say you came to warn him."

"I am sure she did not come to warn me," said Shorty blandly, as he came toward Harvey Good. "Miss Reid did not even know I was here. How could she, when the officers do not even know it?"

"I suppose she came to see Lightning Lewis!" sneered Good.

Shorty stopped near Good, a thoughtful expression on his face.

"You are a lawyer, are you not?" asked Shorty.

"I am, sir," replied Good stiffly.

"In the practice of law, I believe you are influenced by precedents, are you not?"

"In many cases—yes."

"Then find a precedent for this!" said Shorty, swinging a hay-making right fist which connected solidly with the lawyer's chin.

Ann screamed softly as Harvey Good took three stiff backward steps and fell out through the kitchen doorway, knocked cold.

"Lovely gosh, what a punch!" exploded Lightning.

Shorty stepped quickly to the kitchen doorway—where, as though by magic, a crowd of men seemed to pour through the doorway, knock him down, and fall on him in a heap. As they untangled, it was easy to identify them as Jeff Kirk and four of his cowboys. They yanked Shorty to his feet, his nose bleeding, one cheek gashed, his glasses hanging by one bow. Jeff Kirk held him tightly to the wall while some one roped his elbows.

"There!" exclaimed Jeff Kirk triumphantly. "How do you like that?"

"Will one of you straighten my glasses?" asked Shorty. "Without them it is difficult for me to know who to thank for this."

Kirk jerked them roughly into place. He turned and looked at Ann and Lightning.

"So the heroine came out to see him, eh?" he said.

"That's about all from you, Jeff," warned Lightning. "I busted you up once, and I can do it again."

"I owe you somethin' for that," replied Kirk savagely.

Harvey Good was sitting up, nursing his sore jaw.

"You bit off more than you could chaw, eh?" laughed Blizzard Storms.

"Well, now that you've got him roped—what's the next move?" asked Lightning.

"We're takin' him to Dry Lake for the inquest," smiled Kirk.

"Takin' the law in yore own hands, eh?"

"Don't let that worry you, fella. And while yo're restin', you might as well pack up yore *own* stuff. By this time tomorrow, you and them other three misfits will be goin' down the road, lookin' for jobs."

"I'll saddle up a horse for this rooster," offered Storms, indicating Shorty, and hurried down to the stable, where he saddled Smoky.

Kirk jerked Shorty outside, and they boosted him into a saddle.

"You must be afraid of him," said Ann. "Five of you—and him all roped tight."

"Don't let that worry you," laughed Kirk. "We've got him, and we'll keep him."

Harvey Good went with them, still a trifle dazed. Ann and Lightning watched them ride away.

"I ain't goin' to wash no dishes," declared Lightning. "I'm goin' to hook on my old gun and ride to town with you, Ann. As long as I'm fired, I ain't beholden to anybody—and I'm tired of dirty dishes, anyway."

The arrival of Kirk's outfit with Shorty Pollinger caused plenty of interest in Dry Lake, where they were preparing for the inquest. Lige Blackstone took charge of Shorty, warned the Seventy-six boys to behave themselves, and went ahead with their preparations. Harvey Good told his troubles to Judge Reid at their office.

"Do you mean that Ann went out there to see that fellow?" asked the judge.

"That is where I found her," replied Good miserably. "He hit me on the chin."

The judge scowled and drummed on his desktop with his fingers.

"Harvey," he said, "I've discovered that the Strong will is gone from my safe."

Harvey Good's eyes opened widely. "Gone?" he parroted. "Why, that is impossible, Judge."

"I put it in there the day you and Ann witnessed the signature—the day before I left for the East. A few minutes ago I opened the safe, and the will is gone."

"But—but I don't understand, Judge. You have the only keys."

"There are two keys," said the Judge. "Ann has one. I gave it to her to use in case anything should happen to me. It would require dynamite to open that safe. But Ann would not open it—and I have my key."

"That is very queer, Judge. You see, it happens that this Pollinger is the man named in that will."

"You read the will, Harvey?"

"No, I never read it; but you told me the name."

The Judge's bony fingers drummed on the desktop.

"R. S. Pollinger," he said thoughtfully. 'But why the devil did he try to kidnap me? I don't understand it. Why did he kill Tex Cole?"

"Did Jim Strong give everything to this Pollinger?"

"Everything. He hated Jeff Kirk. All he knew of Pollinger was that letter he received from Chicago. But he knows that his sister married a Pollinger."

"Well," sighed Good, "I'm afraid the will would never do Pollinger any good, because he's slated for a mighty long term in prison."

"Which doesn't prove what became of the will," said the Judge. "It is mighty queer. I'd almost—" The Judge's eyes squinted thoughtfully. "Harvey!" he exclaimed. "Do you suppose, when I was kidnaped, that they took my keys—and brought them back—later? Maybe the ransom talk was only a blind."

Good shook his head and felt of his sore jaw.

"I'm going to that inquest," said the Judge, getting to his feet. "You better go and have a talk with Ann."

"I'm afraid not, Judge."

"You didn't quarrel with her, did you, Harvey?"

"The conversation was not exactly pleasant."

"Hm-m-m-m. Well, we'll fix that up. You better come along to the inquest; it might be interesting."

A dance hall on the main street had been selected as the place to hold the inquest. Dozens of benches and chairs had been brought in to accommodate the crowd, and the seats were filled when the judge and his assistant came in. But the coroner invited the old judge to sit with him, and some one produced another chair.

Seated near the coroner and beside the sheriff was Shorty Pollinger. His nose and cheek were swollen, which did not add to his appearance. He was wearing a pair of faded overalls tucked into the tops of his fancy boots, and his shirt had been torn in his scuffle at the ranch.

On one set of front seats were Jeff Kirk and his men, while on the opposite side sat Rosie O'Grady, Brad Ellis, Cinch Cutter, and Lightning Lewis. Behind them sat Ann Reid. Shorty tried to smile at her, but it was only a grimace.

The coroner rapped for order and got to his feet, calling the names of six men to act as a jury. None of the JK nor Seventy-six were included in the jury. As soon as the six men were sworn, the coroner said:

"This inquest has been called to try to determine the responsibility for the murder of Tex Cole last night. Will Lige Blackstone, the sheriff, please take the witness chair."

The sheriff took the brief oath and sat down.

"I don't know much about it," he admitted. "I was in the Cascade Saloon when the shots were fired. We rushed out and found Tex Cole, layin' beside the hitch rack, shot through the heart. I asked the men to note the position of the body, and then we packed him into the saloon."

"In your opinion, was he killed instantly, Sheriff?"

"Just as dead as a forty-five can kill any man."

"Have you ever heard of any reason for any man killing Tex Cole?"

"No, I don't reckon I have."

"That is all, Sheriff. I shall ask Jeff Kirk to take the stand and be sworn."

"What good's an oath to him?" whispered Lightning, loud enough to be heard.

"That's plenty, Lightnin'," warned the sheriff.

Kirk scowled at Lightning as he took the oath. The crowd was inclined to chuckle over that whispered question, but sobered at his dramatic tale of the shooting of Tex Cole.

"It was too dark for me to see the murderer," he admitted. "I don't see how we missed each other, but we did. Then he started to run, and I took after him, but I wasn't fast enough. I took some more shots at him, but I don't reckon I hit him."

"Mr. Kirk," said the coroner, "do you know of any man who might have a real or fancied reason for shooting Tex Cole?"

Jeff Kirk looked at Shorty Pollinger for a moment, but turned to the coroner.

"No," he said slowly, "I don't."

"Cole worked for you?"

"For about six months. He was a top-hand."

"With a six-gun," muttered Lightning.

"Another remark from you, and out you go," said the sheriff.

"That is all, Mr. Kirk," said the coroner. He looked at Shorty, and his brows lifted slightly, as he said:

"Mr. Pollinger, the sheriff told me that you would testify."

"Why—" Shorty stammered. "I—yes, I do not mind."

He walked to the witness chair, was sworn, and sat down.

"Wait a minute," said Rosie, getting to his feet. "This boy has been accused of lots of things, and I want you all to understand that he ain't on trial for any of them. If he knows anythin' about the killin' of Tex Cole, let him tell it—but anythin' else is out."

"Still backin' a loser?" Kirk sneered.

"The cards ain't all been played yet, Jeff," said Rosie coldly.

The sheriff realized that they were very close to open trouble.

"Proceed with the inquest, Doc," he said quickly.

Shorty gave the coroner his full name, and added that he was a nephew of Jim Strong, deceased. Kirk laughed, but sobered quickly when the coroner said:

"Mr. Pollinger, will you tell us how you happened to come here, and just what you know about Tex Cole."

He turned quickly to the crown.

"I am asking that question because of the fact that Pollinger's name has been connected with the shooting of Tex Cole. Proceed, Mr. Pollinger."

"I met Tex Cole in Chicago," said Shorty huskily. It was his first public speech, and he was having trouble with his vocal cords. "He came there to murder me."

The crowd sat up straight. This was getting interesting.

"I got a letter," continued Shorty. "It said that a small dark man who looked like a cowboy was coming to kill me. It also said that my uncle was dead, and had left me the Seventy-six. I had no idea what the Seventy-six might be."

"Who was that letter from?" asked the sheriff.

"Well,"—Shorty smiled queerly,—"I would rather not say, because I am not exactly sure. However, the small dark man who looked like a cowboy came to find me, and I—I knocked him downstairs. In the excitement, I—well, I found later that I had his wallet and gun. In the wallet was a return ticket to Dry Lake. That is how I came here."

The crowd murmured amazedly.

"Who sent Tex Cole to kill you?" demanded the sheriff.

"The letter did not state," replied Shorty.

"That's a lie," declared Jeff Kirk. "Tex Cole wasn't out of the state."

Rosie O'Grady was on his feet, eyes flaming angrily.

"Then how did Tex Cole recognize Pollinger in Oro Grande and try to pull a gun on him?" he demanded. "Where did Tex Cole ever see Pollinger before—unless it was in Chicago? Where did Pollinger get Tex's pocketbook—if he didn't get it in Chicago? Go ahead and answer that, Jeff Kirk."

The coroner rapped sharply on his table.

"This is an inquest—not a guessing contest," he stated.

Shorty was fumbling nervously with the top of his left boot. He crossed his legs, still tugging nervously.

"Then you met Tex Cole again in Oro Grande, did you, Pollinger?" queried the coroner.

"Yes, sir," said Shorty. "It—it was the morning after the night I got lost."

"Lost?"

"Yes," admitted Shorty. "Foolish of me, I'll admit. That was the night I found the dugout where Judge Reid was held captive. I saw him."

Judge Reid got quickly to his feet.

"You say you were lost?" he asked.

"Well, I—I didn't exactly know where to go. I suppose I was lost."

"You saw me there, and did not offer to release me?" roared the old judge.

"You see," replied Shorty hoarsely, "Rosie O'Grady told me that the way to get along in this country was to mind my own

business. He said that no matter what I saw or heard, as long as
it did not directly affect me, I must ignore it.''

''My God!'' exclaimed the judge, and sat down heavily.

''What happened when you met Tex Cole in Oro Grande?''
asked the coroner nervously.

''He tried to draw a gun, and I knocked him down,'' replied
Shorty.

''What was said? What caused him to try to draw a gun?''

''Nothing was said.''

''Neither of you spoke?''

''There—there wasn't anything to say,'' stammered Shorty, still
fussing with the top of his left boot.

''What has all this to do with the killin' of Tex Cole?'' snapped
Jeff Kirk.

''Keep yore shirt on,'' advised Rosie.

The coroner rapped for order again, and the crowd quieted.

''Mr. Pollinger,'' he said slowly, ''where were you when Tex
Cole was killed?''

Shorty swallowed heavily, started to point, but changed his
mind.

''Why, I was beside the saloon, right near the hitch rack.''

''You were? Near where Cole was killed. Did you see him
killed?''

''Yes, I saw him killed,'' replied Shorty calmly.

''Do you mean to set there and tell us you saw Tex Cole killed?''
demanded the sheriff.

''Why, yes, I do.''

''You saw the man who killed him?''

Jeff Kirk was on his feet, tense, white-faced, jerking out his
gun, as he came to his feet. He whirled so that his back was to a
blank wall, the cocked gun balanced in his right hand.

''Go ahead and tell 'em who shot Tex Cole, you damn' lyin'
tenderfoot!'' gritted Jeff. ''You might as well talk fast, 'cause I'm
goin' to down you. Steady, everybody. Don't move. I'm goin' to
kill this horse-faced hoodoo, and then I'm goin' out that window;
and I'll kill anybody that tries to stop me.''

Jeff Kirk was panting, trying to watch everybody. He came a
step nearer Shorty Pollinger—too close to miss. The crowd tensed,
waited. Jeff Kirk shifted his eyes to Shorty and started to elevate
the muzzle of his gun, when a forty-five crashed out, the concus-

sion rattling the windows. But it was not Jeff Kirk's gun; it was Shorty's—and he had fired the shot over the top of his left boot . . .

Jeff Kirk buckled at the knees, turned half-around, clawing for support, and pitched back among his own men. The Seventy-six outfit were on their feet, guns drawn, yelling at Kirk's men to keep their hands off their guns. Blizzard Storms had started to run up the aisle, but somebody tripped him, and he fell heavily, his gun falling under the chairs.

Irish McClung had been watching Bliz, and now he vaulted into the aisle and fell upon Blizzard, while some of the spectators gave him able assistance. The room was in an uproar. The coroner was trying to find out how badly Jeff Kirk was injured, and Kirk was cursing him and everybody else. But in all this uproar Shorty Pollinger still sat in the witness chair, gazing curiously at the efforts of everyone trying to help some one else.

During the excitement Harvey Good left the room—and was never seen in Dry Lake Valley again. Order was partly restored when Ann Reid came over beside Shorty and shook hands with him. The heavy bullet had knocked Jeff Kirk down, but the coroner said he had a good chance of recovery. Men crowded around Shorty Pollinger, questioning him further. The judge and the sheriff shoved their way to him, and Ann handed her father a sealed envelope. He glanced at it, and looked at her in amazement.

"It is Jim Strong's will," she said. "I overheard Harvey Good giving Jeff Kirk some advice on how to beat the will. Harvey told him there were two ways to get the Seventy-six. One was to kill Pollinger before he knew anything about it, and the other was to get your keys and rob the safe of the will. So,"—Ann took a deep breath,—"I wrote to Mr. Pollinger, and then I stole the will out of the safe and substituted a dummy envelope. That is what they stole."

"Well, bless my soul!" exclaimed the Judge.

"My goodness!" exclaimed Shorty. "So you are Ann Unknown!"

"What I want to know is this," said the Sheriff: "Pollinger, you saw Tex Cole murdered, and yet you didn't say anythin'. What was yore idea?"

"Well," replied Shorty, "Rosie told me the way to get along

down here was to pay no attention to things that didn't concern me; so I didn't say anything. Blame Rosie if the code is wrong."

"I'll be—" began the sheriff.

"What *I* want to know is this," said Irish McClung: "You didn't have any gun on you when we brought you in here, Shorty. Where did you get that six-gun?"

"Oh, that!" Shorty smiled weakly. "I had that gun inside the waist of my trousers, when they jumped on me at the ranch, and it slipped down my pant-leg, and into my boot-top. I was trying to get it out because it was hurting my ankle."

"I give up!" snorted Lightning. "I thought I had seen everythin', but I was all wrong."

"Are they all through asking me questions?" queried Shorty.

"Yes," said the sheriff, "we're through—at least, I am."

"Thank you, sheriff."

Shorty got off the stand and walked over to Ann.

"You are a wonderful girl," he told her bravely.

"You are rather wonderful yourself," she laughed.

"Not wonderful," Shorty said slowly. "Merely dumb, foolish and fortunate. The bible says that the meek shall inherit the earth, you know. I'm starting in with the Seventy-six ranch, which is quite a piece of the earth for one person to inherit; and it if had not been for you, I'm sure such good fortune would never have been possible."

"But don't be too meek," she smiled.

"Oh, I'm not. I'm even learning to swear."

"You are?"

"My goodness—yes."

And they both laughed, looking each other straight in the eyes.

Lightning, Rosie, Cinch, and Brad were standing in a group, looking at the two.

"See nothin', hear nothin', say nothin'," muttered Lightning. "He's crazy, I tell you."

Rosie looked at Ann sharply, sighed, and nodded.

"I suppose he is—I wish I was."

About the Editors

Bill Pronzini has written numerous western short stories and such novels of the Old West as *Starvation Camp* and *The Gallows Land*. He lives in Sonoma, California.

Martin H. Greenberg has compiled over 200 anthologies, including westerns, science fiction, and mysteries. He lives in Green Bay, Wisconsin.